W9-BFT-267

Acclaim for Ian Slater

WORLD WAR III
"Superior to the Tom Clancy genre . . . and the military aspect far more realistic."
—*The Spectator*

MACARTHUR MUST DIE
"A most satisfying what-if thriller . . . The plot [is] a full-speed-ahead page-turner. . . . Flashy, fast fun."
—*New York Daily News*

"Searing suspense . . . [A] rousing, splendidly told adventure."
—*Los Angeles Times*

"Taughtly written, this novel is loaded with scenes that will have you grasping the book so tightly your knuckles will turn white. . . . The final scene is a climactic hair-raising thriller."
—*West Coast Review of Books*

*Please turn the page
for more reviews. . . .*

FIRESPILL

"In the right place at the right time with the right story."
—*MacLean's*

"A good, powerful, readable, terrifying, inescapable story."
—*Vancouver Sun*

"An excellent book . . . There's something for everyone in the plot."
—*Canadian Book Review Annual*

ORWELL:
THE ROAD TO AIRSTRIP ONE

"It is doubtful that any book provides a better foundation for a full understanding of Orwell's unique and troubling vision."
—*The Washington Post*

"The best introduction I know of to the life and ideas of George Orwell, [written] with insight, intelligence, and imagination."
—PETER STANSKY, Stanford University
Author of *From William Morris to Sergeant Pepper: Studies in the Radical Domestic*

"Penetrating and illuminating—one of the few treatments of Orwell which is at once completely informed and freshly intelligent."
—ROBERT CONQUEST, Hoover Institution
Author of *Reflections of a Ravaged Century*

By Ian Slater

FIRESPILL
SEA GOLD
AIR GLOW RED
ORWELL: THE ROAD TO AIRSTRIP ONE
STORM
DEEP CHILL
FORBIDDEN ZONE*
MACARTHUR MUST DIE
WW III*
WW III: RAGE OF BATTLE*
WW III: WORLD IN FLAMES*
WW III: ARCTIC FRONT*
WW III: WARSHOT*
WW III: ASIAN FRONT*
WW III: FORCE OF ARMS*
WW III: SOUTH CHINA SEA*
SHOWDOWN*
BATTLE FRONT*
MANHUNT*
FORCE TEN*
KNOCKOUT*
ORWELL: THE ROAD TO AIRSTRIP ONE
(second revised edition)
WW III: CHOKE POINT*

published by Ballantine Books

WW III

CHOKE POINT

IAN SLATER

BALLANTINE BOOKS • NEW YORK

For Marian, Serena, and Blair

Choke Point is a work of fiction. Names, places, and incidents are either products of the author's imagination or are used fictitiously.

A Ballantine Book
Published by The Random House Publishing Group
Copyright © 2004 by Bunyip Enterprises

www.ballantinebooks.com

ISBN 0-345-45377-8

Manufactured in the United States of America

First Edition: April 2004

OPM   10   9   8   7   6   5   4   3   2   1

ACKNOWLEDGMENTS

Once again, I would like to thank Mr. D. W. Reiley for his expertise regarding small arms and associated subjects, my friend David Leask for his communication technology advice, and Mr. Tim Ross, map librarian at the University of British Columbia, who has been unstinting in his help. And as always, I am grateful to my wife, Marian, whose patience, typing, and grammatical skills continue to give me invaluable support in my work.

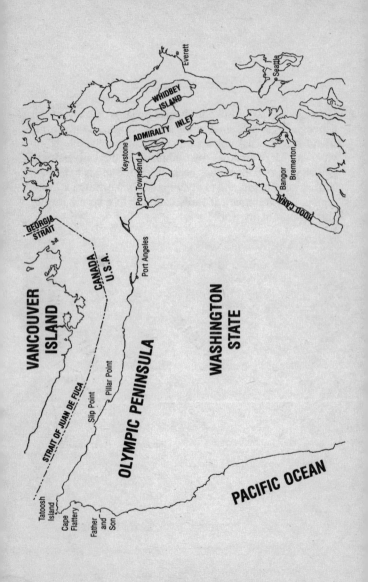

CHAPTER ONE

Direct Action Mission A039
2:00 A.M., Khyber Pass, northeastern Afghanistan

FAST-ROPING DOWN FROM the hot, oily smell of the Pave Low chopper into the Stygian darkness of a frigid ravine, seven U.S. Special Force commandos ran quickly out of the down-blast over snow-dusted rocks toward a six-foot-high, three-foot-wide fissure in the sheer rock face—the mouth of the suspect cave. Pausing fifty feet from the entrance, the Alpha strike trio, with veteran commander and Medal of Honor winner Captain David Brentwood on point, checked out the closet-sized opening through the thermal sights of their Heckler & Koch flame- and sound-suppressed machine guns. Bravo, the backup squad of four commandos, was comprised of Eddie Merton, armed with the team's Squad Automatic Weapon (SAW), two men carrying M-4 carbines, and Jamal "Jam" Hassim, the only Muslim-American in the team, toting a shotgun. The seven-man team of Alpha and Bravo waited two minutes, an eternity in the gritty, dust-smelling darkness. Radiant heat seeping from the cave showed up as white splotches against the emerald green of the commandos' night vision goggles, as did the infrared ID tape on their helmets, sleeves, and ankles.

There was no sign of guards. The seven men waited until they were sure that no one in the area had been unduly aroused by the sound of the Pave Low; that any al Qaeda present would, it was hoped, dismiss it as yet another of the Allied helos that periodically skirted the towering peaks of the Hindu Kush, flying west-

ward through the Khyber Pass into Kapisa Province and on to
the armor-friendly plains north of Kabul. Even in the icy wind
chill, several of the commandos were sweating beneath the
weight of their mission-specific gear, which included ammo
load/assault vest packs, flash bang grenades, additional mags,
flashlight pouch, camelback water bladder, night vision goggles, black Nomex gloves, balaclava, Beretta 9mm sidearms,
and the beloved miscellaneous gadget bags attached to each
man's load vest.

Satisfied there was no movement nearby, six of the seven-
man team—three on either side—entered the cave. The seventh
man, Eddie Merton, armed with the SAW and responsible for
operating the team's HF radio, SATCOM unit, and cell phone,
took up position as planned at the entrance to the cave. Thermal
Satscans, in satellite overflights, had shown that the entry
widened immediately beyond its opening, snaking its way for
four hundred feet into the rock below a razorback ridge. As the
two three-man squads moved cautiously forward in the cave,
Eddie placed his SAW against a two-foot-high rock by the entrance and popped his "baby umbrella"—the black double criss-
cross SATCOM antenna. He then took cover behind the
boulder, from where he could best serve as the DA team's rear
guard during the snatch and grab. For a while, at least, he could
maintain communications with Brentwood and the other five,
each equipped with Saver FM radio and earphone.

Inside the cave, the air was damp, sour, the rock floor strewn
with thousands of marble-sized pebbles blown in throughout
the ages by the fiercely frigid winds that swirled through the
mountain fastness of the Hindu Kush. Despite the weight of
their packs, the commandos' footsteps were all but silenced by
the U.S. Special Forces' state-of-the-art overboots. Made of
black, oil-impregnated leather, Spandex, and slow-recovery
foam, they muffled the sound of the commandos' approach.
David Brentwood knew that soon there would be no reliable radio contact with Merton because of the serpentine nature of the
cave. He glanced at his watch and whispered into his throat
mike. They had been down for three minutes. "Exfil 0230."

"Exfil 0230," confirmed Merton. It meant they had exactly

twenty-seven minutes before the Pave Low returned to exfil-trate the team. Now that the ambient starlight that had been boosted over three million times by their night vision goggles was no longer available, the green monochrome faded, and the Direct Action Team switched on the tiny infrared light at the front of the helmet-mounted monocular unit.

Coming to a dogleg where the cave suddenly narrowed, Bravo held back so as not to crowd Brentwood's strike trio, whose sole purpose was to find Li Kuan—if he was there. A former and corrupt middle manager from NORINCO, the Chi-nese government's arms export company, Kuan's sole purpose was to sell Osama bin Laden's successors depleted uranium for a dirty anti-Satan bomb, a conventionally exploded nuclear waste device that would spew out deadly uranium dust over the terrorist's American city of choice. Li Kuan, the commandoes had been told, should be easily identifiable from a pockmarked scalp, reportedly the result of a sulfuric acid-tube timer for a ni-trate bomb that had prematurely exploded when he was instruct-ing his al Qaeda clients.

In fact, Brentwood had been one of the thirty-eight Ameri-cans who'd had the misfortune of witnessing both the nitrate bomb explosion in Oklahoma City in 1995 and, on furlough in New York City in 2001, the first of the 9/11 hits on the World Trade Center. His sister's husband, a bosom buddy, had been one of the scores of firefighters cremated alive when the South Tower imploded. And Jam Hassim had lost a cousin, a U.S. Army sergeant, in the attack on the Pentagon. Knowing this, General Oakley, of Special Operations Command, told David's team that their anger was "a good motivator. But remember," he'd added, "the mission isn't to waste this prick Li. It's to snatch him, bring him back so Intel can have a 'quiet' word with the bastard. The Chinese say he's also trying to sell his dirty bomb stuff to terrorists in the province of Xinjiang. So you'll save a lot more people if we get him alive. Understood?"

They had, and they'd studied the computer-enhanced photo of Li that Beijing had sent, the only one available. It seemed to them, however, that, aside from the pockmarked bald head, the face was so indistinguishable, it could have belonged to any one of a billion Asians or Eurasians. The team had completed their refresher "run-throughs" at Delta Force's "killing house" at Special Operations facilities at Fort Bragg, where they had also undergone—no, *survived*, Brentwood would have said—the forty-meter inverted crawl in twenty-five seconds; the thirty-three pushups in a minute; the grueling two-mile, seventeen-minute runs in full gear; and the "lovely" hundred-meter swim while fully clothed and in assault boots. Only then would they have met the exacting standards laid down for them by the legendary, now retired, General Douglas Freeman.

Only thirty feet into the cave, Brentwood paused, sensing movement, his hand signals taking over the job of whispered throat mike instructions. Rats scuttled left and right, the stench of the cave now laced with the odor of roasting goat. Jam Hassim could feel warm eddies of air gently brushing the sliver of exposed skin between his NVGs and balaclava. But as yet there was no wood or charcoal odor, no whiff of kerosene, and no white splotch in the NVGs that would indicate the source of the warmth. Perhaps the eddies he'd felt were body heat, Hassim thought. But whose?

The team was trained for speed and daring, but, when needed, caution—all seven commandos were alert for booby traps. He motioned the team forward. They had been down from the Pave Low for only eight minutes. Nineteen to go, and lots to do. Satisfied that the only noise he'd heard was that of the rodents, he checked his watch. After ten paces, though, he thought he heard voices, faint, maybe twenty feet farther in, and signaled the men to stop.

CHAPTER TWO

Northeast Pacific

ON THE FAR side of the world, moving from "quiet" to "ultra-quiet," the 377-foot-long Virginia-class USS *Utah*, the fastest and deadliest attack submarine ever built, was speeding beneath gray seas at sixty miles an hour when one of the four sonar operators in its blue-lit control room spotted an anomaly on his green waterfall screen.

"Contact on surface," he said. "Bearing zero six three degrees. Fifteen thousand yards."

The attack sub's sonar library computer, containing the acoustic signature of every ship afloat, immediately printed: HOSTILE BY NATURE OF SOUND.

"Officer of the deck," ordered Captain John Rorke. "Man battle stations."

"Man battle stations, aye, sir."

The "G-sharp" sounded throughout the *Utah*, and the 134 officers and men scrambled to assigned positions, their Vibram-soled sneakers barely audible, all nonessential equipment quickly "powered down." The deep, gurgling sound of torpedo tubes flooding could be heard by some as the plotting officer's computer crunched the numbers—water salinity, sea temperature, angle on the bow, and the other myriad variables necessary to solve the complex mathematical equations that preceded firing the sub's Advanced Capability Mark 48 torpedoes. The torpedomen removed the WARNING WARSHOT LOADED cards from the notification slots of the two tubes selected for firing. Each tube housed a sleek, black-nosed, 1.5-ton Mark 48 "fish" capable of running at sixty miles per hour for a distance of twenty miles. The warhead was designed not to hit the target dead on, but below an enemy's keel, in order to create a vacuum into which the doomed ship would collapse and sink within minutes.

"Steer course zero six five," said the weapons officer.

"Very well, Weapons," Captain Rorke replied.

The plotting officer checked the proposed vectors on his computer chart. "Shot looks good on plot."

"Very well, Plot," acknowledged Rorke. "Officer of the deck, secure for battle stations."

"Secure for battle stations, aye."

Alicia Mayne, the lone civilian scientist aboard, sat on the flip-down stool just outside the entrance to the Combat Control Center. She was struck once again by the Navy's ritual of dogged repetition, designed to avoid the kind of catastrophic error that had lead to the USS *Greeneville*'s accidental sinking of the Japanese trawler *Ehime Maru* off Hawaii in February 2001. The board of inquiry investigating the *Greeneville*'s grievous mistake had pointedly noted that civilians aboard the sub had crowded the boat's Combat Control Center, and so Alicia was now careful to stay out of the way. She enjoyed simply listening to the vocal confirmation of each order. It evoked a sense of teamwork honed under all kinds of conditions. It was reassuring. And she enjoyed watching Captain Rorke, a lean six-footer—in his early thirties, she guessed—so absorbed by his task that he was oblivious to her presence. Or perhaps so disciplined that he knew she was there but was able to focus entirely on his job anyway.

"Prepare to come to periscope depth," commanded Rorke.

"Prepare to come to periscope depth, aye."

Seconds later, Rorke ordered, "Officer of the deck, proceed to periscope depth."

"Proceed to periscope depth, aye." Everyone was tense; battle stations could last for a minute or an hour. Either way, they were approaching the moment of truth: Was it a drill or would it be an actual firing? Only the navigating officer and the captain knew for sure. In the torpedo room an auxiliaryman bet ten bucks it was a drill.

* * *

David Brentwood hand signaled his five DA commandos forward again; the voices he thought he'd heard were gone. His men had all heard the phantom sounds before on other missions. The wind moaning through the Hindu Kush could play on the imagination, a fact well known for a hundred years by the British regiments who had tried to pacify the wild Afghani tribesmen.

Jam Hassim, with his beloved Remington pump-action at the ready, moved up, but he wasn't happy. There hadn't been any al Qaeda guards posted at the cave's entrance. Then again, why should there be? It was a top secret operation, and the commandos' fast rope infiltration had gone by the book, the noise of the chopper only transitory—by now the most common sound in the war against terror. Besides, the fact that there were no guards could mean that the cave was deserted. The heat signature the team had seen through the NVGs at the mouth of the cave could be hours old, heat ghosts of the kind that remained even after a parked car had left the parking lot, its residual infrared signature like a mirage on a hot day—still extant, though invisible to the naked eye. And Jam knew how many times the Special Forces had been fed rumor rather than hard intelligence because of the now retired CIA boss Admiral Stansfield Turner's obsession with signal intelligence and other gizmology, as his archcritic General Freeman had repeatedly pointed out to the Pentagon. Instead of cultivating more human intelligence, spies around the world, the CIA and other U.S. intelligence agencies had relied too heavily on satellite reconnaissance.

Afghanistan, for example, had only a handful of U.S. agents, unlike Britain, whose long colonial experience in the Near and Far East had yielded more informants. And most of the handful had been hunted down, caught, and tortured to death during the Taliban's reign of terror before 9/11, when reliance on electronic eyes and ears had been able to yield only so much. Since 9/11 the situation been changing, but human spies took time to cultivate, train, and infiltrate.

Now, it struck Jam, as it had Brentwood up ahead, that they could well be on a wild goose chase. Whoever had been ensconced in the farthest recesses of the winding subterranean fissure was probably there only during one of the allied air strikes.

Through his NVGs, Brentwood, on point, discerned a perfectly straight thin white line a few inches above the cave. It passed from one side of this eight-foot-wide section to the other. It was high-tech in a low-tech environment—a photoelectric beam. His hand shot up again, and the other five commandos froze.

Good for Dave, Jam thought. Had he broken the beam, an alarm would have sounded. Al Qaeda and the Taliban belonged to the Stone Age, but bin Laden had taught them to go high-tech wherever possible, and he'd provided the funds. Then again, all allied Special Forces, including the Aussies and Brits, used such early warning devices, and Jam realized that if the cave hadn't been abandoned, they might be closing on another allied SpecOp team taking temporary refuge from the bitter cold. Bad intel? No. He dismissed the thought as wild surmise. It couldn't be.

The cave now narrowed to a six-foot-wide, five-foot-high tunnel that split into a Y. The six commandos, dividing into two three-man squads, bent low, crouching over their weapons as they proceeded farther into the tar-black interior. Brentwood had elected to lead his strike trio into the left spar of the Y, remembering that the satellite heat signature pictures suggested the left-hand fork had been bleeding heat. Jam's trio, including a rifleman, Julio Sanchez, took the right branch of the Y, which Jam guessed might soon peter out. He was right. He signaled his team to backtrack to join the other squad, which meant he was now tail-end Charlie, with Brentwood still on point.

There were fourteen minutes to go when Brentwood glimpsed a baseball-size white blur coming at him from the left flank. "Down!" he yelled, pivoting, swinging his HK and unleashing a burst of 9mm fire. The ear-dunning crash of the grenade's explosion, its purplish white cross combining with the fiery tongue from his weapon, "bloomed out" his NVGs, the white on white temporarily blinding him as his HK sent red-hot rock fragments ricocheting off the cave's walls, over his five prostrate comrades. Three commandos returned fire, pocking the Y's left branch, where Jam now saw a clutch of terrorists.

There were at least eight of them, momentarily illuminated by the detonation of a flash-bang stun grenade tossed by Sanchez on Jam's right. The two commandos to Jam's left were literally shot to pieces as the fire erupting from the terrorists' AK-47s threw them in sharp relief against the rock that formed the cave's cul-de-sac. The terrorists hid behind a shoulder-high barricade of expended ammunition boxes filled with pebbles.

One of Brentwood's trio fell dead, and his right arm was split from below his elbow to his shoulder, streaming blood, as he continued to fire at the terrorists twenty feet away, his HK tucked tightly between his left arm and Kevlar-protected waist. The hydraulic shock of the rounds knocked down al Qaeda as if they were being felled with a sledgehammer. Jam pumped his Remington four times, its 12-gauge sabot slugs smashing through the terrorists' barricade. The force of the slugs was so powerful that three of the four not only shattered the stone-packed ammo boxes and killed three of the terrorists, but also created a deadly hail of pebbles that hit the remaining four terrorists with the equivalent of a hundred or more stones.

Within seconds all but one of the eight were down, the thudding booms of the Remington's enfilade momentarily deafening the three remaining commandos. Smoke and the acrid stench of cordite engulfed the cul-de-sac, then spread out slowly in ethereal layers, wafting like lazy swamp gas out toward the cave's entrance where Eddie Merton, unable to make radio contact with his buddies, wondered what the hell was going on. Only one terrorist was still on his feet, one hand thrust up in surrender, the other trying vainly to stem the spill of his entrails, the red spaghetti-like clump taking on the luminescence of melting ice cream in the four remaining commandos' NVGs.

The stench of feces and urine choked the air, then Brentwood heard a sound like running water—pebbles continuing to spill from the terrorists' shattered ammunition boxes, which had served as their ad hoc sandbags. With Sanchez, who'd thrown the illuminating flash-bang, covering the captive, Brentwood and Jam Hassim quickly checked the seven terrorists on the ground, feeling for a pulse with one hand, the other holding their weapons' barrels against each enemy's throat. The play-dead technique was as old as combat itself, but in the confusion of battle it still worked occasionally, taking a would-be victor, especially a new hand, by surprise. There was a flash in Brentwood's NVGs—the one survivor throwing a knife at Sanchez. As it shot past Bentwood's helmet, Hassim pumped two sabot slugs into him, rendering the man's head mush on the cave's back wall. Now all eight terrorists were dead. And when they checked, none of the men was Chinese. Bad intel? And what to show for it? Brentwood asked himself. Two Americans dead, and the brains of seven al Qaeda splattered against ancient rock. And no Li Kuan.

He took a moment to bend down and do up a loose bootlace. For a moment in this subterranean hellhole of death and gagging smells, he smiled to himself, recalling his dad who, like all parents, occasionally drove their kids nuts by repeating a favorite story or warning ad nauseam. In this case it was the memory of his dad telling him repeatedly how dangerous a loose shoelace could be. Again, the story of the German tenor, Fritz Wünderlich in the 1960s. Coming downstairs one evening in his home to answer his doorbell, Wünderlich, ignoring a loose shoelace, tripped, tumbled down the stairs, and broke his neck. "Just like that," David's father had told him. "Never ignore a loose lace, son."

"No, Dad," he'd replied.

Now, Brentwood heard a sound like tarpaper tearing—a SAW light machine gun. Two bursts. Then a sharp crack like a bull whip.

"Shit!" Jam said, moving fast, back past David and Sanchez toward the tunnel entrance to help Eddie. David followed. But neither of them ran. They knew that an escaping Li Kuan, or whoever it was, could have activated a booby trap somewhere along the six-foot-wide tube that was the cave, which rushed at them in their NVGs, the snaking, gun-smoke-filled enclosure now widening to ten feet, where they could finally stand up. There was another *crack!*

"Down!" shouted Jam, Brentwood instinctively dropping to the rock floor a few feet from the cave's entrance. His flex Kevlar elbow pads absorbed most of the shock, and he smelled the sharp odor of burned cordite issuing from Merton's now silent SAW drifting up like an errant fog out into the pristine mountain air outside the cave. Unlike the cloying perspiration- and rat-soured atmosphere behind them in the cave, the blast of oxygen was at once ice cold and invigorating, though it was laden with fine dust particles that in the NVGs' magnified starlight looked to David like white tracer.

Jam Hassim he saw, was dead, facedown, the back of his head blown off by what must have been the sniper's second shot. Eddie Merton had been killed by the first. What had been Eddie's left eye was now a gaping void, the blood-filled socket a jagged-edged white hole on David's NVGs, rapidly losing its intensity as the snow-cold wind moaning through the Hindu Kush caused the dead commando's body temperature to plummet and his blood to coagulate. David used his infrared night sight to scan the razorback ridge that formed the other wall of the deep ravine. There was a residual heat signature, but no body except the one David was using as a weapon rest—Jam's still warm corpse.

And why? David asked himself angrily. Because he'd bent down to fix a goddamn bootlace. What the hell had happened? Had the man who somehow escaped from the tunnel and shot Merton from behind been Li Kuan? And had he also fired the second shot, which killed Jam? Or had the second shot been fired by whoever had been on the ridge? It was the fog of war— no one would really know until they had the luxury of hindsight, the Monday morning quarterback's clear-eyed view. All David knew for sure now, as he tried to piece it together, was that one of the best buddies he'd ever had was dead because of that goddamn shoelace.

He cussed his old man, then felt guilty and extraordinarily weak, the effect of the blood he'd lost from his right arm over-taking the adrenaline rush of the face-to-face combat in the claustrophobic killing zone in the cave. One thing was for damn sure, he thought. Somehow, somewhere, he was going to nail that son of a bitch Kuan.

He reached for Merton's SATCOM mike lying inert on the ground, only now realizing that it would be touch-and-go as to whether a medevac helo would make it in time.

CHAPTER THREE

THE *UTAH* WAS nearing periscope depth. In combat control, Rorke ordered, "Stand by to shoot four and three."

"Stand by to shoot four and three," confirmed the OOD.

"Up scope!"

"Scope's breaking," announced the watchman.

Now speed was everything. Rorke, cap reversed, eyes glued to the scope's rubber cups, flicked down the column's arms. The cups weren't supposed to be there, the design of the new Virginia-class attack sub having replaced the captain's "old-fashioned" scope, the scope's view through the cups now seen as pictures on TV monitors in the combat control center. However, finding the physical detachment from what they were viewing too unnatural, Rorke and some captains of other Virginia-class subs had insisted on retaining the old drill. His arms draped over the handles, he rotated with the scope, then stopped, his senses super alert, the new-car-showroom smell of the CCCs more powerful than usual. "Bearing. Mark! Range. Mark! Down scope."

Above the soft whine of the retracting search scope, his reflection distorted in its oil-glistening column, Rorke reported, "I have one visual contact." His confident tone, however, masked the fact that, given the northwesterly chop and spray, it was difficult for him to discern the suspected hostile clearly. "Range?" he asked.

"Eighteen miles," came the response. It was four miles short of the torpedo's maximum range.

"Sonar," Rorke called. "Acoustic signature still hostile?"

"Signature still hostile by nature of sound."

"Very well." The automatic sonar modules on Virginia-class subs didn't need operators, but Rorke liked to have a hands-on sonarman on his watch.

"Solution ready," announced the weapons officer.

"Ship ready," added the assistant WO.

"Ship ready, aye," acknowledged Rorke. "Match sonar bearings and shoot."

The firing officer now took over. "Shoot four and three."

Every man in the *Utah* heard the rush of compressed air blasting the two Mark 48 torpedoes out of their tubes, their propulsor jets quickly taking over. Each fish trailed guidance wire from the first of its two compact ten-mile-capacity spools. The existence of guidance wires, Alicia Mayne knew, was a surprise for visiting VIPs, who expected wireless torpedoes in the twenty-first century.

"Four and three running," announced the WO.

"Very well," acknowledged Rorke, having already started the stopwatch that hung about his neck. "TTI?" Time to impact?

"Nineteen minutes, twelve seconds."

As per standard procedure, no one aboard, except the captain and his navigating officer, knew where *their* sub was, let alone the target. All the *Utah*'s crew knew was that they had left Bangor base over a day before, passing through the retracting section of the Hood Canal Bridge. By now they could be off the Alaskan panhandle, or heading for Hawaii. The pressing question on the minds of most of the young crew was whether a crazy Ivan or third world hostile had come to test their potential adversary's state of readiness or to land "illegals"—agents. That was standard procedure for all blue water navies, including that of the U.S. Or, as was part of every U.S. submariner's lore, was it readying to launch a surprise attack, as the Japanese sub *I-17* had when it suddenly surfaced off the California coast on the night of February 23–24, 1942, and shelled the strategic oil installations at Santa Barbara? Plus, every U.S. submariner, like the U.S. Navy at large, like America itself, carried the memory of having been taken utterly unawares on December 7, 1941, and on September 11, 2001, the Navy in particular vowing that neither its surface nor submarine fleet would ever be taken by surprise again.

Bangor Submarine Base, Washington State

"Are you ready?" Admiral Jensen's wife asked him playfully as she slipped into bed beside him. Her plumeria perfume washed over him, her diaphanous peach-colored nightie catching the light teasingly before she switched off the lamp. It was 3:00 A.M., and the fifty-three-year-old admiral, Walter Jensen, Commander of U.S. Submarine Group 9, and his wife Margaret were tired but relaxed. They had returned from a successful if long Navy-hosted reception for over two hundred northwest VIPs, including everyone from Bill Gates to the Greenpeace representatives. With Margaret in tow, the admiral had reassured the movers and shakers of the Northwest, and Seattle in particular, that the U.S. Navy was conscious of its environmental responsibility in the pristine waters of Puget Sound, especially the fifty-three-mile-long, 2.5-mile-wide Hood Canal waterway through which the admiral's nuclear-armed subs egressed into the Strait of Juan de Fuca and the open Pacific. Among the guests were several Canadian politicians from the nearby province of British Columbia, where the southern tip of Vancouver Island formed the northern flank of the vitally strategic strait, Washington State's ruggedly beautiful Olympic peninsula forming the southern flank. Even the "environuts," as they were deridingly called by some in the Navy, seemed satisfied that the admiral was doing everything in his power to assure the environmental integrity of the clear, cold cobalt-blue waters whose emerald islands had attracted urban refugees from throughout America.

The admiral switched off the light. "In all, a good night's work, Chief," he told Margaret.

"We're not finished yet," she replied, reaching lustily for him, squeezing hard, her perfume even stronger now.

"Permission to come alongside?" he joshed eagerly.

"I'd rather you came aboard," she said.

"Very well. Permission to come aboard?"

"Permission granted."

He'd begun his roll to port when the phone jangled in the darkness, its red light showing it was from the base. *Damn.* "Jensen."

"Admiral, sorry to disturb you, sir. This is Duty Officer Morgan."

"Yes?"

"Sir. Star has spotted an anomaly." The duty officer's voice was even, unhurried, thoroughly professional. But the admiral knew that at three in the morning it had to be important. "Star" was base shorthand for "Darkstar," the resurrected unmanned aerial vehicle which, along with the Navy's undersea hydrophone Sound Surveillance System, or SOSUS, was used for COMSUBPAC-GRU 9's real-time security surveillance of Puget Sound and environs. This had been particularly important since the terrorist "Ressam" had been caught at Port Angeles in 2000 crossing over from Canada with a truckload of explosives, intending to blow up Los Angeles Airport.

"Anomaly on land or water?" the admiral inquired, sitting up.

"Water, sir."

"Vessel wake or sub venting?" the admiral pressed.

"None reported in the area, sir. We have the *Utah* out but she's much farther west."

Which meant the anomaly could be a patch of upwelling, a common occurrence on the West Coast, where fresh water leaked upward from seabed springs through fissures in Juan de Fuca's ever-shifting tectonic plate. Because of the fresh water's different salinity, and thus slightly different color, it often showed up as an anomaly, like a slick of oil, readily visible by Darkstar's God's-eye view. Or the anomaly could be the first sign of an environmental disaster. An oil spill.

"You check with Coast Guard Air at Port Angeles?" asked the admiral. With that, his wife turned on her bedside lamp, resignedly sliding over a copy of *Time* from her nightstand.

"All right," she heard her husband tell the duty officer, "keep me posted. . . . No, no, you did the right thing. When the Coast Guard gets back to you, let me know what they say. Perhaps it's just some weird local phenomenon . . . Yes, absolutely, call me either way."

Margaret Jensen, scanning the *Time* interview, knew that her husband's "either way" meant he wouldn't be able to relax enough to have sex, at least not the kind she wanted. He was in line for CNO—Chief of Naval Operations, the U.S.'s highest naval rank—and the smallest "screw-up," as he'd so often reminded her, could scuttle the promotion. He looked apologetically at Margaret. "Sorry about this kafuffle."

She shrugged, trying not to look annoyed but knowing there'd be no orgasmic relief until Walt knew exactly what the damned anomaly was.

"Morgan'll get back to me soon," he assured her.

"Don't think so," she said, still reading.

"Why?"

She turned the page. "Weather channel said there's a low closing in from the Pacific. Fog. Coast Guard planes won't see anything."

"Damn! You're right." He lifted the phone, about to punch the preprogrammed button for the base, then decided against it. Best to wait for the Coast Guard report. Don't overreact. A potential CNO never panics. Pray God it was a simple case of upwelling, and not the first trace of an oil spill from some Liberian-registered vessel having illegally discharged its bilges under cover of darkness to save a few bucks having it pumped off in port.

Fifteen minutes later the phone jangled again. The admiral let it ring twice. "Jensen here."

"Admiral, Duty Officer Morgan. No reports from Coast Guard Air, and their vessels report nothing but the usual run of boater accidents, general assistance calls, et cetera. But they're sending a cutter out to have a look-see. It's dark as sin out in the strait—they'll use infrared."

"Infrared wouldn't show a spill in this weather," the admiral pointed out. "If it *is* a spill."

"No, sir," agreed Morgan. "But they can take water samples." Then the DO posited an entirely different but quite plausible explanation for the anomaly Darkstar had spotted: "It could be a NAWID." He meant a natural air-water interface disturbance caused by a hard rain shower or a school of fish in a frenzy of feeding on plankton near the surface.

The admiral was nodding, thinking about requesting a "side-scan" sonar profile of the sea bottom rather than settling for the ordinary sonar depth reading that as a matter of standard procedure would be taken by the Coast Guard cutter. But to request a side-scan radar profile that would reveal any venting or other anomaly on the sea bed was a costly proposition for the Navy, ergo the taxpayers. And he could be accused of making a mountain out of a molehill. He decided to wait.

"All right," he told Morgan. "Let me know if you hear any more. Request another Darkstar run tomorrow."

"Aye aye, sir. Good night."

The admiral replaced the phone. Maybe the anomaly had been nothing more than a sudden squall of wind. He'd seen that often enough—anybody who'd been on any kind of boat had seen it, an area of water disturbed by a phantom gust ruffling the water, causing it to momentarily take on a different shade of blue, green, or gray, depending on the color of the sky. But Margaret saw that he was worried.

"Go to sleep," she urged, pulling the bedspread playfully up over his head.

"You think I'm overreacting?" came the muffled voice beneath the cover.

She put the magazine aside and switched off her bedside lamp. "Well, you have made a bit of a meal out of it."

He cast off the cover. "A *meal* out of it? I've never heard you use that before."

There was silence.

"You've never used that phrase before," he repeated.

"I don't know," she said in the penumbra of his bedside light. "I must have read it somewhere."

"*I've* heard it before," the admiral said accusingly. "It's a limey expression. That limey admiral, the Brit liaison guy at the base. He's always using it."

"Maybe," she said tiredly.

"But you're never on the base. How would you know?"

There was another long silence before she spoke. "Don't start with me, Walter."

"Start what?"

"Obsessing."

"Goddammit, all I said was that you're never on the base. Are you?" Now he could hear the alarm clock ticking. "Answer me, Margaret . . . Margaret."

She wouldn't.

Dammit! He sat up, couldn't sleep. But she could—through a tornado. Perhaps she's right, he thought. He *was* obsessing again, his Darkstar anxiety expressing itself in veiled accusations about a suspected attraction between her and the limey liaison officer. Like a dog with an old bone, he told himself, his obsessive streak made worse throughout his career by the Navy's insistence, particularly the nuclear navy's near paranoid insistence, that you do everything by the book. Or else. Check, double-check, and check again. Lives depended on it. Oh, use your initiative by all means, but only after you know the rules well enough to know the ones you can break. Of course there were renegades, "cowboys," like the SEALs and Freeman's now-disbanded SALERTs—Sea Air Land Emergency Response Team—who thought they could operate under their own rules. But sooner or later the service—Army, Air Force, Navy, or Marine—reined them in, and they sure as hell didn't make flag rank.

The problem, he knew, was that he was so close to becoming CNO. Settle down, he told himself. This was simply an attack of nerves and self-doubt that at times assailed even the most self-assured individuals, who momentarily, with sweating palms, heartbeat racing out of control, are seized by the unshakable conviction that they're about to be found out, the veneer stripped away, the naked self revealed, warts and all. Jensen wondered if that was why Mike Borda, the Navy's most beloved admiral—a "mustang," a man who'd worked all the way up from the deck to admiral—ended up blowing his brains out in 1998, ostensibly for wearing a medal to which he wasn't entitled.

His eyes now accustomed to the darkened room, Jensen made

his way quietly into the living room, past the smell of hothouse roses, past the faintly visible outline of the model of the new Virginia-class sub, and poured himself a stiff Jack Daniel's, eschewing ice for fear of the dispenser waking Margaret. Or was she just pretending to be asleep? Thirty years of marriage, and there were still times like this when he wasn't sure whether she was genuinely asleep or using it as a means of escape.

"Get a grip," he chided himself. "You're acting like a goddamn ensign before his finals. You're commander of Subgroup Nine, for Christ's sake. C'mon, Walter!"

He started when he heard the phone ring, and took it in the kitchen. "Admiral Jensen!"

"Morgan here, sir. We have a Coast Guard cutter report. No anomaly."

"No spill."

"No spill. Fishheads."

"Dumping!" said Jensen, realizing now that the anomaly had probably been caused by one of the hundreds of fishermen— oops, *fishers*, if you were headed for CNO—who plied the Northwest's waters. They often dumped thousands of fishheads from their catch to save valuable storage space in the boats' freezer, which, given the price of fuel, cost them a small fortune to keep cold. Yes, it was pollution of a sort, he acknowledged, but small potatoes, the fish heads quickly devoured by the sea's predators.

Morgan could hear the admiral's sigh of relief.

"Very well," said Jensen. "Everything's fine then. Good night." There was new buoyancy in his tone.

But back in bed, pulling up the covers, residual anxiety stayed with him. "Everything's fine," he'd told Morgan. The very same phrase he'd used to assure Bill Gates et al. about the pristine waters of Puget Sound. It recalled the advice his uncle used to give him about voicing such blasé assurances. "Say that about your car," his uncle had once cautioned, "and next day the goddamn wheels fall off!"

Flinging aside the bedspread once more, Jensen walked softly back to the living room and called the base. "Morgan. Call Port Angeles. Send out a Bruiser with two divers. See if there's any

evidence of gas venting from the seabed." It was the one phenomenon amid all the wacko Bermuda Triangle theories that
had made a smidgen of sense to Jensen—the idea that at times
enormous bubbles of hydrate gas, "like a fart in a bathtub," as
one chief had indelicately but accurately put it, were vented
from the sea's bottom. Lighter than air, the escaping gas would
not only disturb the water-air interface, but would rise rapidly,
and if there was a "sparker" in its path, such as an aircraft or
boat engine, there'd be an enormous explosion, leaving nothing
on the radar screen.

"A Bruiser, two divers," Morgan confirmed, adding, "It'll be
light in about an hour, Admiral. You want me to wait until—"

"No, send 'em out right away," cut in Jensen. "Besides, it'll
be dawn by the time they get there. Tell them that if they smell
gas vapor, they'll need to cut the motor for the last half mile and
go in under paddle power."

"Yes, sir," Morgan answered, adding, as he put down the
phone, "They'll like *that*."

CHAPTER FOUR

DAVID BRENTWOOD HEARD the deep *brrr* of the bulky
Pave Low coming in over the ravine. He saw the dim outline of
the chopper's portside crash-resistant external auxiliary fuel
tank as the pilot trimmed the craft. Then the tank's silhouette in
his NVGs was lost against the helo's body, the pilot deciding
against dropping antimissile "sucker" flares because a rain of in-
candescent decoys would announce to any hostile in the area
that infidels had arrived. Rules of Engagement meant that
David, in urgent need of first aid, would have to go up first.
Next, the bodies of Jamal Hassim, Eddie Merton, and the four

commandos killed in the cave would be hauled up, followed by Sanchez, the only other survivor besides Brentwood, whose job it would be to hook up the dead. It would take time, it would be dangerous, but Special Forces' first commandment was: "Thou shalt not leave a comrade injured or dead."

Intuitively, David felt badly about insisting that he be the first in line for extraction, but common sense, together with Spec-For's Rules of Engagement, had to overrule his better nature. If his arm could be saved, either by the 18D first response/trauma medic among the chopper's six-man crew or at the battalion MASH unit at Tora Bora base, he could fight again, and go after Li Kuan before a dirty bomb appeared in an American or somebody else's city.

As he ran out to grab the rope lowered by the chopper into the ravine, the .50 caliber machine gunner on the Pave's rear ramp door moved his weapon left to right on the pintle mount in concert with his NVG sweep of the razorback ridge that cut the night sky like a knife blade, no more than a hundred feet away. Sanchez, emerging from the cave's entrance, knelt to cover Brentwood amid the onslaught of dust and pebbles kicked up by the helo's downdraft. The ramp gunner saw a flash at one o'clock, swung his .50 hard left, and unleashed a full burst, the machine gun's deafening staccato overriding the whack of the sniper's armor-piercing round hitting the right auxiliary tank, whose sealant wall did not prevent a leak, but there was no flame. The pilot, wanting to jettison the tank but afraid it might strike Brentwood, who was still on the ground directly beneath the chopper, yelled through his mike, asking if he was hooked up to the SPIE line. The copilot, meanwhile, released a rain of orange antimissile flares.

"Are you hooked up?" shouted the pilot. "Do you copy? Are you—"

"Yes, I am! Go! Go! Go!" And the Pave's bulbous-nosed radar dome and in-air refueling proboscis dipped in unison. The chopper's rear rotor tilted as the Pave rose swiftly above the dark V-shaped cleft of the ravine, the helo's rear ramp machine gunner laying down suppressing fire until the last possible moment, the ramp door closing like the mouth of some airborne flame-spitting dragon. David, still on the ground as the Pave Low took up the slack, clung to the rope with his left hand, his right dangling uselessly.

Then suddenly he was off, his body and boots a tiny exclamation point to the pilot, the commando leader dangling over two hundred feet below the chopper. In fact, Brentwood was only ten feet off the ground, his illusion of height caused by the freezing air roaring into his lungs as wind currents buffeted him from side to side, dangerously close to the narrow ravine's cliffs, like a pendulum's bob. The vapor trail of the Russian-made rocket-propelled grenade streaked up from a razorback hide and was clearly visible to Sanchez at the cave's entrance.

Not being a heat-seeking missile, the RPG's 1.7-kilogram high-explosive antitank round struck the helo below the right engine mount's cowling. Black smoke poured out of the helo, which immediately began losing power. In an instantaneous decision, the pilot jettisoned the right auxiliary fuel tank that had already been hit by the range-finding sniper bullet. The tank dropped like a bomb, but the pilot was right to release it, for now he could see that the tank was afire. David felt the whoosh of hot air as the tank plummeted past him, no more than ten feet away, a second before the chopper rose another fifty feet. The burning tank, smashing into the ground, exploded, vomiting out an enormous pear-shaped orange flame that engulfed the cave's entrance, incinerating Sanchez and Jam's inert body.

"I'm going down!" yelled the Pave's medic, grabbing his trauma pack. The helo's ramp was opening again, its .50 caliber now joined by the helo's right-side 7.62 minigun.

"Go!" yelled the pilot, who fought against the fierce winds coming up from the ravine, which had no doubt been strengthened by the auxiliary tank's explosion. He realized, as the medic must have, that any attempt to winch Brentwood up farther would spell disaster, given the helo's severe "rockabye" motion. Either Brentwood would be smashed against the rock face or, delaying the Pave, make the helo a sitting target.

"Disengage!" the medic yelled at Brentwood.

David didn't have to be told twice, both men falling within seconds of one another from the SPIE line, ten feet to the ground. David rolled onto his injured arm, the pain shooting so fast to his brain that he momentarily passed out, the medic dragging him behind the cover of boulders twenty feet from the cave's entrance. David's pain was so intense, however, that a moan escaped him. "Shut up!" the medic told the Medal of Honor winner, injecting him with a vial of morphine. He taped David's arm and started an IV drip, the wind almost blowing off his Kevlar helmet, which was pelted by small pebbles and dust as fine as talc. But all the medic could think of now was whether the Pave pilot had had time to send a Mayday to Tora Bora, and if so, had they heard him?

"Goddamn CIA," he cursed. They'd given the Afghans hundreds of heat-seeking Stingers to fight the Soviets, and now the missiles were being used to kill Americans. The world was crazy. And now the Russians were helping the U.S. fight the terrorists.

He checked Brentwood's pulse. It wasn't good. Why in hell had the helo stopped dropping flares to avoid Stingers? Probably, the medic guessed, because the copilot was conserving them for the run back over hostile areas to Tora Bora. It occurred to him then that if al Qaeda got to him and Brentwood, he could barter his medical skills and supplies for his survival. "You goddamned coward!" he berated himself aloud. "You're Special Forces, for Christ's sake. One of Freeman's boys. Get a grip!"

He saw David Brentwood struggling with his left hand for the mouthpiece to his camelback, but the water sack had been lacerated either by the firefight in the cave or by shrapnel from the explosions of the helo's jettisoned fuel tank. The medic took off his own camelback but warned David, "Just a sip."

The helo, now free of any encumbrance, rose high and, barely missed by another RPG round, banked sharply to the left for twelve hundred meters, beyond the maximum range of an RPG. From there, the Pave, hovering, its machine guns roaring, aided by infrared searchlights, began raking the razorback, now that the helo had more freedom to move. "Winds are dying down," noted the pilot. "Maybe we could have another go?"

"Why not?" said the copilot, sounding braver than he felt.

"Missile three o'clock low!" shouted the pilot, hauling hard on the Pave's yoke, narrowly avoiding the RPG. The Pave's gunners laid down suppressing fire left to right, the helo banking hard toward the ravine, the copilot warning the medic this would be the last attempt.

The medic was frantically lashing himself to Brentwood when the weighted SPIE line thumped him in the back, sending his helmet flying, knocking him and Brentwood to the ground. "Jesus Christ!" But he was quick enough to grab the line and clip on. The line, now slacker, dragged past him. The Pave's pilot tried to ease the Pave up, but despite the helo's heavy enfilade, another RPG was coming straight at him. He dropped the helo abruptly, and the medic and Brentwood, who had been rising before, were now dumped. For a moment the medic thought the SPIE line had been jettisoned again to save the chopper. The RPG exploded high above them on the ravine's cliff face, sending a rain of rock fragments down on the two men. The whack on Brentwood's helmet was so loud that the helo's winch man swore he heard it above the rotor slap. The baseball-size fragment that struck the helmetless medic wasn't heard by anyone on the Pave as the helo rose quickly, simultaneously winching the two men up.

The dust storm it created sent a gritty, eye-closing wind over the terrorists, who nevertheless kept firing, the Pave taking several hits, none fatal. The ramp machine gunner, shot in the right boot, was unaware of it until he felt the warmth of his foot, the boot filling with blood. Brentwood was dragged hard over the fuselage's lip. The medic, though none of the crew realized it at the time, was dying from a massive hemorrhage in his brain.

CHAPTER FIVE

AS THE FIVE-MAN crew of one of the Port Angeles Bruisers—as the thirty-foot-long rigid hull inflatable boats were unofficially known—readied to put to sea, the crew of the *Utah*, seventy miles to the west of Juan de Fuca Strait, braced for the explosions they expected against the suspected hostile target nineteen miles or so farther west. The hand on Rorke's watch reached zero. Knowing that noise raced through seawater at three to four times the speed of sound in air, depending on the ocean's salinity, the crew were aware it would take twenty-five to thirty seconds for the detonations to reach them—plus a few more for tide and current interference and for torpedo counterevasive tactics, should the hostile have seen the *Utah*'s torpedoes coming and tried to outmaneuver them. At zero plus twenty seconds, no one was worried. At zero plus thirty seconds, nothing. Forty . . .

"Damn!" said the weapons officer. "Looks like we've got a lem—"

Then they heard and felt the blast of the 650-pound high-explosive warheads, followed by the awful sound of bulkheads buckling and collapsing like the bones of some huge prehistoric animal in its death throes.

How many were dying?

Rorke could see the question written on the faces of his young crew, now that the excitement of the hit had passed.

"Relax, gentlemen," he announced, smiling. "We didn't deep six anyone. Just a rusty target hulk rigged to emit hostile acoustics. You did the *Utah* proud." He turned to Lieutenant

Commander Ray Peel, this watch's OOD. "Officer of the deck, emergency blow."

"Emergency blow, aye, sir."

The ballast control operator activated the two "mushrooms"—ballast control valves—the rapid gush of air from the sub's air banks to her ballast tanks so alarming that it made her crew tense again. *Utah* broke surface nose first in an enormous rush of foaming white phosphorescence before she trimmed, her belly coming down on the sea like a broaching whale. The phosphorescence quickly faded, men releasing their hand holds.

Alicia Mayne could see the men visibly relax. She felt it too. As one of the Navy's preeminent torpedo researchers she'd known that at some point during *Utah*'s exercise patrol—her first aboard one of the $1.6 billion Virginia-class subs—there'd be a "shoot" in order for her to study postfiring telemetry data. But she hadn't been told when or where it would take place.

"Why couldn't you have told me beforehand?" she asked Rorke pointedly, albeit with a smile.

"Thought you might alert the crew," he replied. "Take the edge off them."

Now she *was* offended, and Rorke knew it.

"No, no," he said, "not tip them off verbally. It's a person's body language. Just like you're telling me now how pissed you are at me. Besides," he added cheekily, "I thought you might enjoy the suspense."

"*Enjoy?* Not knowing if we were going to be fired on?"

"I figured the experience would give you a greater appreciation of what a torpedo launch is like," he said. "Telemetry is only one part of it. Your knowledge of the human factor could be just as valuable in improving the new Mark 50." He paused. "You notice the strain on the men in combat control? In the weapons officer's voice? When those boys—their average age is twenty-two—are sending out all that information through the wire, one slip, one nanosecond of lost focus, could mean our fish hits a hostile a second too late, giving the enemy time to launch. And that'd be the end of us."

Alicia knew he was right. She *had* felt the gut-tightening "human factor" when the ADCAP had been fired. Seeing how it was done on the sub rather than watching a launch in the lab tank ashore could help enormously in the design, in upgrading the Mark 50. A minute change could buy you that vital nanosecond. "I agree," she told him. "That's why I came along."

Rorke realized then why she was tops in her field. It wasn't just because of her mastery of physics and ocean dynamics. She was quick to concede a point if she thought you were right, not pigheaded like some of her male colleagues. Though obviously proud to have been the first child of a "blue-collar family," as the *Navy Times* had put it, to work her way through college—the "icing on the cake," as her father said, a Ph.D. from MIT—it was clear that, unlike other aspiring postdoctoral students, she wouldn't allow her pride to stand in the way of admitting to a better idea from colleagues. It was one of the reasons, Rorke concluded, that she had been appointed senior scientist in charge of upgrading the Mark 48 ADCAP torpedoes and the Mark 50, the revolutionary ship and *air*-launchable nine-foot-four-inch-long by 12.75-inch-diameter torpedo, which was half the size of the ADCAP and less than a quarter its weight.

"Well, Captain," she told Rorke, "when you start using the 50B, you can forget all about the problems of wire guidance. It'll be strictly 'shoot and scoot.' No hanging about."

"Great, but don't we already have that with the present Mark 50?"

"Yes, but the 50B'll give you fifteen more knots."

Which meant it would have *twice* the speed of the ADCAP.

He was obviously impressed, and ushered her into the wardroom, where a sonar operator had taken in the reams of the two fired torpedoes' telemetry printout for her perusal.

"Like a coffee, Doctor?" Rorke asked. "Hot chocolate?"

Alicia declined. The excitement and anxiety of the launch was all the stimulus she needed to stay awake. "May I ask," she ventured coyly, "where we are?" Before he could answer either way, she added, "I'm guessing on the Nanoose range?" She was referring to the testing range east of Vancouver Island loaned to the U.S. Navy by Canada for firing and retrieval of dummy warhead torpedoes.

"Nope!" he said good-naturedly. "The Nanoose range is so full of sh—er, crap, miles of used wire and other Navy debris. Bangor had to hire Oregon Oceanics to clean it up. We're nowhere near it. We're west of Cape Flattery."

"That's off Washington State, right?"

"Right."

"Most northwesterly point of the continental U.S."

He raised his coffee mug in salute. "Were you on *Who Wants to Be a Millionaire?*"

"Oh no," she laughed. "No—I couldn't stand the strain."

"Ah, too bad." He smiled. "I could have been your lifeline." He said it jocularly but pointedly, sipping his coffee. Their eyes met. He saw her blush like a schoolgirl.

"Ah," she stammered, "how long will it take to clean up Goose—I mean Nanoose—Island?"

He laughed; an open, breezy laugh. "Nanoose *Bay*."

"What—oh yes, of course. *Bay*."

Rorke shrugged. "Month or two. Hall, the guy who runs Oregon Oceanics, works pretty fast. Unlike most government contractors, he doesn't soak the taxpayer. Ex-SEAL and SALERT. One of Freeman's boys."

Rorke could see Alicia hadn't heard of either Freeman, the retired general, or Frank Hall, oceanographer extraordinaire. Or was she still trying to find her feet after his subtle but unmistakable pass?

"Freeman's a tough old buzzard," explained Rorke. "Ex-SpecFor warrior. *Very* unpopular in Washington, D.C. Has a nasty name for bureaucrats."

"Oh?" Then, to show him she was no neophyte, blushing notwithstanding, she asked, "Well, aren't you going to tell me?"

"No, ma'am. It's not for the likes of you."

"You mean I'm a goody-two-shoes."

He paused, putting down the coffee mug. "Yes, ma'am, you are. You're a lady."

She was shocked. On a sub, she'd expected to be treated as an equal by the officers—she had a Ph.D. to make the point. But a *lady*. For a man who captained the most technologically advanced "weapons platform"—that is, "killing ship"—in the world, "lady" struck Alicia as delightfully old-fashioned. "Thank you, kind sir."

He nodded appreciatively. "I'll leave you to your work." He glanced at his watch, as if in sudden need of an excuse to go. "We'll be heading through the Juan de Fuca Strait soon, back to base."

"Fine." She hesitated, then followed him briskly down the corridor. "Thank you for letting me use your stateroom. I'd expected to have to—" She was flustered again. "Actually, I don't know what I expected."

"Doss down with the crew? Now *that* would've taken the edge off them."

With that, he was gone, leaving her in the wardroom, staring at the seemingly endless printout of telemetry. She made a mental note that when she got back to the lab ashore, she needed to do another security check on all her lab personnel—a mandatory requirement for all department heads, ever since Hansen of the FBI had avoided such regular checkups to become the most infamous Russian spy in America's history. And it would be a good excuse to check Captain Rorke's file. He wasn't wearing a wedding ring. But was he engaged? Estranged? It wasn't the sort of question you could ask the crew.

Though it had been a short exercise patrol, Alicia, toiling back in the wardroom with her telemetric data, had become attuned to the slight variation of sound in the sub that indicated a change in speed. Now it felt as if the *Utah* was barely moving. "Are we stopping?" she asked a steward who was cleaning up the wardroom.

"No, ma'am. We're still underway, but we're entering Juan de Fuca Strait. It's always busy, but especially now that it's fall."

"How's that?"

"There's a lot of shipping," he answered.

"There's always a lot of shipping," Alicia said, nonplussed, as she put down her marker pen to take a break from the rows of oceanographic data. "It's one of the busiest waterways in the world."

"Well, you know, it's snakehead time. Asian smugglers bringing illegals across into Canada and the U.S. They try their luck starting springtime. Too cold in the winter. They'd freeze to death in those containers. It's bad enough for 'em being locked in there for three weeks, with other containers stacked on top of them and all around them." The steward picked up empty mugs and swiped the wardroom table with a chamois. "Some don't come in container ships—try to sneak in on some rust bucket during the night with no navigation lights, no lights period. Figure that once they're through the strait and get to where it widens into the funnel of Puget Sound, they're home and away, get lost amid the myriad islands."

Amid the myriad islands. Alicia was taken more by the steward's vocabulary than by what he was telling her. She knew about the ongoing problem of illegals trying to slip into North America, with Canada being particularly known as the softest touch in the world for immigrants. It had harbored everyone from genuine refugees to Nazi war criminals and terrorists, but a steward who used a phrase such as "amid the myriad islands" was intriguing.

"Forgive me if I'm prying," she said, "but have you always been in the Navy?"

"Yes, ma'am. From high school on." He could see where she was headed—he'd been asked the same kind of question before. "I like what I do," he explained. "I'm not really a people person. In this job I know exactly what I have to do. At the end of my watch, that's it. Gives me lots of time to read. That's what I like doing best."

"Aha!" she said, smiling, folding her arms and sitting up straight-backed against the bulkhead in a mildly triumphant mood. It was a moment of exuberant empathy. "You're one of *us.*"

"I'm no scientist, ma'am." But Alicia knew he knew what she meant, and she knew she was flirting. She was surprised at herself, even mildly disapproving, but she was enjoying it. She didn't lack confidence in her job, but she was essentially a shy person, her white lab coat ashore evoking a more impersonal, reserved impression—that of the cool, objective scientist who, if not devoid of emotions, kept them under tight rein. That is, until Rorke had showed up and—

The G sharp sounded again.

"Man battle stations! Man battle stations!"

CHAPTER SIX

HEADING OUT FAST from the Coast Guard station at the end of Ediz Hook in Port Angeles into the fogbound darkness of the fifteen-mile-wide, seventy-mile-long strait, the five-man, thirty-foot rigid hull inflatable Bruiser bucked its way northwest toward the dark, brooding mass of Vancouver Island. Six miles out, the coxswain of the Bruiser began a wide left turn, setting a westward course just south of the "line"—the maritime boundary that divided the west to east strait between the U.S. and Canada.

The twin diesels' "Jacuzzi" propulsion system now at full throttle, the Bruiser headed into the swells that came funneling in from the Pacific, the breakers' first landfall Tatoosh Island off Cape Flattery. The coxswain and his observer, though seated behind the steering console's protective windscreen, were as drenched in spray as the diving-cum-medical/mechanical technician and the two other divers, Rafe Albinski and Peter Dixon. Aft of the platform, they held their air tanks and other equipment while clutching the grab rail against the sea's incessant pounding. Though almost opaque with salt particles, their fall masks nevertheless afforded some protection against the biting wind. There was little conversation, the effort required to be heard above wind, sea, and the RIB's body-bashing progress against the swells at thirty miles per hour being conserved for the dive, which was always a tricky proposition, given the often heavy maritime traffic, the state of the sea, and the strong currents in the strait. Fortunately, Admiral Jensen's request had come at the tide's ebb, giving Albinski and Dixon reasonably stable underwater conditions before the incoming tide made conditions above and below hazardous for both RIB and divers alike.

The coxswain, his observer, and the technician strained to pick up any sign of shipping. Despite the strait being the conduit to Seattle to the south, Vancouver to the north, and much of the Pacific Northwest in between, it was notoriously difficult to pick up the pinpoints of starboard and portside navigation lights, given the sprinkling of shore lights on the U.S. Olympic peninsula or on the equally sparsely populated west coast of Vancouver Island. Besides, in the predawn fog the RIB would be virtually impossible to see by shipping traffic, despite the light the coxswain had rigged atop the boat's air-filter-shaped radar dome seven feet above the stern. On a reasonably calm sea, day or night, the radar's sweep would pick up oncoming traffic, but in this kind of chop, the radar's outgoing signals were often bounced back by high swells and covered the radar screen with "ground pepper" sea clutter. The men's biggest fear was the presence of an oil tanker coming through the strait, en route to Washington's Cherry Point refinery. The quarter-million-ton behemoths, pushing an enormous bow wave before them, were incapable of stopping in under seven miles, despite using full reverse thrusts and their props, and thus obliterating anything and anybody in their path.

Twenty-six-year-old SEAL Peter Dixon, one hand on the grab rail, edged toward the coxswain, asking loudly, "How long?"

"Longer than yours!" yelled the coxswain, grinning in the faint glow of the instrument panel. Dixon's response: a short, loud obscenity.

"A half hour," the technician answered.

"My kidneys are rupturing!" put in Rafe Albinski, Dixon's diving buddy.

"You shouldn't have any by now!" joshed Dixon, a reference to the thirty-five-year-old Albinski's long list of gut-jarring missions, one of the most dangerous being during Desert Storm when Albinski, Dixon, and other SEALs, inserted by low silhouette fast boats, had sneaked ashore, planting timer-equipped explosives and assorted machine gun and small arms noisemakers. When these went off, the Iraqis panicked. Believing that the U.S. Marines in the hovercrafts and other vessels offshore were about to land troops, they called for reinforcements—52,000 of them. The SEAL's colossal feint had thus diverted four Iraqi divisions away from the real Allied offensive.

It had been a tough, exhausting mission, but the truth was, Albinski would have preferred to be on another such covert op than here in the strait. The thirty-foot Bruiser was more than living up to its name, the craft's lower fiberglass hull and nylon neoprene upper hull taking the kind of punishment en route to Darkstar's anomaly site unknown to most surface sailors, even to the old-timers of World War II's Corvette navy, most of them Canadian. They would have recalled the constant battering of the sea against their small ships during the bitter do-or-die Battle of the Atlantic against German U-boats. At sustained periods from thirty to forty miles per hour, the punishment taken by the human body was so severe that more often than not men came back from the high-speed, cold, numbing missions literally bruised black and blue, to say nothing of the long-term effects on their internal organs. Ironically, Dixon and Albinski were relatively warm, the quarter-inch foam beneath their neoprene wet suits having trapped any water entering the suit, their body heat then warming this to create an insulated layer.

Twenty minutes later, as dawn's light suffused the fog and began burning off the mist, the coxswain turned to the two divers, shouting, "Making good time! Be there in five minutes!" Double-checking his console's GPS, he told the technician, "Make ready marker buoy," checked that the RIB's diving light array was working, and quickly switched it off—all lights working as they should. The next time he turned them on, they'd be on station. Dixon reached forward for his black attack board, the size of a child's flotation board, only heavier, embedded with a depth gauge, shockproof digital watch and compass, a four-inch-diameter handgrip slot cut on either side of the board. Counting each kick while watching the dials, Dixon and Albinski would be able to estimate how far they were going on their search pattern of the anomaly grid. As Dixon grabbed for the board, the Bruiser was punched hard midships in a cross swell, flinging him against the grab rail, the attack board clattering onto the platform.

"That'll help it," said Albinski wryly.

Abruptly, the motors died to slow/idle, the RIB's diving lights on.

"After all this," said Dixon, adjusting his face mask, "I hope we find something."

The RIB technician was busy helping the divers with their tanks, weight belts, and the rest, and the coxswain maneuvered the boat to provide as stable a platform as possible against the incoming tide. But once the divers were over, he knew there'd be nothing to do but sit. And wait. For the mechanic, the pitch and yaw of the boat by the marker buoy on station was much more likely to make him feel queasy than the bruising run out from Port Angeles.

In the next minute both divers checked their flashlights and spat on the inside of their face masks, rubbing the spittle about as a condensation preventative, ready to go over the starboard side. Dixon would lead with the attack board.

The crew of the *Utah* were no longer on battle stations, a sonar man having mistaken the sound of a Canadian sub—indeed, the only sub the Canadians had on their west coast—as that of a possible hostile. Alicia had returned to the wardroom, working on the torpedoes' telemetry data, when Rorke reentered and poured himself a coffee. "Hope we didn't frighten you with that latest alert?"

"I wasn't frightened."

He seemed not to hear, continuing, "Repairs to the sub's diving planes changed the Canadians' sound signature as it egressed from Esquimalt. That's Vancouver Island's southeastern harbor."

She knew where it was. It was a big Canadian naval base, full of obsolete warships. "Shouldn't that have been in your listening mike SOSUS computers?" she asked. "I mean, shouldn't the microphones have picked up the sub's new signature?"

"Murphy's Law," he answered.

"On the most sophisticated WP in the world?" she countered with mock severity, her use of WP for "weapons platform" telling him she knew more than he might think.

"Yes," he answered quietly, defensively. It was the first time Alicia had seen *Utah*'s captain look anything like sheepish as he added, "Canucks should have notified us."

"Perhaps they did?" Why was she doing this? she asked herself, her tone with him becoming almost accusatory when what she really wanted to do was endear herself to him. Was it her professional curiosity overriding her amorous intent? Or was it some latent feminist aggressive streak in her that had driven her to the top of her field in a world still overwhelmingly dominated by men? But she didn't like feminists. In her opinion, they were pushy and shrill.

"Perhaps they did notify us," Rorke conceded. "Anyway," he added tersely, "I'm responsible."

Oh damn, she thought, no he's not. But he was adopting the Navy's time-honored stance that whoever was in command *was* responsible. If a seaquake, which happened often enough near the Juan de Fuca plate, swallowed up his sub, he would still be held responsible as far as the Navy was concerned.

"I'm sorry," Alicia said hastily. "I didn't mean to imply—"

"Captain!" It was the officer of the deck, Ray Peel, on the speaker. "Bogey on screen."

"Coming," Rorke replied, striding out of the wardroom.

Now she'd missed the opportunity to apologize, she realized. What had begun as a simple tease had ended in an absolute muddle, precisely the opposite of what she'd intended. She knew a lot about telemetry, but men?

"What's your best guess, gentlemen?" Rorke asked his sonar operators, each one working the scores of vertical lines on his green "waterfall" screen, each wiggle representing a different sound from the cacophony in what most people erroneously imagined was a silent underworld. "Whales?" Rorke suggested. "Shrimp? Distant volcanic—"

"Definitely not a sub," the senior sonar man replied, the others readily agreeing. "It's very weak, sir. But it's there."

"Distant Ivan?" Rorke pressed, meaning the noise might be the remnants of a faraway active pulse from a Russian sub.

"No, sir. Not a sub. No way."

"Very well," said Rorke, his eyes scanning the arc of green falls to his right. "Keep tracking it. Officer of the deck, no change of watch for sonar men while we're on this."

"No change of watch, aye, sir," Ray Peel acknowledged.

CHAPTER SEVEN

THE TWO DIVERS fell back in unison, the cold, backward plunge hitting Dixon's forehead with the force of an ice cream headache in high summer, startling his senses into high alert. Rafe Albinski's reaction was more sanguine. Long experience plus his naturally more relaxed nature allowed him to absorb the facial shock as little more than one experienced during a dramatic change of temperature while taking a shower. It was something which happened to him frequently whenever his seventeen-year-old son, Dirk, against house rules, turned on the hot water tap in his basement shower, momentarily freezing Rafe in the upstairs shower, where Rafe would thump the wall. "Goddammit, Dirk!" Albinski smiled when he thought of Dirk. They were close—except when he turned on the basement tap.

The attack board, its outline surprisingly sharp in the flashlight's beam because of the renowned clarity of the waters in the Pacific Northwest, was already registering temperature, depth, and direction as the two divers began their search. Within five minutes of beginning the grid, the fog-filtered dawn that had afforded them initial light, allowing them to see the variegated colors of marine life passing by, grew faint as they went deeper. Midway along the northern perimeter of their search grid, Dixon, through dim flashes of silver herring, saw the temperature on both the attack board and on the mercury thermometer built into the Coke-can-sized water bottle sampler on the board's right-hand side registering an increase of three degrees. It was a big jump from the norm for that time of year. His left hand on the board's side grip, and letting his flashlight temporarily dangle from his wrist, he used his right hand to scratch *3 degree jump @ 31 feet* on the board's slate, and pointed at the board's thermometer for Albinski to see. Albinski was signaling them up for a surface temperature check.

As they broke through the undulating gray mirror above them that was the sea's surface, they noticed a drop in temperature here too, of half a degree, which they knew would have been enough to register as an anomaly. Dixon gave the thumbs-up to the mechanic on the Bruiser fifty yards away, then both divers descended again.

At forty-five feet they saw that the temperature had changed from three degrees at thirty-one feet to four degrees. Dixon tripped the water bottle through an arc of 180 degrees. Both spring-loaded rubber stoppers at either end clamped shut, trapping the water sample at that depth, the 180-degree fall breaking the mercury column so that the temperature reading now registered on the thermometer would remain the same, no matter how deep or shallow they dived. Dixon scratched the slate board, *45 feet, bottle tripped*. As they went deeper, the temperature rose another degree, though it should have been falling, but the lateral dimension of the anomalous patch at this depth was small, no more than twenty yards across. The whole anomaly grid took the shape of a dumbbell, about fifteen yards wide at its waist and fifty to sixty yards long, the ends of the dumbbell each about thirty yards across. They went deeper still, and the temperature became hotter relative to the surrounding ocean, the diameter of the dumbbell's waist now decreasing to no more than five yards across. From this they were able to deduce that whatever effluent was at work, it was pluming up from the ocean bottom in a conical shape, narrow at its source, widest at the surface, like a double ice cream cone. Albinski hypothesized that the source point of the plume was only a few yards or even feet wide. The one thing they were sure of was that whatever was bubbling up from the depths, its relative salinity compared to the surrounding ocean had no doubt produced the different color effect seen from on high by Darkstar. It was definitely not oil.

Soon Albinski and Dixon were down to 115 feet, pressing the normal safety limits for this section of the strait. Albinski tapped his buddy's arm, signaling them to go up. Dixon was keen to press beyond the normal safety limit, but for veteran Albinski, there was no sense in risking your life if people weren't in danger. This was strictly a recon grid for COMSUBPAC-9, and recon in peacetime wasn't worth risking the bends for. That way, you stayed alive, lived long enough to collect a veteran's full pension and no-exception catastrophic medical coverage for you and your family. Besides, Albinski thought he had a damn good idea what was causing the anomaly.

The RIB's coxswain, his observer, and the mechanic strained to help the two divers aboard the RIB. Albinski and Dixon streamed with water in the gray dawn, like two harbor seals sliding over the gunwales, the Bruiser bobbing up and down in the increasingly aggressive chop.

"Find anything?" asked the coxswain as he turned the Bruiser downwind for the run back to Port Angeles.

"Temperature anomaly," replied Dixon, pulling up his face mask. "No oil, though."

"Upwelling?" the coxswain asked. "Freshwater spring?"

"Can't tell till we do a chemical analysis of the water sample," Albinski replied. "I think it's probably a water tank or refrigeration unit leaking from some old wreck. Not very big. Probably an old trawler. Something relatively small."

"Wouldn't it have leaked out by now, whatever it is?" asked the coxswain.

"No," replied Albinski. "The *Arizona* in Pearl Harbor is still leaking oil from when it was sunk in 'forty-one."

The coxswain shook his head, his voice rising against the brisk wet wind and the noise of spray splattering the RIB's salt-encrusted windscreen. "Coast Guard says they did a sonar run over it. Saw nothing."

"Could've missed it," countered Dixon, dropping his flippers onto the equipment slab. "A hundred yards either way and you'd see zilch."

This possibility, the coxswain knew, would have been more than likely in the old pre-GPS days, but not now. Albinski and Dixon had been given precisely the same coordinates as the Coast Guard vessel.

"Maybe it *is* a simple upwelling," conceded Albinski. "Freshwater or saline from an undersea aquifer?"

"But even the Coast Guard sonar trace saw nothing," countered Dixon. "So how come we get a *temperature* anomaly and the CG doesn't?"

That had Albinski and everyone else on the Bruiser stumped.

As the Bruiser returned to Port Angeles, the coxswain radioed ahead to base. "How long will we have to wait until we get the results of our water bottle analysis?"

"Two hours. Admiral Jensen's given this one top priority."

"It's nothing," opined the mechanic as the coxswain ceased transmission. "Jensen's a worry gut. Glass half empty—all the time. Admiral Gloomboots."

They all laughed at "Gloomboots," a name that stuck for a full hour and forty-three minutes until the Coast Guard's Seattle lab e-mailed Port Angeles the chemical analysis of Albinski's water bottle sample. *Highly toxic*, and proof positive that whatever the source material was that had reacted with the supersaturated saline solution of the sea, it had generated a "significantly high temperature differential of plus or minus four degrees."

Everyone was suddenly a Gloomboots. First question: Why hadn't the Coast Guard water sample revealed any toxicity? Even if the Coast Guard vessel had not passed exactly over the dumbbell zone and somehow missed a clear sonar profile of the sea bottom there, the surrounding water surely would have been toxic enough to have been measured by a Coulter counter that could identify minute parts per million. Second question: Were there any known naturally occurring toxicities of this type on the sea bottom in that part of the strait?

The answer to the second question was no. Oceanographic charts showed no wrecks in that location that might be leaking toxic materials.

Albinski, however, reflecting on his long SEAL experience of invasion beach surveys, was able to offer a reasonable explanation for the Coast Guard vessel not discerning any temperature anomaly. Its prop would have been churning the sea's surface so violently, he said, and sucking in such a flood of colder water from outside the dumbbell perimeter, that any temperature difference could have been so small as to be virtually undetectable, given the mix.

"All right," Jensen told Duty Officer Morgan at Bangor. "Order a *side-scan* sonar." The expense was now warranted, for he knew that if Greenpeace, the Sierra Club, or any of the other environmental organizations got wind of this anomaly—it didn't bear thinking about. And that very morning the Chief of Naval Operations in Washington, D.C., had e-mailed a request for Jensen to forward an updated résumé vis-à-vis his estimation of COMSUBPAC-9's liaison with Puget Sound residents. The CNO was doubtless gearing up in the search for a successor who rated high in PR skills. In the same e-mail the CNO asked Jensen to rate his own performance on a scale of one to ten. Jensen e-mailed that he was a nine. He told Margaret he believed he was a ten but it was prudent to show a little humility.

"Have our two SEALs go back and do a deep dive," he ordered Duty Officer Morgan. Morgan suggested the divers use Frank Hall's oceanics vessel *Petrel II*. The oceanographic ship had all the required equipment for a deep dive, even LOSHOK explosive to send sound waves down for its side-scan sonar should the sonar's electric transponder malfunction. Plus *Petrel II*, more commonly known as *Petrel*, was a civilian ship and a common sight in Northwest waters. A simple press release from Bangor could claim *Petrel* was moving farther west of Nanoose Bay, where it was usually employed to retrieve practice torpedo debris. The release could emphasize the Navy's zero tolerance for scrap metal, especially the miles of torpedo guidance wire that, since the thousands of practice firings during World War II, had until now been permitted to pollute the strait.

"Damn good PR, Morgan," said the admiral.

"And it'll be the truth," Morgan added, elated by the admiral's appreciation. "I mean, this anomaly *is* polluting. Have to clean it up."

"Precisely."

There was silence on the line. "Admiral?"

"Why didn't the CG water sample show anything?" the admiral asked. "This water bottle would have been taken below the prop wash that Albinski was talking about?"

"Faulty equipment?" proffered Morgan.

"Perhaps." But the admiral didn't sound convinced.

"Want the Coast Guard to do it again, sir?" suggested Morgan. "Same vessel. Tell them not to change any of the equipment. Do it just as they did the first time. A double check."

"Good idea."

The Coast Guard steamed over the "dumbbell" in the morning fog and took another sample. It showed a three-degree difference in the water *and* high toxicity.

"What in hell's going on?" Jensen asked Morgan from his study, his voice tired. He hadn't had a wink of sleep since Morgan called in the first situation report. Before the duty officer could answer, Jensen continued, "Where's the *Utah*? Could it have anything to do with this?"

"No way, sir. Last SITREP says that it's heading into the strait as we speak. Over twenty miles to the west. It had a practice target firing. And one false alert. Nowhere near the anomaly."

The admiral paced his office, gazing out at the cobalt blue of the Hood Canal and the wildly beautiful mountains of the snow-topped Olympic peninsula beyond. Something was odd about the Coast Guard not getting any anomalous reading the first time around. No salinity change. No temperature change. "Weird," he muttered. Then the admiral had a burst of inspiration, his voice suddenly losing its fatigue. "It's an old torpedo, Morgan! By God, why didn't I think of it before? Leaking.

Those two divers reported it's a small source area, right? Cone-shaped?"

"Yes," agreed Morgan.

"Damn torpedo's buried in mud, Morgan, that's why Coast Guard sonar didn't pick up a profile! How long will it take those two divers from the RIB to reach *Petrel*?" he asked impatiently. "They would need the ship's special salvage deeper diving gear."

"They could be there within half an hour, sir—it'd only be a short helo hop from Port Angeles to the ship."

"Do it."

"Yes, sir."

"What's going on?" Margaret Jensen asked her husband as he appeared, bleary-eyed, at the kitchen table.

"I don't know," he answered truthfully, less sure about his idea of the torpedo now. Sonar penetrated mud. Still, whether you got a profile did depend on the angle of approach. He knew about Ballard's difficulty in finding the *Titanic*. Still . . . God, he wished life was simpler. She slid the *Seattle Post Intelligencer* toward him. "Dammit, Margaret, just once I'd like to get the paper in one piece. After you're finished with it I can't find a damn thing."

She poured him coffee. "It's probably nothing."

"It's *something*," he said, turning the paper inside out until he finally found the social section.

"There's a good photo of you," Margaret told him, "on page two."

He grunted, but turned to it nevertheless. She was right. Both of them looked good—though she'd never admit it. He couldn't remember Margaret ever saying she'd taken a good photo. Couldn't remember *any* woman saying she liked her photo. Something always wrong with their damned hair. But there they both were, standing next to the wonder boy Gates himself. "It's something toxic," he told her.

"How long before you know the cause?" she asked, without looking up from the funnies.

"Tonight possibly. Divers are going down."

"Again?"

"To the bottom. Civilian research vessel."

"I should hope it's before nightfall."

He said nothing, turning the paper noisily back to the front page. China and Taiwan were on the boil again. Beijing, resurrecting the confrontations of the fifties and sixties, when the PLA had shelled the Taiwanese islands of Matsu and Quemoy, was warning Taipei not to proclaim independence. If it did, Beijing said there'd be war. The admiral shook his head. The U.S. should never have agreed to defend Taiwan, he thought. If push came to shove, there'd be a war against China as well as the war against terror. War on two fronts—any military's worst nightmare.

"Isn't that dangerous?" Margaret pressed. "Sending them to the sea bottom in those conditions?"

"Yes."

"I'll say a prayer."

"Thanks."

Margaret folded her hands and closed her eyes. He envied her faith. He'd lost his long ago. Some commanders, like the retired nuisance, General Freeman, hadn't, but even Freeman's faith was qualified, his adage being, "Love thy neighbor and keep the son of a bitch in your sights."

As Jensen worried and his wife prayed, the oceanographic ship *Petrel* was casting off from Nanoose Bay and Albinski and Dixon's chopper was heading for it, to land directly on the upper deck's helo pad.

CHAPTER EIGHT

Suzhou, China

OVER SUZHOU, THE ancient canal city of eastern China, the morning mist and smog had turned the autumn sun into a hazy saffron ball, but apart from this, the October dawn had begun much like any other. From around the algae-streaked arch of Wumen Bridge and the myriad *hutongs*—the alleys leading away from the Grand Canal—came the usual sounds of people on their way to work: the crush of jangling bicycles, shouted greetings, the noise of children and the sound of bird sellers. The smoggy air was heavy with the vinegary odor of urine on damp earth and the stench of *feng che*, the night soil carts, mingling with the warm, sweet aromas of the sidewalk stalls selling fresh *mantao* buns, hot soybean drink, and the oil-fried breakfast twists of *youtiao*.

The hunched rider of one of the *feng che* carts passed an old man in a faded blue Mao suit, his chin stubbled, teeth brown and crooked, a homemade cigarette dangling from his lips as he sat on his haunches on the dirt sidewalk outside a dingy, clay-walled house. A small boy, emerging from the dark interior of the house, watched the old man spreading an oil-stained rag before him on the sidewalk and placing on it an odd assortment of screws, small levers, and tire puncture kits. The old man's sinewy hands sifted through the bits and pieces like some aged carrion bird picking over a carcass. Now and then he made a strangled coughing noise, took the drooping cigarette from his mouth, spit, wiped the dribble from his mouth with his wrist, and looked up at the endless river of bicycles streaming to and from the arch of the Wumen Bridge. As always, the cyclists heading to the bridge slowed as they drew level with the old man, for it was here they dismounted and began filing off to the right. There, instead of having to lift and carry their "Flying Pigeon" or "Forever" bicycles up over the stone stairs, they used the narrow, gutter-deep troughs running up and down the arc of the bridge, enabling the dismounted riders to wheel their bikes next to them as they climbed the stairs up and over the arch of the bridge down toward Panmen Gate. High above the gate, red-flagged battlements towered forbiddingly over the crumbling ruins of nearby Rugang Pagoda.

It happened when a small boy, one of the many children who were now running and laughing through the crowded alleys, dashed past the old man and down the embankment steps to the right of the bridge. For a few seconds, urinating into the fetid green water, he was unaware of the commotion that was beginning up on the bridge. A clump of cyclists, head and shoulders barely visible above the bridge's stone balustrade, began shouting, gesticulating wildly down at the him. *"Gan kuai! Gan kuai!"* Grab a pole!

Only then did the boy look up and out at the canal and see the floating lump gyrating slowly in the shadowed eddies beneath the arch. At first he thought it was the body of an infant girl, the infanticide of baby girls as common in Suzhou as in any other province of China, whose strictly enforced policy of one child per couple gave preference to males.

A crowd of onlookers was gathering quickly about the embankment, and as they pulled the body ashore, its sodden Mao suit now an inky blue, the head lolled down like a wet, black mop. Some of the more curious onlookers bent low, peering between the legs of others. A noisy khaki motorcycle and sidecar pulled up, its two traffic policemen in crumpled, baggy white uniforms. They walked over importantly beneath the shade of the sycamore trees, ordering the crowd of drab blue- and gray-clad workers aside. While appearing to move away, the crowd merely moved around, staying more or less where they were until a small blue Jinlin truck arrived, carrying four members of the People's Liberation Army. They were from General Chang's Nanjing Military District's 12th Army, and along with new olive-green uniforms and medals for valor in Tiananmen Square and against the mass protests of the Falun Gong sect, their uniforms sported the new gold shoulder boards of rank.

The soldiers, bearing AK-47s, started shouting orders, but even then the crowd moved reluctantly, some sullenly, to let the soldiers through. One man well back in the crowd asked aloud whether the People's Liberation Army had come armed because they intended killing more of their fellow Chinese or because they were afraid to come among the people unarmed. Someone else, incensed at the comment, shouted that he didn't blame the soldiers for defending themselves these days. Another two of them had been found garroted in the *hutongs* in just the past week, presumably by Xinjiang/Kazakhstan terrorists or members of the "counterrevolutionary" Liu Si Minzhu Yundong—the June 4 democracy movement. Or by the Falun Gong.

As the two policemen searched the body's sodden Mao suit, the four soldiers found it increasingly difficult to keep the onlookers from pressing in, and the soldiers' officer, a young lieutenant, told the policemen to hurry things up. After a quick glance at the dead girl's green identification card, one of the policemen handed it up to the PLA lieutenant.

"*Da bizhi!*" he said. A Big Nose, a foreigner.

The photograph showed a young woman, eighteen years old, five feet four inches, hazel eyes and brown hair now turned black by the water, the engaging smile of the identification card in marked contrast to the gruesome matted hair and bloated corpse that had just been dragged from the canal. The PLA lieutenant showed the photo to his gawking comrades, announcing loudly, "*Meiguoren xuesheng.*" American student. He was disgusted. It was common knowledge that foreign students and "rebellious antisocial elements" among the Chinese students often had postexamination "five-star" beer parties, got blind drunk, fell into the canal, and drowned.

After finishing work, Charles Riser, the attaché for cultural affairs at the U.S. Embassy in Beijing, returned to his apartment in the diplomatic compound near the Friendship Store on Jianguomenwai Daijie. He smiled when he saw the red light blipping on the message machine as he walked in. He'd insisted that Amanda—"Mandy," as he always called his daughter—leave any messages on the home tape machine because the voice mail at the embassy, which like all voice mail was stored on computer chip, could be tapped at leisure by China's feared Gong An Bu— the Public Security Bureau. But because of the relatively old-fashioned message machine he'd had installed at his residence, the Gong An Bu wouldn't be able to retrieve a call once it had been made, unless the they were actually tapping his home line twenty-four hours a day, seven days a week. But he knew he wasn't that important.

He said hello to Mrs. Tse, his *ayi*, who cleaned and made

dinner for him. Mandy had left two messages: one that Charles realized he'd forgotten to erase from last evening, which said she and fellow "totally stressed-out" students—as she put it in her wonderfully mellifluous voice—taking a break from Beijing Culture and Language University in Haidan district, had finally reached Suzhou after a terrible flight on China Air to Hangzhou. They would be in Suzhou for two or three days, depending on the vicissitudes of China Air.

A later second message, obviously from her cell phone, given its broken-up transmission, sounded urgent: "Daddy . . . Wu Ling . . . loaded . . . as usual . . . told me Chang . . ." A rush of static, like fish frying, then: "—tralize . . . or . . . wes . . . kind of deal . . . the mill . . ." More static. Then silence. She sounded frightened.

For his "little girl," as he still called her, to risk the call instead of waiting to tell him whatever it was in person, meant that she must have known she was being followed—or worse, that she might not reach home. Mrs. Tse handed Charles his evening scotch and Evian. He took it like an automaton, didn't say, "Thank you," something he'd never failed to do before, and ran the message back to note the time of her call: 2:00 P.M.

He rang the Beijing Culture and Language University. "Our general office is closed for the day and will reopen . . ." Charles Riser tried to recall her teacher's name. Damn! He should have paid more attention to what she'd told him whenever she came home to visit on the weekend. Where was she staying in Suzhou? All he remembered was that the students had to take a flight to Hangzhou first because there was no airport in Suzhou. *Darn it,* what *was* her teacher's surname? But then, how would a name help him? As cultural attaché, he was only too aware of the massive problem China had with surnames, there being basically only five, creating a nightmarish problem for bureaucrats and businesses alike. One of the few ways overseas Chinese had overcome this problem, and one Riser had encouraged as cultural attaché to the U.S., was to adopt a variety of Anglicized first names so that they became "Homer Wong" or "Irene Li," and the like.

At nine-twenty that evening Charles received a visit from a

Gong An Bu man who read a note aloud saying that the Suzhou coroner's office regretted to inform him that his daughter "Amanda"—he pronounced her surname as "Wiser"—"has drowned dead in Suzhou Canal."

Stunned, Charles could only ask frantically, "Where is she?" If he'd thought about it for a moment, the answer was obvious—the Suzhou morgue—but the shock had hit him like a battering ram.

"I do not know," answered the Gong An Bu man, who added after a few seconds, "Offices will be closed now in Suzhou."

Within seconds of the man leaving, Charles was calling the *wai shi*—the foreign affairs branch of the Gong An Bu—using whatever influence he thought his status as American cultural attaché might exert. The Chinese government, despite all their blather about equality among the people, were, after the Japanese, the most status-conscious crowd Riser had encountered in Asia. While waiting interminably on the phone, he was stressed both by the tension of waiting for the next official up the ladder to respond to him and by the knowledge that someone, maybe one of Mandy's friends, was trying to get through to him. God Almighty! What was happening to his family?

First, his wife Elizabeth had died just two years before. Why? Charles never found out. Mandy, then seventeen, had been inconsolable. All they were told was that it had been a hit and run at night, on the rain-drenched New Jersey Turnpike. Though running late to meet Charles for Mandy's high school graduation in Rockville, Elizabeth had apparently seen a car ahead of hers pulling off to the side, taillights flashing, an elderly woman slumped over the wheel. She pulled off to the shoulder, used her cell phone to call 911, then getting out to help was struck by another vehicle. The impact hurled her over the guardrail and thirty feet down an embankment. A witness, another motorist, said it was a Jeep that had hit her, a Jeep with a gun rack attached to the cabin, trying to pass the vehicle in front on the inside, crossing the shoulder's safety line. In the downpour there'd been no chance for anyone to see the killer's license number, and given the volume of graduation traffic on the turnpike, there'd been no hope of a trace. All that Charlie Riser, graduate of Yale majoring in Fine Arts, could think of then was that it had been a Jeep *with a gun rack.* Hunters. Guns. Violence in America. All the high school shootings. It was one of the reasons he'd applied for the Beijing posting after Mandy graduated from college, to give her a year or two abroad in another culture, without guns.

The operator came back on the line—no one from the university could be reached. The whole of China, it seemed, was asleep. The operator, however, perhaps because she felt some empathy for the Big Nose, added, "Suzhou is really under Nanjing Military District's 12th Army."

Charles phoned 12th Army's headquarters and was told its commanding officer, General Chang, would not return till tomorrow. Stymied, he ran the message again. He skipped "Daddy"—it was too painful—and tried to concentrate on what he thought were the key words. "Wu Ling . . . loaded . . . as usual . . . told me . . . tralize . . . or . . . wes . . . kind of deal . . . the mill."

Wu Ling and Chang were no mystery. One of Mandy's friends, Wu Ling was the mistress of General Chang, a man in current disfavor in the eyes of the Chinese government because of a bungled high-seas attempt by him and rogue Russian cohorts under the Russian General Kornon to hijack the prototype of the U.S. superfast RONE computer. The attempt had been just barely thwarted by U.S. oceanographer Frank Hall and the former Special Forces SALERT buddies of General Freeman.

After Charles had been introduced to Chang during the annual Moon Festival, he discovered that Chang's mistress, Wu Ling, just happened to be enrolled in the same international relations and language courses at BCLU as Mandy. No surprise—every American official's kin were routinely targeted by the Gong An Bu, to be befriended in an effort to gather information about American attachés—spies—in Beijing. Riser knew, of course, that the CIA did precisely the same thing to Chinese college students in America whose parents worked in the Chinese Embassy and consulates throughout the U.S. Like his Chinese counterparts in Washington, he also forwarded anything of interest he picked up at unofficial functions. But his daughter—that was out of bounds. Thinking about the message, he wondered if "or" was part of "either or" or was "or . . . west" northwest? Was "mil" military? It was the first thing he thought of in the post-9/11 world. Or was it a grain "mill," a meeting where some kind of massive trade fraud deal was about to be consummated?

Ten minutes later his phone rang and he snatched it up. It was General Chang expressing "deepest sympathy for your loss" and promising the assistance of Nanjing's 12th Army, whose command included Suzhou, in finding the "antisocial elements responsible" for Mandy's death. There was a terrible silence in Charles's apartment, the home where he and Mandy had laughed and cried and held each other when, after he'd brought her to China, their loss of wife and mother sometimes overwhelmed them.

"So you believe," Charles said slowly, "that she was murdered?"

"Of course," replied Chang, his bluntness at once appreciated and resented by Riser. "This police report from Suzhou," continued the general, "is—how do you Americans say?—a cover-lift?"

"Cover-*up*."

"Yes, a cover-up. The Suzhou police don't want to admit the murder of a foreigner. Bad for tourists. Suzhou depends heavily on tourists."

Riser found himself nodding without speaking, a wave of nausea engulfing him.

Chang said, "Forgive me for prying at this time, Mr. Riser, but was your daughter carrying valuables?"

Charlie Riser was about to throw up. "A robbery? I mean, you think it was a robbery gone bad?" Somehow, not that it made any real difference, Charles found it easier to consider a robbery gone wrong than a straight-out murder.

"Suzhou says no," answered the general, "her *xue-sheng zheng*"—her green card—"was still on her, but perhaps it was still a murder for money, the thief not knowing what to do with the green card. No matter that there is much more tourism these days, the fact is, Mr. Riser, very few Chinese have ever seen a foreigner in the flesh and they would not know what the green card was. Even if they did, they would have to sell it to a foreigner. This is very dangerous."

Chang had a point.

"Leave it to me, Mr. Riser. I will investigate further."

"Thank you, General."

Perhaps, he thought, Chang's offer of assistance was purely self-serving. After Chang's failure with the Russian Kornon to get the RONE supercomputer, the general was probably trying to rehabilitate himself in the hierarchy of Chinese intelligence, to prevent the kind of international strain the murder of an American official's daughter would undoubtedly place on Chinese-American relations—relations which were never good at best, and worse than usual right now because of Taiwan's ever-growing assertive industrial and military strength. Though unlike Kornon he hadn't been "transferred"—that is, exiled to Xinjiang, China's Siberia, as punishment for his failure to grab the latest American technological breakthrough—Chang, like Kornon, would no doubt have to do something spectacular to get back into the good graces of his superiors. Helping Beijing avoid American charges of China's ineptitude in the matter of solving the murder of a young American woman would certainly do the trick. It might put Chang firmly back on the road toward becoming party chairman, head man of China.

In any event, Charlie Riser didn't care about the fact Chang might be helping him just to ingratiate himself with Beijing. The point was, Chang was the one party official who was at least trying to get to the bottom of it. And for that, God bless him.

CHAPTER NINE

Bangor, Washington State

WHILE ADMIRAL JENSEN anxiously waited for the result of Albinski's and Dixon's second dive, he filled in time with an unannounced inspection tour of the submarine base on Hood

Canal, instructing his driver/aide Davis to begin with the "James Bond" house. He meant the huge Magnetic Silencing Facility shed built over water, at the base of which the Trident Boomers and Hunter Killer subs entered in order to be degaussed. This process wiped off their magnetic signature through rows of enormous electrical coils, thus reducing their vulnerability to enemy detection.

Jensen was also inspecting his base's Explosive Handling Wharf, another enormous shed built over water. In this one the forty-four-foot-long, seven-foot-wide Trident D-5 missiles, with their distinctive royal-blue fiberglass protective domes, were being loaded into each of two football-field-long, 18,000-ton Tridents, or boomers. Each boomer held two rows of twelve missiles. Atop each missile sat fourteen five hundred–kiloton reentry vehicles, each housing a thermonuclear warhead. Thus, each boomer was capable of striking, over a range of eight thousand miles, 192 different targets, all of which could be hit from just one U.S. submarine. And each of these 192 bombs was ten times more powerful than the one dropped on Hiroshima. Now, of course, Japan was one of the U.S.'s most reliable allies in Asia. And China, which had once fought with the U.S. against Japan's imperial expansionism, was considered by Washington to be its biggest single threat, notwithstanding America's ongoing war against terrorism.

Satisfied with the efficiency level at both the MSE and the Explosive Handling Wharf, the admiral was driven the mile or so south along the shoreline road to the triangular-shaped Delta Refit Pier, with its docking facilities for two boomers and room for another one in its dry dock. Jensen, continuing to reassure himself that all was well—as it needed to be for a prospective CNO—headed for the "mange," the deforested clear-cut areas in the otherwise heavily forested seven-thousand-acre site where the stocks of C-4 and D-5 missiles were housed deep underground. He worried about the vulnerability of the area, despite the presence of the heavily alarmed security fence that ran around the huge base. He'd assured Washington after 9/11 that even though the "manges" were as visible from the air as any clear-cut area in a commercially logged forest, they were safe.

The protective sheath around the missiles was so far underground that no bomb—not even their own state-of-the-art guided bunker-busting GBU-15s—could penetrate. Except a nuke.

The secure phone in his Humvee rang. It was the 0800 to noon watch duty officer reporting another anomaly. It spooked the admiral, though he took care not to show it as he waved nonchalantly to the skipper of the sleek tug that was gently nudging a boomer into position in the azure blue water that lapped peacefully against the Delta Refit pier.

Switching to open voice so his aide in the Humvee could hear him, Jensen asked the duty officer for more details of this latest Darkstar photograph.

"It's in the same general area as before, Admiral—a bit farther north, in the direction of our San Juan Islands."

"Where exactly?" Jensen demanded as his aide brought up the Canadian Hydrographic Service 1:80,000 scale chart of Juan de Fuca Strait. It showed the waters between the Olympic Peninsula and Admiralty Inlet to the southeast, and north to the edge of the 172 San Juan Islands.

"Exact position," reported the duty officer, "latitude forty-eight degrees twenty-two minutes and three seconds, longitude 123 degrees and four minutes."

Jensen's aide punched in the coordinates and immediately had a red circle on the map, depth reading plus or minus 364 feet.

"How big an area?" asked Jensen.

"Irregular shape—discoloration—'bout two hundred yards in diameter—"

"Wait a minute," said the admiral. How the idea came to him, he didn't know. Maybe it was the jolt of his breakfast coffee, waking him up after the long night. "Enter 'Kelp beds location,'" he instructed the aide, explaining how such discoloration could be caused by large vessel traffic through the strait, ships' bow waves pushing brown kelp before it was scattered again by wind and current.

In milliseconds the laptop's screen was pockmarked with brown splotches along the long western coastline of Whidbey

Island north of Hood Canal and in the funnel-shaped area of sea bounded by Whidbey in the west and narrowing eastward into the long Juan de Fuca Strait between Vancouver Island and the Olympic peninsula. Still, Jensen was so anxious about his possible promotion that he ordered the Coast Guard to check it out, and started imagining everything from a hostile sub being in the area to hostile antisubmarine mines being placed on the bottom—which, when he thought seriously about it, made no sense. For one thing, there was the extensive underwater SOSUS microphone array the U.S. Navy had in the area, as well as all around the Pacific. For another, this second anomaly's location, which was now being investigated by Albinski and Dixon, was not in the egress channel for his subs, unlike the first location. But to be absolutely sure, he demanded that the Coast Guard do a depth-sounding run of this new anomaly, as well as a visual check. Yes, he told himself, admittedly it was a very small area. The duty officer said it was a hundred yards or so across in the 625-square-mile area. But again he thought of Admiral Kimmel, C in C Pacific, who hadn't been given the report of a radar anomaly north of Oahu on the morning of December 7, 1941.

He called the duty officer. "Any report yet from the deep dive at anomaly one?"

"Not yet, sir. *Petrel* is on station now."

"Very well," said the admiral. "I still think—"

He was interrupted by the DO. "Sir, Coast Guard has seen kelp in the vicinity of anomaly two."

"By God," said Jensen, turning to his aide. "Why didn't anyone else think of kelp beds before me, Davis?"

The aide shrugged. "Not as smart as you, Admiral."

Jensen laughed, the first time he'd done so in over forty-eight hours. "You sucking up, Davis?"

"I'd like a posting to Hawaii, sir."

"Well, you're not gonna get it." They both laughed. Ahead was the Explosives Handling Wharf. At its apex, two fully armed Marines manned an M16 machine gun behind sandbags. Another two stood guard as line handlers, in their orange life preservers, as tugs secured boomer SSBN 659, the USS *Will Rogers*, into which one of the big, white, tree-trunk-diameter

D-5 missiles was about to be lowered. Jensen was once again aware of the awesome responsibility he had. Little wonder he worried about everything, from the safety of the missiles to the guards on his sub base's perimeter.

"Must have been kelp," he assured Davis. Though Davis said nothing, the admiral sensed that his assistant wasn't convinced, which uncaged his obsessive streak once again. "All right, then," he told Davis. "Call the DO. Have him send a burst UHF message to the *Utah* and have Captain Rorke pick up a sample of that damned kelp from the site on his way into base."

It was 1100 hours when the admiral's Humvee pulled up at the Trident Refit Facility. It would be hours yet before he'd hear anything from *Petrel*. He glanced at the forest on the other side of the 2.5 mile-wide canal, and the Olympic Mountains beyond. Wild and beautiful. Inside the TRF shed there was no sub, but a search periscope that carried cameras and radar sensors was being tested along with a smaller attack periscope. Nearby, a boomer's 8J scope was having its hermetic seal checked for any possible water, air, or gas leakage.

Looking at the boomer, preoccupied with thoughts about his own days at sea during the Gulf War and the mixed emotions he used to experience on his way out from the base during the eight-hour, fifty-five-mile-long transit up through the canal and the strait into the Pacific, Jensen didn't see the Marine guard and his German shepherd dog coming around the corner of the building. The dog suddenly lunged at him, snarling, baring his teeth. Jensen stopped dead in his tracks. The guard, jerking the dog's leash, apologized. Jensen swallowed hard. "It's all right, soldier. Good to see you doing your job."

"Yes, sir."

Aide Davis saw that the admiral's hand was trembling. Jensen's cell phone rang. "Christ!" His aide walked discreetly away. "Jensen!" the admiral barked into the phone.

"Duty officer, sir. Coast Guard reports nothing unusual. They suspect you're right. Darkstar must have picked up a floating kelp bed. They say kelp can act like oil on water—smooths out a patch so it looks calm compared to the surrounding chop. That would register an anomaly."

"Very well," said Jensen, his voice strained.

"Everything all right, sir?" inquired his aide.

"Yes," answered the admiral. "Seems as though Darkstar gave us a false alarm. That damn thing's too sensitive. Like the temperature gauge in my SUV. Damn thing changes every hundred yards."

His relief after the adrenaline surge caused by the German shepherd, together with the Coast Guard's confirmation of his kelp theory, suddenly gave the admiral a burst of confidence, if not an unusually aggressive, almost arrogant air. During his inspection of one of the boomer's exteriors, he pointed to an abrasion on the sub's anechoic coating—the rubber sonar-absorbing layer applied to the hull to reduce the possibility of detection by enemy sonar pulses. "Make a note, Davis. I want that fixed."

"Yes, sir!"

"Not ASAP," the admiral added and, in his buoyant mood, added his favorite Churchillian phrase: "Action this day!"

"Yes, sir."

Churchill had been very popular since 9/11, the President and his speechmakers having borrowed freely from the great Englishman's World War II speeches.

By the time the shot-up Pave Low, heading south, taking sporadic small arms fire along the way, approached the sun-drenched airfield at Tora Bora, its engines sounded more like a harvester shucking wheat. Hydraulic fluid was bleeding from its belly against the blue Afghan sky and the snowcapped peaks of the Hindu Kush.

Like all such snatch and grab missions, Brentwood's had been a secret operation, but not now that fire trucks, ambulances, and padre were on Code Red, and with rumors flying about the Medal of Honor winner having screwed it up. The stories bandied about the camp temporarily put to flight the stagnant air of insufferable boredom that forms the interregnum between battles.

"Poor bastard," said a tank gunner as he watched Brentwood being stretchered through the blazing heat into the MASH unit, where the soft whirring of the air-conditioning unit delivered a different planet to the Afghan desert. It was a cool place where

Brentwood fought the trauma team "heavies" who tried to strap him down in pre-op, the morphine now losing its battle with the invading horror of consciousness—a time-distorted frenetic attack on his conscience in which he wanted to rush back into the cave and save his buddies. And then the shot of sodium pentathol took over, the cave closing in, smaller by the millisecond, until all light was gone. The monitors' whirring and the periodic alarms of intravenous pumps were heard only by the trauma team in their fight to first save his life and then, if possible, preserve the use of his right arm.

They saved him and the shot-up arm, but the main brachial artery had been severed, and though sewn up with over thirty stitches, it was remarked by Surgeon Major Ainsleigh that this Captain Brentwood's career in the military was now over.

"Lucky bastard!" It was an OR orderly incognito behind his surgical mask, possibly a reservist who had signed up for the adventure of weekend bivouacs and the few extra bucks, not for full-time service in what the "'Ghanistan" troops called "Boring Boring." Their hope was, now that the war on terrorism was winding down, at least in Afghanistan, they'd soon get news they were going home. Back home where a six-pack wasn't against the will of Allah, where a girl was free to go out with whoever might ask her and let a man take off more than her veil.

CHAPTER TEN

GENERAL CHANG WAS as good as his word, calling back by three-fifteen. "Mr. Riser, I have some information about your daughter," he said. "As you probably are aware, my niece, Wu Ling, is—was, excuse me, please—a good friend of your daughter."

"Yes," Riser said, though he had never personally met the general's "niece." "Has she any information?"

The general wasn't used to such directness. In China, one took longer to get to the point, and it was considered impolite to rush. But then again, the general told himself, if someone had murdered *his* daughter, he would be just as impatient for information as was the American. "Wu Ling said she was with your daughter at the Museum of Opera and Theater when she called you."

"Does she remember what my daughter said?"

"A little, I think. That is why I'm calling. She told me it was very noisy. Tourists." He added a lighthearted self-criticism of his fellow countrymen. "Chinese tourists. Very loud." Riser had the will but lacked the energy to laugh openly. "Ah," continued the general, "it may be helpful if you spoke to my niece."

"Is she with you?"

"Yes."

"May I speak to her now?"

"Of course." There was a pause as the general summoned her.

Wu Ling tried to be helpful, but it was hopeless; her English was poor, and she spoke a dialect of Cantonese, not Mandarin, the official language of government and of cultural attachés. And with Riser unable to see her body language, any attempt to splice Mandy's segmented message into something cohesive was impossible. Could he meet her? he asked the general.

"Unfortunately, we are in Suzhou for the next week. Perhaps when we return to Beijing we could arrange—"

"No. Now," said Riser. "I can fly down to Hangzhou then catch the train to Suzhou." Riser heard a rapid, loud exchange between Chang and his "niece." He had never gotten used to the din of Chinese conversation; at times it felt like being assaulted by a human ghetto blaster.

"Wu Ling," Chang apologized, "is very saddened by Miss Riser's death. She does not want to dwell upon it."

"I understand," said Riser, "believe me—" Charles paused to regain his composure. "—but I wouldn't take much of her time. I would be *grateful* for even a half hour. I'll catch the early morning flight." Riser heard Wu Ling agree, albeit reluctantly.

"Perhaps," added Chang, clearly sensitive to Riser's mood, "we could meet somewhere quiet. The Garden of the Master of the Nets. You know it?"

"Yes," said Riser. "Tell Wu Ling I appreciate it. This is very kind of you, General. I won't forget it. Neither will my government."

The truth was, his government didn't know about him going to Hangzhou because Riser knew there was no way his boss and the American ambassador would sanction a trip to Hangzhou tomorrow. It was the day of the Moon Festival, an important all-China, mid-autumn celebration during which cultural attachés posted in Beijing should have remained in the capital, not traveled six hundred miles away to the south, no matter what personal reasons they might have. Besides, China and the U.S. were not on good terms. As usual, there was the perennial tension over the human rights issue in Chinese-occupied Tibet, the ever potentially explosive issue of Taiwan, and now Beijing struggled with the problem of the "Stans"—the countries of central Asia that bordered China. They included Tajikistan, Afghanistan, Kyrgyzstan, Kazakhstan, and Pakistan, with their huge Muslim populations. In particular, there was the problem of Muslim terrorists in China's far northeast region of Xinjiang. In that vast province, almost four times the size of Texas, many of the terrorists were believed to have been financed by al Qaeda.

Charlie Riser, forgetting that he was still on the phone with the general, was surprised to hear Chang speaking. It was a kind of absentmindedness that had frequently overtaken him since Mandy's death.

"Wu Ling," said the general, "tells me that your daughter desired it very much—the garden."

Desired? thought Charlie. It was such a beautiful, albeit unusual, way of putting it.

"Yes," Riser said. "I look forward to it." The thought that he would be walking in a place where his daughter had so recently been was strangely comforting and saddening at the same time.

As usual, China Air was running late. En route to Hangzhou, Riser, irritated by the surliness of a flight attendant, recalled how the nascent airline used to test applications for the job. "Honest to God," the embassy military attaché, Bill Heinz, had told him, "four turns in a swivel chair. If you didn't get dizzy you were in." It was the only airline Charlie knew—from a flight he'd once made to Xian to see the famed buried Stone Warriors—that had landed the aircraft with food trays still down and not cleared. On one flight, both pilot and copilot managed to lock themselves out of the cockpit and, drawing the curtain separating flight deck from passengers, proceeded to bash their way back in by means of a fire axe.

He was relieved when he saw the early morning lights of Hangzhou, still sparsely lit by Western standards. Most of them were clustered east of the West Lake, a long string of lanterns marking the Sudi Causeway, which seemed to be running uphill north to south across the four-square-mile lake as the plane banked, the blackness of the lake dotted here and there by the firefly dots of ferries and sampans.

After the gritty Mongolian dust storms that perennially blanketed Beijing and irritated his contact lenses, it was the fresh, sweet air of Hangzhou's surrounding hills that first struck Charles as he stepped off the plane. The second thing he noticed was the abundance of colored lanterns—Hangzhou would of course be required to celebrate the anniversary of Mao's revolution, but much of the bustle in the city was in preparation for the Moon Festival.

At the Hangzhou rail station there were no soft-seat-class tickets left. Envisaging riding "hard seat," jammed in with masses of "cawking," spitting comrades in a blue haze of cigarette smoke and shouted dialects, Riser told a taxi driver the price he was prepared to pay in yuan for the eighty-mile cab ride to Suzhou. The driver snorted as if the proposed price was ridiculously low. Riser began walking to the next cab in line when the first driver relented. Even so, he wrote down the amount so there could be no "misunderstanding" when they reached Suzhou. *"Ni hùi shuo yingwen ma?"* he asked the driver. Do you speak English?

"Bu shuo," the driver said, shaking his head.

"Zhèci lüxing yào hua duochang shíjian?" How long does it take?

"Two . . . maybe forty hours," the driver told him in English, grinning in the rearview mirror. A comedian.

Charles gave him a smile, though he didn't feel like it. The fact that the teeming life of China, of the world, was going on outside without the slightest concern for his daughter's death seemed monstrous to him. But part of the reason he put his Walkman earphones on again was not so much to shut out the world, but to try to make sense of Mandy's urgent, static-saturated message that he'd taped and replayed at least twenty times. And to hear her voice. And, yes, in part, to black out the teeming, uncaring world, to close his eyes to the passing fields of morning, to retreat like a migraine sufferer, withdrawing from his pain into the cave of darkness. In drawing the shades against the indifference of the world, against its harshness and unrelenting glare, he could see her again, hear her voice. His memory of her and his need for vengeance were the only things that made it possible for him to go through these China days. But he couldn't escape the urgency in her tone.

"Daddy . . . Wu Ling . . . loaded . . . as usual . . . told me Chang . . . tralize . . . or . . . wes . . . kind of deal . . . the mill . . ."

He only hoped Bill Heinz could help.

At first Riser had resisted passing on a copy of the garbled conversation to the military attaché. It seemed to him like giving up something, his daughter's last words, an intensely private thing, to a stranger. But maybe the appropriate agencies could make something of it? Since 9/11, the atmosphere in the embassy had been as paranoid as that in America itself. And so, while not yet recovered from the mind-numbing shock of Mandy's murder, he sought what the media called "closure," while knowing there could never really be any following your child's death. Which was when he had typed out a memo, including the message, to Heinz.

CHAPTER ELEVEN

AT THE SURFACE, the tough fiberglass Kirvy-Morgan diving helmets that Frank Hall's *Petrel* crew had gotten for Rafe Albinski and Peter Dixon were a bright canary yellow atop the SEALs' black neoprene dry suits. Under the suits, they wore their Navy-issue clothing as they dove to reinvestigate Darkstar's first reported anomaly, only this time they would be going much deeper, literally trying to get to the root of the problem.

Within fifteen feet, the canary yellow diving helmets were a light pastel. Another twenty feet, and Frank Hall—his right hand wheeling clockwise, telling the two adjacent winch men to keep lowering—could no longer see the helmets. His eyes shifted instead to the two blocks at the apex of the square A-shaped derrick, the depth needle on each block moving smoothly, registering the two divers' descent. Each of the SEALs' umbilical cords consisted of a half-inch black air, or Kluge, hose, a thin communication wire and nylon tethering rope. They had passed easily over the block's wheel, a coarse, chalky white powder rising from both divers' cables as dried salt particles were spat out by the uncoiling tether rope.

In the nether world 180 feet down, the two SEALs saw the high intensity light of their halogen lamps suddenly speared by a sixty-foot-high forest of kelp moving in a strangely beautiful yet Quixotic ballet, parts of it swaying gracefully side to side in the main east-west current, other strands of the amber plant quivering rebelliously, the rasping sound of frond upon frond faintly audible to the divers' external mikes. Dixon, though the junior of the two, wasn't at all fazed by the sight of the massive kelp barrier, which was so wide their halogen beams couldn't find a perimeter around which they might circumscribe the forest. In fact, Dixon thought it a "cool" diversion, and he radioed Rafe Albinski, "Man, that's pretty!"

Albinski agreed, but he'd lost colleagues to this "pretty" stuff. Like fishing line that could entrap divers, he'd seen this mesmerizing ballet of giant shadow and light turn ugly, the vertical forest breaking up in intertidal flux, collapsing in a morass of interweaving vines. It could be a huge mesh in which men had became quickly entangled, their air used up much faster than normal if they'd succumbed to panic, and then ended up suffering, gasping as hopelessly as a fish trapped in a net.

But they passed through the kelp, turning their mikes' volume down to drown out the irritating abrasive sound of the kelp chafing itself. The immediate drop in the noise level was a welcome respite, so much so that when Albinski felt a juddering sensation against his umbilical air hose, he assumed he'd merely swum against an unseen stalk on the kelp perimeter, and guessed that the impact registered all along the snaking air hose, communication wire, and rope to *Petrel*'s compressor, over 180 feet above them. Then he felt a tug, more like a yank, on his umbilical, causing him to rise several feet before descending again.

Something also sent a shudder down Dixon's air umbilical, but it had not been nearly so strong. "You feel that, Rafe?" Dixon asked his dive buddy. But all he heard was a faint noise like a tap left running. Remembering that he'd squelched the volume button against the kelp, he turned it up. Now he heard a roaring sound as if a dam had burst—perhaps the noise of a bubble cascade picked up by Albinski's mike—so loud it would surely drown out any sound of Albinski confirming a sudden and potentially fatal imbalance of pressure caused by whatever had whacked his umbilical and been thwarted by his helmet's nonreturn valve automatically shutting off, preventing a surge of water into his air hose.

The vibration in Albinski's umbilical's communications wire was so intense that Frank Hall, standing on *Petrel*'s aft deck, saw the A-frame's block bucking violently. He could also hear the splitting of individual strands of the umbilical's tether rope, throwing off droplets from the visible part of the tether line with such force that the shower of water particles hissed as they peppered the waves. The tension meter needle on the A-frame's block was shivering ominously, its point in the red "overload" zone.

Hall turned to Albinski's winch man. "Bring him up!" Dixon's umbilical looked all right.

The fact that Albinski didn't answer Hall's radio call wasn't necessarily conclusive, because Hall knew that Albinski was a pro and might be breathing in air from his Bail bottle, the small, one-hour auxiliary tank that working divers strapped to their back. But without the insulation of air that kept Albinski warm earlier in the dry suit, there was a pressing danger of irreversible hypothermia.

"Rafe!" Frank shouted again, trying to penetrate any semiconscious barrier that might be closing in on the diver, the ex-SEAL oceanographer thinking reflexively to give the diver that extra shot of hope that sometimes made the difference of a few lifesaving seconds.

"All right, Pete," Frank informed Dixon. "We're bringing you up too."

"Copy that."

Petrel's officer of the watch turned the vessel further into the wind to prevent her from rolling too much in the "ball-freezing wind," as the bosun referred to the easterly.

Fourteen miles to the west, Captain Rorke was overseeing his deck party, including Alicia Mayne, carefully descending *Utah*'s vaneless sail down to its base from which to take the water sample requested by Admiral Jensen. It would show no unusual seasonal temperature variation, confirming Jensen's hypothesis, at least in his own mind, that the problem had been current-driven kelp beds, the huge sea plants' own salt and other chemical constituents causing both anomalies sighted by Darkstar.

"Son of a—" began Dixon, abruptly cut off in mid-sentence during his ascent by the noise that, to Frank Hall's ears, sounded like the sustained hiss of a water jet. He heard Dixon gasp,

"Flooding!" followed by a gurgled "Got it! Nonreturn valve closed. Thank Christ!"

"You on Bail bottle?" came Frank's anxious inquiry.

"No. I'm sucking my dick!"

"Didn't know you had one," riposted Frank. It eased the tension momentarily, but why did both divers have trouble with the supposedly foolproof nonreturn valve? Damn thing should have closed immediately when water tried to enter the air lines.

Hall raised his canvas-gloved right hand, moving his forefinger quickly clockwise through the salt air in the seaman's traditional "up fast" signal to the hoist men, both winches now singing in unison. It would be six minutes till Albinski and Dixon were up, water spitting from the A-frame's block and winch drum alike.

Then, suddenly, both winches began to labor, the umbilicals of both divers under enormous strain, the tension meter needle on each winch having swung hard right into the red, quivering. The winch man for Albinski's line donned protective goggles. If the line broke above the surface under the strain, it would come across the deck like a bullwhip. "We're near overburn, Frank," the winch man warned.

Frank's hand was still circling furiously. "Then fucking overburn! Go till there's smoke!" He switched channels to the dry lab. "Lab, you getting this on the trace?"

"Yes, sir. Sonar's recording."

"Well?"

"Two suits in a huge tangle."

"Both hoses severed?"

"Can't tell in all this kelp shit."

"As high density profile as you can."

"We're on it, Captain." The shift from "Hall" or "Frank" to "Captain" measured the mood of urgency that had taken over *Petrel*'s crew of sixteen. Several of them in off-duty wet gear, now that it had begun to rain, coffee mugs in hand, were gathering at center deck aft of the dry lab's overhang, from where they could keep one eye on the A-frame's two blocks and one on the stylus racing across the sonar trace paper. The glacially slow reverse spin of the depth meter told them the two SEALs should reach surface in about five minutes, a few grim side bets being made on Dixon's and Albinski's chance of survival. The onlookers tried to make some sense of the sonar image, but like untrained eyes looking at aerial recon photos, the black and gray shadings against the white paper seemed nothing more than that.

"Smoke!" It was Dixon's winch man. Everybody had expected Albinski's winch to be the first to evidence malfunction since he'd been the first in trouble, but Frank recalled that the Dixon winch was older. The winch man slammed his foot down hard on the brake pedal.

The A-block's depth needle stopped abruptly and Frank screamed, "Slower, you idiot! Tap it!"

Given the enormous weight of the kelp that had wrapped itself around the umbilical, such a sudden brake could exert enough torque to snap the cord as easily as an impatient fisherman jerking his line against a snag.

Albinski's winch man was standing up now in his tractor spring seat for a better view of the A-block meter.

"Sorry, Captain!" said Dixon's winch man. There was obviously nothing they could do till the block cooled.

A crewman was rushing out of the dry lab toward the smoking winch with a foam-nozzle fire extinguisher. "No!" yelled Frank. "Get back in the lab!" Christ, that's all he needed, foam on the winch drum—soap on a rope, lose the vitally needed friction grip of the cord against the drum. "Try it now!" Frank ordered Dixon's winch man over the agonized scream of Albinski's winch.

Now the sonar showed the two divers at about the same depth, eighty-five feet, a "short dip" in the ocean compared to the dives Frank had supervised over the Marianas Trench, which was so deep it could swallow Mount Everest with another five thousand feet of water to spare. But right now the two SEALs, though in much shallower water, were in a much more dangerous situation—a dead weight lift.

"Smoke!" Now it was Albinski's umbilical, but this time the winch man pumped the brake pedal to a stop, the winch hauling up Dixon groaning, the umbilical taut, completely devoid of any slack.

"Smoke!" Dixon's line was overheating again, threatening to snap at any moment, the tether rope's strands starting to "split ragged," as the bosun explained to the cook's young gofer. All bets as to how long it would take were now off. If both divers had gotten to their Bail bottle in time, there was still the question of their energy, nitrogen, oxygen, helium, and air running out.

"Sir?" It was *Petrel*'s second officer. "COMSUBPAC-GRU-9's on the line. They want to know—"

"Not now."

"The admiral's asking—"

"Not *now*!"

CHAPTER TWELVE

"NI HAO," CAME the greeting. At first Riser didn't recognize the general. The commander of Nanjing's 12th Military District had donned the traditional drab blue workers' Mao suit instead of his uniform. Wu Ling, also in the drab blue uniform, looked on shyly.

"Ni hao," replied Riser, extending his hand and nodding to Wu Ling. The general's eyes smiled, and the sparse apology for a mustache momentarily became a straight line, his tobacco-stained teeth highlighted by expensive gold crown and bridge work, his breath so pungent it could have stopped the Shanghai Express. Riser wondered if his own breath was offensive. Mandy would, *had*, occasionally reminded him, "Daddy, I think you need a mint." And since her death—the same thing had hap-

pened after Elizabeth's fatal hit and run—he'd let personal habits slide, didn't give a damn if he'd showered twice a day anymore, polished his shoes, or done the other things he habitually did.

"I am sorry," the general said, "that the flight to Hangzhou was delayed. China Air is not very punctuated."

"Punctual," said Riser, immediately regretting the correction, which many Chinese, particularly higher-ups like Chang, often resented as typical of "Big Nose" arrogance. But Chang laughed easily at his mistake. "Punct-you-all?"

"Yes." Riser smiled, seizing upon the general's good humor to get to the serious questions he wanted to ask, and for which he'd risked the wrath of his boss by foregoing the official Moon Festival festivities in Beijing. Wu Ling trailed behind them, so deferential that it was immediately obvious to Riser that she was not going to be the source of much helpful information.

In the courtyard of the inner garden, Riser suddenly had a powerful sense of déjà vu, so much so that despite his impatience to find out what Chang knew about Mandy's death, he stopped walking, staring at the lanterns and the master's study with its distinctive Ming furniture. He had seen this before, with his wife, but he and Elizabeth had never been to China, let alone Suzhou, together.

Chang was still talking. "I wanted to meet you here. One needs tranquility before—" He saw that Riser had fallen several paces behind him, the attaché's face reminding the general of the British politician Tony Blair, creased with worry lines that momentarily gave him the appearance of a much older man, an effect highlighted by the bereaved cultural attaché's uncharacteristically unkempt appearance.

Riser turned his gaze from the master's study in the garden to the general. "Yes?"

"Perhaps you are not ready?" suggested Chang.

"For what?"

Obviously the American hadn't heard him. "To go to the morgue."

Wu Ling, Riser saw, had tears in her eyes, fighting hard to control her emotion.

"No," Riser told Chang. "I'm not ready. But I have to, I suppose."

"Quite so. I thought the garden might give you a chance to revive your spirits first. Perhaps I should have arranged it the other way around."

"No, no, I'm sorry. I didn't mean to be rude, but I've just—I feel as if I've been here before with my late wife."

"You are correct."

Riser stared at the general, completely nonplused.

"Some years ago," the general explained, "this courtyard was copied in every detail and displayed in New York at the Metropolitan Museum."

"When?" asked Riser, relieved by the possibility that his mind was not imagining things but merely remembering a real, happier time—his Sunday visits to the museum with Elizabeth and Mandy. "Going to church," he used to call it, the highlight of their week, Mandy transfixed by Monet's *Haystacks*.

"I think," replied the general, "it was before your daughter was born."

"Yes." Charles forced himself to return to the present. "What have you found out?"

"She was murdered, Mr. Riser, but I do not think it was for money."

Charles felt his bowels turning to ice. His doubts about Mandy's death had been difficult enough to deal with, but confirmation of his suspicions that she had been randomly attacked— He had to sit down on the stone bench and take a deep breath.

"Perhaps you should not go to the Suzhou coroner." The general meant going to the morgue.

"Yes," said Charles. "I have to see her. Can we go now?"

"If you wish," said Chang, surprised by the energy of Riser's request coming so quickly after what had clearly been a body blow.

"I want to get it over with," Riser told him, sensing the general's surprise.

Outside the Garden of the Master of the Nets, the general resorted to small talk in an effort to amortize the American's pain, explaining to Charles how the garden had been named after a government official so fed up with bureaucracy that he'd decided to abandon his world and become a simple fisherman, casting his nets. Charles appreciated Chang's efforts, and he did understand how the official had felt; how, like so many, he had yearned to be free of it all, as he himself did now—free not only of the bureaucratic world, but of the world itself.

On their arrival at Suzhou's morgue, Wu Ling remained in the car. The building was renovated but still bore all the elements of the brutal Soviet architecture of the 1950s. Chang and Riser passed through a small, cluttered, smoke-filled office. There were three computers, but no one at them, two of the female clerks staring at the "Big Nose," the other preoccupied, doing her nails. The coroner, Mr. Wei, was out, one of them told General Chang, apparently not recognizing him out of uniform.

It was the grim, overpowering smell of antiseptic that first struck Riser. Further inside, however, the morgue looked and sounded disconcertingly gay, with Moon Festival paper lanterns strung all about and Chinese opera wailing from Suzhou's Chinese Central Television channel. Copies of *Renmin Ribao—The People's Daily*—the country's propaganda organ, outdated editions of the *Shanghai Star*, and several tabloids he'd never seen before, featuring front-page pictures of nudes soaking up the sun on some "unnamed" southern beach, were strewn about. Either there wasn't much to do in the Suzhou morgue or it was overstaffed. Had the Gong An Bu seen these ideologically impure publications? Either that or they hadn't been here at all.

There was a short, sharp exchange in dialect between coroner Wei as he returned and the general, an assistant in a bloodstained lab coat quickly gathering up the tabloids and scurrying out to the cramped front office. As if by way of apology for the festive, rather lackadaisical air, or so Charles thought at first, Chang walked over to the TV, seemingly to turn it off, but he surprised Riser by turning the opera up even louder. The high, nasal whine of the *dan*—the female roles played by men—reached such a pitch that Riser was sure he was in for a splitting headache, even though he was more or less conditioned by now to the appalling noise pollution levels in which most of China carried on its business.

"I like opera," Chang told him loudly, while scribbling something on a piece of notepaper and waving Riser over toward the far bank of aluminum freezer trays. "I particularly like this one, 'The People's Justice.' Do you know it?"

"No!" said Riser, so forcefully that it betrayed his irritation, though he'd no sooner said it than he realized that Chang was probably creating what in the embassy they called an ad hoc "special classified intelligence facility"—a rubber-mounted plastic bubble with anechoic coatings, from which no sound could be detected by either beam mikes aimed through glass from outside a building or from fixed mikes hidden in the room.

The experience of having to identify Elizabeth's body still vivid in his memory, Charles steeled himself to be ready when Wei pulled out the cold, calico-sheathed aluminum slab.

There was a delicate lace of ice about her hair. Worried she'd be so cold, Charles gently brushed the frost back from her forehead. The opera was reaching hysterically high levels, and, already queasy from the overpowering antiseptic—a peculiarly sweetish, astringent odor which he knew he would never forget—he said nothing.

Chang, indicating the bruising on her head, spoke quietly in English, as if not wanting any of the coroner's staff to hear. "Say nothing. She was tortured. Raped. Massive internal bruising." With that, the general stood up, pushed the slab in partway, and reaching up, drew down a fifteen-by twenty-four-inch paper bag, taking out a blue Mao suit and a smaller jeweler's packet, spilling out a digital Casio watch and a locket. "Her personal effects. One watch, one locket. You must sign here. Ah—" added Chang awkwardly, "—there is a fee. I am sorry. Twenty yuan."

No doubt it was another foreigner rip-off, but Charles, rummaging beneath his shirt in his money belt, didn't argue. He owed Chang a lot more for telling him the truth.

"I think you need a drink," said Chang.

Charles nodded.

In a small pavement restaurant near Barberry's Pub Café on Liangxi Road, Chang told Charles, "I've found out more since I called you. We think she was tortured because of a message she was trying to get to you."

Charles wasn't taking it in, unable to evict the sight of ice in her hair. So cold and final. Now the general was saying something about "stupid girl." "*What*?"

"Wu Ling," answered Chang. "I've told her never to repeat anything she hears me discussing with Beijing, but I guess it was a—" Chang paused, trying to think of the English word. "—a *juicy* story. About Li Kuan."

The general saw the name meant nothing to Riser; understandably, given the fact that Kuan was a common enough name. Either that or the American cultural attaché was still deep in shock at just having confronted the bleak reality of his daughter's death. She was—had been—a beautiful woman. "Li Kuan—the slag merchant," Chang explained.

Riser, his mind still with his daughter, looked across at the general, refocusing. "Yes." Everyone at the embassy knew about Li Kuan, the slag—leftover radioactive waste—dealer who was hawking the deadly material reclaimed out of everything from spent fuel rods to medical waste, with which terrorists could make a cheap radioactive bomb. And not all of Li Kuan's merchandise was slag. Some, Bill Heinz said, was high weapons grade material stolen from poorly monitored Soviet installations. Riser vaguely recalled Heinz telling him that some "HWG material," as they called it, had been housed in buildings that lacked the most basic video surveillance. All of which made Li Kuan one of the world's deadliest salesmen.

"What's he got to do with Wu Ling?" inquired Riser.

"Wu Ling and her BCLU friends were having a drink at Barberry's Pub. Very popular among—"

"Big Nose students," said Riser.

"Wu Ling went to the ladies' room," explained Chang. "There was a lineup. She overheard a student from Xinjiang province—it's our most northwesterly province. It borders on four of the seven Stans. Kazakhstan, Afghanistan, Uzbeki—"

"I know where it is," said Riser.

"Many Muslims in the area," continued Chang. "Wu Ling heard this student say soon the American and Chinese infidels would pay for their ungodliness, that there would be military attacks in the Northwest. You see, the Muslim fanatics believe anyone who isn't Muslim—"

"I know," said Riser impatiently. "We remember 9/11."

"Yes, of course," said Chang apologetically. "Well, these friends said this Li Kuan had done a deal with holy ones from Xinjiang to Taiwan, that soon their wrath would be unleashed against America and China, that the world would be run instead by the holy ones. I think in English you call them the 'moolas'?"

"Mullahs," said Riser. "So?"

Chang leaned forward, his breath reeking of black bean sauce. "Wu Ling told your daughter and her other friends."

Riser could guess the rest. "The fanatic or his friend realized they'd been overheard and followed Wu Ling and Mandy out of the pub."

"Yes."

"But only Mandy was—"

"Attacked, yes. Perhaps because she was the only American. The terrorists are more afraid of Americans than Chinese. They watched the Iraqi War on CNN. But I don't doubt they intended to kill my Wu Ling and the other students who might have overheard them. But there was much confusion. Wu Ling said many other students came out of the pub. The assassins escaped. By now they are probably in Shanghai, or Xinjiang." Which meant, Riser realized, they would never be found.

"You think it was just beer talk?" Riser asked. "About attacks in the Northwest?" He was thinking of Mandy's frantic phone message. "The Northwest of China or America?"

Chang shrugged. "What puzzles me is, what were two Muslim fanatics doing in a pub?"

Riser hadn't thought of that. Muslims—fanatical Muslims—were forbidden to drink alcohol. "Terrorists have no patent on hypocrisy," said Charles.

"True," agreed Chang.

Riser got up from the table. "I'll pass the information on to Washington."

"Good. It may be nothing," said Chang, "but I will also pass it on to Beijing. The problem is, Mr. Riser, we must be careful."

The inflection Chang gave to "we" was clearly meant to refer to China, *not* America.

"I thought Beijing's policy was to be tough on terrorists."

"Yes," said Chang as they walked back out to rejoin Wu Ling, "we agree with your President. But Beijing must be careful. If it were to attack the terrorists in Taiwan, for example, it could be accused by Washington of using antiterrorism as an excuse, a pretext, to take over Taiwan."

Riser nodded and extended his hand. "You've been very kind to tell me all this, General. I won't forget it."

The general brushed it aside. "If it was my daughter—"

"Yes," said Riser, more sharply than he intended, but he was already thinking of revenge for Mandy's murder. The scum had tortured her.

For a man who was his country's *cultural* attaché, a man presumably more sensitive to the finer things in life, he was taken aback by the depths of his hatred, by his seething desire for vengeance against whoever had killed his daughter. But the more he listened to Mandy's last call, to the fear in her voice, its urgency, the evidence of her courage, the less he cared about the propriety of his thirst for revenge. He wanted the killer or killers—what would be the best he could hope for? Execute them the way the Chinese did it—a shot in the back of the neck? No, that was too quick.

CHAPTER THIRTEEN

IN BEIJING, THE U.S. military attaché, or "MA," as Bill Heinz was called, was trying not to be curt. He was naturally sympathetic to Riser's loss, but dammit, didn't the cultural attaché realize the possible import of Mandy Riser's last message? "You should've told me about this right away, Charlie."

"I did," responded Riser, his voice echoing in the embassy's enclosed security bubble. "I left you that memo before I flew down to Hangzhou."

"Memo? A few words—something about a 'Wu Ling . . . nor . . . wes. . . . ' C'mon, Charlie, I can't send this to the agency. They'll think I've gone China cuckoo. Too long away from the States."

"How about the notes I left you about what General Chang told me?"

"Shit, Charlie, don't you remember the flap in five-oh-two?"

Charlie had to think, military attachés preferring "Milspeak" to English. Five-oh-two? "May, two thousand and two—what about it?" said Charlie.

"Jesus, Charlie," Heinz said more cordially. "What do you CAs do all day anyway? Listen to Peking Opera?"

Before Riser could answer the jest, the military attaché hurried on. "May two thousand and two, Charlie. Congressional hearing on the security gaps before 9/11? How come al-Midhar and Al-hamzi, two of the pricks who took over American Flight 77 and crashed it into the Pentagon, had been identified by the Agency in Kuala Lumpur as al Qaeda operatives—as far back as January oh-two—but we didn't pass the info on to the FBI or State Department? And how come the FBI itself failed on one of its own agent's tips to find out why so many Arabs were taking flight training courses in the U.S.? How come our own Navy secretly builds research vessels and doesn't tell brother agencies about it?"

Heinz answered his own long-winded question. "Interservice rivalry, yes, but just as often, Charlie, it's because people simply don't pass on the intel *in time*!"

Charles looked nonplused.

"What I'm saying, Charlie, is that soon as Chang told you about those terrorists talking about slag in—" Heinz glanced down at Charlie's notes. "—Borberry's Pub—"

"*Bar*berry's."

"Yeah, well, Charlie, for a cultural attaché your handwriting sucks. Point is, old buddy, you should have called me on the hotline immediately. Like, right away! Xinjiang's back-to-back with K-stan," continued the military attaché, meaning Kazakhstan. "And Kazakhstan, Charlie, is *oil*. Three hundred million barrels a year. Most of it's been piped to Russia, but that's changing—fast. China's Petroleum Corp. wants in on the tit. New deposits in the Caspian Sea puts Kazakhstan's reserves to eighteen billion barrels. That, old buddy—now remember this, Charlie—equals three-quarters of the *U.S.*'s total reserves. So we want into K-stan too—cut our dependence on Saudi Arabia et al. A lot of U.S. companies have already invested there. Problem is, among the 228 million people who inhabit the Stans, there are a lot of Muslim fanatics, and not just al Qaeda. Some of these terrorist crazies are stirring it up in K-stan. With one dirty bomb—"

"I'm not that dumb," Riser told his colleague. "No one wants them to set the oil wells on fire."

"Or the pipelines. You let one *martyr* get away with blowing himself up next to a pipeline and it starts a trend."

"You can't punish him," Riser said wryly, "if he's dead."

"Correct. Which is why your info from Chang is red hot, because it's telling us, Washington, D.C., that if there's any sign of Li Kuan, who one of our SpecFor Direct Action teams was supposed to waste in Afghanistan but failed—" Heinz took a breath. "—if there's any sign that Li Kuan and his henchmen are stirring the pot along the Chinese/K-stan border, Beijing's going to kick ass and take names. And Uncle Sam had best stay out of it. Let the PLA get Li Kuan and his mob."

So now Charlie Riser saw something he hadn't before—that while it was nice of Chang to help him cut through the red tape and tell him what happened to Mandy, the general, and thus Beijing, had also seen it as an opportunity to use him as a conduit to the U.S.'s Beijing military attaché, thus informing Washington that Li Kuan, who'd given this SpecFor team the slip, was now headed for the K-stan–Chinese border and/or Taiwan to trigger chaos in China and the oilfields. But hopefully not chaos in America.

"So," proffered Charles, "the Chinese don't want the U.S. to interfere, should they have to wield a bit of stick."

"Correct," said the military attaché. "Oh, in case you're

tempted to get a big head about being the chosen messenger, don't. The Chinese have been feeding us this line for a while through other channels. Not officially—too much danger of leaks to pain-in-the-ass human rights types who'd march on the U.N. if they knew. But if Chang's right about Li Kuan moving to K-stan, we could see SMA there any minute."

"SMA?" Riser asked, knowing it was the MA's acronym for substantial military action, but wanting his colleague to explain it in English.

"Substantial—"

"War," cut in Riser. "In Central Asia—or even Taiwan, if that's where Beijing thinks the terrorists are about to strike. Beijing still sees Taiwan as a province of China."

"Taiwan's a long shot," said the MA, climbing out of the embassy's ICB bubble on the way to the code room. He was going to send this message himself.

Charlie could still see the spidery white frost in Mandy's hair, covering her once lustrous sheen with a web of old age, years before her time. If anything good could possibly come of her death, maybe it would be Beijing's messages to Washington, D.C., via his conversation with General Chang, to give Beijing a free hand against Li Kuan, to hunt him down and kill him.

On *Petrel*, the afterdeck, an island of light in the evening darkness, was illuminated by the arc light atop the A-frame. Albinski's and Dixon's umbilicals, which had earlier been groaning through the A-frame's left block, now had to be stopped every few minutes to clear kelp from them as fast as possible. Then Albinski's winch man called, "Thirty feet to surface." A murmur of excitement passed through the dozen crewmen huddled around the dry lab, only Frank Hall's work party of six men, including the bosun, allowed on the apron of steel directly beneath the A-frame's block.

"Twenty feet to surface."

"How 'bout Dixon?" asked one of the deck party.

"Another sixty-four," answered the diver's winch man, at once grateful for the cooling that each kelp-clearing stop afforded his winch's motor, but worried too, like everyone else, whether the divers—if they were still alive—had enough air left in their Bail bottles to wait out the seemingly never-ending kelp clearance, the weed at times so thick about the umbilical that it wouldn't pass through the block.

"In sight!" announced Albinski's winch man. There was a loud cheer as bubbles erupted in an undulating circle of light that moved up and down the choppy surface like a sodden white sheet, the rain sweeping over it.

"Steady!" Frank cautioned the winch man. Sometimes in the excitement of a surfacing, the winch man miscalculated the rate of hoist during the final seconds of haul in which a diver emerged from the density of sea. His weight in air, if the winch man hadn't geared down fast enough, could suddenly cause him to swing like a freed pendulum, smashing into the ship's stern. "Steady! Steady!" said Frank.

"Holy shit!" It was one of the work party, literally taken aback when instead of the fiberglass helmet he'd expected to see, what was emerging from the sea was like something out of a horror movie: a huge, glistening mass of kelp. Some said afterward it was the size of a VW Beetle—an exaggeration, but it was big, the enormous fronds looking like the tentacles of the giant squids that other oceanographers had found off New Zealand. As yet, no sign of Albinski.

"Don't just stand there!" bellowed the *Petrel*'s bosun. "Get the pikes onto it."

Frank Hall switched his mike channels. "Sonar?" he asked. "What else do you see besides the kelp?"

"Nothing sir. We're too close to it. No definition—just a big blob of kelp obscuring the whole damn trace."

Four of the work party had thrust out their pikes, the long-handled boat hooks grasping Albinski's umbilical four to five feet below the A-frame's starboard block. The men prevented a dangerous pendulum by using counterforce, pulling the umbilical in as *Petrel*'s stern dipped in the swells, pushing against it as the stern rose atop the next swell. Two of the deck party were slicing at the kelp, torn between going so fast that they'd sever the umbilical or so cautiously that they'd lose the race against what they knew must be Albinski's emergency air supply in his

Bail bottle. And all the while, Dixon's umbilical was moving at an agonizing snail's pace through the A-frame's portside block, its "smoke" stops and quivering tension meter needle testimony to the winch operator that he too was hauling in a massive load of kelp.

"You know," said an off-duty crewman standing anxiously by the dry lab, "they use kelp to smooth out ice cream?" The outrageously inappropriate comment was presumably the only way he could deal with his own mounting anxiety.

Dixon's winch man didn't bother to respond. All his attention was on Albinski's umbilical, which was swaying port to starboard and back like a hanged man's rope, the umbilical's thin communication wire missing, the black air hose, though, looking intact.

"Good!" he said aloud.

"What?" said the "ice cream" man, his shadow cutting across the winch drum. "Oh yeah. Amazing stuff, eh?"

"Get outta my light!"

Suddenly, there was a tremendous splash astern, foaming seawater cascading down on the work party, swirling and running out about their feet through the scuppers with furious speed. Two men were sprawled on the deck, cursing and trying to get their wind, when Frank, grasping *Petrel*'s starboard rail, shouted, "Bring 'im in slowly." Albinski's neoprene suit looked bigger than it should have been, his helmet still obscured by an errant swath of kelp that took on a bright cherry color in the arc light.

"Mother of God!" said the bosun, his tone immediately casting a pall over the deck crew.

Frank was helping up one of the men who had been downed in the splash caused by the enormous ball of kelp that had suddenly given way under the pike's probing and plunged back into the sea. "In easy," he said in a tone as gentle as the soft rain that continued to fall, its shadows slicing the deck lamp's light like a black snow.

The cherry-colored helmet contained all that remained of Rafe Albinski. The tremendous sea pressures, set upon him when his one-way nonreturn valve failed to shut, had crushed his body, expelling the ninety-eight percent that was water, pulverizing the remaining two percent of bone, skin, and organs into a paste that was forced by the indifferent laws of physics up the ruptured tube that had been his dry suit into his helmet. What had been his dry suit was now an obscenely bloated Michelin-tire-man figure that, having expanded as it rose to the surface, was disgustingly urinating from a hundred different pin-sized holes.

Two of the deck party had dropped their pikes and run back amidships, being sick over the side, for which Frank Hall would dock them five hundred dollars each. If he'd still been in the Navy, he would have insisted on formally charging them. He knew that ex-SEAL Albinski would have understood his fellow SEAL's action. By deserting the afterdeck, albeit in shock, they had left the work party short-handed with a fellow SEAL's umbilical cord still ascending, when every man in the work party was needed in order to tear off block-choking kelp that Frank fully expected to see wrapped about Dixon's line.

"In sight!" called out the bosun.

"Shit," said the ice cream man. "This bastard's bigger'n the other one." Fortunately he meant the kelp entanglement and not Dixon's dry suit which, once the kelp was cut off, was revealed, unlike Albinski's, to be as form-fitting as it should have been. Even so, with seawater pouring off it, it wasn't certain whether it was puncture-free. It was only when they saw Dixon's eyes, exhausted-looking yet obviously cognizant of what was going on, that they knew his nonreturn valve had continued to function properly.

As Frank disengaged Dixon's fiberglass helmet from its O-ring neck assembly, Dixon was shivering so badly he couldn't speak, his lips purple. But Frank knew the young SEAL desperately wanted to say something: to ask whether his diving buddy was okay. And if not, why?

CHAPTER FOURTEEN

WHEN THE MACHINE-CHATTERING newsroom at CNN headquarters in Atlanta received the report from its Kabul correspondent of a bomb having exploded northwest of Jinhe, no one had any idea where it was. Besides, bombings by terrorists, separatists, freedom fighters, whatever they called themselves, were a dime a dozen, and unless an incident seemed to have any direct bearing on the U.S.'s wider world war against terrorism, it simply didn't make the cut for the news. But a professional sifter in the newsroom was paid to keep tabs on the location of all place names coming in on the media feed, in the event that some out-of-the-way hole in the wall suddenly became prominent. The sifter, clacking away on his computer, heard one of the anchorwoman's assistants add, "Kabul guy reports Chinese troop movement along the border."

"What border?"

The Kabul correspondent spelled it for her; all these "Stans" that sounded alike in central Asia had never meant anything to the American public. Before the wars on terrorism in Afghanistan and Iraq, such countries were ignored by the world in general, relatively few people even knowing they were breakaway republics from the old Soviet Union.

"Along the border with Kaz-akh-stan," said the sifter.

"Here it is," put in another assistant. "Jinhe—some burg 'bout eighty to ninety miles from the Chinese border with Kazakhstan. Looks like it's on the only rail link between the two countries."

"U.S. have anything near it?"

The sifter enlarged the computer map. Jinhe was in Kyrgyzstan, immediately below southeastern Kazakhstan. "Apparently we have a big air base there. Let's see." He tapped the mouse. "At someplace called Manas. Three and a half thousand of our guys."

"Personnel," the anchor told the sifter.

"Yeah, right. Base has been there since 2002—puts us in range of Tajikistan, Afghanistan, Iran. . . . Man, who'd believe it? Most of these Stans used to belong to the Ruskies. Two hundred and thirty million, more than one and a half times the population of Russia. Now we've got a *base* there—fighters, transporters, and tanker planes."

"Hey," added the anchor during a commercial break. "Russia is now a member of NATO. Chew on that."

"World war against terrorism," said the sifter, by way of explanation. "Politics makes strange bedfellows."

"The enemy of my enemy is my friend," said someone else.

"All right," joshed the anchor. "Enough with the proverbs. How big was this bomb attack in this Jinhe?" He glanced at his recessed computer screen.

"Our guy in Kabul," replied the sifter, "says it blew apart the rail tracks for a mile or so."

"Any American citizens killed or injured?" It was the news producer in the booth.

"Don't know yet," said the anchor, shuffling his papers, ready to move on to the next item, but not before hearing a staff member voicing his curiosity about the explosion being so large as to have taken out a mile or so of track.

Within a half hour of the predawn bomb attack on the rail link northwest of Jinhe, between China's far northwestern province and oil-rich Kazakhstan, two Chinese Group Armies, 112,000 men—a fraction of the PLA's three million—crossed the one-thousand-mile-long border on a three-mile front northeast of Jinhe, each army of 56,000 men with their own air engineering and artillery support. In Urumqi, Xinjiang's drab smokestack capital of 1.5 million, 270 miles east of where the two armies were crossing into Kazakhstan, another bomb exploded in a mailbox outside the Holiday Inn, killing three people and injuring a dozen laborers on their way to work early in the morning. This bomb, authorities suspected, was probably meant to explode later, in the morning rush hour. As sirens wailed through the city, the Gong An Bu began rounding up the list of usual suspects, Muslim separatists from among the Muslim Urghurs, who made up 7.3 million of the province's seventeen million inhabitants and had always considered the Han Chinese to be invaders, since as recently as 1955 over ninety percent of Xinjiang's inhabitants were non-Chinese. But now over half the population were Chinese, sent westward in droves by Beijing, who wanted to secure the province, in part to use the salt lake Lop Nur, in the vast area of Xinjiang's Turpan Basin, for further nuclear testing.

The two Group Armies dispatched from the Tacheng subdistrict in Lanzhou, one of China's seven military regions, met only sporadic resistance in the form of AK-47-toting Muslim Urghurs. The latter used Red Arrow antitank guided missiles, which, despite multiple firings whose backblasts and burned solid-propellant blossomed and crisscrossed in the dusty air, took out only eight of the PLA's upgunned T-69s. These Russian-made PLA tanks, with their laser-sighted 125mm cannons, decimated forty-two of the Muslim rebels' old Russian 100mm T-55s, whose three-rounds-a-minute and thousand-meter range could not stand up to the bigger bore, six-rounds-a-minute T-69s. And this despite the fact that many of the Kazakhstanis' old Soviet T-55s had been equipped with reactive armor. The terrorists and nationalists in the Kazakhstani forces had placed high hopes in the reactive armor, whose explosive slabs would detonate when hit by a PLA's T-69 armor-piercing discarding sabot round. But inferior manufacture of the reactive armor meant that it failed to stop the APDS's ten-pound, foot-long dart from penetrating the Kazakhstanis' T-55.

In Kazakhstan's new capital, Astana, 390 miles northwest of China's invasion—or "policing incursion," as Beijing preferred to call it—the ruling Communist party boss, a sullen pro-Russian leftover of the Cold War and the Soviet Union's collapse, did not join the Muslims or the PLA, afraid of the deep and still active Muslim hatred of Russia and the PLA's institutionalized distrust of Moscow. Besides, the Muslims made up almost half the city's population, and the most radical elements were known to make common cause with China's Muslim Urghurs. What the Communist party boss did do, however, was try to contact the elusive Li Kuan. The party boss had connections with old comrades in Russian nuclear facilities who had difficulty making enough money to put bread on the table.

Later that day, in Washington, D.C., the President expressed outrage at the PLA's violation of Kazakhstan's territorial integrity and said he had called in the Chinese ambassador. China's two Group Armies were now fifty miles into the arid steppe of Kazakhstan and kept advancing, albeit slowly, determined to rout every Muslim terrorist out of every crack and cave. The aim was to form a buffer zone between the two countries and secure the vital oil and rail lines between the two from terrorist sabotage, which Beijing said was clearly in both Kazakhstan's and China's national interests.

The U.S. State Department and the White House, in rare agreement, were secretly reaching the same conclusion, despite the President's public expression of dismay. The surge of over a hundred thousand Chinese regulars over the Xinjiang-Kazakhstan border was alarming to some of Foggy Bottom's experts, but a state of open rebellion in China that could ensue should Beijing fail to go after the terrorists was a much worse scenario. As Eleanor Prenty, National Security Advisor, knew, in every administration—indeed in any government—stability won out against chaos every time.

"If you think Yugoslavia breaking up was complex," she told the President, "imagine what the disintegration of Xinjiang would be like." She paused to take out the map of Central Asia she'd had faxed over from State. "There are fourteen national minorities over there," she continued. "Sooner or later, amid all the Muslim rioting, we'd be caught up in it because of our base at Manas in nearby Kyrgyzstan."

"But," said the President, always insistent on playing devil's advocate in his decision-making, "Muslim rioting might break out across *all* the Stans *because* the Chinese have crossed the border."

"Granted," conceded Eleanor. "There could be widespread rioting throughout the Stans and the Muslim world in general. But if Beijing fails to act decisively and go in now after the terrorists' staging areas, it'd be like us sitting still and doing nothing after 9/11. That vital section of rail track destroyed by that terrorist bomb was over two miles long." Eleanor glanced down at her SATRECON report. "Two point six miles, to be exact. And all in one hit, Mr. President—not sequential explosions. We have our problems with Beijing—the perennial human rights issues, especially in Tibet, versus our pro-China trade lobby, who keep arguing, with some merit, that the best way to improve human rights in China is to trade more with them, engage them economically. Beijing's been careful not to announce its intention to cross the border because it would have brought out every human rights activist, and no doubt the Europeans, telling us we should step in, through the U.N."

"And," put in the Chairman of the Joint Chiefs, Sam Wentworth, "the last thing we want, Mr. President, is a war on more than one front. Afghanistan and Iraq were quite enough for us to handle. It'd be a logistical nightmare, no matter how small the operation. I'm with Eleanor on this one. It's China's war on terrorism. And to put it quite bluntly—"

"You ever put it any other way, Sam?" There were smiles from the other armed services chiefs.

"I guess not, Mr. President," the chairman responded gracefully. "My point is, the PLA's strike into Kazakhstan takes the heat off us militarily all the way to the southwest in the Hindu Kush and gives the Euros someone other than the U.S. to whine about."

"Euros? You're excluding Great Britain, I hope."

"Of course," said the chairman, it being a particular point of gratitude in the White House that Britain and most of the British Commonwealth countries, particularly Australia, had stood by America's side in past crises.

"Well then, we're agreed," said the President. "We continue with normal expressions of concern. Beyond that, wait and see."

"The Russians'll be pissed," warned Wentworth. "Former republic and all that."

The President shrugged. "Do they want to be in NATO or not? Besides, they're no fonder of terrorists than we are. They don't like the Chinese, but they want a steady oil flow. Stability."

"Thank God," interjected Eleanor Prenty, "we had unofficial warnings about China's intended move and weren't taken by surprise."

The President nodded. "That girl, Riser—"

"Yes, sir, Mandy Riser."

"This country owes her a lot."

"Yes," agreed CIA head John Norris, who was ever ready to protect his agency's turf in the bureaucratic war spawned by the White House's push to consolidate intelligence agencies after 9/11 into a new giant Department of Homeland Defense. "But the agency had heard other unofficial signals of the Chinese build-up in the Northwest."

"I meant," said the President, "her hearing that this slimebag Li Kuan was working in Kazakhstan. Your agency dropped the ball on that one. Thought he was in some damned cave in Afghanistan?"

"We're sure he was there, Mr. President. But he got out before we could nail him."

"Like bin Laden. Well, how'd he get to Kazakhstan so quickly?"

Norris explained that if Li Kuan had gotten to Istanbul or Pakistan, he could have caught a Pakistani Air flight to Astan in a matter of hours.

"Well, whatever, but it was that poor girl who gave us the intel that the bastard was in Kazakhstan. And we know now after the rail line hit that Li Kuan's clients there have quite a conventional explosives wallop. If he manages to sell them the slag for a dirty nuclear bomb, we're all in trouble. Let's hope the Chinese get him."

"Yessir."

Norris was tempted to explain that it had been the Chinese General Chang who had actually told Charlie Riser, the U.S. cultural attaché in Beijing, that Li Kuan was reported in Kazakhstan, but he didn't press the point. It would have seemed too pedantic.

"John," the President said to Norris, "how are our Chinese surveillance flights going? Any problems?" The President could never bring himself to call the Aries II surveillance flights what they were—U.S. spy missions. One of the Lockheed Martin Aries had been shot down in April 2001, the crew held as POWs for a while by the Chinese.

"Flights are doing fine, sir. Chinese don't like 'em, of course. Keep sending up MiGs to try and intimidate our boys."

"Okay, but tell our Air Force guys to be careful. Last thing we need is another international incident now."

"Yessir."

As the meeting ended, the President, heading off for a press conference, asked the Chairman of the Joint Chiefs, "How many men did we lose in that Li Kuan mission?"

"Seven, sir. Six Special Forces on the ground. One from the chopper, a medic, during evac."

The President's jaw clenched as he shook his head. "Only one survivor, then?"

"Yes, sir. Ex-Medal of Honor guy. David Brentwood."

"Ex?" said the President.

"Yes—ah, well, yes. Story is, he choked."

CHAPTER FIFTEEN

TEN MINUTES AFTER the President had given his televised press conference the switchboard received a call from retired general Douglas Freeman, the George C. Scott lookalike who had been conscripted from the "retired" list to go on a sponsored goodwill tour for the troops in Afghanistan.

The general knew very well that his ad hoc phone call from Tora Bora was definitely not the way to make contact with the

White House. Retired officers, even four-star generals, were supposed to follow normal channels, like everyone else. Write a letter. But even as a young officer, long before he had become a legend and what was known as a perennial PITA—pain in the ass—to Washington's bureaucrats, Douglas Freeman had adopted Von Rundsted's advice to an up-and-coming Wehrmacht oberleutnant, namely, that "normal channels are a trap for officers who lack initiative."

"White House. How may I direct your call?"

"Yes," said Freeman forcefully. "General Freeman here. I'd like to speak to the President. He knows who I am."

That was the problem; the President certainly did know about the general, who, though retired, felt free, "like any other goddamned citizen," as the general once put it, to give advice to the CEO who ran the world's only superpower. Freeman wasn't an arrogant man, but he was known to be as persistent as an M1, America's main battle tank, the kind he had led during the famous winter battle in which, outnumbered by Russian-made T-80s, he'd ordered a running retreat in what was initially regarded by his men and an appalled Pentagon watching on live satellite feed as a blatant act of cowardice.

The operator directed the general's call to Public Relations, who in turn promised to connect him to a presidential aide.

"Presidential *aide*? I don't want some damn gofer who picks fluff off the President's suit. This is a matter of national urgency, goddammit!"

"I'll direct your call to Ms. Prenty's office. She's our National Security—"

"Yes, I know who she is. I gave a visiting lecture to her IR course at Emory in Vir—"

Ms. Prenty was "unavailable." Would the general leave his number, and a member of her staff would—

"Goddammit!" exploded Freeman, slamming down the phone. Two minutes later he called back. It took him four more White House operators to reach the one he'd sworn at. She'd sounded so young. "May I ask your name, ma'am?"

"I'm Operator Eight, General."

"Yes, well, look, I apologize for my rudeness." A long, long silence. Goddammit, she wants me on my belly, thought Freeman, like Eisenhower wanted Patton on his belly before he'd forgive the general for slapping a soldier he'd accused of cowardice in Sicily. Patton sent Ike a damn turkey—big son of a bitch—for Christmas. Didn't make any difference. Ike kept him out in the cold. Freeman knew he had the same problem. Temper. But goddammit—He took a deep breath. "Us older guys get a bit cranky now and then. Sorry."

"Old or not, General"—the bitch, he'd said old*er*, not old—"it's still no excuse for rudeness."

"No, no, it isn't. You're quite right." Then a short shot of his own. "Operator *Eight*, you're quite right. My profoundest apology. I'd be very grateful if you'd have one of Eleanor's people call me back." The "Eleanor" should help, he thought.

"Your name again, Colonel? Nicholas Feedman?"

Colonel—

Operator Eight heard an expulsion of air like a tire deflating. "Name is Freeman," the tightly restrained voice answered her. "General Douglas Freeman, as in 'land of the *free* and the home of the brave,'" *which if you want to help keep it free, you dozy dame—*

"Would you like her voice mail, Colonel?"

"I'll call back!"

Old! she'd said. He was sixty, for crying out loud. Douglas MacArthur was still active at seventy-two. Younger generation didn't know a damned thing. Appallingly ignorant of the past, both geographically and politically. He recalled the young woman on NBC's *Late Show* who'd thought it was the French who had attacked Pearl Harbor. And NBC hired her later as a reporter! So how in hell could they be expected to know who he was, about the stunning victory he'd pulled off years before during the U.N. intervention in the Russian taiga, a victory so brilliantly executed, so particularly reliant on his command of the minutiae and sweep of military history, that his exploit had fired the imagination of every soldier in the army.

One of those soldiers had been a young lieutenant called David Brentwood, who had gone on to win the coveted thirteen gold stars on the pale blue ribbon that signified he had joined the hallowed hall of warriors, the elite. Some wore the medal easily, part of a willingness to take life as it came to them; others, like Brentwood, accepted it with deep reservation born of a private conviction that in another place, at another time, they might just as easily have disgraced themselves. And now Freeman had heard that Brentwood was here at Tora Bora.

David Brentwood lay in the MASH's post-op recovery tent, his right arm wrapped in virgin-white bandages, his bloodshot blue eyes squinting out through the triangle of his tent door up into the hard blue of the Afghan sky and the distant Hindu Kush. Brentwood had already court-martialed himself. He was too intelligent to wallow in the charge of cowardice—he knew he'd done his best. But he *was* guilty of something. Any mission leader who takes in six of the most highly trained men on earth and loses every one of them, plus the helicopter medic . . . Yes, he knew the medic probably would have survived if he'd been wearing his Kevlar helmet, which undoubtedly would have protected his head from the impact of the falling rocks. David dragged himself up higher against the pillows, his pajamas soaked through with perspiration. They'd given him a couple of Oxycodone pills three hours before, but the pain that even military physicians, who should have known better, insisted on calling "discomfort" because it made *them* feel better, was so intense, he felt on the verge of passing out.

Normally, he would have been delighted to see his old commander among the visiting morale-boosting USO party. But this day, as he saw a Humvee approaching along the Afghan plain then coming to a stop in a rush of gritty dust that swept in front of the vehicle, enveloping his tent, the pain of his wound assailed the Medal of Honor winner and temporarily rendered him speechless when he spotted the unmistakable figure of Douglas Freeman emerging ghostlike from the cloud. By way of compensating, he gave the general an awkward left-handed salute.

Freeman, wearing his Afrika Korps cap, returned the salute with the familiar swagger stick he'd been given as a token of appreciation by members of the British Special Air Services. He had known the renowned but publicity-shy elite British commandos long before they'd unwittingly burst upon the world's consciousness in London on May 5, 1980, executing the perfect and dramatically televised takedown of hostage-holding terrorists in the Iranian embassy. Following the example of U.S. Colonel Beckwith, Freeman had always insisted his Special Forces teams be involved in joint Delta/SAS exercises in the grueling terrain of Wales's Brecon Beacons, as well as in Fort Benning, Georgia.

"To the bone, I hear?" said Freeman, indicating David's bandaged right arm as he took off his Afrika Korps cap. Putting it down on the end of the bed, he remained standing and unsmiling.

Given his pain, David found talking difficult, and his tone was uncharacteristically apologetic. "One or two places—" he told the general. "Splinters. It'll mend."

"Witch doctors tell me you're finished for combat."

"That's what *they* think. I need to get my hands on an—" He winced with the effort. "—on an F2000."

Freeman merely nodded, his manner affirming nothing more than that he was familiar with the revolutionary Belgian assault rifle. Designed for the new world disorder in which a soldier one minute might be a U.N. policeman helping to maintain enough order to distribute food in some drought-ravaged third world country, and in the next be engaged in a vicious firefight with rebels, the 5.56mm weapon had been designed to accommodate snap-on, snap-off modules for different situations and to accommodate these modules quickly and easily. In this way, the F2000 avoided having many of the fixed add-ons that gave so many other modern weapons a "Christmas tree" look. There were other snap-on, snap-off assault weapons, but Freeman knew immediately why David was hoping for the ergonomically designed Belgian piece. The F2000 was not only well-balanced and easy to carry, but was "ambidextrous amenable" in both firing and carrying mode, the cocking handle being on the left of the receiver. The relatively light—less than eight pounds—twenty-seven-inch-long rifle was especially suited for combat in Central Asia. In this vast region, where weapons themselves were under constant assault by the fine grit of dust storms sweeping out of the Gobi and other deserts, the F2000, whose access points, including its cocking slot, were sealed, was the natural choice.

"It doesn't look pretty," said Freeman. David thought the general meant his bandaged arm, until he continued, "But it's compact and does the job. Clip-on grenade launcher. Thirty-round M16 pattern mag."

"Yes."

There was an awkward pause, David ending it with, "Has a fire control system they say is foolproof."

Freeman grunted. "Whenever they say a thing's foolproof, you'd better start looking for the fool."

David laughed, but it was forced, both men veteran comrades in arms using their natter about the F2000's specifications as a stand-in for the subject they were both avoiding. It was distinctly un-Freeman-like to step around painful questions. Indeed, it was his unflinching willingness to confront unpleasant situations head on that had contributed in no small measure to his legend in both the military and Washington, D.C. The wounded Medal of Honor winner wondered how long the general could hold his fire.

"Started exercising?" asked Freeman.

"Yes. Trying to cut down on the pain pills."

"Don't, if they help you get through exercises. Knew a guy once—would never take pills. Rambo type. Thought he was going to win the game all by himself. But couldn't fit into the team. Wouldn't pass the ball."

"Uh-huh. Know the type. Remember—"

"Wouldn't take pain pills," cut in Freeman. "Not even a damn aspirin. Thought it was wimpy. Being a sissy. Out on an exercise one night up at Fort Lewis, he got a goddamn headache from the howitzer batteries uprange. Must've been a migraine. Wouldn't take a pill. Got so damn disoriented by this migraine, saw the steps, made so much noise going through the brush, couldn't concentrate, and gave the whole squad away. Reds nailed us before we could hit the kill house."

"Steps?" asked David.

"What? Oh, yes. Steps going up in front of you like a serrated castle wall. It's called the 'castle'—an aura a lot of migraine sufferers see before an attack, distorts their vision. Usually the steps come with a background of green—most beautiful damn green you've ever seen. You take the pills *then*, you've got a chance of beating the headache or at least reducing the severity—"

The general stopped, the abruptness confirming what Brentwood had already realized. "You suffer from them, General."

Freeman, the *soldat extraordinaire*, or what his enemies called "soldier eccentric-aire," nodded. "Never told anyone that before. Strictly between you, me, and the gate post. Understood?"

"Of course." It had been the best the general could do in approaching the as yet hidden subject of his visit, delaying the unasked question by dredging up the story of the man who wouldn't take medication and of how he himself was a secret migraine sufferer. It was a kind of "I understand pain too" quid pro quo. So now he could ask the question, soldier-to-soldier. Seven commandos in. Six commandos dead.

"So what went wrong, David? You fuck up?"

David moved awkwardly in the bed and, pulling out his bedside table drawer with his good left hand, unscrewed a smoke-grenade-size vial and lifted it to his mouth, swallowing two more Oxycodone.

"That bad, eh?" said Freeman, taking the vial from him, screwing the top back on, dropping it into the drawer.

"It was a shoelace," said David cryptically.

"*Shoelace*? You starting a quiz program? What the hell does that mean? You tripped, fired your weapon, is that what happened?" He paused. "Blue on blue? That what we're talking about, David?"

"No, sir, I didn't shoot my own men. Though I might as well have."

"Hey!" snapped the general. "I don't want any sniveling crybaby, mea culpa, poor-me, self-pitying shit. What'd I tell you boys—all my boys? Look at it square on. You've always stood up. Taken full responsibility. Goddammit, I wrote you up for the gong. Saw the President pin it on your chest, remember? But taking responsibility isn't the same as making a clear analysis. I haven't read the goddamn AAR." He meant the After Action report. "I'm *retired*, remember? Bastards don't let me see anything 'cept the damn USO schedule—when some blond big tits is going to work up the boys so they spend the next week beating their meat 'stead of keeping their mind on the job. All I know is that seven of my boys went out and six didn't come back. What went wrong? What're the AAR's 'Lessons Learned'? We're gonna be in this godforsaken place for years, no matter what the White House says. Stuck here and in the other six Stans. Same in Iraq. What can we learn from your experience, Captain?"

David explained about the shoelace—the damn German tenor—how it was that Jamal got ahead of him as they'd run for the entrance.

"So that accounts for why this Jam got it instead of you. Nothing else." Before David could reply, the general asked, "You think Li Kuan was there?"

"I don't know, General. Light was pretty bad. Didn't see any pockmarked guy."

"But you think they were waiting for you?" the general pressed. "A trap?"

David shrugged, his legs relaxing, the Oxycodone giving him a buzz. "We spotted one sensor. Could've missed others, maybe tripped one."

The general nodded, gazing out at the Hindu Kush. "Lost your confidence?"

David's forehead creased. It made him look much older, puzzled. "I don't know. Sometimes I think no. Other times—"

"At night?" said Freeman, turning around.

"Mostly," replied David.

"Don't think too much. Set an exercise goal—push yourself harder every day but don't use it as penance. Channel it for Operation Payback."

"Haven't heard of that."

"Neither have I," said Freeman, "but it'll come. You heard about the Chinese—going into Kazakhstan after the terrorist staging areas?"

"Saw a bit on CNN."

Freeman pulled out a khaki handkerchief and began roughly polishing the goggles he habitually wore in the region. Wrapped around the old khaki Afrika Korps cap—a gift which, like the goggles, had been passed down from one of Rommel's staff— the goggles made him look like the famed Desert Fox himself, especially when he rode in one of the open Afghanistan Humvees, standing up and using the .50 caliber machine gun as an armrest that vibrated noisily as the vehicle sped across the Afghan plain.

Freeman placed the goggles around the peaked cap. "I still maintain an extensive list of contacts in the forces," he told David. "Keep tabs on what's going on. Saw the report Beijing's military attaché sent Washington. Said a young American girl was murdered because she overheard a couple of Li Kuan's al Qaeda boys talking about making trouble in China's Northwest—Xinjiang. Given what the President just said on the box, I take it Beijing figures we won't object to whatever the PLA does because it'll be fighting terrorists."

"We're all against terrorists," said David.

"The Beijing attaché says this young woman, Riser—if I remember correctly, Amanda Riser—overheard these two creeps in a place called Barberry's Pub Café in Suzhou."

"Suzhou?" David couldn't place it.

"About four hundred miles south of Beijing, on the Grand Canal," said Freeman. "Point is that Barberry's Pub Café is a *bar*."

David was ensconced in the initial euphoria of the Oxycodone smothering the pain, finding it difficult not to close his eyes and luxuriate in the temporary escape. But he was far from what the unit's pharmacist would call "Zombiefied." "Uh-huh," he responded, gazing out at ice cream clouds rising majestically in the endless blue of the Afghan sky. "Muslims, especially fanatical Muslims, don't drink. They certainly don't go to bars."

"Right," said the general, slapping on his cap and pulling out a business card from his load vest. "You need to talk, David, you can reach me at this number. It's the USO."

"I'd have thought Washington would have put you back on the active list."

"They won't even return my calls. Still pissed at me about the first Iraq war. Told 'em Bush Senior should've given Schwarzkopf the green light to roll on into Baghdad and kill the son of a bitch. Remember the old lube an' oil change commercial, 'You pay me now or you pay me later'? Not going to Baghdad then meant we gave 'em twelve more years to build up their terrorist networks and finance al Qaeda."

"You should call 'em about the bar," David said, his gaze held captive by the majesty of the ice cream cumulonimbus rising and spreading into a line of bruising anvils. There was going to be, as Jamal would have said, "one mother of a storm" over the Hindu Kush. It would be an icy rain. He was thinking about the Barberry's Pub Café again. "General?"

Freeman was pulling the goggles snugly below the Afrika Korps cap as the normally reserved Brentwood, in a painkiller-induced devil-may-care tone—one he'd normally use for a fellow Special Forces warrior and not a general—repeated forcefully, "Why don't you call our military attaché in Beijing? About the bar?"

"I will."

With that, the general collected his swagger stick. "Soon as I get back to USO HQ."

"Where's that?" asked David.

"Tora Bora," replied Freeman, and gave a swashbuckling salute with the swagger stick, as Rommel might have done. Douglas Freeman despised what the SS and other Jew-hating Nazi scum had done, but in the Wehrmacht, the German army, there had been some soldiers of honor, and for Freeman, Rommel had been one of them.

David tried to write his weekly letter to his wife Melissa, but it was difficult—he told her he hoped he could handle an F2000 and convince them he was still battleworthy. For encouragement he drew on all the "impossible" diagnoses he knew and which were habitually cited by Special Forces as examples of grit overcoming extraordinary personal difficulties: Adolf Galland, Germany's top air ace, had only one eye—cheated on the eye chart exam. How could he do that—fly a Messerschmidt

109 and later, in 1945, the Me 262, the worlds' first jet fighter, with just one eye? He would have had no spatial perspective, no depth of field. And Douglas Bader, the Brit. Lost both legs in an air crash before the war. They said he could never fly again. "Not in a fighter, old chap!" He did, became an ace, was captured by the Germans, escaped so many times the commandant confiscated his tin legs.

But David's all-time favorite was a man who had nothing to do with war, but with the combat of the soul: Lance Armstrong. Testicular cancer, lung cancer, brain cancer, and he fought back to win the toughest race in the world, the 2,160-mile-long Tour de France. Five times in a row! Most Americans, besotted by football, hockey, and basketball, didn't comprehend the Herculean stamina and iron will that it took to be first among hundreds of the world's elite cyclists. Some fool Frenchman complained, "But 'e is on chemicals."

"That's chemotherapy, you idiot!" came another American's reply.

So, dammit, David thought, he could sure as hell learn to stay in the fight, to do what he'd been trained for. For now, however, his letter to Melissa would have to be painfully typed out on a computer, then sent to the unit censor, since e-mail contact with home had been temporarily suspended because of terrorist hackers who'd penetrated the U.S. Army's computer network. The physical effort of having to type with his left hand afforded him much more time than he usually had to think about what he wanted to say to her and, most important, what to leave out. Besides, he knew he'd have to lead into it—cushion the news of his savage wound.

Dear Melissa,

Greetings from nowhere. This has to be the most forsaken place on earth. God was punishing somebody when he made this sun-baked jumble of rocks and dirt. Our unit G2 tells us it's about the size of Texas. I asked him how many square miles of water there are and he just laughed. Zip. Zero. Nada. You see a tree here, you practically die of shock. And the people. I keep thinking when I was a kid—bashing the

*fridge to close it and saying there was too much damn food
in there. Dad got after me for cussing and tore a strip off me
for saying there was too much food—how great it was to live
in a country where I could say that. "Poor" doesn't even begin to describe the people here. A lot of them haven't even
got shoes, sandals—anything. Had one of them, a scout, on
one of our missions. It was 35 degrees, just a tad above
freezing, and he had nothing on his feet. Least we didn't
have to do that at—*

He was about to write "Fort Benning," but censored it himself
and instead put "camp."

*I can't like them, though. Remember how all the media
used to talk about Northern Alliance against the Taliban?
Well, at the end of the day I wouldn't give you a dime for any
of them. Most of them are still nothing but mercenaries—sell
their own mother. Change sides like they change shirts—
which, come to think of it, isn't a good analogy. I've never
seen one of them wash, let alone change. But you get what I
mean—no loyalty at all to one side or the other. It's all filthy
lucre. Sort of like our Congress—ha, ha! On the other hand, I
know we have to be here. After 9/11 we had no choice but to
hunt the Taliban and al Qaeda down. And then go get Saddam. You remember the day one of our guys climbed up on
Hussein's statue and they pulled it down? And I'll tell you
one thing, we're going to be here for years, and no matter
what our politicians say. We pull out now, after having
thrown out the Taliban, the creeps'll come back from their
hideaways in Pakistan in six months and we'll have terrorist
training camps all over. The present government we put in
wouldn't last for a week if we weren't here. Look at the assas-
sinations of officials since we've been here. And anyway, I
don't trust one sect more than the other when it comes to any
idea of reform. The way they still treat women—no better
than baggage. That's getting better now but it's going to take
a long time. What gets me is the Afghans say they want an end
to war but the first thing they want to get their hands on is a*

Kalashnikov. It's like Northern Ireland and all those other places, I guess—fighting's become a habit. Sometimes I don't think they know what the heck they're fighting for—it's just what they know how to do.

Anyway, sweetie, these are some of the reasons I'll be glad to get out of the place, which brings me to the big news: I'm coming home! High time, eh? Got some shrapnel in the right arm. It's slowed me down a bit so they're shipping me to Fort— for some R and R. You know, some physio—hot tub, that sort of stuff. Before you know it I'll be good as new— back in the unit.

He ached, needed to tell her how badly he felt about losing his men, but he knew she'd worry about him worrying—and what could she do? "You can tell me anything, David," she'd told him. "I don't want you carrying the load all by yourself, honey. No matter what it is. Okay?"

"Okay," he'd agreed, but how could he explain it to any civilian? And she was alone. All he could do was write the six KIAs' next-of-kin, and knowing that they'd all write back to him, thanking him for his thoughtfulness in writing them, made him ill. And they'd trust him all the more because he was a hero, a Medal of Honor winner, which made him inwardly cringe.

He signed off with "Lots of love to everyone," kisses and hugs, aware that he hadn't told her how long his R&R at Fort Lewis in Washington State, and therefore their reunion, would be.

At USO Headquarters at Tora Bora, where he could use a secure land line, the general called the Beijing embassy, asking for the military attaché. He was transferred to Riser instead, and introduced himself, adding, "Sorry about your girl, son."

"Thank you, General. You wanted to speak to the MA. He's out at the moment. Friendship Store."

Freeman knew the place—overstaffed by semicomatose Chinese salesgirls who were about as enthusiastic about selling merchandise to "Big Noses" for urgently needed U.S. dollars and euros as they were about joining the PLA's reserves, which had begun to decline as the younger cell phone–Internet generation of Chinese became less enamored with the PLA's slogan of "Unite against the running dog lackeys of the right" and more interested in getting the latest burned American CDs.

"General, he's just come back," said Riser, handing the phone to Bill Heinz, who respectfully heard the general's concern about the Muslims in a bar, the same point General Chang had brought up with Riser and thus indirectly with Heinz.

"Good point, General. I see you're sharp as ever. I still remember your tip-off about the Patriot missile. But it's not unusual for Muslim terrorists to go to bars." The MA was calling up his computer file on all suspects thought to be involved in the planning as well as the execution of the 9/11 attack. Among them were three men who were at a skin palace, The Pink Pony, a Daytona Beach strip club featuring "totally nude XXX naked dancers," the night before the attacks on the WTC and Pentagon.

"Huh," responded Freeman. "Those fundamentalists sure get around town."

"Sure do, General. 'Course, those three suspects might not have been drinking, unlike Li Kuan's boys in Suzhou."

"Guess not," said Freeman wryly. "Too busy slobbering over pussy at the Pink Horse."

"Pony."

"Whatever, drinking or perving, seems as if they're using bars and strip joints to fit in. No doubt their religious sensitivities are offended. They're just whoring and boozing out of a sense of duty."

"Probably," laughed Heinz. "Maybe getting a taste of the seventy-two virgins they'll get when they hit us again."

"So the info from Suzhou isn't suspect just because the Muslims were hitting the sauce?"

"Not as far as I'm concerned."

"Thanks for your time."

"My pleasure, General."

When Bill Heinz replaced the phone, Charlie Riser asked him about his reference to the general and the Patriot missile.

"Freeman," Heinz explained, "cottoned on to a bizarre fact—

that in a certain range the Patriot missile could be accidentally launched by a baby's scream. Freeman warned them. They did tests. He was right."

"They fix it?" asked Riser.

"Oh, yeah. Real quick."

Charlie Riser was impressed. "Anything he doesn't know?"

"Yeah," answered the military attaché. "How to get on with politicians and their staff. Too blunt."

Indeed, it was the general's prickly relationship with the present administration which was responsible for Eleanor Prenty's delay in returning Freeman's call to her. Besides, SATPIX taken over the darkness of the far western Pacific were coming in fast and furious, showing cluster "blossoms," explosions of light, near the line of the South China coast, specifically in Shantou and other bases in Fukien Province. Both the NSA and CIA had alerted Eleanor, but she'd decided not to wake the President until she realized that the lat/long coordinates of these "blossoms" were actually *on* the Chinese coast. The explosions caught by the satellite's zoom eye were revealed to be in Shantou, Dongshan, Xiamen, and Pingtan—all major PLA navy bases directly across the strait from Taiwan. "Sea scratches," long white lines, could also be seen through the intermittent cloud cover offshore, the wakes indicating that the vessels were approaching the Chinese coast.

Then the red "Red" phone from Beijing rang. Zhou Zhang, the premier of the most populous country on earth, urgently needed to speak to the President of the most powerful nation on earth. Eleanor buzzed the interpreter and the President himself, and noted that it would now be early dawn in China.

"Hello, Mr. President," was the first and last English phrase the Chinese premier used, because he knew there was no room for error, or the slightest misunderstanding. His message, a courtesy to the President, was the same message his ministers for defense and the interior were now conveying to their counterparts in Europe and Russia: The Chinese mainland was under attack by the forces of renegade Taiwan, which was obviously taking advantage of China's preoccupation with its northwest-

ern terrorist problem to launch a sneak attack against China's
eastern seaboard.

The President had no sooner thanked the Chinese premier for
advising him of Beijing's point of view than Eleanor handed
him a decoded "Eyes Only" transmission. Both the NSA and
CIA were reporting that the Nationalist government in Taipei
was emphatically denying that it had ordered any attack against
the Communist Chinese mainland.

"All right," the President told Eleanor. "But how about the
offshore Chinese islands? The Nationalist-held islands are
within spitting distance of the mainland. What's going on there?
Every day the Communists shell the Nationalist island of Kinmen with propaganda pamphlets, and the Nationalists are
bunkered in a complex you wouldn't believe." He took off his
reading glasses, dropping them tiredly on the Oval Office desk.
"Ever since 1949 they've been at loggerheads."

CHAPTER SIXTEEN

Taiwan

A TYPHOON ALERT had been issued at 3:50 A.M., the typhoon expected to make landfall at Shihmen at the northernmost tip of the 240-mile-long, leaf-shaped island of Taiwan,
which varies in width from its tapered five-mile-wide southern
extremity up through its eighty-five-mile-wide waist, to the
northern end of the leaf, where the distance from west to east
coasts is about thirty-two miles.

In the small village four miles east of Shihmen, the wife of
fifty-one-year-old Moh Pan awoke in the predawn darkness,
foisting off her husband's groping hands from beneath their

bedroll. "No," she said firmly. "It's time." It was already five o'clock.

"A few minutes?" he pleaded.

"No. After."

"After?" Moh snorted. "*After*, I'll be dead!"

"You always say that." She was out of bed and, though the same age as Moh, moved with the energy of a much younger person. Opening the door, her voice rose above the roar of the black sea. "If I had a mushroom for every time you said you'd be dead, I'd be so rich we wouldn't have to pick them."

Moh turned away grumpily, cursing the necessity of picking the damned mushrooms between five and seven every morning, the two-hour slot affording the right temperature and humidity for coaxing the valuable fungi from their dark sheds to their prime market size, no more than an inch in diameter. Any later than seven and the mushrooms would be worth much less at the market in Shihmen. Mumbling at his wife's rebuttal of his sexual advances, Moh, who was a little hard of hearing, now pretended to hear nothing she said, blaming the unending crashing of the surf against the rocky shore a quarter mile down from the village that nestled in a small, wind-blown dell at the northernmost end of the island. The high surf there marked the tail end of the most recent typhoon, one of the many hurricanes that periodically assailed the island and battered its spectacular east coast. Here, enormous cliffs dropped from wild, bird-filled skies sheer to the violent creamy-edged sea, absorbing most of the typhoons' power in the form of torrential rains and winds, which, after lashing the island's mountain spine, were less ferocious when they reached the more habitable and heavily industrialized lowlands of the west coast.

Even there, however, the prevailing easterlies of the typhoons were still strong enough to favor Taiwan's daily leaflet-filled balloon and loudspeaker war against the mainland, a propaganda battle that had continued every odd-numbered day since 1958, Mao's mainland Chinese having built the world's biggest speakers in an attempt to outshout their wind-favored Nationalist enemies entrenched on the hills and coast of Kinmen Island. The latter's name meant "Gate as if Made of Gold," for it was seen as the gate controlling the adjacent seas off the Chinese mainland. The island, formerly known as Quemoy, bristled, as did Matsu, with updated U.S. Patriot surface-to-air missiles. The ferocity of the Communists on the mainland who wanted to regain Taiwan and all its islands could be measured by the fact that on Matsu and Kinmen the Nationalists still felt obliged to enforce martial law and maintain the presence of their 150,000 Taiwanese troops. So self-sufficient and self-contained were these islands, which served as early warning radio and radar listening posts for Taiwan, that in addition to enough food, water, ammunition, and medical provisions to last months without resupply, they even had their own currency.

As Moh Pan reluctantly dragged himself out of bed at a few minutes after six, he glimpsed what he thought were metallic glints at the gray edge of the world, about forty miles due north of Shihmen. At that moment on Kinmen, 173 miles westward across the Taiwan Strait, the military headquarters was abuzz with consternation over what night vision binoculars on Kinmen's western side had revealed was a flotilla of Communist PLA navy fast-attack Houxin and Huangfen patrol boats heading eastward toward Kinmen. Though capable of thirty-two and thirty-five knots respectively, the Communist attack boats were approaching the Nationalist island slowly, only to make a U-turn back toward the mainland at high speed, leaving clearly visible wakes of phosphorescence in the plankton-rich sea. Meanwhile, Matsu HQ was receiving frantic inquiries from Taiwan's Tsoying Naval Base, a hundred miles eastward, which in turn was receiving urgent inquiries from the U.S. State Department and the Washington intelligence community. The latter, despite their eye-in-the-sky spy satellites and other gizmology, couldn't figure out exactly what the hell was going on.

Walking to market, pulling the cart full of mushrooms, Moh Pan looked north again to see whether he could see any ships, or had it been the glint of aircraft? Perhaps he should call Shihmen's Civil Defense Office. "Do you have your cell?" he asked his wife.

"Battery's dead," she answered. "You forgot to recharge."

"Of course," he countered. "And I suppose I'm to blame for the typhoon too?"

She refused to answer. He just wanted to start a fight. He was giving her the evil eye.

Paying no attention, his wife tightened her scarf against the rising wind.

On Kinmen, where Moh Pan's son, Ahmao, was doing his National Guard service in the army, the Nationalist garrison was completely nonplused. Did the sudden maneuvering by the Communists patrol boats presage an attack? Or were the Communists merely taunting the Taiwanese as they had so many times during their so-called "military maneuvers," using elements of their PLA navy and PLA air force fighters, mere seconds from Matsu and Kinmen and only eight minutes from Taiwan itself? Such maneuvers, in this case by attack patrol boats from China's East Fleet, were no doubt designed not only to rattle the nerves of the Nationalists, but to serve as a constant reminder to the Taiwanese that Beijing believed Taiwan was nothing more than a renegade province that sooner rather than later would be forced to rejoin the Communist mainland. And on that day, Taiwan would be forced to give Beijing back the enormous treasure Chiang Kai-shek, Mao Tse Tung's mortal enemy, had taken with him and his Nationalist Army across the straits in 1949. Beijing had been encouraged since 1978 in its dream of reunification when U.S. aid to Taiwan and U.S. recognition of Taiwan as an independent nation ended, and then a year later, in 1979, when the U.S.-Taiwan national defense treaty died. Even so, every President from Harry Truman, who, despite his reservations about Chiang Kai-shek—whom he called "Cash My Check"—to Bill Clinton in 1996, had at times dispatched a CBG, carrier battle group, up into the Taiwan Strait to keep the uneasy peace between the two antagonists. And now the President and his advisors thought it prudent to repeat his predecessors' cautionary move, as one of the first questions every President asked in times of impending crisis was, "Where are the carriers?"

The carriers, thought to be outmoded in twenty-first-century war, were floating U.S. air bases that were now more important than ever before, given the number of U.S. overseas bases that had been closed once the Cold War had ended, a war in which the U.S., like the Soviet Union, had made many an unsavory deal with a tin pot dictator in order to prevent one another from gaining an advantage in the other's hemisphere. The current occupant of the White House had quickly discovered that in the war on terrorism, which involved so many different flashpoints, even the might of the U.S. Navy was stretched thin. America's twelve CBGs were spread far and wide, standing off "the powder keg of the Middle East"—Afghanistan, Iran, as well as the new Iraq, to say nothing of the far-flung U.S. missions to combat terrorists and their myriad bases throughout Central and South America and amid thousands of islands of the Indonesian and Philippine archipelagos. Then there were missions in Pakistan and throughout the Africas, where American citizens were being kidnapped, murdered, or threatened.

In all this, the carriers served as stand-ins for all the land bases the United States had lost in post–Cold War client countries that now felt they could go it alone. Especially troublesome to the U.S. Navy, however, was the loss of the huge complex at Subic Bay in the Philippines. And so it was that this President, with a mandate to continue waging the war on terrorism until the terrorists were beaten, knew more than any President since JFK about where his twelve carrier groups were at any one time.

"Eleanor, all of our carriers are overextended," the President said over the phone. "Do we have any available in dock?"

She didn't know. A quick call to the CNO's office in Washington, the transit coding causing a delay of only 1.5 seconds, gave her the answer. There was one in Bremerton, Washington State's big maintenance yard. It was the USS *Turner*, a Nimitz-C class flat top, a nuclear aviation carrier.

"The *Turner*." The President nodded. "Western Pacific Fleet?"

"Yes, sir. In for overhaul."

"What's its completion date?"

Eleanor, phone still in hand, relayed the question to CNO, then informed the President, "Estimated time of completion, five days."

The President shook his head. "No. Tell them they've got twenty-four hours. I want the *Turner* to join the *McCain*, which I believe—" He brought up the CNO's map on his computer screen. "Yes, there's the *McCain*. South China Sea. I want *McCain* to steam north to the Taiwan Strait ASAP!"

And it was so ordered. The *McCain* would steam north immediately, the *Turner* to leave Washington State in the Pacific Northwest within twenty-four hours.

"The *Turner's* CO didn't like that, Mr. President," proffered Eleanor. "Said it's almost impossible to speed up overhaul from five days to one."

"He doesn't have to like it. He only has to do it."

"Yes, sir."

"Get me the *McCain*'s CO, Growly."

"Admiral *Crowley*," Eleanor reminded him diplomatically.

"No, *Growly*," riposted the President. "Always bitching about how much more we give the other armed forces. He's a pain in the butt."

"Like Freeman," put in Eleanor's junior aide.

"Exactly, but Freeman's retired, thank God," replied the President, overhearing.

"Know their jobs though," said Eleanor Prenty, giving her junior aide, who looked ready to join in the dissing of Freeman and Crowley, a withering look. It told the aide he had best hold his tongue, though Eleanor realized she was being hypocritical. She'd not only ignored Freeman's phone message to call him, she'd forgotten all about it. Freeman, despite his legendary status among military types, was regarded as a "has-been," and the truth was, he had no political clout at all. In short, he was of no consequence to the administration's agenda.

"You through to *McCain*?" the President asked impatiently.

"Not yet," she replied, the image of the Nimitz-class carrier in her mind's eye. The carrier was named after the Vietnam hero, Senator John McCain, who, after being shot down by North Vietnamese Communists, being held prisoner, and tortured in the "Hanoi Hilton" for years, would not cave in. Dragged out in front of the blinding TV lights in Hanoi with other American prisoners as Communist propaganda, McCain was blinking so much that it looked as if he might have a damaged retina. In fact, his apparent affliction was the personification of defiant cool, his blinking a Morse code message to those at home watching that what the Communists were saying was a load of BS.

Admiral Crowley was now on the line, his voice gruff as usual. He had to respect his Commander in Chief, but he detested politicians.

"Admiral!" said the President heartily, scrolling down Crowley's file on screen in front of him. "How's your boy Richard doing? Must be his final year at Annapolis?"

"Yes, sir," came the admiral's reply.

"Has his heart set on Fallon, I hear?" continued the President. Fallon was the top gun school in the Nevada desert.

"Well," answered the admiral, "he'll have to learn to walk before he can run."

"I'm sure he'll make it," the President said, adding, "main thing is, Admiral, he's following his passion. We parents can't hope for much more than that."

"True."

"Admiral, there's some kafuffle up in the Taiwan Strait. What we're getting from Beijing and Taiwan is 'they started it first, not me' stuff. You no doubt have been getting the traffic?"

"Commies are accusing Taiwanese marines of going after one of their offshore islands. Taiwan denies it. Taiwanese are accusing Chinese Communist patrol boats of going for one of *their* islands."

"That's it. Now I want you to take the *McCain* up there and put yourself between those two. Our other carrier groups, as you know, have their hands full at the moment."

"Exactly," said Crowley sternly. Was there an implicit criticism of the White House's failure to push Congress for more naval appropriations in his tone? It was difficult to tell—he was normally gruff.

"Yes," said the President noncommittally. "Well, Admiral, we're already fighting World War Three against terrorists around the globe. The last thing we need is war on another front. We have to be extraordinarily careful."

"I know the drill, Mr. President. Fire only in self-defense. No preemptive strikes."

"You've got it, Admiral. Beijing's terrified of any revolt that might spread. That's why they're so down on these Falun Gong groups, et cetera. They're afraid of a chain reaction—a repetition of Tiananmen Square—spreading through China like wildfire, particularly now after Beijing's had to loosen its grip somewhat and allow some budding capitalism. They're afraid they won't be able to keep control of it."

"I've got the picture, Mr. President," Crowley assured him, somewhat impatiently. Crowley, like Freeman, had a distinguished combat record, and their bluntness belonged more to the tradition of Admiral Bill Halsey and George Patton than to the kind of diplomatic expertise required in a multinuclear-power age where the intemperate remarks of Indian and Pakistani politicians about each other, for example, had taken everyone to the brink.

High up in the *McCain*'s island that overlooked the carrier's four and half acres of deck, the diminutive Crowley, who at just over five feet had barely made it into the Navy, put down the phone. The admiral was under no illusion that the President had been prompted—by an aide, probably—about his son's expectations for top gun. Still, it was nice. The admiral would never ask for special favors from the President—that was strictly against his code—but hell, it didn't do any harm that the Commander in Chief of the most powerful nation on earth knew your son's name and where he wanted to go.

The sun was losing altitude in the South China Sea, a grand illusion as the world turned, the six thousand men and women who crewed the *McCain* and her air wing hearing the pipe sounding, "Now darken ship."

Hundreds of miles to the north of the *McCain*, in Shihmen on the northern tip of Taiwan, Moh Pan bent low against the advance force eight winds of what had now been officially tagged as Typhoon Jane. Inside the Civil Defense office, Moh waited patiently for his turn to speak to the female clerk, a knockout from Taipei, her ash-black hair pulled back tightly, passing through a silver clasp. Her smile revealed the most beautiful teeth Moh had ever seen in a woman, and her figure was so magnificently proportioned, like the singer Chyi Yu, that he welcomed the wait. In fact, he insisted an elderly woman from his village go before him. He knew his wife would have insisted he demand instant service— his sighting of possible enemy ships or aircraft off the north shore possibly signs of yet another mainland Chinese incursion into Taiwanese sea and air space. Of course, Moh told himself, they could have been Taiwanese ships or aircraft, but it was wonderful standing here, just watching the young clerk breathe.

When his turn came to report, it would be important, he advised himself, to be thorough, not to rush. Perhaps, in the interests of Taiwan's national security, he should show her on a map approximately where it was off the coast he had seen these "glints"—ask to see a high-scale map of the region, a pictorial accompaniment to his verbal report. A chance to demonstrate what everyone had always said about him—that he should have been an illustrator for the law courts in Taipei, where photographs of the accused were forbidden and readers had to rely on still-life sketches of the accused or victim. Perhaps she would like him to do a sketch of her. In a few strokes he could capture the essential aspects of the face. Moh felt himself becoming aroused.

He noticed a young couple in from his neighboring village sniggering at him, the girl cupping her hand in front of her mouth, whispering to her boyfriend, then trying unsuccessfully to stop her giggling. Moh saw the boyfriend staring at him, saying something, which sent the girl into another fit of giggles, the boyfriend sniffing the air as if there was something malodorous in the room. Moh realized they were probably laughing at the smell of the fungi fertilizer, the couple looking down on him in his overalls as if he was a pig farmer. The two idiots didn't deserve defending, he thought. He had a good mind to forget it, to walk out. But he stayed, and not just to enjoy the sight of the pretty clerk. He'd do it for his son stationed on Kinmen and for all the other young men and women who were worth defending and who were putting their lives on the line. Still, it irked him—the couple were the kind of college-educated yuppies whom Mao had sent out to the countryside during the Cultural Revolution and made work, the communes puncturing their arrogant self-assurance with real labor so they'd respect those who'd built the Revolution. Moh didn't like the Communists, but sometimes . . .

Anger had overtaken his normal passivity, but now the loyal mushroom grower concentrated on the girl's breathing again, his eyes closed from fatigue and the fantasy of having her in the dark, cool shed. From outside, a gust of gale-force wind rattled the office door. She would cling to him, frightened of the storm, the howling winds, the electric-blue lightning crashing around them, and he'd hold her, comforting her, telling her all would be well.

By the time Moh Pan reached the Civil Defense counter, his fantasies about the beautiful clerk had been sabotaged by the young couple sniggering at the smell of his work clothes. When he reported to the clerk that he'd seen some kind of aircraft or ships off the north cape, any confidence he might have had that they were Chinese Communists evaporated. She thanked him for the information and gave him a smile, but there was nothing remotely sexual in it, merely a young woman's courtesy toward an older man. He was old enough to be her father, his son Ahmao on Kinmen young enough to be her husband. Moh felt dejected—immeasurably old—exacerbated by the feeling that the world had passed him by. Outside, a gust hit him with such force it blew him back against the glass, rattling its frame. Now he *wanted* to go back to the mushroom sheds for refuge. He saw his wife coming out of the market crowd, counting her money, the red currency startlingly vibrant against the nondescript gray of the town square.

"Did you tell them?" she asked perfunctorily, without looking up from the bunch of hundreds.

"Yes."

"What did they say?"

"Nothing."

"You have to recharge your cell."

"Yes," Moh Pan agreed obediently. If his cell had been charged, he wouldn't have had to walk all the way into town and get a chance to see the young beauty.

"They were probably ours anyway," said his wife, stuffing the money into her purse, the sea wind billowing her scarf.

"Yes," agreed Moh Pan. "A big waste of time trudging into town."

CHAPTER SEVENTEEN

AFTER HELPING HIS deckhands extract what had been Albinski's dry suit, now looking like a black, flattened toothpaste tube, oceanographer Frank Hall decided he had to take a core from the sea bottom—see if a hot vent's plume of superheated water was responsible for the kind of turbulence that would have fatally loosened the two divers' air hoses and twisted the kelp around the umbilicals.

Young Peter Dixon, whey-faced, being sick in one of the dry lab buckets, didn't hear the ex-SEAL-cum-oceanographer approaching the bright island of the stern's deck lights, seeing only Frank's shadow looming over him.

"Where's Albinski's attack board, Bud?" he asked Dixon, putting his arm on the young diver's shoulder.

Dixon looked up from the bucket, wiping his mouth, as if he hadn't heard the *Petrel*'s captain, or rather, that he'd heard him but couldn't believe the man's insensitivity. "Piss off!"

Frank understood, but he was captain—he shouldn't, *couldn't*, let his emotion cloud the issue. "I need to see what the temperature variant was down there. It could tell us whether a sudden release of vent pressure or whatever had anything to do with it."

"What's the difference, man? He's dead."

"You're not." Dixon was supposed to be a SEAL, not a baby. "Where's the board?"

"Guess it's over there," said Dixon, indicating the shining pile of brown vegetation beneath the A-frame, where the long tendrils of kelp had been cut away from what had been Albinski's dry suit.

Frank gingerly extracted the attack board from the pile of water-slicked tendrils, cut the nylon fishing line by which it had been attached to Albinski's arms, and handed it up to the bosun.

"Mother of—" began the bosun in shock.

Scrawled on the attack board's slate was one word: *Minisub*.

Frank strode to the deck's intercom mike midway between the winches. "Bridge?"

"Bridge here. Go ahead."

"Call COMSUBPAC-9. Urgent. Send chopper immediately." Next Frank turned to the bosun. "Assemble the crew. Dry lab. Everyone except watch personnel."

It wasn't until the bosun saw Frank working the tumblers on the dry lab's safe that he realized why Hall hadn't ordered the bridge to transmit the discovery of a hostile minisub in American waters directly to COMSUBPAC Jensen. The *Petrel*, as a civilian vessel—though contracted by the Navy and using a Navy transport helo in its hangar—had no coding computers aboard, and anyone could have picked up a plain language transmit, including those aboard the hostile. The helo would have to take the message.

This delay in getting the message to Admiral Jensen by chopper was to prove fatal, however. In retrospect, to some critics it was far more damaging to the United States in the near future than the not so sensible delay caused by the decision in December 1941 to send the warning of an imminent attack on Pearl Harbor to Admiral Kimmel by telegram.

In the next hour the President let it be known publicly, via the TV and cable networks, that in order to "calm down the rhetoric between"—He had wanted to say, "between China and Taiwan," but Eleanor Prenty convinced him to change it. "—the *People's* Republic of China and the *people* of Taiwan," he had dispatched elements of the 7th Fleet to the Taiwan Strait—the *McCain*—and that because of commitments elsewhere in the ongoing war against terrorism, he considered it prudent to send the USS *Turner* and its battle group as well. This announcement, the President hoped, would send a clear message to both potential combatants to back off or risk the ire of the United States.

It was a monumentally bad decision because it was based on insufficient information: first, about who exactly was attacking whom, and second, on not yet having received the information, because of *Petrel*'s helo delay, that a hostile sub had apparently penetrated the "American littoral," or coastal waters, well within the two-hundred-mile limit, a limit extended in modern times, updating the old three-mile limit derived from the fact that in the days of sail navies, the maximum range of a man-o'-war's cannon had been three miles from shore.

The President was not the first occupant of the White House to have made a bad decision against the onrush of escalating developments, nor, because of the unforeseen consequences of his public address, would he be the only President—like JFK during the Cuban Missile Crisis—who would come to think that it might be his and America's last decision.

There was harried activity aboard the *Turner*'s core battle group, which, under the overall command of Admiral J. Bressard, was made up of the Nimitz-class carrier itself, two guided missile Aegis cruisers, a four-ship destroyer squadron, the replenishment vessel *Salt Lake City*, plus two nuclear attack submarines—one of them Captain Rorke's USS *Utah*. The battle group was ordered to maintain station, ready for immediate turnaround. Ten ships in all, nine of them already leaving Washington State's naval base at Everett and the Bremerton yard, the group's replenisher to follow as soon as she was "choc-a-bloc" with supplies, in the words of her highly efficient, no-nonsense captain, Diane Lawson. Fuel for the huge, 98,000-ton *Turner* was no problem, its two Westinghouse nuclear reactors having enough power to drive its four shafts for ten to fifteen years, or for a million nautical miles, before the fuel cores needed to be replaced.

Below, in the carrier's garage-smelling hangar deck—nearly one and a third times bigger than a football field and three stories high—an army of mechanics of the carrier's 2,800 air wing personnel were feverishly getting ready for the arrival of the air wing from Whidbey Island. This would consist of eighty-five aircraft, including twenty F-14 Tomcats, F-18 Hornets, A-6E Intruders, E2 Hawkeyes, EA-6B Prowlers, S-3 Vikings, and six Seahawk helos, the last of the urgently recalled ship's personnel on leave having readied the ship only forty minutes before she'd cast off from the Bremerton yard.

The *Turner*'s CBG deployment to join *McCain* was seen by some young Americans on the liberal left as "excessive," even "bullying," in nature, but the beginning of the twenty-first century had taught many Americans, and not only those in the country's armed services, that it was best to contain a danger rather than let it fester unchallenged as happened to the Taliban in Afghanistan. And 9/11, showing terrorists reaching into the heart of America itself, had certainly influenced people as well.

The White House, meanwhile, was receiving "Presidential Eyes Only" traffic from the U.S. Embassy in Beijing, General Chang having advised Bill Heinz that the Gong An Bu believed Li Kuan's terrorists might have penetrated American seaports, particularly on America's west coast. Chang said that suspected Xinjiang and Kazakhstani terrorists "under questioning" by the Gong An Bu had revealed that small suicide inflatable boats and dirty bombs, possibly hidden in SeaLift containers, had been smuggled into American and possibly Canadian waters.

Aboard the USS *Turner*, in what at the time seemed an unrelated and banal incident, Admiral Bressard was told that the fan room located on the third deck, port side, was experiencing some difficulty, which meant air circulation wasn't up to par. The world being divided into those who are always too hot and those who are too cold, the "hot" mechanics were complaining so much it was suggested that the two enormous steel doors dividing the hanger into three distinct areas be opened. The officer of the deck refused. The idea of having the two huge doors closed in these hectic hours of getting underway was that if a fire or explosion occurred in one or more of the planes or from the ordnance—of which there was three thousand tons, in addition to the ship's 2.68 million gallons of aviation fuel—the doors would seal off the hangar into three distinct zones, each as survivable as the other two thousand watertight compartments throughout the twenty-three transverse and longitudinal bulkheads.

Admiral Bressard looked ahead into the darkness of the Juan de Fuca Strait and at the two protective Aegis cruisers. The one off to his right was all but invisible against the rugged mass that was the southern coast of Vancouver Island. The silhouette of the other Aegis, on the *Turner*'s left flank, was lost against the coast of Washington's Olympic peninsula. Then came the 4,315-ton Arleigh Burke–class destroyer squadron, two abaft and two astern of the carrier, and up ahead one of the two escorting flank attack submarines, the smallest vessels in *Turner*'s battle group. But having twelve vertical launch tubes for nuclear warhead Tomahawk cruise missiles, each of the converted Lafayette-class subs packed a powerful punch. The other sub, maintaining station farther west, moving slowly at sixty feet below to join the battle group, was Rorke's 7,800-ton *Utah*, none of its crew happy at having been so near yet so far from home.

Alicia Mayne was the unhappiest of all, keen to get off the boat onto terra firma and back to her lab. She liked Rorke and the super politeness of the *Utah*'s crew, a naval tradition whether on sub or carrier, where long, narrow passageways, needed to make room for more equipment and close living quarters, demanded exceptional courtesy. But Alicia yearned for the lavish comforts of a full-size bedroom, the sheer pleasure of a walk outside, the sensuous feel of rain on one's face. No matter how much modern commentators emphasized the roominess of the 377-foot-long, thirty-four-foot-diameter Virginia sub compared to other subs, it was still a submarine, a cooped-up world in which the normal rhythms of life ashore are lost. Only the "redded out" lighting, making the submariners' eyes more able to adjust from red to the darkness, should they have to surface, told them it was night in the world above.

Alicia could smell steaks cooking in the galley, and she heard the whir of the big mixer mashing potatoes and the thud from what she guessed was something bumping against the hull, forward and below the sail. Then all hell broke loose.

The explosion shook the *Utah* like a toy, things crashing everywhere, burned wires smoking, and suddenly the pastel blue of the wardroom walls bulged out in huge blisters from the intense heat. She could hear men yelling and screaming, the sub still shaking so violently that what she took to be dust falling was in fact fine particles of pipe-wrap insulation squeezing through multiple fissures in the pipes' sheathing. From a broken elbow joint, superheated jets of steam sliced across the passageway in which she could already hear doors and hatches slamming shut, turning the long, cigar-shaped sub into a series of watertight compartments, so that whatever section had been hit might be effectively sealed off from all others.

Alarms continued to sound, the OOD calling for damage reports as Rorke ran from his stateroom to Control and other men rushed to their stations. Rorke could feel the sub desperately trying to assume her emergency up angle in order to surface, but the forward ballast tanks were obviously damaged. In fact, there was a gash approximately three and a half by one foot wide on the starboard bow tank between the chin's sonar array and the sail. The pumps seemed unable to evict the torrent of water required to give the *Utah* the positive buoyancy she needed to rise, which she had to do quickly before becoming so heavy she'd be driven to the bottom. Rorke immediately ordered all engines stopped, diving planes at surfacing elevation, and the crew ready to abandon ship.

The starboard-side bulkhead of the battered forward tank was showing spider fissures visible only on the control monitor's zoom, and in the few seconds it took for the operator to tell the OOD about it, the spidery fissures had gone to a "visible web," the tiny cracks emitting powerful pencil-lead-thin jets of water. Rorke quickly realized that with the air pressure coils in the ballast tank ruptured, there was no hope of the *Utah* surviving, unless he could somehow achieve an emergency blow. In its present fragile state, the boat hovered dangerously close to negative buoyancy. If that happened, it would plunge, reaching breakneck speeds, plummeting past its crush depth and smashing into the seabed, its air-filled chambers popping like tin cans under the sledgehammer weight of the ocean.

In a matter of milliseconds the explosion of the seabed-planted mine had not only ruptured *Utah*'s ballast tank, but generated a pulsating white-domed bubble of carbon dioxide and methane gas that struck the aft bulkhead above the prop. The speed of the explosion's shock waves, excited by the prop's normal cavitation or bubble-producing motion, created a partial vacuum. The sudden whack of the explosion's pressure wave, traveling at Mach 4, deformed then oscillated the entire structure of the sub, in effect whipping the boat, ripping bulkheads away from their longitudinal stiffeners, and causing massive flooding.

Now that the integrity of a half-dozen previously watertight compartments was breached, the flooding could not be contained, and thirty-two officers and men in departments aft of the sail drowned within minutes of the roaring deluge invading their home. The encased pipelike housing for the SOSUS "python" was torn asunder from the sub's flank like some long worm tube, breaking up, its contents of black, oil-encased "hockey puck" microphones spilling into a frenzy of white water. It marked the catastrophic end of one of America's preeminent warships, a weapons platform that had contained more than twice the firepower of all the ordnance dropped by all combatants in World War II.

Rorke had ordered Beaufort life raft drums released, and Alicia Mayne to be the first out of the sail's hatch. She'd been through the drill often enough, but actually doing it, hitting the cold, ear-dinning horror of a battering in total darkness, was terrifying. Her body was caught in the vicious vortexes of contrary forces from the sinking boat and the boiling sea, and further battered by debris, her arms flailing, breath failing, her nostrils clogged. Her chest seemed about to explode, and her lips felt as if they were afire in the fierce upstream of acidic effervescence that was now highly poisonous due to the chemical reaction between seawater and the dying sub's gutted battery compartment.

The resulting greenish-yellow clouds of dirty chlorine that had already suffocated a dozen or more of Rorke's crew were now visible as a smudge on Darkstar's routine overflight, the explosion itself heard by the handful of isolated settlements on both the American and Canadian sides of the fifteen-mile-wide strait. Some of the submariners who, in fate's strange grasp, had popped through the chaos of swirling sea and debris to the surface of the strait, were relatively unharmed. The screaming of others was a terrible testimony to the burns and injuries inflicted by the firespill spreading across the previously black surface of the sea, its flames illuminating hundreds of pieces of debris, the unidentifiable shapes, some afire, floating around and around Alicia and everyone else who'd made it out.

Alicia involuntarily opened her mouth to scream as a corpse, its head all but severed, floating beside the body, bumped into her on the downward slide of a cresting wave. Her mouth, however, made no sound, and instead sucked in the scum of oil and a slippery, cold, choking substance that made her gag. It could have been a mélange of canned or frozen food that had exploded from containers as the *Utah* imploded from the mine's pressure wave, but convinced that she'd swallowed human flesh, albeit inadvertently, the thought gripped her with an overwhelming revulsion. *"Captain!"* she screamed. But all she could hear was the agony of survivors and of the dying, and then a wave crashed into her, pushing her into the burning oil slick.

Through his binoculars high in the *Turner*'s island, Admiral Keach, the overall commander of the carrier's battle group, could see the oil slick moving up and down like a fiery island, illuminating the final seconds of the *Utah* before she disappeared piecemeal below the heaving crimson-slashed surface of the strait. Keach had already ordered the carrier's rescue Sea Knight helicopters aloft. Standing firm against the instinctive desire of all his battle group's sailors to rush to help their stricken comrades from the *Utah*, Keach ordered all other elements of the battle group to stay where they were until further notice. On *Turner*'s bridge, Ensign Myers, though trying to hide his disgust with Keach's decision, murmured his disapproval. The admiral took it as a chance to educate the officer as well as to chastise him for not keeping his feelings to himself. "Mr. Myers," he said. "What would you do as captain of one of the Aegis or destroyers? Go full steam ahead?"

Myers, surprised by Keach's acute hearing, given the noise of the last helicopter taking off from *Turner*'s flight deck, had no time to react before the admiral was answering his own question. "Yes, you'd be the hero and dash ahead to help your fleet buddies. A noble sentiment, Mr. Myers, but what caused *Utah* to go down? Internal explosion? Torpedo? Friendly fire? A mine?"

The ensign was nonplused.

"Remember the *Kursk*!" added Keach. "Accidental firing in their own torpedo room."

Already the *Turner*'s sensor arrays were monitoring the air for any radioactive leak from *Utah*'s reactor. That would be a double whammy—a lethal cloud of radiation sweeping over the entire battle group plus the enormous catastrophe that would assault the millions of Americans who inhabited the Northwest's pristine mountains and coasts. What's more, if the water from the countless streams and rivers that raced down from the high peaks of the Rockies and Cascade ranges to the sea-stack-dotted coast of Washington, Oregon, and northern California were contaminated, most of the western United States would die.

"COMSUBPAC-9 on the scrambler line, sir," *Turner*'s Admiral Bressard informed Battle Group Commander Keach. "I think it's Admiral Jensen himself."

Keach took the phone from Bressard, Keach's tone correct but not noticeably friendly. They had both dated Margaret, and Keach's ego was as big as any of *Turner*'s air wing pilots. He hated losing.

"Admiral," Jensen told Keach. "I've just received a disturbing message from the oceanographic ship *Petrel*. They sent it down by helo—no encryption capability."

"What is it?" asked Keach.

"*Petrel* reports a possible hostile in the strait."

Keach was so dumbfounded, all he could say was, "*Utah*'s gone, Admiral. Don't you know—" He stopped, realizing there was a very good reason Jensen wouldn't know what had happened to one of his attack subs. The subs didn't make regular check-ins—such transmissions could immediately give away their position to an enemy.

"I *know* that . . ." began Jensen, his voice trailing off in a mumble. Keach was struck by the sudden metamorphosis. What had been the voice of a self-confident commander a moment before had vanished. Jensen was a man on the edge.

"Torpedo or mine, I'd say," Keach told Jensen, "but could have been internal. Or a hostile. I don't know."

There was no response from Jensen, but Keach knew he was still on the line. "I have to go, Admiral," said Keach, who immediately ordered a warning flashed to every ship in his battle group. The captain of the Aegis cruiser on his left flank asked for confirmation as to whether it was a "mini" or "midget" sub. Keach said that he had already requested confirmation of this in plain language message to the *Petrel*'s captain.

All Frank Hall could tell Keach, however, was what Albinski had written on his attack board—"Minisub"—the diver obviously not having enough time to put anything else down before his life was snuffed out.

"What's wrong?" Margaret asked when Walter walked in, gray-faced, as if he had literally aged overnight.

"A disaster," he replied, with the kind of deliberation that had always alarmed her. A "disaster" for Walter in what she called his "worrywart moods" had come to mean anything from the possibility of having to replace the muffler on his beloved Porsche to hearing that one of his Hunter Killers was in deep trouble somewhere in the Pacific.

"You look awful, Walter."

Wordlessly, he flicked on CNN, and there it was, the lead story. How did those media bastards find out about this stuff so quickly? More than a headline, the news flash was taking over the entire 11:00 P.M. newscast. Not many details, but repetition ad nauseam of a "tremendous explosion" being reported by Seattle's CNN affiliate; the high-profile anchor, Marte Price, claiming that it was believed to be one of the Navy's ICBM "boomers"—Trident submarines. Normally,

Jensen would have been scornful of the misidentification, quick to point out that it was a "Hunter Killer attack boat, you idiot," but all he could think of now was to say a silent prayer that Keach was able to have *Turner*'s Sea Kings and every other available helicopter in the battle group rescue as many of *Utah*'s men as possible, and how he, COMSUBPAC-GRU-9, so recently at large in Seattle's society circuit as guardian of Juan de Fuca's and Puget Sound's pristine environment, would be offered up by the White House as the sacrificial lamb for the catastrophe.

"Kimmel's reputation was destroyed," Jensen now told his wife, "when FDR fired him as CINCPAC after the surprise attack on Pearl Harbor. Doug MacArthur had been just as guilty, in fact *more* culpable of ignoring warnings about an attack on Clark Field in the Philippines—parking all his damned planes in clumps, easier to guard, and easier for the Japs to *destroy* the next day. But fate was on Doug's side—FDR didn't have anyone else available on our east perimeter to take command." Kimmel, he knew, had died in obscurity, and when MacArthur did get fired by Harry Truman for wanting to cross the Yalu from Korea and bomb China's staging areas, he came home a hero, got a ticker-tape parade the likes of which New York had never seen. He slumped into his TV chair, saying, "They'll crucify me, Margaret."

She went to the kitchen and began making coffee. It would be a long night. Finally, her hand on his shoulder, she asked quietly, "How many men were aboard the *Utah*?"

"A hundred and thirty, give or take. A woman aboard too, one of our scientists. Torpedo specialist."

Margaret bit her lip, thoroughly ashamed of herself. "Torpedo specialist" had made her think of a joke she'd heard among the Navy wives—torpedoes and penises. How could one think of such a vulgar thing at a time like this? Same thing, she remembered, when she was a child. Went to church every Sunday, frightened sometimes by the urge to yell out the foulest things. The more she tried to block it out, the worse it became. Walter said such things to her only when he began kissing her between her—

"Rorke," said Walter softly. "He's the skipper."

Margaret nodded. As the wife of an admiral, she got to know most of the skippers. Like her husband when he was younger, they awed her. The responsibility of young men like John Rorke, who drove the nuclear-powered steam engines that carried the power to destroy worlds, impressed even someone from the rarefied air of Radcliffe College.

"Keach," Walter said suddenly. "Your old beau. He's safe on the *Turner*. The carrier."

"Oh, yes."

They were both wrong. Six minutes after the last rescue helicopter had left the *Turner*'s darkened flight deck, three warhead mines, their release fuses initiated by the enormous downward push of the *Turner*'s 98,000 tons, detonated. The near simultaneous explosion of the mines caused what Alicia Mayne would have called a "geometric" rather than "arithmetic" progression, in that one plus one plus one did not equal three, but much more, the pressure wave so powerful that it lifted the huge warship into the air. It wasn't by much, indeed it would have been barely perceptible to the naked eye, even in daylight, but it was enough to create a fissure running up from the great ship's keel, or spinal column, to several decks above, in effect breaking the carrier's back. Many survivors of the *Utah*, eight miles to the east, foundering amid the floating debris of the sub, unable to gain a purchase on any floatable wreckage and who had only life vests, were concussed into unconsciousness by the shock waves that sped through the water from the stricken *Turner* at nearly 3,000 miles an hour.

Below on the carrier's flight deck, in the cavernous hangar, which, save for the rescue helos, did not yet house its air wing— the latter's fighters, fighter-bombers, attack and recon aircraft, following standard procedure, having not yet flown to the carrier from Whidbey Island's naval station—the crew witnessed an astonishing sight, one unique in the annals of naval history. Because their blast door was down, separating their section from the other two hangar zones, what appeared in front of them on the port side was not the huge wall that normally separated their hanger section from the support structures outside, but a jagged, ten-foot-wide gash four stories high, running from below the waterline all the way up to the hangar deck. Through the gash, the astonished crew could see the glittering diamonds of the Big Dipper. They could also hear a deluge as millions of gallons of roiling seawater rushed in. It sounded like a dam opening its spill gates, so at first no one could hear the screams and death throes of over seven hundred men and women, who, from the deep-set engine/reactor room through the aft berthing spaces, catapult equipment spaces, air filter cleaning shop, and aviation equipment storage, were drowning. The aft stern section of the carrier had been split asunder as if some giant had fire-axed the left rear side of the "boat."

Despite the superb honeycombed watertight compartmentalization of the carrier, the massive damage meant that designated escape routes no longer existed in the maelstrom of twisted aluminum and steel. The portside list of the carrier was evident within minutes. Hundreds among the carrier's six thousand were sucked out to sea and drowned. Others were burned alive in the scores of fires within the wreckage, the mines' simultaneous explosions not allowing time for these victims to don life jackets and get out.

In Aft Bay 3, crew were moving quickly to take advantage of the ten-foot-wide, V-shaped gash, which, like the unsinkable *Titanic*, was never supposed to happen, given the ship's three-inch high tensile steel. Scores of off-duty personnel, including sailors, still in their boxer shorts and T-shirts, along with female air mechanics and a female fighter pilot in shorts and tank tops, had formed a bucket brigade, stretching from the rear of Hangar 3. They passed life jackets and white oil-drum-sized Beaufort containers, which were quickly tossed overboard, falling over sixty feet past the burning, smoke-choked lower compartments. When the Beaufort drums hit the water, their CO_2 cartridges triggered upon impact, inflating the orange-glow tent rafts that were capable of holding from six to twelve people or more, depending on canister size, each raft ingeniously stocked with emergency flasks of fresh water, Power Bars, salt tablets, morphine syringes, aspirin, acetaminophen, and toothpaste-sized tubes of nontoxic, oil-based sun cream which in a pinch could be consumed as a high source of protein. In addition, there were a hand-held GPS unit, flares, saline-generated lights, palm-sized energy beam locator with batteries, and, providing survivors were in a nonshadow satellite cone, a cell phone.

The sight of the battle group's flagship, split keel to hangar deck, was devastating enough as the media arrived en masse in Port Townsend. Some, such as Fox and Britain's ITN, went farther west along the wild and sparsely populated coast of the Olympic peninsula's northernmost boundary to cover the story.

Just east of Port Townsend, a clutch of Middle Eastern networks and some European correspondents set up their gear, barely able to conceal their euphoria at the sight of the world's only superpower humbled by the grievous damage to the aircraft carrier and the outright sinking of one of its premier warships. As if on cue, detritus continued to bubble up from the pressure-flattened wreckage that used to be the USS *Utah*. Everything from ragged slabs of the anechoic sound-absorbing tiles that had coated the sub's exterior to the crushed body parts of U.S. submariners floated to the surface.

CHAPTER EIGHTEEN

THE SHOCK HIT America with the speed of light, on every TV in the country. Word of it got to incarcerated terrorists as well, who were overjoyed by the death and destruction wrought upon the "Great Satan." The terrorists immediately saw what the Pentagon was slow to recognize—that this naval disaster, within the home waters of the United States, was a catastrophe more serious than the attack of 9/11, whether or not the number of lives lost was greater. Bombing buildings by crashing planes into them was one thing; the British, as New York mayor Giuliani had recalled at the time, had suffered far worse human and material losses in the terrible Nazi blitz of 1940. But strategically and tactically, this attack on the carrier in the Strait of Juan de Fuca had achieved something that shook the government and the military to the core. The enemy had penetrated to the very center of an American carrier battle group, despite its overwhelming firepower and state-of-the-art electronic surveillance. The group, whose whole raison d'être was to protect the carrier, had been brushed aside.

In particular, the White House wanted to know how neither of the billion-dollar Aegis cruisers had detected any unusual underwater activity, along with the sub-hunting destroyers, escort frigates, and the Lafayette-class submarine which, along with the *Utah*, was supposed to have made any such attempt a near impossibility.

Eleanor Prenty had never liked the war room, or what the staff called "the basement." It had all the "gee whiz" stuff, but though smoking there had long been banned, she swore you could still smell cigar ash from time to time. And despite its no-expense-spared accoutrements, the room still felt like a bunker. The decor had certainly done nothing to ameliorate the President's mood.

"C'mon, gentlemen," he demanded. "What the hell's going on? Two—*two* of our capital ships sunk within—"

"The *Turner*'s still afloat," the CNO corrected him.

You dork, thought Eleanor.

"Yes, Admiral," said the President. "But have you seen the pictures? It's been gutted—top to bottom." He was correct, for by now the V, which had reached as high as aft Hangar Bay 4, had expanded under the sustained strain of the initial separation of the bulkheads and was visible as a ten-to-fourteen-inch-wide cleft running the full width of the flight deck, revealing equipment spaces immediately below. And the track for one of the forward catapults was severed.

It was fast becoming apparent to anyone watching CNN, which numbered almost as many who had witnessed the 9/11 implosion of the World Trade Towers, that the *Turner* might well come apart, separating, as Marte Price diligently pointed out, along the cross deck line of arresting wire number two. The image that caught the public's imagination, however, was that used by an excited Seattle commentator for CNN who opined that the damage to the *Turner* resembled an enormous "pie-shaped wedge." To illustrate his analogy further, the commentator displayed the dramatic picture from the sixties showing how an A-shaped bow had knifed into a thousand-passenger Canadian ferry in the Strait of Georgia. "We are witnessing war in our home waters," NBC declared solemnly, a truth echoed not as solemnly, and indeed joyously, by stations throughout the Arab world.

"Mr. President," interrupted an aide, "our surveillance flights confirm an invasion force heading from the Chinese mainland toward the Nationalist offshore islands of Kinmen and Matsu."

The President was already visibly shaken by the sinking of the *Utah* and the attack on the *Turner*—no list of survivors had yet reached him. The aide's news only deepened his consternation. "Well, right now, Richard," he said, "we have to prioritize." It was a word he usually disliked, but he didn't have the time to think of a better one. "The American military has been taken completely by surprise, and my first job is to defend the United States." He had already grasped what the think tanks at the Hoover Institution and the National War College would soon be impressing upon TV's talking heads, namely that if terrorists could penetrate the nation's military defenses, they could launch attacks against civilian targets at will—anywhere in the United States.

"Do you think they'll attack Canada?" the Army chief of staff asked.

"No," Homeland Defense director Harry Hawthorn replied. "Canada's immigration policy's a joke. Terrorists *love* Canada. They won't attack Canada—be fouling their nest."

The President nodded his agreement, but he had more important things to worry about than Canada. Besides, everybody already knew the score regarding Canada, its government the quintessential wimps. Full of good intentions, but in world affairs—no viability at all. The country, if you could call its disparate regions that, depended entirely on the United States for North American defense, droning on about "soft" power while the government in Ottawa continued humiliating its small but brave military through such wanton neglect that when Canadian peacekeepers were actually called upon to do something, the Canadian military didn't have a single air-worthy plane to transport them. Hopeless. The President wanted no more discussion about Canada.

"How far is the carrier from Port Townsend?" he inquired of no one in particular.

"Fifteen, twenty miles west-nor'west in the strait."

"Is that all?"

"Yes, sir."

"Son of a— Who's your man up there, Admiral?" he asked the CNO.

"Admiral Keach was commander of the battle group."

"You heard anything from him that we don't already know?"

"No, sir. He's missing."

"*Missing?* I thought he would have been up in the island."

"He was, Mr. President—over by the bridge's starboard wing lookout. Word is, the force of the explosions flung them both overboard. Apparently, the lookouts on the fantail suffered the same fate. Rescue helos he'd sent out earlier to pick up any *Utah* survivors hadn't yet returned to the *Turner.* Anyway, it was pitch-dark."

"They would have been wearing life jackets, though," said the President.

"The two lookouts at the stern, yes, sir, but I don't know about the admiral."

A sky-blue folder with the presidential seal, containing a thick pile of pages, was placed in front of the President. On the first of the 230 pages was the heading CVN TURNER—PERSONNEL. There were six thousand names, a quarter of them asterisked with either *KIA* or *MIA.* The very battle group he'd intended to use to prevent a war in Asia, in a world already at war against terrorism, now lay immobile in the Juan de Fuca

Strait. And for one overwhelmingly simple reason: the proudest and most powerful navy in the world had been grievously wounded and humiliated by a bunch of mines, weapons that, the U.S. mining of Haiphong notwithstanding, elicited the kind of contempt in naval officers as that accorded a backshooter in the Old West.

"If terrorists can sink two of our capital warships before we can even reach our littoral seas," wrote the *Wall Street Journal*'s editorial, "what possible defense can we expect from the Navy?"

US SUB SUNK was the less erudite but more effective verdict of the tabloids.

As first editions hit the street on the East Coast, it was 3:00 A.M. in the Straits of Georgia and Juan de Fuca, where the rescue effort of hundreds of small boats, together with a dozen U.S. Coast Guard patrol vessels and Canada's two coast guard cutters, had begun.

Mayhem quickly followed in the wake of good intentions, as congested sea traffic, strong tides, and fog combined to endanger the would-be rescuers. Indeed, the fog was so thick that it obscured even the monolithic carrier, which, with her power cut, the gash in her side expanding till it was now over eleven feet wide, seemed beyond saving. The crippled leviathan's aft section, from Elevator 4 to stern, looked to Admiral Bressard as if it would detach itself from the rest of the ship at any moment. The bone-grinding sounds of more bulkheads giving way, mingled with the cries from sick bays now rendered useless as air flows in the carrier—superheated by burst steam pipes leading from the reactors—made it necessary to bring hundreds of the wounded, many already suffering from severe scalding, up onto the forward flight deck. There, as corpsmen and other medics performed triage, surgeons did what little they could under the circumstances, the navy chaplains all but overwhelmed administering last rites. And yet, as the CNO and everyone else knew, there had been no battle in the strait—no enemy sighted.

During the massive if largely ad hoc rescue effort, which the media was referring to as "America's Dunkirk," the *Turner*'s captain, like all his fellow commanders in the CVBG, were ordered by the CNO to remain in DEFCON—Defense Condition—1. Maximum force readiness.

"Cautious," said the *New York Times*.

"Scared," said *Le Monde*.

Everyone on the remaining ships of the CVBG was increasingly nervous following the fate of *Utah* and *Turner*. It seemed that both the *Times* and *Le Monde* were right, the ships not daring to proceed through the strait for fear of three possibilities that Aegis analysis sensors now suggested but could not confirm: simultaneous detonation of five mines, two against *Utah*, three against *Turner*, either combinations of pressure/acoustic mines or coil rod induction fused bottom mines; a much more advanced, highly sensitive and comparatively cheap triple-axis fluxgate magnetometer-triggered mine; and finally, that the *Utah* and the *Turner* had been blown up by sensor mines measuring the electric current sent into the sea by the electrochemical reaction generated when steel hulls slice through iron-rich salt water. This latter type of targeting, however, was considered least likely by the Aegis electronic warfare officers, given the presence of the anechoic coating on the *Utah*, which would have minimized the metal/seawater electrochemical reaction.

For the Pentagon, the question of what type of mines had been used against the two warships was crucial to any planned defense in the future, because obviously neither of the comparatively sophisticated underwater defense systems aboard *Utah* and the Aegis cruisers had worked.

All right, the CNO asked, but what or who had laid the mines? A "mini" or "midget" sub? If mines had been laid from an unmanned mini, where was the mini being controlled from? All U.S. and Canadian submersible companies had been cleared. And if it had been a manned mini or midget sub, then where was its "milch cow," its mother supply ship?

Amid the winking of scores of rescue boat lights in the mist-shrouded strait, the sailors, offloading wounded into a Coast Guard cutter, saw one of the lights for a second become as bright as a struck match. It was the backblast of a missile streaking toward the huge gash on *Turner*'s aft port side. The speed of the missile registered by the computers on the Aegis nearest *Turner* was Mach 1.9, which meant it reached the already gravely wounded carrier in .3 seconds, the blink of an eye. Even so, the Aegis's Phalanx close-in weapons system, with its state-of-the-art, superfast radar-guided response, did intercept. It was disastrous however, the impact of the incoming missile and outgoing 20mm ordnance resulting in a fiery rain of white-hot debris that showered *Turner*'s island, knocking out its cluster of vital antennae and radar dishes. For this reason, a second missile, fired a millisecond later, was able to disappear into the cavernous V cut, exploding at the waterline. Six minutes later the order was given to abandon ship. She would not hold.

At 0431 the 95,000-ton carrier, tow lines attached, began a twelve-second death roll to port. Two tugboats—one out of Vancouver, the other from Seattle—were unable to release their lines quickly enough. One was dragged under, and the other, its line already taut, whipped through the air like a toy as the *Turner*'s stern inverted, the oceangoing tug slamming into the carrier's prop like a box of matchsticks, the tug's crew flung into the maelstrom of the carrier's immense propellers.

CHAPTER NINETEEN

FROM CHINA'S COAST province of Fukien, the PLA's sixty Xian H-6 medium bombers that attacked the offshore Nationalist island of Kinmen, about one-eighth the size of Rhode Island, did not come directly from the west, as expected. Following the PLA's thousand-gun artillery assault, a prelude to what Kinmen's Nationalists anticipated would be the invasion, the ChiCom bombers, augmented by 120 Q-5 ground attack aircraft and protected by three hundred-plane swarms of PLA Shenyang J-5 Fresco interceptors, flew south of Fukien, not east toward Kinmen.

The ChiCom pilots, using their own hilly Amoy Island, ten miles directly west of Kinmen, as a screen, turned their fighter-protected bombers westward in a sixty-mile crescent, sweeping in low over the arc of Liaolo Bay on the island's forty-mile-long southern coast, thus attacking the Nationalists' heavy fortifications on the island's northern shore from behind. Only now did Taipei and Washington realize that the fast Chinese attack boats, seen earlier on SATPIX as white scratches heading east from the Chinese mainland, had been a feint, making the Nationalists on Kinmen think the ChiCom fast attack patrol boats were the forward elements of a head-on invasion of the island from the west. This had duped the Nationalists on Kinmen to rush the bulk of their north coast garrison to the southernmost shores, thus leaving their flank exposed.

As Freeman and the rest of the Army's USO team packed up for their flight back to the States, the general sent an e-mail to David Brentwood, who was to be sent home from Tora Bora for R&R, telling him, "I'll come to see you back in the States. Fort Lewis is pretty close to this Northwest chaos, and I'd like to have a look-see for myself. Washington sure as hell doesn't know what's going on. It just occurred to me that probably the best place to meet would be in Port Townsend, right on the Strait of Juan de Fuca. Will confirm later. By the way, I don't think the towelheads are behind this at all."

If that last phrase didn't get him the attention of Homeland Defense, Freeman thought, he'd eat his Afrika Korps cap.

Army surgeons at Tora Bora, eschewing the kind of false hope that some of their well-meaning civilian colleagues often felt compelled to give patients, told David bluntly that his military career was over. "The lower part of your nerve plexus in the right arm has been destroyed, unfortunately—so badly damaged that even the best vascular surgeon can't repair your arm beyond forty percent of its function. Better to face that now,

Captain," said one of the specialists, who, as an afterthought, asked, "You a religious man, Brentwood?"

"Foxhole convert," David quipped, a little too flippantly, given his sardonic smile, for any of the three surgeons to believe him.

"Religion sometimes helps patients to adjust," the surgeon said.

David resented his tone. He saw it as an atheistic condescension toward someone the doctor considered simpleminded. "I don't believe in miracles," he responded, and immediately regretted giving ground.

"Well, I think you'll enjoy your R and R at Fort Lewis." An awkward silence ensued until the doctor added, "The Pacific Northwest is big timber country. Lots of logging—one of the most accident-prone jobs in the world. A lot of good surgeons and rehab right at Fort Lewis's doorstep."

"Ah, I think he wanted his rehab in Hawaii!" joshed one of the other doctors. "Somewhere a little warmer."

David gave them the smile they expected.

"You ever been in the Pacific Northwest, Brentwood?"

David wondered where he should begin. Obviously they hadn't read his military record. "Yes," he said simply.

Approaching Washington State, the military transport was escorted in from a hundred miles out by two F-18s out of McCord, the Northwest under the highest alert since the Cuban Missile and 9/11 crises.

After landing at SeaTac, David walked past the Fort Lewis driver who was holding the BRENTWOOD sign, consulted "Surgeons" in Seattle's yellow pages directory, and caught a cab downtown.

Dr. Paul Gonzales, a surgeon from the famed Brazilian clinic used by many Hollywood celebrities, was more suave than the three doctors at Tora Bora and disagreed with their diagnosis. Surgery, he told David, could not be expected to restore more than a maximum of thirty percent use in his right arm—"in the fingers, no more than twenty-five percent."

"Shit!" said David, in an uncharacteristic outburst. "How about physiotherapy—you know, rehab and—"

Gonzales shrugged. "You'll have to do that just to maintain

the minimum range of movement you have. If you don't, you'll lose it."

Brentwood knew the doctor meant his arm, but he already felt as if he'd lost everything. A one-armed soldier.

"Of course," Dr. Gonzales continued, "your left arm will take over some of the functions of your right. A squeeze ball will help somewhat. Keep exercising the stiff hand as much as possible to retain what motion remains."

"A *squeeze* ball?"

A stunning print of Cot's *Storm* hung on the doctor's pastel-gray wall, the glances of apprehension on the faces of the two lovers fleeing through the foreboding and beautiful forest arresting David's attention. Despite the danger all around them, there was hope in their eyes. And he needed hope now, the kind Melissa had given him through the long months of separation. He needed her now, but the nightmare of the cave, the death of his six comrades, was too heavy upon him to go to her yet.

Gonzales's second examination was merely an act of courtesy. "I'm sorry," he said.

Douglas Freeman, true to his e-mail, turned up in Port Townsend's East-West Café for lunch. It was the only place open since the scare. But David Brentwood wasn't in the mood to eat, and neither was the general, beset by what seemed an endless MTV video blaring from the TV in the corner of the restaurant. Agitated, but trying not to show it, the general was convinced that Washington, D.C., was merely spinning its wheels while the West Coast burned, and that more attacks could be in the offing. "They think," he told David, "that this damn minisub, or whatever the hell it is, has shot its bolt."

"Well," said David, "they might be right, General. A carrier and a nuclear sub isn't too bad."

Both men picked unenthusiastically at their appetizers, brought to them by a young, sullen Vietnamese woman who was complaining bitterly and loudly to a customer who looked like a regular, ". . . is because we Asian. FBI, Home Defense, come here. They think we terrorists. Blow up ships. We good citizens, Mr. Norman. We good citizens of United States."

"I know, Sally. They're just checking everyone out."

"They check *you* out?" she asked, furiously wiping off a table at the back of the restaurant.

"Well, I don't—" began Mr. Norman.

"See?" the woman said, using her white cloth as a pointer. "They no ask *you*. They think we terrorists. Not good for customers."

"Neither," Freeman told David, "is yelling," the general pleased to see that his and David's main dishes were being happily delivered by one of the two Vietnamese waiters whose smiling dispositions were a welcome respite from "Sullen Sally."

The general, however, always a stickler for personal hygiene, scowled in disgust. "Did you see his fingernails?" he asked Brentwood, who, as unobtrusively as possible, pulled his right hand from the table, resting it in his lap, not sure of the state of his own fingernails. "Goddammit," continued Freeman, "those two guys look as if they've been in a brawl."

"Maybe over Sally," joked David, trying to find as many cashews as he could in the mixed vegetable, chicken, and rice dish.

"Well, she roughed them up pretty good," said Freeman. "Look at their wrists. And the one who served us—looks like she tried to strangle him. Either that or cut his throat. Great bloody welt around his neck."

"I wouldn't like to tangle with her," said David.

Freeman hadn't realized that Sally had overheard some of their comments, and she opened up on him. "I no beat anyone, mister. They," she said, indicating the two waiters, "go down, help pull sailors from the sea. That how they get burn."

David was embarrassed. Hadn't Freeman heard about the local Dunkirk effort? Hundreds of people coming from all points on the sparsely populated coast to help in the rescue of the survivors, often at great personal risk, many of the rescuers having to wade out into burning oil slicks to reach the victims.

"Dey have burn all over body, helping sailors."

"I'm sorry," Freeman said. "I didn't realize. You've done a great job. Thank you."

Sally pointed back at the restaurant kitchen. "We give hot food to saved people. Many hours."

"Yes," said an abashed Freeman. "I'm sorry, miss. I was way out of line."

David nodded, about to give his heartfelt thanks, but before he could respond further, they had visitors. Two morose-looking men in shades had entered the East-West Café and were walking toward their table.

"FBI or Homeland Defense," Freeman told David, who was taking a sip of his green tea.

The agents identified themselves, and without any apology for interrupting the two men's meal, explained that a NSA computer phone scan had picked up Freeman's e-mail to Captain Brentwood, and would the general be good enough to explain his comment, of which they had a copy, that "I don't think the towelheads are behind this at all."

"By 'towelheads,' gentlemen, I meant Arabs," Freeman told them. "Yes, I know that their 9/11 attack was brilliantly coordinated and executed. But they used *our* planes, *our* technology. But do you know how many people this strait thing up here would require—what kind of operation you would need for *military* targets? Not Trade Towers, gentlemen, but two capital ships. Scores of the bastards—that's what it would take to pull it off."

"Who then, General?" asked one of the agents.

"Don't know, son," Freeman replied. "But I've been reconnoitering the area on my own. Not enough towelheads around. Haven't seen one damn A-rab on this coast. Not one."

"So you don't think it's Muslims?"

"I didn't say that. What I am saying is that with all our carrier groups already spoken for on so many different terrorist fronts—Middle East, East Africa, West Africa, the Philippines, et cetera—we'd only have the *McCain*'s battle group to referee the Taiwan Strait, because we're boxed in here. The most powerful nation in the world can't move its warships out of the Northwest through this choke point because we don't know what the hell's going on."

"What would you suggest we do?" asked the older of the two agents.

"Tell the government to give me access to Darkstar. I'll use my own team."

"Your team?"

"SpecFor boys. You just get me the authority—tell this Admiral Jensen to let me use Darkstar. I've got a few ideas."

Once he'd heard this, all David could think of was getting back to Fort Lewis to see whether the endless exercising he had done since Afghanistan would prove the doctors wrong— whether through sheer will he could make his hitherto dead right arm, specifically its recalcitrant elbow, bend enough to support the front weight of the new F2000 bullpup rifle.

It didn't matter who had started the war in the Taiwan Strait, the PRC—People's Republic of China—or the ROC—Taiwan. If Taiwan fell, the quake through the world's financial markets, especially that of the U.S., was certain to plunge the West into its worst recession since the collapse of '87.

"Admiral," the President appraised *McCain*'s Crowley, "you're the only flat top we've got in this ball game. I'll do what I can to bleed off elements from the Gulf and elsewhere, but if you wait for them to join you I suspect it'd be too late."

"I understand, Mr. President. We'll give a good account of ourselves."

"I know you will. Your boy excited?"

It took Crowley aback that a President, in the midst of such a clear and present danger to the nation, was nevertheless so alert to the fact—the non–politically correct fact—that young men and women from West Point to Annapolis would see in the terrible act of war in the Strait of Juan de Fuca against their country the opportunity of a lifetime. Military men understood youth's eagerness for combat. But for a civilian like the President, with no military experience, to be equally aware—though obligated, as the nation's Chief Executive, to do all he could to stop the war—at once pleased and alarmed Crowley. However eager the uninitiated soldier might be, Crowley knew that the more a soldier saw of his grizzly trade up close, the less he wanted to see. Except for those like Douglas Freeman, who, in the darkness of his inner journeys, had recorded illegally in his combat diaries, that, "God forgive me, but, like old Georgie Patton, I do so love it." The sting of battle beckoned to him, the ever-present call of Thermopylae, of being one of those who, on some great and terrible day, would save the nation in its hour of peril.

And here in Port Townsend, in his hotel bathtub, Douglas Freeman contemplated America's present peril, the greatest, it seemed to him, since the nation teetered on the verge of destruction—the White House in flames, the British columns advancing, the Continental Army in bitter retreat. The call reverberated in him as deeply as it had in Churchill, another great aficionado of bathtub contemplation.

Wet facecloth over his "George C. Scott" face, the only noise that of his breathing and occasional ripple, he tried to put the pieces together like a chess player surveying the board, the clock ticking as he attempted to solve the deadly puzzle, to forestall the enemy's next move. He tried to recollect everything, like every pawn on the table, which alone might contribute little or nothing to the puzzle but which once all assembled, brought willfully together in the mind's eye, might reveal the who, what, and why of it all.

The shrill ring of the bathroom phone evoked a curse worthy of Aussie Lewis, who'd been the most profane of Freeman's SpecOps boys. Whipping the facecloth off, he barked, "Freeman!"

It was Eleanor Prenty. He softened his tone, though still irritable at the interruption to his train of thought. "I've been informed of your request for Darkstar access. Admiral Jensen has been told to assist in any way possible." She paused.

He refused to fill the silence. Let her wait—about damn time she returned his call.

"We've received a communication from the Chinese," she continued. "Their intelligence reveals that Li Kuan, the—"

"Yes, I know who he is," cut in Freeman, trying to maintain his train of concentration and struck by the irony that when he'd been practically begging the White House to talk to him, he couldn't get past Operator *Eight*, and now, precisely when he didn't want to be disturbed, they were—

"Beijing has information that suggests Li Kuan is behind the attack on *Utah* and *Turner*. If so, he could have a dirty bomb."

"Then he would have used it."

"Not if he's *here*."

Jesus.

"Your thoughts, General?" Which told him that, as before 9/11, no one in Washington had any more idea of precisely what was going on than he did. They were even seeking the opinion of retired generals. "I'm going to need some help. I'll call a few of my boys. I'll get back to you."

"Thank you, General."

Well, that was more like it.

CHAPTER TWENTY

THE DENSE WHITE smoke rising from the hilly spine of Kinmen Island was the result of artillery smoke rounds fired by both Communist and Nationalist forces as the battle was joined. Most of the fighting was taking place on the green high ground overlooking the strands of beaches on the less verdant western shore of the island, whose pinched half-mile-wide waist accorded the island a shape that navigators throughout the *McCain* battle group referred to as the "bow tie."

Its highest point, the eight-thousand-foot Mount Taiwu, rose in the middle of the bow tie's eastern segment. Here, Chinese paratroops, their transports having skirted Kinmen's two south-side airfields, were engaged in bitter, often hand-to-hand combat to capture the high ground to quickly establish and secure observation posts and fire bases from which they could lob 100mm mortar and 105mm howitzer rounds down upon the Nationalist forces dug in along the island's northern and eastern defensive perimeters. The bulk of Sky Bow II missiles for Kinmen's defense had been situated on its northern and western shores, where the ChiCom invasion was anticipated. But now ChiCom paratroops, who began falling like confetti on the ridges about the base of Mounts Taiwu and Shuhao, had attained complete surprise.

Sky Bow missiles fired from the Nationalist island's more heavily defended northern and western shores did bring down a clutch of six high-flying ChiCom J-5 Fresco Interceptors. But the missile flight arc of the Sky Bows fired up at the heights of Shuhao and Taiwu mountains and the hilly spine in between could not execute the abrupt C turn it would need to hit the lower flying ChiCom interceptors and ground attack aircraft. They came in low over the South China Sea, bombing and strafing the southern shore's two vital airstrips.

While the ChiCom paratroop transports continued to unload their men, mortars, and multichute, quick-assembly howitzers at precariously low altitudes, their low-drop zones pushed safety margins. Carrying at least 130 pounds of weapons and equipment, in addition to their own body weight, the paratroopers were jumping from the scores of transport planes at six hundred feet, in order to use the bulk of Taiwu and Shuhao mountains as protection from Nationalist ground fire.

All over the island billions of black beetles, known as *chun*, rose in panicked crescendo as the normally tranquil air, disturbed only in the recent past by loudspeaker propaganda from the Chinese mainland, was now resonant with the noise of gunfire—the *chunk* of 60mm and 82mm mortars, and the unrelenting thudding of howitzers laying down covering fire and fire for effect, from both ChiCom and ROC forces. The Nationalists, over 25,000, dug in along the entire length of Kinmen's western and northern shores as ROC armor moved toward Mount Taiwu and adjacent high ground in the island's mideast sector. Here, a forward battalion of Nanjing's Armored Division, one of those in the twenty percent of the PLA's First Class Training Units, now dropped eighteen triple-drogue-chuted mobile howitzers. Each gun was capable of firing flat or high trajectory rounds while on the move at 34 mph, and was also equipped with up-graded infrared night vision and a 7.62mm machine gun.

Initially, the eighteen mobile howitzers caused alarm at Kinmen Nationalist HQ, the ChiCom howitzers unleashing a deadly fire on the line of Nationalist bunkers and trenches at will. Then dots began appearing on Kinmen's east coast radar screens. They were the ROC's own fighters, American-made F-18s, screaming westward high above the Taiwan Strait, the 127-mile distance between Taiwan's Ching Chuan Kang air force base on Taiwan's central west coast and Kinmen closing fast, the estimated time to enemy contact three minutes.

A swarm of fifty ChiCom Nanchang fighter-bombers and sixty H-6s—ChiCom versions of Russia's glazed-nosed Tupolev TU-16 medium bombers—were now pounding Kinmen's defenses with six-hundred-pound cluster bombs, their aerial onslaught met with dozens of ROC surface-to-air missiles. From a distance on the big screens of *McCain*'s Tactical Flag Command Center, the contrails of rockets and planes, and bursts of one-in-four red tracer arcing gracefully through the mayhem, looked like a huge and colorful video game. But it was a deadly, no-holds-barred struggle over whether Communist China, with overwhelming if temporary air superiority, would take Kinmen, Taiwan's first line of defense.

Then the ROC's F-18s, engines screaming at Mach 1.2, joined battle, coming in from the sun at three o'clock low. They unleashed their air-to-air missiles with such precision and accuracy that the five ChiCom H-6s were hit and downed in the first twenty-two seconds of battle. It sent the entire ChiCom bomber swarms, 253 planes in all, retreating to the mainland's coastal air space, which, even for the farthest ChiCom bomber and fighter escorts, was mere seconds away, and thick with SAM batteries that till now had remained silent for fear of hitting their own aircraft. Once the bulk of the returning Chinese bombers and escorts crossed the coast, however, the scores of ChiCom surface-to-air missiles opened up, the ROC's F-18s in hot pursuit, popping orange "sucker" flares. Descending slowly, like fairy dust that belied their serious intent, the flares drew off the

ChiComs' heat-seeking missiles, whose infrared-seeking heads
had mistaken the sucker flares' intensive heat for that of the F-
18s' exhaust.

"They're running!" announced a young ROC pilot.

"For now," his wing commander replied. "But for how long?"
The ROC air commander, a pilot of long experience, knew that
what he was seeing was Mao's famed hit-and-run guerrilla land
tactics being ably applied to aerial combat. And he was aware,
as he knew his ChiCom enemies must be, that the overriding
problem for the Taiwanese fighters was that they couldn't loiter
as long as the ChiCom planes, which were much closer to their
bases, only a few miles away on the Chinese mainland.

When the Taiwanese fighter pilots heard their low fuel alarm
and turned back to Taiwan to refuel and rearm, there would
have to be other Nationalist squadrons to relieve them, thus
stretching their resources in what was quickly becoming a war
of attrition. As if to underscore his concern, the Taiwanese wing
commander caught sight of a dozen or so smoking plane wrecks
scattered around the base of Mount Taiwu. He had no way of
knowing whether they were ChiCom or ROC fighters that had
risen up from Kinmen's two southern airfields before the
airstrips were cratered, save for one clearly evident "red star"
tail, visible in thick green foliage.

Unless hostilities were either called off by Beijing, or some
kind of diplomatic cease-fire came into effect under U.S. guar-
antee, this coastal war situation could quickly escalate to a catastrophic ICBM exchange between Kinmen and Taiwan, the
stand-ins, as it were, for Beijing and Taipei. Realizing this, the
Taiwanese wing commander knew he must emphasize to Taipei
that if Kinmen was not to fall—on one hand a human disaster,
an enormous strategic and military defeat on the other—the
ROC must keep fighters aloft over Kinmen. To lose this aerial
battle would only encourage Beijing to go further.

As thirty Chinese Communist J-11 fighter interceptors—in
reality Russian-made Sukhoi-27s—rose from their Fukien
airstrip to meet Taiwan's squadrons of Mirage 2000s, the
ChiCom pilots of the PLA air force were confident of victory.
The two Lyulka afterburning turbofans on each of their J-11s

could deliver more than twice the thrust of the Taiwanese Mirage's, rocketing the Communist fighters to Mach 2.35 versus the Mirage's 2.2. Plus the Russian Lyulka engines could take the ChiCom J-11s, with their A-10 Alamo and AA Archer missiles to a service ceiling of 59,000-plus feet, over four thousand feet higher than the Taiwanese Mirage, though both planes' climb rates were comparable at around 59,000 feet per minute.

When ChiCom ground control alerted their J-11 pilots of a new development—a squadron of Taiwanese F-16s scrambling from Taiwan's Ching Chuan Kang Air Base—the Communist pilots remained unfazed. The ChiComs' Sukhoi-27s would still outnumber the Taiwanese challengers by two to one. Indeed, the ChiCom fighter pilots welcomed the news, knowing that their Russian-made aircraft outmatched both the ROC's Mirage 2000s and their American-made F-16s in both power thrust and service ceiling. Even the highly touted American F-18s, which the Taiwanese were holding back in hard-shell revetments for Taiwan's last line of defense, were not as fast as the J-11s. And studies at the China-French Friendship Polytechnic at Harbin had shown that the J-11s would defeat the American-made plane more than fifty percent of the time in tight-turning, dogfight engagements.

But as any driver knows, a vehicle is ultimately only as good as its operator, and unlike their mainland enemies, the Taiwanese, because of their buoyant economy, had been able to give their pilots all the air time they could log. They had also been able to purchase the expensive high-tech simulators needed to train a cutting-edge air force; though, in a strange irony, even the best aviators, it was noticed, often became violently airsick in simulators—a condition most of them had never experienced in actual flight. In addition, the best ROC pilots had spent time in the United States by means of a politically hush-hush U.S.-ROC pilot exchange program at Fallon's top gun school in Nevada. There, high above, and sometimes precariously low, over the Nevada desert, the best Taiwanese pilots from the ROC Air Force Academy flew daily against America's elite aviators, many of whom had seen active service in both Gulf wars and in Afghanistan. And though relatively few of the

Americans there had been in actual dogfights—that is, in one-on-one aerial combat—many had experienced the real-life, gut-wrenching, adrenaline-surging terror of surface-to-air missile attacks as they fought up to nine G's in the life-or-death drama of evasive maneuvers where they used all the skills taught to them at Fallon.

From high above the blue of the Taiwan Strait, the ROC F-16 pilots could see both the line to the west, where the deep blue of the ocean met the brown effluent of the Chinese mainland, and the dirty, greenish-brown haze of the combat-polluted zone above and around Kinmen, whose eastern sector was smothered by artillery-laid white smoke. The usual westerlies, however, were blowing the smoke quickly back over Kinmen's western side, effectively hiding the ChiComs' howitzer and mortar positions, but simultaneously shrouding the positions of the four Taiwanese infantry battalions who were now moving up and away from the island's northern and eastern shore and the very positions they had so assiduously practiced to defend. They were moving toward the ChiCom paratroopers who had come in the back door and now occupied the island's high ground. But with neither army on the island's western side able to see one another through the man-made fog, the usual confusion of war was exacerbated into utter mayhem.

Both the ChiCom and ROC infantry, normally well-conditioned, began firing at anything that moved in the smoke. The situation was further confused by the close similarity of both sides' khaki/green field uniforms, which the PLA and ROC had begun copying from the Americans in the late 1990s, and which were markedly unlike the plain PLA green still used by the Chinese armies now routing the Muslim fundamentalists in Kazakhstan. While the new camouflage clothing used by both armies on Kinmen was admirably suited to the brownish green foliage of Taiwan, the ChiCom coast, and offshore islands, the all-but-identical uniforms escalated the usual danger of "friendly fire" to pandemic proportions in the battle.

With both sides continuing to lay smoke during a lull in the westerly winds, the entire island was shrouded in a pungent, bruise-colored smoke reeking of cordite and gasoline exhaust from armored personnel carriers, mobile artillery haulers, and tanks. Vehicles moving through tinder-dry scrub began a series of fires, whose growing ferocity was due to the panic-born thoughtlessness of an ROC infantry platoon moving up toward Mount Taiwu to dislodge a dug-in section of ChiCom machine gunners. The ROC platoon, having been already badly mauled by sniper fire and now down to about twenty men, found their way blocked by a wide rush of splotchy-leafed and highly toxic *yaorénmāo*—"people biting cat" nettles—and also came under heavy ChiCom machine gun fire from thick woods on both flanks. Rather than remain exposed in the relatively open nettle space, a corporal—the platoon's lieutenant and sergeant having already been killed—yelled for the platoon's flame thrower to torch the nettles, probably hoping to use the resulting smoke as a blind as well as to clear a way through. As the disembodied orange tongue of liquid fire arced into the nettles, the fire, fanned by the resumption of the winds blowing westward from Taiwan, swept forward so rapidly through the trees that it overtook the ChiCom machine gunners. They were forced to abandon their heavy two hundred–round box magazines in an attempt at retreat. The sickly sweet stench of the ChiComs burning alive mixed with the smell of incinerated equipment.

At the same time, billions of the ubiquitous black insects swirling skyward to escape the smoke that covered the island began to explode, the resulting rapid firecracker noise mistaken by younger soldiers on both sides for the sound of the ChiComs' lightweight CQ automatic rifles. It was a burst from one of these rifles, known among U.S. and other NATO forces as a 7.5-pound M-16 "rip-off," that felled Corporal Ahmao Pan, the youngest son of Moh Pan, as he led his rifle section against a ChiCom sapper unit that had quickly braved an intense, overlapping field of ROC mortar fire near the ROC's big bunker near Pupien on the island's northern side. The impact of the 3.56 gram bullets, their muzzle velocity among the highest in the ChiComs' armory of infantry weapons, blew away Pan's chest and stopped what up till then had been his section's spirited charge against the enemy sappers.

The pause enabled the ChiCom engineers to place satchel charges against the bunker. The detonations failed to wreck the bunker but created such enormous and simultaneous concussions that the bunker's ROC defenders were so badly disorientated that they failed to prevent two hundred ChiCom marines from rappelling ashore from Mikhail-B heavy transport helos. The Communist marines captured the huge bunker complex with virtually no opposition.

Within minutes another fleet of Mikhail heavy transport helos arrived, flying at no more than a hundred feet above an increasingly choppy sea that presaged the coming onslaught of Typhoon Jane. The transport helicopter pilots carefully watching the precipitous fall in barometric pressure had already seen satellite pictures showing the towering green columns of rain and debris that were picking up speed after having been initially slowed from 135 miles per hour to 100 mph as they passed over islands in the Philippine Sea. "Jane" had sucked up houses, entire villages, and automobiles two days before in Luzon, spitting them down miles away as the massive weather disturbance, siphoning off the power of smaller systems, continued its destructive course toward Taiwan. The CNN anchor, Marte Price, echoing reports from the East Asian network, announced that Taiwan was reportedly in for what the Chinese traditionally called a "*super* typhoon."

CHAPTER TWENTY-ONE

DOUGLAS FREEMAN HEARTILY despised the media in general, regarding them in an infamous address to a graduating class at Emory as "a bunch of lily-livered liberals" who should be told about wars only when they were over. On CNN, Marte

Price had reported his comments as an "antiliberal tirade," noting that he'd been booed by the student body. The general laughed it off. He and Marte were old friends, though diametrically opposed politically. As he once commented to Norman Raft, his 2nd Army quartermaster, with uncharacteristic embarrassment, he and Marte Price, who had been a reporter in the field during several of his wars, were "what you might call, ah, chemically aligned."

"What the hell's that mean, Douglas?" Raft replied. "You screwed her?"

"Damn woman was going to write some nasty stuff about my Sea Air Land Emergency Response Team," Freeman said, "and for reasons of national security, I had to launch a, ah . . ."

"Preemptive strike."

"There you go. For the good of the Army."

"Was she a good fit?" asked Raft.

"Like a 105 in the breech."

"A *105*!"

"Metaphorically speaking," Freeman responded.

"Oh, then it was more like small caliber—"

"That's enough, Norman. Don't you have to order some water pumps?"

It was an old joke between them, a reference to the tragic failure of a five-dollar cooling component in the British army's tanks during the initial and disastrous campaign against Rommel in the Western Desert. The small, defective part had been responsible for terrible losses as overheated engines conked out and became sitting ducks for the Afrika Korps 88s. It was one of the reasons that Freeman, to the disapproval of fellow senior commanders past and present, occasionally sported his distinctive khaki Afrika Korps cap—the swastika removed. The cap reminded him of the two vital attributes of any country's great lieutenants: first, the ability to get inside your opponent's head, to think like him tactically as well as strategically; and second, to remember that God *is* in the details, the water pumps, for instance, without which an entire armored division could grind to a halt. These were details most overburdened generals left to their army's quartermaster and Freeman always attended to himself.

But now it was time to get a detailed map of the area and to call the team—or, as he liked to refer to them, the old Special Forces "gang." There would be no small talk now that Freeman was sure that the Navy—indeed the United States—was in even more danger than it feared.

Aussie Lewis in Los Angeles was the first to get the call.

"You in for a job?" Freeman asked him.

"Location?" replied the laconic Aussie Lewis, refusing as always to admit surprise.

"Washington State," Freeman said. "Picking apples. You fit?"

"A mile with full kit, in under ten. How's that?"

"Adequate." It was part of the code. "Now this is crucial: What's your current waist?"

"Thirty-one. Thirty-two after lunch at Hooters."

So he *was* fit. "One more thing . . ." said Freeman.

"I'm waiting."

"Will Mommy let you go?"

Lewis ignored the taunt. "When?"

"Tomorrow, 1600. You have your own Draeger?" He meant the special chest-mounted rebreather unit and air tank which, unlike other diving gear, would not release telltale bubbles that could betray your position to the enemy.

Next, Freeman called Sal Salvini in Brooklyn, asking the same question. The answer was, "I'm packing now."

Choir Williams, who had settled in the quiet little town of Winthrop, nestled in eastern Washington's Cascades, the wilderness mountain chain that ran south of Mount Baker near the Canadian-U.S. border, received the last call. But by the time the general dialed him, the Welsh-American who'd never lost his accent had already been contacted by Aussie Lewis.

"Williams here!" he answered the phone. "A fine lick of a lad I am. Fit as a rugby fly-half and a devil with the ladies!"

There was a polite pause. "Mr. Williams. It's Pastor Keen-heart here. Perhaps I've caught you at a bad time?"

"Ah yes—well, ah, no—Pastor."

"The choir at Winthrop St. Andrews wondered if you'd be so

kind as to lend us your fine eisteddfod tenor voice for our Thanksgiving service."

"Ah yes, of course. Sorry, Pastor, I thought—I thought you were an old pal of mine. Yes, of course I'd be happy to assist, though I could be out of town."

"Oh, that'd be a pity, because two of our soprano ladies wanted you to bang them!"

"General?"

Choir answered Freeman's questions, including giving his waist size, and as he had with Aussie and Salvini, Freeman told him to bring "Draeger" along, as if the latter were a person. Choir inquired about David Brentwood, the other member of the old team. Would he be going also?

"No!" It was so emphatic that Choir was taken aback—they had always worked as a team. He didn't press further. And, being a single man, there was no "Mommy" consideration for Choir.

When Eleanor Prenty heard a message on her answering machine from Freeman—"I know what's going on"—she called him immediately, her earlier reluctance to return his calls or seek his advice having vanished in light of—or rather, the darkness of—the *Utah* and *Turner* having been sunk. No one in COMSUBPAC-9 seemed to know anything other than what oceanographer Frank Hall had informed them: that SEAL diver Rafe Albinski had apparently spotted a mini—or could it be a midget?—sub before his suspicious death, and that Admiral Jensen had therefore requested an airlift of the Navy's small NR-1B research sub from the Atlantic coast to Whidbey Island, where it could be launched to help in the investigation.

Freeman explained to Eleanor Prenty where he thought the sub was by referring to what he called the reverse-seven shape of the Olympic peninsula's coastline, which appeared in the Cape Flattery quadrant of the 1:110,000 maritime chart of the Juan de Fuca Strait where he'd spotted the simple four-word entry "Hole in the Wall." It referred to a sea cave in the extraordinarily rock-pitted coastline.

"A cave!" Eleanor said, struck by the general's perspicacity.

But she immediately pointed out to him the difficulty of getting enough divers to search almost one hundred miles of some of the wildest coastline in North America. All available divers were already needed to scout every port and dock—

"I've already made calls," Freeman cut in, "to three or four of the best SEAL SpecOp guys in the country."

"*Three or four?* It'd take hundreds more," she said.

"You're right," Freeman replied.

Eleanor was taken aback by his agreeing with her and his friendly tone. "So," she said, "I suppose you have an alternate plan."

"Yes ma'am." This was the problem he'd solved in the bath. "COMSUBPAC Group 9's UAV."

She thought for a moment—military types were always throwing around their acronyms for equipment, and it gave her pleasure to surprise him. "Unmanned aerial vehicle?"

"Right."

The National Security Advisor felt elated.

"I want to have Darkstar do an infrared run west from Pillar Point to Cape Flattery, then south to a place called Father and Son. Fifty-seven miles in all."

Eleanor was trying to locate the place names on her wall map. No luck, but she'd already grasped Freeman's idea. "Hot spots," she said. "The UAV photographs the fifty-seven miles of coast, and any hot spots indicating human habitation can be investigated by our divers. Right?"

"You've got it. Darkstar's pix are digital disc so we can get real-time feed."

"I'll have the CNO contacted right now to order—"

"Ah," cut in the general, "maybe you could have your Admiral Jensen call the CNO."

Eleanor hesitated. It'd make more sense for her to—"You want Admiral Jensen to get the credit."

"Well, hell," Freeman said, "poor bastard could use some. Media, everyone, wants someone to blame. Someone to crucify. Maybe he was derelict. I don't know. None of us'll know till we have time to investigate. Time for that later. Right now we need to go after the sub and its hideaway."

She was beginning to like the gruff, bluff legend they sometimes called George C. Scott because of his uncanny resemblance to the Oscar-winning actor who had made such an indelible impression with his acclaimed portrayal of Patton, one of Freeman's boyhood heroes. "That's very generous of you, General."

He mumbled something about "there but for the grace of God go I," and asked her to let him know when Darkstar was airborne and to give him a password for his laptop's entry to the UAV's real-time IR transmits of its surveillance flight.

CHAPTER TWENTY-TWO

AT THE FIRING range at Fort Lewis outside Tacoma, the setting sun had thrown pine and spruce trees into stark relief. Over Puget Sound, the strait, and the symphony of mountains, cumulus, and seacoast, there was a pink-lavender beauty so redolent with the smell of forests and pure air from the perennially snowcapped Olympics that it would have seemed the wild imaginings of some fantastical painter but for the fact that it was real.

America remained traumatized, its Navy humiliated, its self-esteem bombarded by the unrelenting anti-American foreign press scoffing at the Navy's continuing embarrassment about what to do in the strait. With two capital vessels gone, the *Turner*'s battle group, or what was left of it, was "like a man caught in a minefield," the *New York Times* editorialized. "He can neither go forward nor retreat, having seen his most forward comrades on the *Utah* and those behind him on the *Turner* blown up. In short, the Navy is paralyzed."

But on the firing range at Fort Lewis, David Brentwood's only concern at the moment wasn't what the editorialists were saying but that his lame right hand was refusing to play its part, its fingers bunched in an immovable, stubborn fist. The Humvee's driver, who had brought the Medal of Honor winner to the range, opened the back door to grab the only new ambidextrous F2000 assault rifle at Fort Lewis.

"I'll get it," said David, subdued, his tone devoid of any trace of sullenness or ill-temper, but characteristically quiet, showing as much concern for the other man's embarrassment as for his own.

"Oh, sure," said the driver, stepping back.

First problem: The assault rifle had no mag. Rules of the range: no weapon to be loaded until shooters were in the stalls or on the mound.

But even the simplest job—snapping in the mag—proved harder than David had anticipated. As his sister, an Army nurse, had so often said, "The things you take for granted!" her work with the wounded having relentlessly driven home the point.

The F2000, constructed of molded polymer and modern in appearance, wasn't a pretty weapon. It was thoroughly ugly, in fact. Though ergonomically correct, its modular design looked more like a child's stubby gray Lego construction. Despite its aesthetic shortcomings, however, it had been the Bullpup's carrying handle, allowing the well-balanced Bullpup to be carried with equal facility by left and right handlers, that gave David hope. He should be able to grip the weapon tightly enough, by jamming it between his left arm and side, to control its three-round bursts. After considerable sweat and remonstrations against his dangling, uncooperative right arm, he was able to cradle the weapon for burst fire. Then, in an act of sheer will, using his good left hand to literally drag the dead lump of fingers that had been his right hand across to the front underside and through the loop formed by a half-inch-wide rubber band suspended from the gun's barrel, he managed to lift the relatively light eight-pound weapon high enough to assume a shoulder firing position, should he be tested for single-shot accuracy.

He fired four three-round bursts from the waist position, the driver watching the man-size target through the range binoculars. While the group of three 5.56mm bullets all hit the target, they were too widespread. Still . . .

David readied for the shoulder shot, trying gamely to camou-flage his pain beneath a forced grin. "Good to be shooting again!" he told the driver.

"Uh-huh." The driver's attention had shifted from the line of targets to the arrival of another Humvee. "Son of a—it's George Patton!"

Freeman, as usual, was well turned out, khaki shirt and trousers immaculately pressed. Together with the snappy peak of his khaki Afrika Korps cap, his gear made him look ten years younger. But the general was not a happy camper, and his dri-ver, loaned by Fort Lewis's CO, wisely remained in his Humvee. David's driver came to attention, giving the retired general a smart salute. Freeman returned in kind without break-ing stride, as if arriving to inspect the 2nd Army. "A word with Captain Brentwood."

"Yes, sir," David's driver replied, quickly absenting himself, heading toward the other Humvee.

"General?" said David, slipping on the safety.

"We've got bad news. You're a diver, right?"

"Yes, sir."

"Good. Need your advice."

That was something David liked about Freeman. He never hesitated to seek the counsel of others—those below him in rank, particularly those who, like him, had been in the field.

"What's the problem?" David asked, grateful for the chance to lower the 2000, resting it against the gnarled trunk of a pon-derosa pine.

"Told National Security Advisor Prenty that maybe the sub had its lair in a cave or some other indentation in the coast from Port Angeles down past Father and Son."

David knew about Port Angeles, of course, but, apart from the Bible, not Father and Son.

" 'Father and Son' are a couple of sea stacks off the Olympic Peninsula's west coast. I suggested Jensen, COMSUBPAC-GRU-9, run his UAV Darkstar along the coastal sea caves."

"For IR hot spots," David said, immediately extrapolating from Freeman's remark that what would be needed was a diver-capable SpecFor team to either execute a swim investigation or an abseil insertion from a helo, as Brentwood and his team had done in the Hindu Kush.

"Exactly," confirmed Freeman, his hand flashing out with surprising speed, capturing a fly, which he then flung ferociously against the ponderosa. "Anyway, Darkstar is in pieces. Overhaul. Won't by flyable till tonight, 2100."

David glanced at his Swiss issue watch. "That's only four and a—no, five hours away. Not long."

The general gave the grunt of a man whose rationality was losing to his impatience. "*Turner*'s battle group—what's left of it—is still sitting out there in the strait."

"How many planes'd we lose on the *Turner*?"

"A few—none of the fighters, thank God. Hadn't flown out from Whidbey Island. Carrier only takes 'em aboard once the boat's clear of the strait and in the open sea."

"If I were the terrorists, I would've waited," opined David. "Hit the carrier at sea—likely to get most of the fighters in the hangar deck and topside."

"I agree," said Freeman, taking off his Afrika Korps cap, running his fingers through a shock of silvery gray hair. The general slapped his thigh with the cap. "Got any ideas of what to do while we're sitting on our bums waiting for Darkstar to be reassembled?"

"Hovercraft," said David. "They're equipped with IR scopes for night searches. Helos too—but I'd go for the hovercraft. Low flying helos—even by pilots from the Coast Guard familiar with the coasts—aren't as good as hovercraft. Hovers are at eye level with any cave or indentation. Helos have to avoid sea stacks. Especially hard to see at night."

Freeman nodded in full agreement, already striding back to his Humvee, grabbing its phone. Coast Guard HQ in Seattle told him they could let him have three hovercraft, the remainder of the squadron still busy searching for survivors among the more than 389 MIAs still unaccounted for.

"When?" asked the general over the phone.

"We'll need authorization from Admiral—"

"Hey!" David could hear the general's sharp retort. "You jokers listen to me. We've lost a Nimitz carrier, a state-of-the-art Virginia, and most of the people aboard them, and you want some goddamn piece of paper so you can go look for the sons of bitches who did this? If we lose any more because you—"

"Orders are going out now, General," cut in the duty officer's voice. "As we *speak*."

"Good, I'll need real-time digital feed of any hot spots the hovercraft get on their video."

"No video, I'm afraid, General. Strait's too rough."

Like most people who hadn't ridden aboard one, the general, despite his extensive military exposure, harbored the illusion that a hovercraft traveled smoothly over the water on the air cushion.

"Well—hell, then, have them notify me if they see anything that looks suspicious."

"Roger."

"Let's hope," Freeman told David when he put down the phone, "that nothing hits the fan between now and midnight."

"Amen to that," said David. Having rested during Freeman's tête-à-tête with the Coast Guard, he now clicked a new mag into the F2000, keen to show his old boss just how well he could handle the Bullpup with one good arm.

Freeman, eschewing any of the ear protectors in the stalls, plugged his ears and shouted, "Go!" upon which David unleashed three bursts, all on target, if the target had been a barn door. Certainly nowhere near a sufficiently tight group for the SpecOps qualification.

"How about the grenade launcher?" Freeman asked casually as he lifted the rope-secured range binoculars and studied the grouping.

David had been so intent on overcoming the problem of firing the F2000 with one arm, he'd forgotten about the grenade launcher. It was the essential clip-on module for anyone using the assault weapon, for anyone in a SpecFor group.

"Not yet," he told the general. "I'll clip it on now."

"Good."

David smiled, but inwardly felt a rush of gut-knotting anxiety, a condition virtually unknown to the Medal of Honor winner in the years prior to the disaster in the Afghan cave. He had good reason to feel apprehensive. The F2000's grenade launcher weighed another two pounds.

It might not have seemed like much, but "ask a pregnant woman what another two-pound strain on her breast means," as a Fort Bragg drill instructor had once said to him, Aussie Lewis, Choir, and Salvini.

"Stop it!" Aussie had said. "You're driving me nuts!"

The DI had had their attention. "When you're aiming a weapon with a launcher attached from the shoulder, it's like saying, 'Hold on a second, I'll tie a brick to the barrel. Makes one hell of a difference."

Now, David's driver came back down from the Humvee to give him moral support. In his plummeting mood, David ill-advisedly pressed the point by adding, "What other damn module does this thing have?"

"Clip-on bayonet," said Freeman.

"Like me to get one for you, Captain?" offered the driver.

"That'd be nice," David responded. "Any other clip-ons?"

"Ah, lessee," said the driver, not getting David's sardonic tone. "I'll go back up to Stores, grab the fire control system, night vision scope—you want all of them, sir?"

"Sure, why not? Don't want to miss any fun."

The driver's laugh trailed off when he saw the tight grimace of pain that had swallowed the captain's smile.

"Don't hurry back," said David.

As the Humvee took off, its dusty wake shrouding him in what he elected to regard as insult upon injury, the SpecFor captain was simultaneously aware that he was giving way to a disgusting wave of self-pity. He lowered himself to the ground for a rest, pushing his back hard against the gnarled pine.

"Hey, Smiley!" It was a distinctly Australian voice, the accent not lost despite Lewis's twenty years as an American citizen. "What you doin', mate? Playin' with your dick?"

"Thought you'd be here sooner," David replied as Aussie gave the general an informal salute.

"So did I. But the wife insisted we have a farewell quickie.

You know me—I wanted to *skedaddle* to *Seattle* right away, but you can't deny pussy. It's unconstitutional."

David forced a grin, which was difficult for either the general or Lewis to see now that the light was fading. Aussie squatted down like an Arab, posterior well off the ground, a lesson learned long ago in the Australian Outback to avoid what Aussie used to describe to his fellow SpecFor buddies as "bloody creepy crawlies."

"I heard about the screw-up in 'ghan. Not your fault, Harold. Bad intel. A setup. You guys were suckered, plain and simple. You aren't the first team to lose out to that friggin' ghost."

David looked over at his old comrade in arms. "You think Li Kuan's a ghost?"

"I dunno," confessed Aussie, snapping off a stalk of passpalum grass and biting on it. "Tell you what, though—I ever run across the ghost, I'll put a long burst through the apparition— see if the fucker bleeds."

In the silence that followed, the three warriors could hear the rustling of the grass and pines.

"I lost six of 'em, Aussie."

It was as if the breeze had abruptly ceased.

"I heard," Aussie said, spitting out the chewed passpalum. "Everyone but you. Right?"

David, not known for dwelling on what could not be changed, was clearly dwelling on it.

"I've got a couple of Kleenex here," said Aussie. "Trouble is, they're all screwed up into those unusable balls you have to throw away. But I'll tell you what I can—" Aussie slapped a mosquito dead on his forearm. "Little bastard! Anyway, I can go get a coupla towels and we can sit here all night and have a big cry. Or we can get off our ass and go have a few beers. Hear there's a Hooters in Tacoma. Tits bigger'n—"

"I have to master this 2000. Apparently, it's got a grenade launcher and bayonet module as well as—"

"Well, use your friggin' brains, *Captain*. Rig up a friggin' sling—shoulder or neck. Could carry your mother-in-law in that."

David heard the Humvee coming back. "A sling. G   I never thought of that!"

"Geez," Aussie mimicked him. *"I never thought of that."* Then he segued to an old commercial, adopting the voice of its aged actress: " 'I've fallen down and I can't get up!' Course you didn't think of a sling, you twerp, 'cause you're still in mea culpa mode. You believe in God—all that stuff—don't you?"

The general walked into the woods, smiling approvingly at Aussie's frontal assault on his buddy's uncharacteristically fragile psyche.

"Yes," David said seriously. "I do believe. So?"

"Well, you're still alive, mate, 'cause he's not finished with you. Get up an' get goin'."

David's driver was walking down from the Humvee with his arms full of 2000 clip-on/add-on modules.

"Ah, Santa Claus!" said Aussie. "Right, Davy boy, rig a sling. Give you my belt, but since my waist's only a thirty-one, me being so fit to dive with the Draeger an' all . . ."

David began unthreading his belt.

"Oh, that's a good idea, Dave," Aussie joshed. "One bum arm and now you're gonna try shooting with your pants down. What the hell you doin'? I said rig a sling, not expose yourself!"

It was the first real smile that had graced David's face since before Afghanistan.

"Salvini told me you'd been hit in the arm," continued Aussie. "I dunno—looks like you fell on your fucking head!"

David and the driver were laughing now. Aussie handed David a length of polyester rope normally used to attach the range binoculars to the firing stall. The rope sling worked well for support but the shooting was still bad—nowhere near SpecOp standard. In fact, nowhere near boot camp level. But Freeman and Aussie knew that anything to build back his self-confidence was important, even if it had to be made clear to David that there was no way he could be designated "operational" and endanger a team with what was essentially a bum right arm.

Admittedly, Brentwood's handling of the grenade launcher was a surprise, its weight all but nullified by the sling and by David hugging the F2000 hard to his left side. The lobbing of four grenades he fired was surprisingly accurate, well within the acceptable limits for the firing of 40mm projectiles. The next test, however, the bayonet, which could not be successfully thrust or parried with the sling, was a different matter altogether. The weight of its steel blade, extending far beyond the assault rifle's barrel, created a punishing torque on David's left arm. His forehead beaded in perspiration, he was about to try yet another one-arm thrust when he, Aussie Lewis, and the Humvee's driver felt a violent rustling above them and were engulfed by a whirlwind of leaves, dust, and other assorted debris choking the air. This was followed by a thunderous clap.

It had been the magazine of one of the Aegis cruisers exploding, following the detonation of a magnetic signature mine. The ultramodern, reinforced blast wall, built to protect the ship's arsenal of ship-to-ship, sea-to-land, and sea-to-air missiles had given way, the cruiser blown apart with such unmitigated violence that it lit up the strait off Port Angeles with a fiery intensity that turned evening to midday. The rain of white-hot metal hissed so loudly that it startled already shaken inhabitants as far east as Port Townsend and the adjacent Kitsap peninsula. The sound raced northeast to Vancouver, south across Admiralty Inlet, and down Hood Canal, reaching Admiral Jensen at Bangor Base seconds before those across the Puget Sound in Seattle, Tacoma, and Fort Lewis heard it.

"Holy shit!" said Brentwood's driver.

By the time General Freeman had exited the woods, in such haste that he'd forgotten to zip up, Washington, D.C., government switchboards, particularly those of Homeland Defense headquarters, were jammed by terrified callers. What in hell was the government doing about it, and what about the nuclear reactors on the Aegis? If the Aegis had been "blown apart," as CNN said, didn't that mean its reactor had disintegrated as well? And if so, wasn't there immediate danger of fatal radiation through the entire Northwest?

For the first time since the American Civil War, Americans began a massed exodus, only this time from the Pacific Northwest, something their Founding Fathers couldn't possibly have envisaged. En route, they swallowed iodine capsules in the hope that it would either prevent or at least offset what many feared would be the beginning of a massive cancer pandemic triggered by deadly radiation. AMERICANS ON THE RUN, tabloids from Damascus to Paris trumpeted, the most sympathetic foreign headlines coming from Australia, Britain, New Zealand, and Canada. Most European papers, after expressing horror at the destruction of yet another American "superwarship" and lamenting the loss of all aboard, quickly resorted to tarted-up versions of the old "root causes," "blame the Americans" harangues of post-9/11.

Going against the tide of frightened Americans, Freeman, having taken his leave of Aussie and Brentwood, returned to Port Angeles, the repaired Darkstar due to take off at 11:37 P.M. Booting up his laptop, he saw a flickery blue screen. No pictures, however. "Darkstar, my ass!" he thundered so loudly his Port Townsend hotelier heard him from the lounge. "Dark*crap* is more like."

Then the infrared feed came through.

"All right, then," Freeman said gruffly.

Against the infrared's grayish coast he could see bubbling, dime-sized, whitish hotspots and fishing boats' exhaust heat. "You've got balls!" he told the screen, referring to the fishermen. "Three ships sunk and you guys are still trawling for dogfish. I'll be—"

Wait a minute, he thought. *Fish.* Naval slang for torpedoes. Were the terrorists on trawlers as well? One eye on his computer screen, Freeman turned to the phone, punching in the numbers for Coast Guard Coordination in Seattle, alerting them to the possibility of trawlers and other fishing vessels—factory ships, perhaps—having torpedo-firing and/or mine-laying capacities.

When the Coast Guard commander got a chance to interject, which, given the general's rapid delivery, was not for a full two minutes, he told Freeman, "General, that was the first thing our divers and boarding parties looked for—*above* and *below* waterline. We also checked all the Beaufort drums on deck to make sure they contained life rafts and not mines. We were also looking for terrorists."

"Oh," responded the legend, answering, as if he was a member of the British General Staff rather than a retired American warhorse, "Good show, Commander."

"Yes," said the commander. "Not all of *our* members are retired!"

"What in hell does that mean?" growled Freeman.

"Have to go, General. We're running escort for the Navy's pullback into Puget." The commander hung up.

"Hello?" thundered Freeman. "Hello? You cheeky son of a bitch!" He turned to the laptop, and above its screen caught a glimpse of himself in the motel room's mirror. He hadn't thought about the possibility of Beaufort life raft drums being used as mine containers. "Huh," he said, looking at his reflection. "Not so damn smart after all, eh, General?"

Watching Darkstar's feed, he could see more bobbing, dime-sized white spots contrasted against the serrated-gray-wall coastline and the huge Olympic land mass beyond.

Where the lingering warmth of the land, released from the base of Mount Olympus, met the radiant heat of the cooler ocean, fog had formed. It now began permeating the myriad nooks and crannies and wider bays all the way from Port Angeles west to the violent surf of Tatoosh Island off Cape Flattery.

As the big Pacific swells exhausted themselves, crashing in punishing waves of foam against the black, precipitous cliffs of Tatoosh, Freeman could hear the mournful sounds of foghorns through Darkstar's amplified sound feed. Darkstar's bottom screen text informed him that Tatoosh was one of the most densely populated wild bird sanctuaries in the world. But right now the general couldn't have cared less about the sanctuary or any of the others situated south of Cape Flattery down the Washington coast as far south as Cape Disappointment, off the equally dramatic Oregon coast. Instead, his attention was confined strictly to Darkstar's present east-west feed, the UAV's pictures coming in from its low vectored flight between Port Angeles and Tatoosh. They were speckled with more than a dozen hotspots in what were supposedly unpopulated areas. By the time Darkstar reached the end of its flight path just west of Tatoosh, its IR feed became thicker with hotspots. These were smaller than the bobbing hotspots of fishing vessels' radar masts and the like but appeared to the general significantly more numerous.

The phone jangled.

"Freeman!"

It was David Brentwood calling to ask if he had more details, via Darkstar, about the explosion. The officers' mess at Fort Lewis, he explained, was a hive of contradictory rumors, CNN camera-equipped choppers from the news networks apparently not yet on the scene. Some were saying CNN's crews were chickening out because of the fear of radiation.

The general, concerned as he was by the sudden increase in the number of hotspots on the IR feed, was nevertheless encouraged by Brentwood's tone. He knew that curiosity about the world beyond oneself was a sign of recovery from post-traumatic stress disorder. Perhaps with Aussie's help Brentwood had finally accepted the hard truth that he was finished, not only in SpecOps but for the regular forces as well. Surely the Medal of Honor winner now realized how downright irresponsible it would be for any commander, extant or retired, to send an injured man into combat, endangering the lives of all those around him because of his handicap—or what, Freeman thought, politically correct reporters would call his "limb-challenged" ability. Even worse, in the general's view, would be the danger posed to David's comrades' by their preoccupation with his safety rather than with the mission objective.

"David," the general said, "I'd like you and Aussie to get up here to Port Angeles. Salvini and Choir are due momentarily. Tell Aussie to bring his Draeger."

"Roger that," said David. "I'll bring mine too."

There was silence on the general's end.

"Can you hear me, General?"

"What? Ah, yes, yes. Bring your tank. Sorry—I'm glued to an IR printout of the coast," said the general, and seeing the hotpots multiplying, added. "Could do with you boys' advice on this. Something strange going on."

"Metal debris from the destruction of the Aegis?" suggested Brentwood. "Lot of it would still be pretty hot even in the sea."

"Some of that in the sea, I agree. But this is all over the place. On Tatoosh Island?"

"Where's that?"

"Bird sanctuary. No one allowed near it but our UAV. It's showing hundreds of hotspots. Like damned confetti."

"Is this Toosh Island anywhere near where the Aegis blew up?"

"No. Much further west. 'Course, most of the hotspots I'm seeing could be body heat from the thousands of birds. Got every species here from little stormy petrels to giant albatross. But there's other stuff too—bigger'n damn houses—along supposedly *unpopulated* stretches of the coast."

"Close those drapes!"

Freeman was startled by the police bullhorn, but he walked over to the window and closed the curtains, stealing a glance at the dark strait. Not a single light was visible, where only shortly before it had been crowded with naval ships. The remainder of what had been the *Turner*'s battle group were recalled and now steaming back down through Puget Sound to its home port in Everett, the group's remaining attack sub slinking back unheralded to the protection of Bangor Base.

In Bangor, Walter Jensen was standing outside the blacked-out Admiral's House, waiting for the sub's return. "What a humiliation," he told Margaret, who stood silently by his side, her hand gently moving back and forth across his steel-tense back as he stared into the fog-clogged darkness of Hood Canal. "Battle group didn't even get past the choke point. It—I'm finished," he said quietly. He waited for her to cloister him as she always did. But Margaret said nothing.

Walter Jensen was telling the truth. His chances of becoming CNO, replacing the soon retiring Admiral Nunn, had been destroyed, along with the careers of a sacrificial slew of officers unable to explain why on their watch the United States Navy, with all its billions of dollars' worth of computers and other electronic wizardry, including aircraft-borne forward-looking infrared scanners and magnetic anomaly detectors, had failed to pick up either a heat signature or magnetic disturbance from the midget sub reported by SEAL diver Rafe Albinski.

* * *

A caller into Larry King's interview with CNO Nunn, which Freeman had on in the background as Aussie and David arrived, was graciously trying to help Walter Jensen and, by extension, the Navy and the U.S. armed forces in general, by surmising that even with all the scientific know-how available "it must be a much more difficult job to detect a midget sub than a regular one?"

"Yes," agreed Nunn. "And if I could take your analogy further, searching for a midget sub would be like looking for a single automobile dumped on the sea bottom as opposed to, say, looking for an Amtrak train."

The next caller quipped, "If you're lookin' for an Amtrak, Admiral, all you have to do is check with CNN—see where the latest derailment is. They're goin' off the rails 'bout one a day. And if—" King cut him off, obviously displeased with his call screener. The next caller identified himself as a former electronics warfare officer, and said the MAD—the "stingray" tail on any of the battle group's early warning planes or ASW helos— could easily have missed the midget because MAD's range of detection was limited to a third of a mile, "for 'bout six or seven hundred yards max either side of your track. That's only 'bout as far as a par five."

"That's a bogey ten for me," quipped Larry, trying to ease the tension, the admiral smiling.

The note of levity, however, backfired, the caller becoming irate. "I don't see anything funny 'bout it. We've lost more Americans in that Juan de Fuca Strait than we did on 9/11, and we're gonna lose more if we don't find out what the [blip] is going on."

"You're quite right," King responded. "How about the other detection gear, sir? This FLIR—forward looking infrared. How good's that?"

"It's fine," said the mollified caller. "But again, how high are you flying? Best thing is to get satellite surveillance for that."

"Didn't Admiral Johnson—" Larry began.

"Jensen," the CNO corrected politely.

"Sorry, yeah, Jensen. He said he got satellite-reported anomalies in the strait early on and had 'em checked out."

"Yes," answered the CNO. "He dispatched a UAV."

"A Predator."

"No, another type," answered Nunn.

"Can you tell me what kind it was?"

"No."

"It was—" began the caller, but King used his delay button to call up a commercial, CNO Nunn visibly relaxing and thanking Larry during the break. "A retiree, right?" mused King, "stickin' it to his old employer. I'm gonna get crap, though, for cutting him off. Censorship, blah blah blah . . ."

Nunn shrugged. "People generally understand it's not a good idea to tell the enemy what kind of surveillance we've been using."

King didn't comment. Truth was, the Navy didn't think it was a good idea to tell anyone anything anywhere, except come appropriations time on the Hill.

The red light was back on. "Admiral," asked King, "you think the midget sub is still with us? In our waters? Maybe it's gone. Hit the Aegis cruiser—that'd be three in a row—and ran?"

Nunn was caught unawares. Everyone, even the maverick Freeman, was operating on the assumption the enemy sub was still there.

"Ah, well, I doubt it's gone, Larry. A midget sub doesn't move that fast underwater and hasn't got anywhere near the range of a normal-size sub."

"Garbage!" It was Douglas Freeman, who, now with Aussie and David Brentwood, was listening to the King interview while still watching Darkstar's flight south of Tatoosh Island down the wild beauty of the Pacific's pounded coastline. Here and there, streaks of white appeared on the grayish screen, not surf, but isolated, pristine beaches that marked the verdant and rocky edge of America.

"What d'you mean, 'garbage'?" asked Aussie.

"CNO's saying midget sub hasn't got enough speed or range," Freeman replied, his eyes still fixed on Darkstar's feed. "Damn Piranha-class midget can do near ten knots and run for over a thousand miles. If it's one of those, it could be halfway to Japan by now."

"So you think the midget's taken off, General?" put in Aussie.

"No. Why should it? Last kill less than twenty-four hours ago. Still undetected. Son of a—" Freeman pointed at Dark-star's feed. "Get a load of this, boys." The general pulled his head back from the screen to give them a better look. There was a knock on the door, a pause, then four sharp, rapid taps. Free-man pushed back his chair, strode quickly to the door, looked through the spy hole, and opened the door a crack, but left the chain on. "I gave at the office!" he quipped, then slid off the chain and opened the door fully.

"What we got, General?" It was Salvini.

"Trouble," said Freeman, shaking hands with the "Brooklyn Bad Ass," as he called Salvini.

Choir Williams, following, smiled. "General."

The three men walked over to the laptop, David and Aussie exchanging greetings with the two newcomers, Aussie asking Salvini, "Who's your fat friend?"

Choir Williams was in fact the slimmest Aussie had ever seen him, as trim as all of them except the general, who, as an invet-erate jogger, was in remarkably good shape for his age, despite a slight post-middle-age paunch which he insisted was "heredi-tary muscle." There was an awkward moment as Sal and Choir realized David Brentwood could shake only with his left hand.

"Well," pressed the general, his impatience and wish to avoid any further embarrassment to David disallowing his four ex-SpecFor boys any opportunity to catch up on what each other had been doing in "peacetime"—a word they habitually uttered with the same contempt as did a grounded fighter pilot, "what d'you make of these?" He'd asked Salvini and Choir before they even put down their bags and heavy Draeger rebreathers. "Feed is coming in from south of Cape Flattery."

"Piloted recon?" asked Sal.

"UAV," explained Freeman. "Hot-spot feed. And we got a lot of small hot spots—the salt shaker effect on Tatoosh Island—off Flattery. Birds, yes, but other big hotspots that Aussie thinks are media news trucks, among other things. More big hotspots down on the Pacific coast. Must be over forty so far, and we haven't reached Father and Son yet."

"Seals," said Salvini.

For a moment the general, tired, thought he meant "SEALs."

"That so?" said Aussie doubtfully.

"Yeah," said Salvini confidently, looking about the motel room for something to drink. "Surprised you haven't got more of 'em on that trace."

"Seals?" said Freeman, whose vanity habitually denied he was surprised by anything.

"Yeah," repeated Salvini, his hands flapping in a bad imitation of the sea mammal. "You know, Flipper? Caves must be full of 'em."

Seldom had Sal, Choir, Aussie, or David seen Freeman so taken by surprise.

"Sea caves are full of 'em," continued Salvini. "That's why the IR hot spots you're seeing are so big."

"Well," Freeman began, "that's no damn good! I figured on having you guys swim in and check out anything that might be the size of midget sub, but dammit—we haven't enough people to investigate every damn cave up and down the coast." He paused, fixing an anxious brow on Salvini. "How in God's name do you know this, Sal? *Seals?* You're from Brooklyn, for God's sake."

"The zoo," said Sal. "Not seals but sea otters. Used to take my sister's kids in the evening. Took my squad IR goggles for fun so the kids could see the critters all nestled up in their lairs. Big white blobs just like on your IR feed right there. They huddle together."

"Aw," said Aussie, "you don't know dick! Could be anything in those sea caves."

"Yeah," conceded Sal nonchalantly. "But if you look at the feed's scale—" He leaned closer. "—two inches to the mile. It's got to be some pretty big mammals." He paused, joshing Aussie, "Maybe they're elephants!"

"Oh, very droll, Sal," said Aussie. "Ha! Ha!"

"Wait a minute," interjected David. "Sal could be right, General. The midget sub could be using a seal colony as infrared cover."

Choir good-naturedly dismissed the idea of the enemy, whoever they were, using the collective heat signature of mammals as IR cover.

"And what d'you know about mammals, Choir?" challenged Aussie. " 'Cept for those Welsh tarts you used to bed."

"I'll ignore your *antipodean* vulgarity."

"Antipodean. I'm an American citizen, you Welsh turd!"

Freeman, ignoring Aussie's joshing, pressed Choir for his explanation of why terrorists wouldn't use such a cave.

"Noise," answered Choir. "Ever hear the racket those creatures make? It's worse than Aussie's snoring."

"So," proffered the general, "what we need to look at are the caves *without* a hot spot. A cold cave's where the sub's mother ship, its milch cow—a trawler, whatever—stashes its food, torpedoes, mines, diesel fuel. An otherwise empty cave. Sub comes in literally 'when the coast is clear.' Surfaces inside the sea cave, resupplies quickly, and heads back out."

"Maybe," suggested David, "that's why the Navy hasn't seen any signs of the midget surfacing for air replenishment."

"Darkstar saw it," Freeman corrected him. "That's why Jensen dispatched that RIB with those divers Albinski and—" He thought for a moment. "—Dixon." He sighed in exasperation. That General Blackmore had been right when he told the West Point graduates that nowadays you'd have to be part detective to be a good soldier.

Freeman played back the stored IR feed, looking now for cold caves, those whose residual daytime-stored heat signatures were so slight he'd passed them over. It was a dispiriting exercise. The cold cave count rose to 278, and Darkstar hadn't yet reached the big Father and Son sea stacks south of Cape Flattery. Would the Navy have enough time to search them all before the sub attacked again? Or was Larry King's suggestion accurate, that perhaps the terrorists' sub had had its fill of death and destruction now that the decimated battle group had retreated.

"Cold caves, gentlemen," he said, "with an anomaly near them. *That's* what we're looking for."

CHAPTER TWENTY-THREE

IN THE HINDU Kush, more fighting had broken out as a resurgent Taliban battalion, financed out of Pakistan, was infiltrating back into Afghanistan to destabilize the nascent U.N.-protected government in Kabul, which in fact was mainly a U.S. operation. The Taliban leaders' timing was brilliant—to strike when the U.S. Homeland Defense was consumed by a massive public panic attack even greater than that of 9/11. If the terrorists, or whoever, could easily attack America's guardians, who could guard the guardians? The one qualified hope, media pundits such as CNN's Marte Price were saying, was that "as terrible as the attack on our Navy is, it's so far been confined to military targets and not defenseless citizens."

"Silly woman!" opined Freeman, one ear listening to CNN, the other to the suggestions of his four SpecFor warriors brainstorming about how to narrow the search for where the sub might be hiding. "Marte should know better than that. Some poor son of a bitch civilian's probably dead already, caught in that rain of shrapnel when the Aegis blew up."

The general was right and wrong. A civilian night watchman, Carlito Vincennes of Cherry Point, had died three and a half minutes after he'd seen a light, which he thought was either out in the strait or in the woods across the bay. It had looked to him like a camera flash. Then he saw that it was a narrower beam of white light. A missile coming straight for him. "Incoming!" he screamed into his walkie-talkie. "Twelve o'clock low!"

The ensuing line of explosions that engulfed the Cherry Point refinery, as row upon row of storage tanks blew, killed Carlito and twenty-three other civilian nightshift workers. It also produced an enormous firestorm on land, the burning oil disgorged from the destroyed storage tanks flowing into the sea and forming a ten to fifteen acre firespill whose black columns of choking smoke and flames did a macabre dance hundreds of feet into the air. The heat was so intense that surrounding forests and bitumen roads caught fire as if by spontaneous combustion, trapping hundreds of families in the long lines of refugee vehicles already fleeing the rumored danger of radiation leakage from the sunken Aegis carrier and the *Utah*.

But where had the missile come from? "Incoming twelve o'clock low" had confounded Cherry Point's head of security. As a reserve member of the Washington State National Guard, he'd understood "twelve o'clock" meant something had been coming head-on at Vincennes. But from which direction, land or sea? In short, what direction had Vincennes been facing? Sea or land?

It was only later, after 120 square miles of prime Northwest trees had been destroyed by the fire and the town of Birch Bay, near Cherry Point, was a charred, smoking ruin, that the already overstretched Coast Guard was able to triangulate the vectors from various reports about a "flash of light." They deduced that the missile had been fired from the sea. So much for the midget having had its fill. It was, in fact, even more audacious. The reports of two trawlers—one Canadian and the other American—estimated that the "shoot and scoot" firing of the skimmer had probably taken no more than four minutes, including a possible crash dive.

Freeman at least now felt confident that the midget sub's pen probably lay somewhere between Port Angeles and Cape Flattery.

Aussie Lewis, Brentwood, and Salvini agreed with the general's hypothesis, which revolved around the simple but unchanging requirement in war that the closer you were to your supplies, the better.

"No Wal-Marts south of Flattery?" said Choir in his lilting Welsh accent.

"Exactly," confirmed Freeman, calling COMSUBPAC-GRU-9 to turn Darkstar around back toward Cape Flattery. From the cape it could do another run along the seventy miles of coastline to Port Angeles, Freeman lowering the IR intensity recognition level. "Cold caves with a nearby anomaly," Freeman repeated. "That's what we're looking for."

"General, where's that Navy NR-1B research sub?" asked Aussie.

Freeman glanced down at his watch, the bags under his eyes evidencing his lack of sleep over the last twenty-four hours. "It should be here by now."

In fact, the Globemaster III ferrying the U.S. Navy's research sub had landed at the Air Naval Station on Whidbey Island, one of the most beautiful islands in America, and among the longest. The highly classified midget sub was the one Bill Heinz had in mind when he complained to Charlie Riser about the kind of secrecy, interservice, and interagency rivalry that prevented vital information from getting to the right people in time, as had happened before 9/11.

While in the process of deplaning from the giant transport onto a wide-bodied Mack hauler normally used to move houses up and down the island, the Marine guard platoon of thirty men aboard ten Humvees were ordered to establish and maintain a "No Go Zone," even on the naval station's own runway, to provide a moving protective moat of a hundred yards in diameter around the small nuclear-powered sub. With "Deadly Force Authorized," anyone, uniformed or civilian, violating the NGZ was to be shot. The problem, however, was that since the arrival of and transport of the sub was designated "Secret," how could anyone be expected to know about the NGZ? It was bureaucratic nonsense, but so worried were the Navy and Homeland Defense about another attack following the Cherry Point disaster, that the rules of antiterrorist warfare, in the words of Homeland Defense director Harry Hawthorn, would have to be "amended as necessary." Whether such amendment, however, lay within the provenance of the Marine guard officer on the spot, or with COMSUBPAC-GRU-9's Jensen, or with the commandant of the Marines, was not clear.

Jensen, having arrived and placed himself in the lead Humvee, had been fretting for hours about the safe delivery of the NR-1B sub to the launching ramp at Keystone. He was con-

vinced that not only had his CNO hopes gone down with
Turner, *Utah*, and the Aegis cruiser, but any hitch en route to
the ramp would mean the lesser but just as personally painful
humiliation of demotion. When his cell phone rang, he started
as if jabbed with a cattle prod. His driver, a gum-chewing
Spanish-American, PFC Mendez, pretended not to notice.

"Margaret!" he snapped censoriously.

"CNN's reporting that John Rorke and that scientist—"

"Alicia Mayne."

"Yes. They've been found. Adrift on some wreckage, CNN
says. Picked up off Vancouver Island, being taken to Port
Townsend's hospital. John Rorke looks rough, but he's all right.
He vindicated you on CNN. Said there was absolutely no warning when *Utah* was hit. The woman's not so good, burns from
the waist up, apparently. There was an oil slick on fire after the
boat had sunk." Margaret paused. "That CNN woman, Marte
Price, has been calling, left I don't know how many messages. I
think you're going to have to say something, dear. She called
again just before—"

"When I get home," he said sharply. Margaret could hear the
background noise of the Humvee and knew he must be with a
driver. "I'll send get-well cards and condolences to all the
Utah's boys and their families. And to Alicia Payne—"

"Mayne, with an M."

"Yes," said Margaret. "I'll try to see her. What a dreadful
time it is, Walter. All those families."

"Admiral!" the Humvee's radio blared. "Bravo One Charlie
One." It was an incoming message from the first of the twenty
outriders assigned to protect the NR-1B on its way to the Keystone launch ramp. "We have a bogey five klicks from you."

"Describe," cut in the convoy's Marine commander.

"Keep moving," Jensen told his Humvee driver.

"Refugee column," said the Bravo One. " 'Bout two hundred
meters long on the road. Estimate ten to fifteen vehicles. Looks
like mostly families. Fifty, sixty people."

"Admiral?" said the Marine major. Jensen knew the major
was asking him who he wanted to exercise tactical command.

"It's your call, Major," Jensen told him.

"Yessir." The major instructed, "Bravo One, get all those people out of the vehicles and off the road—hundred yards away at least. Make sure no one—repeat, no one—remains in the vehicles. Dogs, cats—nothing. I'll send replacement riders from Bravo Three to scout ahead of you while you take care of this."

"Roger that!" confirmed the Bravo One leader, who had already begun telling his men to move the refugees out of their cars and pickups into the adjacent field.

"What?" bellowed one of the refugees, an elderly man. "That's a damned cranberry bog in there—under two, three, feet o' water. We got kids here!"

"Move off the road now!"

"Come on, Ralph," a woman told the man. "Do as they say."

"Thank you, ma'am," said the cop, one of the local policemen with knowledge of the area who'd been seconded to assist the Marines guarding the convoy. "There's a good reason for it."

"Damn well better be!" growled Ralph, but the cop and his other four comrades in Bravo One were relieved. Everyone's nerves were on edge. Some of the police riders' own families were leaving the island. "*American* refugees," one of the cops had said. "It breaks your heart."

"How long we got to wait?" asked Ralph.

"No more'n an hour, chief."

"Jesus Christ—you know how cold it is in those damn cranberry bogs?"

"Ralph, c'mon! No sense in arguin'. They got the guns."

It was 1:00 P.M., and Charles Riser, who'd been unsuccessful in attempts to get through to General Chang, whom he hoped might have learned something more about Li Kuan's whereabouts, had caught the red-eye flight to Nanjing. He'd been waiting impatiently outside Nanjing Military District HQ since 9:00 A.M. Once more he pressed the button. General Chang's aide-de-camp, a smartly turned out young captain in sharply creased field greens, appeared, and again Riser asked politely to see the general.

The response was in immaculate Mandarin: "The general is in conference and cannot be—"

"For four *hours*?" pressed Riser. "You did tell him it was urgent?"

"Yes," Mr. Riser," came the reply, this time in perfect English, the sudden switch from Mandarin calculated, Riser thought, to surprise him.

It did. By the time he'd thought of a follow-up question, Chang's aide had closed the door. Again Riser heard the slide of the dead bolt. "Damn!" Now he was absolutely sure Chang wasn't in Nanjing. Had they arrested him?

Meanwhile, the U.S. embassy in Beijing was receiving complaints about Riser's persistence. Military affairs, Nanjing reminded Bill Heinz, were not Mr. Riser's concern. Finally, Bill Heinz asked to see the ambassador, and told him, straight out, "Mr. Ambassador, I like Charlie Riser as much as anybody else, and I realize the death of young Mandy has undone him. But we all have our problems, and we have to move on. He's making a damn nuisance of himself with the PLA."

"Thought that was *your* job, Bill?" said the ambassador flippantly.

Bill Heinz flashed his diplomatic smile. "This time he took off to Nanjing to see General Chang."

"On our time or his?"

"Ah . . . his. Took two days' leave, but—"

"Our money or his, Bill?"

"Haven't checked, sir. But the point is, if we don't rein him in, State's going to get a formal complaint from Beijing and we'll be in deep shit, pardon my English. And we need all the help we can get from China in this war against terrorism."

"You're right, Bill. I'll have a word with him."

"Thank you, sir. I'll call him, tell him it's official. He's to come back immediately."

Charlie's exasperation at not being able to see Chang, the only Chinese official who'd really tried to help him after Mandy's death, got worse with China Air's delayed departure to Beijing.

Typically, there was only one attendant at the China Air

counter to calm the throng of impatient travelers. "What's the problem?" asked an Australian backpacker. "Where's the bloody plane?"

The girl threw up her hands. "China Air all in a mess."

"You're right there, sweetheart," said the Australian. "How 'bout some tucker—you know, food? We've been waitin' here for bloody hours. You owe us a meal, I reckon."

Other backpackers joined in, most of them trying to leave China as quickly as possible, before the war with Taiwan trapped them. Taiwanese missiles could hit all of China's mainland coastal airports and Beijing. Riser stayed out of the counter squabble. The U.S. cultural attaché wasn't hungry. The only reason he ate at all was to keep his strength up for his mission to track down Li Kuan and the thugs who'd murdered his daughter.

The crowd closing in on China Air's lone clerk was so dense, a wave of claustrophobia passed over him.

"Mr. Riser?" The voice came from somewhere deep within the increasingly angry mob. Charles couldn't see her but knew immediately it was Wu Ling, Chang's mistress, who had also been Mandy's closest friend in China. Then he spotted her. There was fear in her eyes, but he sensed it wasn't from the threat of the mob getting out of control, a fear every "long-stay" foreigner in China had experienced at least once in China.

Suddenly, the crowd withdrew from the counter, like a wave sucked back into the sea, taking Wu Ling with it. A half-dozen or so airport staff had arrived behind the crowd and were carrying precariously stacked boxes of dinners. Several people were trampled underfoot and there was screaming and general mayhem. It took Wu Ling several minutes to get free. She told Charles she didn't have much time—that the Gong An Bu were following her.

"What's wrong?" he asked. As her perfume washed over him, he could see Mandy. They had both worn—what was it?— Guilin Mist.

"The General," she began, buffeted to and fro in an eddy of the mutton-and-rice-crazed crowd. "He has been arrested and put in—" Her English suddenly deserted her.

"Prison," Charles said.

"Yes. In prison. It is very bad."

"Why was he—"

"The army in Kazakhstan is being pushed back by the terrorists."

"So he's the scapegoat?" said Charles. "He's being held responsible?"

"Yes. Responsible. I must go," she said, and disappeared into the throng.

No doubt, Charles thought, the Gong An Bu had been following her.

On the flight to Beijing, the pilot announced that the PLA had won a great victory. The island of Kinmen had fallen to the combined might of the PLA defense forces, and the party was confident that total victory over the "breakaway province" of Taiwan would be attained within a matter of days. The plane erupted in applause and raucous self-congratulations.

"What about those bastard terrorists in Kazakhstan?" someone called out.

A man from first class entered coach class. He didn't look like a high-level party functionary to Riser, but more like a Gong An Bu agent. There was a thuggish air about him despite the well-tailored Mao suit. He talked to the man who'd raised the question about the PLA's offensive against the Muslim terrorists in Kazakhstan. The man, a short, pasty-faced individual, looked terrified, the man from first class bending over him.

Charles ordered a Tsing Tao beer. He needed to relax. Everything was getting too hyper. Confusing. Should the U.S. be backing the PLA offensive in Kazakhstan if China had started a war against Taiwan? Whatever the situation, surely the U.S., in its own interests, if not those of the Taiwanese, couldn't let the island nation be governed by the Communists. It was America's airstrip in East Asia. The Cold War, Charlie mused, for all its anxiety, was at least clearer, or seemed so. But sipping his beer, he concluded that probably in every war, including this one, the present always seemed confusing, as confusing as the jigsaw puzzle of World War I, which, with benefit of hindsight, seemed remarkably easy to understand. In fact, as any historian knew, it had been a puzzling complex of alliances, backroom deals, and parties who were friends one month and enemies the next—*plus ça change, plus c'est la même chose.*

He remembered his grandfather, one of the very few World War II veterans still alive, telling him about the utter confusion during that war when it came to who was on whose side. Italy was against us, then with us. The Romanians switched back and forth, some Ukrainians fought with the Nazis, and France was Britain's great ally, but not Vichy France. Churchill ordered the British navy to sink the great French fleet in North Africa, killing French sailors, allies only weeks before, to ensure that the Nazis could not use the French fleet once France had fallen. Louis Mountbatten, Supreme Commander of Allied Forces in the Far East, accepted the Japanese surrender in 1945, only to turn around and rearm the Japanese, using them as an ad hoc police force throughout Burma and Southeast Asia to prevent rioting mobs, the very people Mountbatten had been fighting for a few weeks earlier.

Great or small, Charlie decided, all war was byzantine, and all he cared about was living to see Li Kuan, like Saddam Hussein, hunted down and killed. That wasn't confusing.

CHAPTER TWENTY-FOUR

Port Townsend

"I NEED SOME fresh air," announced Aussie. "Anyone else?"

"I'll come," said David.

Sal and Choir, ignoring scatological insults from Aussie about Welsh wankers and Brooklyn Dodgers being lazy, elected to catch some sleep in the motel room Freeman had booked for them down the hall.

Outside, the streets were all but deserted, only patrol cars
with slit wartime headlights moving slowly to enforce the cur-
few. A few dark shapes were visible in the weak penumbra of
police headlights as people scuttled here and there, briefly silhouetted as they quickly slipped in and out of stores for emergency supplies. The Coast Guard—Canadian as well as
American—were assuring the population via radio and TV that
there was no danger of leaking radiation from the sunken vessels—that all the reactors on nuclear-powered U.S. warships
were built to such rigorous standards that "there is little possibility of a split in the reactor."

A motorcade passed by Aussie and David, including a Navy
staff car bearing Margaret Jensen on a mission of mercy to
Woodgate Hospital. Her intention was to show fearlessness in
the face of the radioactivity scare and visit as many of the victims as she could. First she wanted to see Alicia Mayne and the
other survivors of *Utah*.

Also, concerned about the welfare of the survivors of the
sinkings, the commander of Fort Lewis had called Freeman,
telling him it would be a good idea to have Medal of Honor winner Brentwood make himself useful at the hospital. "Be a
damned good morale lift for our men and women. And it'd take
him out of himself."

"Good idea," agreed Freeman, thinking, *You wily polecat*—
can't let the Navy grab Marte Price's attention. Army Medal of
Honor winner beats an admiral's wife any day of the week, and
the Chiefs of Staff at the Pentagon would like what Fort Lewis
did. "I'll send him up, General," said Freeman.

"How'd he do with the Bullpup?" the Fort Lewis commander
inquired.

"Not well," said Freeman bluntly, tired from watching Darkstar's feed.

"So now he knows," said the commander.

"Not sure about that," said Freeman.

"Have him wear the ribbon, Douglas."

Freeman called David on his cell phone. "Captain, get your
butt up to the hospital. You are to go about, shake hands with
those poor bastards, and *smile*! You know Marte Price?"

"Yes, sir. Skirt with the big tits." It wasn't David, but Lewis, listening in as usual.

"Lewis?"

"General?"

"You get back here. Monitor the UAV rerun. You've had enough fresh air."

"Roger that."

David flipped the cell phone shut. "Old man," he told Aussie, "didn't like that. What you said about the CNN reporter."

Aussie shrugged as they headed back past the ferry terminal. To the east lay Whidbey Island, where, if all went well, the Navy would be launching the NR-1B. "Don't shag any of the nurses up there!" he called back to David, who was already ascending the hill toward the hospital, pretending not to hear.

David knew his mission to the hospital was merely to smile and say a few words of encouragement. But after Afghanistan, he felt like a fake.

The exiting air from the hospital's wards hit him in a toxic blast of charcoal-reeking burned flesh, oil and antiseptics. Mounds of soiled and blood-soaked sheets, blackened and singed naval uniforms, and ruined clothes that had belonged to civilians caught up in the infernos of the multiple disasters were now piling up in the corridors faster than the frantic staff could dispose of them in already overflowing Dumpsters. The ash of the hospital's incinerator fell outside like gray snow as the staff worked overtime to cremate limbs and flesh contained in thick "recycled" paper shrouds designated by hurriedly wielded marker pens as "unusable," any possible skin graft material being rushed in sterilized containers to the refrigerators. It was a scene so suffused with urgency and horror that David turned around to leave. The last thing anyone in this hospital needed was some Medal of Honor winner getting in the way when a split second's delay in inserting an IV tube or in any of the surgical lifesaving procedures the ER staff were carrying out could cost someone their life.

"Captain Brentwood? David Brentwood?" The woman's voice was accompanied by a glare of light from a shoulder-held KEMO TV camera, a scruffy looking, gum-chewing technician in obligatory faded jeans, and what Freeman would have called a half-ass beard, approaching David. The reporter, despite the long, rushed trip from Atlanta, looked as alert and as well-coiffed as any well-rested anchor. She extended her right hand, her left clasping the phallic-shaped mike. "Captain, I'm Marte Price."

Before he knew it, David was shaking hands with the woman. She was taller than she looked on TV, where her legs, shapely as they were, were not on display; unlike her bosom, which had stopped many a channel surfer dead in his tracks. Her height added to her aura of vivacious authority. Despite his annoyance with her sudden and what he considered rude interruption, David felt a surge of excitement in his loins. Her sexuality, her perfume, was so alive and contrary to the misery and death surrounding them that he had no control over the kind of excitement she infused in him, a kind he'd not known since long before his near-mortal wounding in Afghanistan.

"Would you please move that contraption," came a doctor's angry voice. "This is a hospital, not *Hollywood Squares*."

Marte smiled graciously and asked where she might conduct the interview with Captain Brentwood, who was visiting his "wounded comrades." The doctor, oblivious to the correspondent's charm, raised his lab coat's blood-spattered arm and pointed brusquely to an orderly behind them, near the elevator. "Ask him."

"Thank you. Captain Brentwood's a Medal of Honor recipient," Marte said, "and—"

But the doctor had already walked away, informing incoming paramedics that they'd have to use their ambulance gurneys as beds for their patients. "No more room."

Marte Price worked her charm on the orderly, who steered them to a room down by a supply room.

"They're all dead in there," the orderly said. "It'll be quiet, though."

After entering the dark room, there was something wrong with the light switch. Marte's cameraman, turning on his video's light, started in fright. So did David. "Jesus!" said the cameraman. A man was standing by one of the beds. "Who are you?"

"Captain Rorke."

Marte Price's shock at hearing the strangely disembodied voice in the nearly dark room was immediately pushed aside by her realization that she'd lucked out. "Rorke? John Rorke?"

"Gold, Jerry," the cameraman told Marte. "Pure gold."

She knew it. Forget the wounded. An exclusive interview with the *Utah* captain—they'd have to find his cap, she thought, or one like it, wet and oily, if possible—would be more impressive. "Can we bring in more lights?" she asked Rorke.

"Maybe one. No more. She's in enough pain already. It'll blind her."

David Brentwood, his eyes now accustomed to the semidarkness, the pervasive atmosphere of burned oil and flesh about him and the *wokka-wokka* sound of rescue helicopters, still bringing in wounded, was momentarily brought back to the cave during the Pave Low's approach.

Now, in the glow of the other light that was brought in, he saw the patient, her face badly scorched, a skull cap of white bandages where her hair had been, and a semi-oval, torso-length frame, like a wooden cage, from her neck down to her waist. Rorke, seeing David's concern, explained to him that the frame was to keep the sheet from touching the part of her that must have been burned above the waterline as she struggled, like hundreds of others, to escape the encroaching firespills spawned by ruptured hydraulic lines on the sub.

David sensed that Rorke's vigil was more than that of a commander trying to comfort his crew. "What was she doing on the sub?" he asked softly. He knew Congress was pushing for women on subs, since other countries had already initiated such a program, but David guessed this would be the first female combat death on a sub.

Rorke didn't answer, and it took a few seconds for David to realize that the skipper of America's most potent weapons platform—the *ex*-skipper, rather—wasn't refusing to answer but was suffering from tinnitus, the ringing in the ears that so often followed the noise of massive detonations. In Rorke's case it had been the horrendous roar of explosions that ripped his prized boat apart and killed most of his crew.

"What was her job?" David asked Rorke, his voice raised above the noise of the cameraman setting up.

"Civilian specialist," John Rorke replied.

David nodded knowingly. "What's her name?"

"Alicia," said Rorke softly. "Alicia Mayne," and David understood, in a flash, that Rorke had been in love, *was* in love, with the dying woman.

In one of those moments that sometimes only complete strangers share in the darkened interior of a night flight or train, knowing they'll probably never meet again, when the heart is unashamed and free, Brentwood, a man whose natural inclination was to always mind his own business, never to intrude, asked, "Can she hear you at all?"

"If I lean close."

"Stay close," David told him. "Close as you can."

David knew Rorke didn't want to be part of any interview but probably felt duty bound to do so. David walked over to Marte Price. "Let's do a ward tour," he said. "I'll speak to some of the wounded."

She thanked him but said that first she wanted an interview with Rorke.

"No, you do me with the wounded."

"Captain Brentwood, I'll decide when and who—"

David looked over at the submariner. "Captain Rorke will do an interview with you. CNN exclusive. In an hour." He turned to the cameraman then. "Let's go down the corridor, try to keep out of the staff's way—" He had to stop talking until the thudding of a Coast Guard chopper's blades faded from the hospital's parking lot. "I'll give you an interview. I'll give you my background on the way," he told Marte Price.

Marte saw there was no arguing with this Brentwood. He'd come across initially as a lamb—now he was a lion. This medal thing had gone to his head. "I've already got your background," she said. "You're supposed to be the shy and retiring type. The 'Aw, shucks' hero."

"Do we have a deal?"

"An *exclusive* with you, Captain Rorke?" Marte asked. "Fox guys are everywhere."

"Exclusive," agreed Rorke.

Before he left the room to join the PR rep, Marte Price, and her cameraman in the blinding white light of the corridor's heavy traffic of hospital staff, David spoke quietly to John Rorke. "You need anything, Captain?"

"I don't think so."

"You were last wounded in Afghanistan, right?" Marte Price asked David as they moved down the hellish corridor.

"Yes," he told her. "That's right."

"At Tora Bora?"

"Yes."

"Can you tell me what happened?" In the public ward, they could hear the desperate cries of the wounded not yet treated with painkillers, pending diagnosis from doctors who, despite help from the Whidbey Island Navy medics, remained overwhelmed.

"We're out of morphine!" a harried nurse reported. They'd all begun calmly and professionally, but the sheer fatigue of overload was drowning the best intentions.

"Use Demerol."

"It's gone."

A drugged young submariner was pleading with a doctor not to amputate his leg. It had in fact already been taken off, but he was feeling the phantom sensation of it, his arms and legs bandaged so heavily that he couldn't remove the sheet or bed covers to check, and everyone else was too busy.

With Freeman asleep, Aussie Lewis had been monitoring the IR feed from Darkstar's last leg home between Cape Flattery near Tatoosh Island eastward to Port Angeles when he noticed what appeared to be a sea-air-interface anomaly very close in to the coast, which was indented by caves, both hot and cold. The zoom didn't help much because the number of pixels making up the picture diluted the color of the surrounding sea as well, so there now appeared a less distinct variation between the color of the suspected anomaly and the water about it. But the zoom did show him that the patch he'd zeroed in on wasn't so much circular as a tadpole shape.

On his own recognizance, Aussie called the Coast Guard at Port Angeles, keeping his voice low, so as not to wake Freeman, whose sheepdog-like snoring reverberated through the motel room. He explained what he'd seen and on the general's behalf requested that the Port Angeles Coast Guard station send out a fast RIB to have a look-see.

"Are you nuts?" he was told. "We've already lost a guy. Besides, we've got every Bruiser out. They're still bringing in sur—" The man stopped abruptly. Aussie could hear voices in the background. Then someone else came on the line.

"Have you tried the oceanographic and torpedo recovery vessel *Petrel II*? It's been busy picking up people too, but it's pretty well equipped. If it's in the area, it could probably drop over a bottle. I'm guessing you want a water sample for an isotope match? That'd tell you whether it's oil or garbage."

"Or both. You got it," said Aussie. "If it's an oil spill and there's no match for it in the Coast Guard's isotope register, then we'll know it's from an intruder. And if that's the case, I'll bet it's the sub."

"I can call *Petrel* if you like," offered the Coast Guard officer.

"No sweat, I'll do it. Frank Hall's the skipper, right?"

"You know him?"

"Ex-SEAL buddy of mine. Taught 'im everything he knows."

"Fine," said the officer. "Listen—sorry about the guy who answered. He lost his wife on the *Turner*."

"Poor bastard," said Aussie. "He shouldn't be on duty."

"I know, but we need everyone we can get. 'Sides, he's hell-bent about staying on. Wants to get even."

"Don't we all. Thanks, buddy. I'll call the *Petrel*."

"What's going on?" asked the general, sitting on the edge of the sofa, yawning, his shock of silver-gray hair disheveled.

"Possible sea-air anomaly on the Darkstar trace," Lewis told him. "Close inshore."

CHAPTER TWENTY-FIVE

AS TOUGH AS he was, oceanographer and ex-SEAL Frank Hall could not bring himself to "drive" *Petrel,* as he tersely put it, "straight through" the fogbound waters of Juan de Fuca Strait that he was sure still contained scores of bodies. Accordingly, he had given *Petrel*'s second mate instructions to strip the stern's A-frame of the practice torpedo retrieval tackle and replace it with a quick-snap release line with which *Petrel* could tow her twelve-foot-long Zodiac. With the third mate, Sandra Riley, and two men aboard the Zodiac, it could be cast off from *Petrel*, if need be, to pick up any survivors or bodies that Hall or his look-outs on *Petrel*'s bridge might see en route, or to get a quick water sample from the Darkstar anomaly for isotope comparison.

Six and a half miles from the air/sea tadpole-shaped patch, the *Petrel*'s starboard lookout did see something orange bobbing up and down in the fog-shrouded chop. Hall doubted it was a body—it looked more like a piece of debris. Nevertheless, he alerted the third mate to its position, heard the loud two-stroke-like roar of the Zodiac's outboard, then saw it as it sped bumpily past *Petrel*, its bow smacking hard against the waves, which was the price of being out of sync with the frequency of the swells. As a result, the third mate and her two crew were jarred from head to foot, a splatter of spray thrown up by the Zodiac along with a whiff of its gasoline exhaust swept onto the bridge by a westerly wind coming in from the open sea through the choke point between the Olympic peninsula and Vancouver Island, the wind starting to disperse the fog.

"Couldn't be much louder," said the bosun, looking down at the Zodiac. "Glad we're not on a silent mission."

"Uh-huh," replied Frank. "But I like it loud in our work." He meant torpedo retrieval. "If I can't see it, I can hear it."

"True," agreed the bosun, his legs wide apart, his torso leaning forward against the bridge's brass rail as he fixed his binoculars on the orange object. "Son of a bitch, it's a zip-up."

"What?" asked the portside lookout.

"You know, thermal survival suit. Arctic rated. Like a waterproof sleeping bag. Zips up to your eyes. Float on your back—right, Skipper?"

"If you're lucky," said Frank, "and don't get concussed face-down before you hit the water."

"Zodiac's just about on it. Reckon whoever—"

"Torpedo!" screamed the station lookout. "Two o'clock! Two hundred yards," which was the limit of *Petrel*'s visibility.

Frank hit the stern thruster button, felt the ship surge another three knots, and spun the wheel right, to the starboard quarter. A fast white streak, two feet wide, passed parallel to them on the left side, less than five feet from *Petrel*'s hull.

"Holy shit! Holy—"

"Be quiet!" Hall told the lookout. "Keep a sharp watch. There could be a pair."

"Jesus!" said the lookout, despite Hall's admonition. He was whey-faced, as was the portside lookout, the latter's eyes big as saucers, staring down at the sea.

"Hey!" It was the cook on the intercom. "That fucker was a dummy, right, Captain?"

"Don't know," said Frank. "Weren't notified. Could be a communication screw-up."

Down aft on the stern deck, several off-watch crew who'd been observing the Zodiac fading away in the distance as *Petrel* closed on the anomaly two miles away were also arguing vociferously about the torpedo.

"It wasn't live, for chrissake," asserted the winch man who'd hauled up Albinski's grisly remains. "It was one of ours."

"How do you know?" an oiler buddy challenged, throwing a wipe rag at him. "You were asleep, you fat fart!" Laughter erupted from the group; a little too hysterical, the bosun thought. It was the kind of response he'd heard while serving aboard a fleet replenishment ship during Desert Storm, the sort of laughter that was more a release of tension after a close miss than because of anything funny.

Hall appeared on the bridge's starboard wing, immediately recognizable by his Navy toque, yellow wet-weather jacket, and hailer. "Everybody back to work! I want six additional lookouts, two for'ard, two midships, two aft. It's possible there might be more survivors."

"Yes, sir. Any news from the Zodiac about the zip-up?"

"No, not yet."

"Was that a live torpedo, sir?" asked an oiler emerging from the galley.

"I don't know," replied Frank. I'll find out." With that, he returned to the bridge.

" 'Course it was live," said one of the deck crew as they began to disperse. "That's why he wants more lookouts, right?"

"Don't sweat it. He told us he's on to it. He'll tell us as soon as he knows. He's a straight shooter."

"Yeah," mumbled the departing oiler. "Like the guy who fired that damn torpedo."

"Can barely see our Zodiac now," commented the first mate, his binoculars back on the Zodiac. "But it looks as if they're hauling someone aboard."

"Anomaly one thousand yards," reported the first mate.

"Prepare for station," Frank announced on the ship's PA while punching in SLOW AHEAD on the computer console.

Petrel's third mate's voice crackled into the chart room aft of the bridge, her voice of exhaustion and depression giving way to an oxymoronic report to Hall: "Survivor—dead!"

"Bring 'im in," said Frank, who now made a GPS check. It showed that due to winds and tidal shift, *Petrel* was a quarter mile west of the oil spill—if that's what the anomaly was. He corrected course, watching the sweep arm on his amber radar screen picking up the tiny blip that was the despondent third mate and the two crewmen returning to *Petrel* with the bright

Day-Glo survival suit. The corpse was of a dark-complexioned man, late forties or perhaps younger, looking older because of the bluish pallor of his skin. A man whom no one on the *Petrel* recognized, like so many of the dead they and the Coast Guard had fished out from the strait in the last forty-two hours.

For a moment, as he thought about all those who had died in the frigid waters, Frank remembered his granddad's favorite hymn: "Oh hear us when we cry to Thee/for those in peril on the sea."

His thoughts were suddenly put to flight by a voice invading *Petrel* on the radio's shipping channel for ferries, the voice screaming for help. It was the first officer aboard the *Georgia Queen*, one of the five-deck-high, five-hundred-vehicle, two-thousand-passenger ferries that daily plied the waters of Georgia Strait on the thirty-mile run between Vancouver Island and Vancouver on the Canadian mainland.

Perhaps the Canadians, whose west coast ferry fleet was bigger than the entire Canadian navy, had believed that all the attacks so far had taken place in American waters, he thought, and believed they would not fall victim to whoever was wreaking havoc with their neighbor. Theoretically, their assumption might have been well-founded. After all, though some Canadians were killed in the 9/11 assault on America, Canada itself had remained untouched.

But no longer, for as the torpedo fired at *Petrel* missed the oceanographic ship, it continued on at fifty-plus knots, by Frank Hall's guesstimate, and in apparent free running, rather than active or passive acoustic mode, for another fourteen miles, crossing the U.S.-Canada line, passing through a pod of Orcas that fifty or so passengers on the ferry had braved the foul weather to see.

Among the whale watchers, a retired British naval petty officer who'd seen action in the Falklands war of 1982, witnessing the sinking of the Argentine battleship *Belgrano* by torpedo, raced along the ferry's upper deck to the bridge, yelling, "Torpedo, starboard beam!" The mate, on the bridge of *Georgia Queen*, against all intention and training with the ferry corporation, became so rattled by the radio officer's hysterical Mayday that he failed to turn the vessel in time. The torpedo struck the ferry starboard aft, the force of the explosion lifting her stern clear of the water, over a hundred cars, SUVs, and eighteen-wheeled freight trucks sliding en masse, smashing into a hill of cars.

Trailways buses and motorcycles piled up against the huge curving doors and ramp, a flood of gasoline and diesel fuel from ruptured tanks suddenly reversing course, rushing aft as the ferry's stern fell back into the sea. This in turn lifted the bow at a precipitous angle moments before the vessel broke in half, the two sections drifting apart, hundreds of passengers on each of the three decks spilling into the sea from the violence of the separation.

It was as if a buzz saw had neatly cut through the model of a ship, only here the avalanche of toy-size figures and vehicles dropping into the ocean were not toys. The sickening thuds the Coast Guard and 911 operators were hearing in the background of frantic cell phone calls for help were the sound of men, women, and children, some of whom had jumped, striking the hard metal of either sinking vehicles or the metal of the lower decks.

Among the two square miles of oily flotsam and debris, the bodies of a baby Orca and several sea otters could be seen along with dozens of drowned cats and dogs that, by regulation, had been required to be kept below in their owners' vehicles during transit. Dead guide dogs were also among the animals hauled aboard by the crews of rescuing Coast Guard cutters. Only one guide dog, a black lab, survived, swimming for all its might, vainly trying to drag its owner, an elderly woman, to safety aboard an upturned Beaufort raft. The exhausted dog, unable to get purchase on the oil-slicked rubber surface, kept falling back into the water, the earlier lustrous sheen of her coat now looking like an oil-matted pelt as she drifted further away.

It was CNN's shot of this dog, taken by Marte Price's cameraman after they'd left the hospital, that arrested Charles Riser's attention, along with that of millions of other viewers. For Charlie Riser, the dog's black, matted coat bore an uncanny resemblance to the photographs showing Mandy's hair after she'd been pulled from the Suzhou canal. It galvanized his determination to press Bill Heinz to find out where Chang was imprisoned.

Aboard *Petrel*, now within a hundred yards of the tadpole-shaped oil slick picked up earlier by Darkstar, the third officer, Sandra Riley, whose discovery of the dead man in the Day-Glo survival suit had badly shaken her, nevertheless felt duty bound to ask Hall, "Shouldn't we turn about, sir? Go help the Coast Guard pick up survivors from the ferry?"

"No," said Frank. "Not till we get that water sample for Freeman. That could be crucial."

"To whom?" the mate snapped. "Freeman. That guy's just like Patton an' all those other glory hounds. They only care about—"

"Calm down!" Hall said, just as sharply. "The water sample could save a lot more lives than those lost on that ferry. If we don't find an international isotope fingerprint in this slick, it means that the oil's an outside batch and belongs to some vessel that doesn't want to be identified. Like a midget sub. Got it?"

"Sorry, Captain."

"No need. You're tired. We all are. Go down to the galley, grab a cup of java, take a breather and—"

Frank stopped talking and cut the *Petrel*'s engines. She was in the slick, and from the starboard fold-out platform just big enough for a man to stand on, he saw his bosun hook up the safety chain rail and raise his right hand, moving it in a clockwise circular movement, the signal for the winch man to start lowering the fifty-pound, quarter-inch cable through the block above the platform. Frank heard the whine of the winch, saw the lead weight penetrate the sea's choppy surface and the bosun give the stop signal as he reached out from the platform and affixed the Neilsen reversing sample "bottle" to the wire. Satisfied that the bottom wing nut clamp was secure on the cable, the bosun next attached the grenade-sized brass messenger, a sleeve weight that, once struck by another messenger sent down the wire, would trigger the sudden upside down flip of the sampling bottle, breaking the mercury column on its side-mounted thermometer and thus preserving the exact temperature reading at that depth. Albinski had had such a thermometer on his attack board.

The bosun gave the "Take her down slowly" signal, and the Neilsen bottle was lowered under the oil slick. There was a heavy thud, felt by Cookie in the kitchen, as the winch man braked. The bosun fixed the trigger messenger to the wire, let it fall down the cable, heard the clack of the impact and saw oily black bubbles fizzing to the surface only seconds after the bottle had tripped. "Bring her up!" he shouted to the winch man, who couldn't hear him but followed the "Up! Up! Up!" motion of the bosun's hand. As the bosun unclipped the bottle, he almost lost his grip on the bottle's oil-slicked casing.

Only then did Frank Hall turn *Petrel* about and head at full speed northward to assist in yet another forlorn rescue task, this time around the sunken ferry. One of the Coast Guard ships would be able to do a preliminary isotope "presence" test. If there was no isotope match-up, it was almost certain that they'd zoned in on the sub's area, and the Juan de Fuca tide flow charts would allow Freeman's SpecFor team to backtrack to where the spill had started.

CHAPTER TWENTY-SIX

MOVING BRISKLY DOWN the carrier's six steep, grated aluminum ladder wells that led from the CNN *McCain*'s island to the gallery deck, immediately below the carrier's flight deck, Admiral Crowley walked quickly forward through the quarter-mile-long cream-colored corridor. The six thousand crew members referred to it as the "steeple chase," due to the scores of oval-shaped and watertight doors that had to be passed through at some risk to knees—if you were short, like Crowley—or your head—if, like Petty Officer Sarah Dugan, you were among the taller crew members.

Turning at right angles to the main axis of the boat, Crowley entered a cross passageway that took him farther inboard. Crew with photo IDs clipped to their uniforms turned aside to allow the admiral to pass, for despite the enormous size of America's largest ship, her corridors were relatively narrow. Every inch of available space was needed to house the millions of pieces of equipment needed for *McCain* to carry out its mission: to transport America's big stick into the Taiwan Strait to contain the war between China and the ROC before the conflict widened in Asia and drew the already overextended U.S. military into what the Pentagon told the President would be a "logistical abyss."

Crowley, now approaching the nerve center of the 96,000-ton carrier, was leaving the gray area of the ship and entering what the crew called "blue tile country," which housed the highly sensitive data-linked command and control functions of the carrier. These included the Combat Information Center, where Crowley was now headed, the Joint Intelligence Center, and the ultrasecret SSES, the secret signals exploitation space, a highly sophisticated electronic snooping and worldwide computer spy shop that could provide the captain with links to all U.S. intelligence agencies and infrared satellite surveillance of enemy movements on the ground. All the information collected in this relatively small but securely guarded unit could be linked to the big screens and consoles in the other four independently housed command and control units. All these units were bathed in a perpetual cool blue light—hence the nickname "blue tile country"—the temperature kept low in order to keep the banks of computers and electronic equipment from overheating in their high intensity 24/7 operation.

The moment Crowley entered the Combat Information Center, he reached for his well-worn lamb's-wool-lined World War II bomber jacket and zipped it up to the neck. "What've we got?" he asked the CIC duty officer, John Cuso, whose calm expression, made faintly ghoulish in the cool, bluish light, concealed his concern. His tone was thoroughly professional, worthy of the aviator's code he still lived by, despite having been permanently grounded after a burst blood vessel during a basketball game that had ended his days in his beloved Tomcat.

Cuso drew Crowley's attention to the big blue situation board, its surface crisscrossed with vectors and blips, showing the position of *McCain*'s present combat patrol, the carrier group now leaving the northernmost waters of the South China Sea, passing into the southernmost limits of the Taiwan Straits. Cuso pointed to the biggest blip on the screen. It was coming in from the northeast. "Sir, this typhoon out of Japan is picking up speed. Lost some energy during landfall over Japan, but on encountering less friction over the Sea of Japan, its winds have increased to 120 miles an hour. By the time we enter the Taiwan Strait—"

"Air's gonna be full of all kinds of junk," interjected Crowley.

"Yes, sir. It'll be like a giant vacuum cleaner if it passes over Taiwan. And we're in late fall—end of the harvest in the fields on the western side of the island'll mean all kinds of debris."

"Plus the damn fires our satellites show over Quemoy."

"Kinmen," Cuso corrected his boss. Crowley was old school, had flown Skyraider infantry support in Vietnam and, like others of his generation, the old Chinese names stuck. Cuso didn't like correcting him, but some terrible mistakes had been made on bombing missions by getting the names mixed up. The one the instructors had always used as a warning at the flight school was Bangor, Maine, and Bangor, Washington State.

"Then we'll have to make sure everyone in the air wing knows," said Crowley, "emphasis 'Brown Shirts,'" by which Crowley meant plane captains, not the brown jerseyed helo captains who wore the same color but sported red helmets to differentiate them from the white-helmeted plane captains whose job it was to be "mother" to his or her particular aircraft.

In fact, John Cuso, the black sheen of his skin speckled by goose bumps from the chilly atmosphere of the CIC, had posted a "dirty air" alert. It meant that flight deck personnel were to be particularly vigilant for foreign object debris on the walkdown of the flight deck that preceded every launch. All the personnel's eyes, as well, had to be protected by goggles. And the 1,092-foot-long, 250-foot-wide rubberized, nonskid deck was to be closely inspected for anything, no matter how small, which would quickly destroy a multimillion-dollar jet engine if sucked into its intake.

A beeping invaded the low hum of the CIC, John Cuso hearing, "We have a leaker," one of the electronic warfare officers informing CIC that an unknown aircraft coming out of the northeast quadrant had violated the battle group's air space. Computer analysis vectors leading to and from the X blipping on the powder blue screen put the bogey's speed at Mach 1.4. The *McCain*'s Combat Air Patrol of four F-18s was flying at thirty thousand feet, already on an intercept course, the intruder up to now having evaded the *McCain*'s battle group's radar by flying at plus or minus two hundred feet above the sea.

"A skimmer?" inquired Cuso calmly, confident that the *McCain*'s Combat Air Patrol, on strict radio silence, would be within visual contact in ten minutes.

"Don't think it's a skimmer, sir," answered an EWO, his computers, together with the target acquisition system, telling him the bogey was too fast for an enemy cruise missile, and an intermittent profile of the cross-sectional area, glimpsed by the carrier's radar, was too large for faster pilotless vehicles.

"How sure are you?" Crowley pressed the electronic warfare officer.

"That it's an aircraft, not a skimmer? Ninety percent sure, sir."

Crowley was tempted to break radio silence and take the consensus of his two Aegis cruisers and the destroyers that made up the *McCain*'s protective screen, but his natural curiosity was sidelined by his responsibility to deny any potential adversary the exact position of his battle group. Cuso knew the admiral's decision was probably at odds with the White House's wish to let Beijing and Taipei know that the "police" were coming, as it were, to stop the fighting. But with the disastrous events that had sunk three of the U.S. Navy's ships in the Strait of Juan de Fuca, Cuso favored his boss's caution. Both men, like the six thousand people in *McCain* plus the thousands more manning her battle group, had personally known many of those killed and missing. Besides, in five minutes *McCain*'s CAP would establish if the bogey was a hostile, and if so, shoot it down. And if the CAP didn't make the kill—though why, Crowley couldn't imagine—then either the battle group's formidable Aegis cruisers, Arleigh Burke destroyers, or the duo of fast attack submarines most certainly would.

Typhoon Jane's winds had increased speed to 125 miles an hour, and Admiral Crowley, returning to Primary Flight Control, six stories above the flight deck, heard the typhoon's advance gusts howling around the carrier's superstructure as the huge airfield kept plowing into the Taiwan Strait at 32 knots. The planes parked on the flight deck were chained down as tightly as those in the hangar deck, the huge, gray ship trembling in its lower regions from the reverberations of its four nuclear-generated steam engines, which were driving the four massive shafts of the carrier and all aboard her into harm's way.

The four Super Hornets of *McCain*'s Combat Air Patrol peeled off high above the bogey. It was still flying so low that as Lieutenant Commander Chipper Armstrong's F-18 Super Hornet broke through the thick gray nimbostratus that was preceding Typhoon Jane by 230 miles, he made visual contact with the speck moving southeast toward the carrier's battle group. The blip on his radar and its concomitant altitude reading seemed at odds, however. His radar was telling him the bogey was 150 feet above the deck, or sea level, his eyes looking through the sun visor of his helmet telling his brain that the unidentified craft was within arm's reach of the wrinkled gray sea. In the backseat of the Hornet, Chipper's RIO—Radar Intercept Officer "Eagle" Evans, so-called because of his exceptional daytime vision—flicked on his digital reconnaissance camera, selecting zoom and link-up to Chipper's right-hand digital display indicator so that Chipper could now receive real-time images of the bogey.

"It's an ROC," said Evans. "Taiwanese. An F-16. That's a Fighting Falcon to you."

"What the hell's it doing here?" asked Chipper.

"Lost his way?" proffered Evans. "Check out its left wing's flaperons."

"I see 'em," said Chipper Armstrong, his eyes following the line of dime-size bullet holes that extended all the way forward of the Fighting Falcon's rear ventral fins to the leading edge of the fighter's cropped delta wing and up to the plane's big telltale bubble cockpit. The Hornet's zoom caught a blinding flash from the Falcon's bubble, which was the "gold" sprayed inside to stealth the aircraft from radar waves.

"That gold just freaked out the zoom," RIO Evans commented, the presence of the pneumonic gray stratus doing little to reduce the gold bubble effect. "I think his nav equipment's shot to hell, Chipper."

"Could be," responded Armstrong. "From those holes forward of his ventrals, I'd say he took a full burst in the kidneys."

"Can you see him?" asked Evans.

"Negative, but it's the damned gold cockpit."

Armstrong moved the stick hard left to give the Hornet's disc camera a less direct angle of approach, the Falcon looking to Armstrong as if it was still on a straight, perhaps auto-controlled flight path. His assumption was confirmed by the Hornet's left digital display, telling him the Falcon was 108 feet above the sea and three miles below the *McCain*'s CAP, its speed 914 mph. Armstrong's four Super Hornets, descending at Mach 1.1, simultaneously moved out of their line-abreast combat pairs into the more open fluid four formation, its two leaders—Armstrong on the left, "Rhino" Manowski on his right, scanning forward, each of their wingmen behind them and off to the side, their responsibility being to watch fore and aft of the four Hornets' formation.

Chipper Armstrong and his RIO, on the front left of the formation, were ten thousand feet from their CAP's right-hand leader and his RIO. The distance between each leader Hornet and wingman, however, was much closer, this spread between leader and minder no more than a thousand feet. This left Chipper Armstrong and Rhino Manowski as the front pair of the fluid four formation, freer to concentrate on the ROC Taiwanese Fighting Falcon that seemed devoid of human guidance.

"He's moving," announced Eagle Evans, Chipper's RIO, Chipper fighting a sudden wind shear that was shooting up in excess of 200 knots per hour. It violently buffeted Armstrong and Evans's Hornet for four seconds, the strength of the phantom's "upblast" no doubt having enveloped the Fighting Falcon with such force that Armstrong and his wingman aft left of him came to the same conclusion—that any movement they'd glimpsed in the Falcon's cockpit almost certainly had been due to the ROC pilot's body being shaken by the hammerlike blows of the wind shear column colliding with the Falcon's air drag, putting the Falcon momentarily into "bone-shake" mode before its autopilot computer effected flap and "Hi" stabilizer corrections.

"I dunno, Chipper," said Evans hesitantly. He thought he'd seen the ROC pilot move forward from the Falcon's maximum thirty-degree recline position. But he wasn't sure, which meant he wasn't sure whether the pilot was alive.

Evans's hesitation was a manifestation of the doubt born the day after he and Armstrong had completed their six-week-long cadet Aviation Preflight Indoctrination course at Pensacola, Florida. Both men, along with dozens of other hopefuls, passed their rigorous Aerodynamics, Survival, Physiology, Escape, and Navigation training tests. But Evans learned that while he'd been rated "above average," he'd flunked the test for Navy aviator nighttime vision. At twenty-three, he saw it as a colossal personal failure, despite the instructor's slap-on-the-back advice that the responsibility in the backseat was huge. "Damn pilot can't do much if he doesn't know where the hell he is, Evans."

Evans had given the appropriate "Right Stuff" smile.

" 'Sides," added the instructor, "once your tours are up, you're gonna be one helluva lot more employable than an aviator. Fighter pilots aren't in big demand among civilian airlines. You will be."

Evans had nodded, remaining unassuaged. For Navy aviators, pilots, and RIOs, flying a civilian airliner was referred to disparagingly as "flying a bus."

Back in the present, Evans thought that maybe Chipper was

right. Perhaps the ROC pilot hadn't moved and had the Falcon on full auto. He hoped so, because if the pilot was hurt too badly to eject, then the auto was his only hope, at least as long as his fuel lasted.

By now the blue screens in *McCain*'s inner sanctums were showing first four, then eight . . . twelve . . . sixteen . . . twenty-four bogeys entering the *McCain* battle group's no fly combat zone at a point fifty-six miles east of Oluanpi, Taiwan's most southerly point. Neither Admiral Crowley nor his battle group staff had any idea why Taiwan's air force would be there, when Taiwan's ROC pilots were committed to protecting their island's western approaches, particularly at Kinmen Island. If the bogeys turned out to be Taiwanese, they would be classified as friendlies and nothing to worry about, either for Chipper Armstrong's CAP, 170 miles northwest of the carrier, or for the battle group itself. But then the *McCain*'s SSES—the Ship's Signal Exploitation Space, the innermost sanctum—reported detecting, via Satellite Infrared Data Uplink, an unmistakable Triple E—enemy electronic emission—pulsing from the twenty-four bogeys that were now directly south of Oluanpi.

Crowley knew this could mean only one thing—that the bogeys were now indisputably "hostiles," ChiCom aircraft completing an end run down Taiwan's east coast and around its southernmost point in order to sandwich the Taiwanese pilots who, low on gas, would be returning from the combat zone over Kinmen. Which meant the twenty-four ChiComs had refueled while in the air, a feat that, given the high advance winds of Typhoon Jane, was not only gutsy, but evidenced an in-flight fueling capability that neither the *McCain*'s battle group nor Taiwan's air force had thought the PLA air force was capable of. This, despite an intel report that some illiterate mushroom digger up in Shihmen had claimed he'd seen "glints" of what he thought might have been low-flying aircraft out to sea.

Admiral Crowley ordered his remaining eight Hornets aloft, to be followed by a fourteen-plane FITCOMPRON—Fighter Composite Squadron. This included twelve F-14 Tomcats and an EA-6B Prowler, already overhead, as was an E-2C Hawkeye, which could continue to act as an adjunct for *McCain*'s ultrasecret signals exploitation space. The Prowler's crew of four could jam enemy signals and in general cause electronic chaos among the twenty-four hostiles.

Crowley ordered Armstrong and his wingman Rhino Manowski to stay and shepherd the ROC Falcon, while the two other Hornets in the fluid four were to break off and head northeast to join the *McCain*'s Hornets and Tomcats. The squadron's mission was to get between the returning ROC fighters low on fuel and the ChiCom hostiles.

"Shit!" complained Eagle Evans, who, like Rhino Manowski and his RIO, had been left out of the FITCOMPRON. "I want to be in the fight."

"What fight?" said Chipper Armstrong. "Rules of Engagement, Eagle. Remember? Our boys are supposed to get in between the two Chinas, to be peacemakers—airborne referees. Who wants that job? End up getting shot at by both sides if you're not careful."

"Well," came in Manowski, "I'd rather some action than being a *shepherd*!" His RIO was of the same mind, and they both glared jealously as the other pair of the fluid four peeled off and went to afterburner, racing to rendezvous with *McCain*'s composite fighter squadron. But the breakaway duo knew that with too much speed, they'd be too low on gas to make it back to the carrier if their loiter time between the returning ROC fighters and the ChiComs was longer than ten minutes. By which time the ROC guys from Kinmen would be heading back to refuel on Taiwan's west coast at Ching Chuan Kang Air Force Base, seventy-five miles northeast of Taiwan's Pescadores Islands, the latter approximately halfway between Taiwan and the Communist mainland.

For Chipper Armstrong and Evans, metallic-gray nimbostratus lay ahead, Chipper doing a visual check of his head's-up display for heading, airspeed, and altitude. The advisory, caution, and warning lights bottom of the HUD screen would automatically flash and sound in the event of impending malfunction, but "ye olde visual," as his top gun instructor at Fallon used to say, was always advisable. "Remember, son, *you're* flying the beast! Beast ain't flying *you*!"

Chipper's main concern was the Super Hornet's "short legs"—its gas-to-weight ratio—which necessitated operations officers wrestling daily with the critical "weapons-to-drop-tank" equation. The Hornet's relative lack of internal fuel space, compared to other fighters, was referred to as IFO—"If only!" As a compromise, Armstrong and Manowski's planes had been equipped with a clip-on underbelly fuel tank in addition to the two drop tanks, one on each wing's outer stanchion, where they would normally have preferred to carry air-to-air Sidewinder missiles, or two laser-guided bombs.

On *McCain*, the operations officer, like everyone in the Combat Air Patrol, had no way of knowing how long this "Bizarro" friendly Falcon could stay airborne. If Crowley'd had his way, he would have ordered Chipper and Rhino to join the twenty-two-plane posse now vectored to intercept the twenty-four ChiCom hostiles forty miles west of the Penghu Island group, off southwest Taiwan, before the ChiCom planes had a chance to down the near empty ROC Falcons, which were also defenseless, having expended all their ordnance over Kinmen. Crowley's other option—his wish, in fact—was to recall Armstrong and Manowski. This was stymied, however, by a political necessity—the President could not be seen deserting a staunch ally in need, even if it was just one pilot. Any reluctance to stay with Bizarro would, as John Cuso advised, be a propaganda coup for America's enemies, who were already gleeful with the stunning victories of what Arab television, radio, and press were now calling the "mighty midget" sub that, with the massive conflagration at Washington State's Cherry Point refinery and the forced evacuations of thousands of Americans, was continuing to humble the Great Satan.

"There he goes!" said Evans, his voice so loud it startled Armstrong in the front seat.

"Jesus, Eagle—"

"No doubt about it. *Right* hand is definitely moving—sliding along the canopy seal—for support, I guess. Hand must be shot up pretty bad—trying to edge it forward along the seal so he can let it drop down onto the stick." The eagle-eyed Evans, though not having realized his dream of being a fighter pilot, was recalling that the Falcon's control stick, unlike in most fighters, wasn't on the center line, but was instead located on the right console.

Now Chipper could see it too, though it was difficult to spot, given the F-16D's near opaque shining gold bubble. Evans was correct, and their Hornet's wingman confirmed his observation. "Eyes of an eagle, ol' buddy," Rhino complimented him. "Eyes of an eagle."

"Yeah," responded Evans, "but not the eyes of an owl." No one but Armstrong picked up Evans's oblique allusion to his aviator nighttime vision test.

To the four Americans' astonishment, the Falcon's pilot managed to turn his head, albeit slowly, to his right, his left hand raised slightly in a "thanks" salute.

"Hey hey hey!" called Rhino excitedly, simultaneously giving the Falcon a thumbs-up. "You go, girl!"

"Girl?" It was Rhino's RIO. "Bullshit! You can't tell a guy from a skirt underneath a bone dome."

"She's got her visor up," retorted Rhino. "You see that, Eagle?"

"Yeah," said Evans, "but a lot of young Asian guys can look to us like a woman. You know, no facial hair, small physique."

"I can see her boob bumps in the g-suit," said Rhino.

"Pull the other one," kidded Evans.

"I'd like to pull 'em both. Hey, you guys, Taiwan's not the only country with women on the joystick. We've got 'em too, remember?"

"Not many," cut in Evans.

"We've got 'em, though," cut in Rhino's RIO. "Call signs— 'Pussy Galore,' 'Titty Galore'—"

A gravelly voice that sounded right next door but was Admiral Crowley over three hundred miles away entered the conversation. "Chipper, Rhino, knock it off." The *McCain* was no doubt doing its thing, scanning, plucking radio signals out of the ether at will, alerting Crowley to the presence of one or all three of *McCain*'s women pilots in the Combat Information Center.

"Focus," Crowley added grumpily. "Report on Bizarro?"

"Bizarro looking good," reported Chipper crisply. "Possible . . ." He paused. Was it a he or a she? What the hell did it matter anyway? "Possible that Falcon will be able to make our roof." "Roof" wasn't exactly code, but using colloquialisms like this instead of saying "able to reach our carrier" was more often than not effective in confusing ChiCom listening posts.

In *McCain*'s Combat Information Center, Admiral Crowley was concerned about the rock-bottom morale of the U.S. Navy after this last week. It had enveloped him as much as if not more than the six thousand officers and crew on his boat. No one could afford another mistake, though just how anyone could be blamed for not having detected the small but deadly predator hiding somewhere in the eleven hundred square miles of Juan de Fuca, and now apparently Georgia Strait, was not all clear. Of course, everyone aboard had his or her own theory of how such a small target lurking in the depths could so easily have escaped detection. There were six thousand theories aboard *McCain* alone, though the pointy heads—the electronic warfare elite—had all but unanimously concluded that the midget sub must be covered in revolutionary state-of-the-art anechoic sound tiles with the sonar absorption capability of cottage cheese. It didn't surprise Crowley. Hell, the U.S. had done it with the radar-absorbing tiles on the latest stealthed fighters and bombers.

The "little black guy," as the tall, six-foot-three John Cuso was affectionately called by the *McCain*'s CIC staff, was also concerned. He had become as perennially cautious as Crowley, despite his life on the edge in his previous incarnation as a fighter jock. Perhaps his caution, like his boss's, was in part the result of simply growing older, when one began to lose the air of invincibility, the universal conviction of youth that *they* wouldn't be the one to "get it," that the unthinkable fate would be visited only upon the incompetent and the hesitant.

Cuso, his skin still goose-pimpled by the cold air-conditioning in the CIC, cautioned the admiral that this "Bizarro"—another informal code word to confuse hostile eavesdroppers—might be a ChiCom pilot in a captured ROC Falcon from Kinmen Field.

"For what purpose?" asked the admiral.

"To decoy our CAP away from the ChiCom hostiles who slipped around the bottom of Taiwan and who, if everything is on cue—" Cuso looked up at the CIC situation board. "—should be encountering our boys pretty soon."

"Well, John," answered Crowley, "if Bizarro is a decoy, which I doubt, he or she managed to sucker us only for a while. But we're on to the hostiles now."

"Yes, but if we'd had Chipper's CAP farther northeast as the hostiles came around, we'd have scattered them there."

"'Ifs' don't help us, John. Our CAP had to investigate Bizarro, who they think is a wounded Taiwanese pilot. My gut instinct is that it's exactly as young Evans says—a friendly, shot-up, scared, on auto until he or she recovers enough to be able to land that sucker. And my guess is he's low on gas."

Cuso nodded at this last conclusion. "I think you're right there. The vectors suggest he, she, must have only—"

"CAP to Mother." It was Armstrong's voice. "Are we to escort Bizarro to the roof?"

"One moment, Chipper," said Crowley.

"If that Falcon's shot up—" began Cuso.

"Goddamn, John," retorted Crowley. "They can see the bullet holes in it, tail to canopy. It's a miracle the bird's still in the air."

"What I mean, sir," continued Cuso, "is that his auto might be whacked for a landing anywhere, let alone a carrier."

"I'm not risking him landing on the roof, John. I'm not risking any of our crew on the deck." He grabbed the spiral cord mike. "Mother to CAP. Negative for the roof. You'll have to have Bizarro eject for pickup. I say again, Bizarro to eject for pickup." Crowley put the mike in its cradle, asking his "covey" of electronics weapons officers, "What's our CAP's ETA?"

"Twenty-five minutes, sir. Possibly a little less. SSES advises SATRECON shows strong tailwind."

"That from the typhoon?"

"Yes, sir."

"Good for Armstrong and Manowski coming home, but that means strong headwinds for FITCOMPRON."

"Yes, sir. Gusts up to seventy miles per hour."

Confirming his officers' verbal report, the admiral, like every other commander in his carrier battle group, looking up at their big blue screens, could see that his FITCOMPRON was slowing because of the headwinds. Contact would now be made in fifty seconds, the CIC computers also projecting a rapidly increasing rate of fuel consumption. Crowley ordered three of his six S-3B Vikings to be brought up by their elevator and gassed up, their antisub warfare crew to ready the aircraft for its other function as aerial refueler, should the Hornets and Tomcats—particularly the Hornets—become dangerously low on Avgas after having to buck the winds of the advancing typhoon.

"No way the Chinese Communists started this punch-up with Taiwan," Crowley told John Cuso. "Who in their right mind would risk any kind of invasion, knowing a typhoon is gonna hit them in the face?"

Cuso was noncommittal. A lot of the world wasn't in its right mind, including his mother-in-law. "Maybe Beijing was caught with its pants down. Didn't believe the weather forecast. Or maybe the ChiComs figured that now would be when an attack would be least expected. Like MacArthur at Inchon," continued Cuso, "and that Freeman retreating with his armor in that blizzard, then—"

"Angels approaching hostiles," announced a weapons officer calmly, his relaxed tone belying the tension building in the skies over the Penghu Islands, where *McCain*'s twenty-two fighters' job would be to break westward, but not before they made visual contact with what SSES's satellite-catalyzed radar had designated as "hostiles." Only then could *McCain*'s twelve "Hummer" Super Hornets and F-14 Tomcats break left, heading eastward to act as what the White House was pleased to call a "buffer zone" between the two Chinese air forces, the Pentagon Rules of Engagement forbidding the Americans to fire unless fired upon.

CHAPTER TWENTY-SEVEN

MOMENTS AFTER THEY reached the air space above the Penghu Islands, which had been only mere dots on the Hornets' and Tomcats' radar screens, *McCain*'s squadrons received a shock. Ahead, in the "box" of twenty-four hostiles, red stars emblazoned high on tailfins and wings, were two types of aircraft. *McCain*'s planes were a mix too, but the ChiCom "box" consisted entirely of Russian-made aircraft. Twelve of them were pale blue, wave-flecked gray MiG29 fighters—NATO designation "Fulcrum"—the remainder a dozen Sukhoi-30s, fighter-bombers. Both Fulcrums and Flankers were as fast as the Americans' Tomcats, and over 300 mph faster than the Hornet.

"Shit! Russians!" exclaimed the Tomcat leader, Lieutenant Colonel Gene P. Crouper, "Drummer" to his fellow aviators.

"Negative!" cut in the nasal radio voice of Commander Johnny Reisman, or "Hummer One," leader of *McCain*'s twelve Super Hornets and overall commander of FITCOMPRON. "Those red stars are barred," he said, by which Reisman meant that the red stars on the Fulcrums and Sukhois had a bar painted on either side of the star, the insignia of the ChiCom air force, not the Russian air force.

"You sure?" pressed Drummer.

"Positive," Reisman assured him. "Russkies are broke. They've been selling assets off all over."

"Okay, but why the Flankers?" asked Drummer Crouper. "I mean, fighter-bombers."

"Got me," answered Johnny Reisman, "but they've seen us— got the message. Let's break east, go play referee."

"Roger that," said Crouper. "I hope we can persuade—"

"What the—they're jinxing us." Drummer was only half right, for while the twelve Fulcrums, the best fighters Mikoyan-Gurevich ever produced, had broken fast left, coming hard at the Americans, the twelve Sukhoi-30 Flanker fighter-bombers were continuing north northwest.

Reisman saw what was up immediately. The twelve Russian-made ChiCom Flankers were carrying Kh-17 "Krypton" air-to-surface antiradiation missiles and TV-guided 1,100-pound bombs on their ten hard points. This told Reisman, and now Drummer Crouper, that the ChiCom left hook mission wasn't just about flying down Taiwan's east coast and around its southernmost tip below the ROC's radar screen in order to engage returning low-on-gas Taiwanese Falcons and Mirages headed home to refuel.

"Bandits jinxing us thirty-eight miles," announced Tomcat's Drummer.

"Swing away," ordered Reisman. "Do not engage. I say again, *do not engage!*"

"Shit!" observed Reisman's RIO. "Every damn pilot in the world knows jinxing's a direct confrontation—"

"Break right!" shouted Reisman, and every fluid four in the American box swung away in a unison that rivaled the Navy's elite Blue Angel Hornet formation team. And every pilot hated the break. Running away from their sole reason for being—to fight.

"And every driver on our side," Reisman reminded Tomcat leader Drummer Crouper, "knows our mission. We're tasked to be peacemakers. That's all. Just let 'em know we're here."

"Drummer to Hummer One. They're coming at us again. Thirty miles."

"Break due west," said Reisman, his voice sounding tight, the increased G force pressing hard on his chest, he and his two squadrons making a hard left turn once more. And then Reisman did something neither he nor many other fighter pilots had done in their career—he flicked from his Fighter Composite Squadron's radio frequency to 243.000, the Coast Guard Mayday channel, which all pilots—ChiCom, ROC, and anyone else aloft, and, most important, the carriers—would have open. If a dust-up was about to occur, Reisman wanted everyone to know who shot first so that no U.N. son of a bitch would be able to complain about U.S. aggression. Whether he liked it or not, Reisman was trying to implement the White House's policy—a totally unrealistic one, in his view—of trying to play referee between the two warring Chinas.

Cuso and Crowley in *McCain*'s CIC were duly astonished. "What the hell—" the admiral began, then paused, listening.

"Crazy to taunt us like that," said Cuso, watching the blue screen. "Don't they remember what happened to the Libyans?" It was a reference to the downing of two Libyan MiG 23s in January 1989 who were brash and brave enough to jinx a pair of Tomcats off the *John F. Kennedy*.

Crowley could feel his blood pressure soaring with the sense of urgency in the plane-to-plane chatter, frying noises of static surge, and labored breathing of his pilots in their exhausting turns as they ran from the ChiComs.

"Bogeys jinxing *again* twenty-six miles!" Cuso and Crowley recognized it as Tomcat leader Drummer Crouper, his "again" so emphatic that it conveyed all the frustration of the FITCOM-PRON's aviators at being ordered by Reisman to evade rather than engage. Crowley was more conscious than anyone on the ship that while pilots might speak to their RIO or other crew members in a completely informal manner, he or she knew that whatever you said on interplane radio could be heard by everyone in the squadron and on the carrier, that it was your reputation on the line. Drummer's "again" was telling everyone that he thought the squadron had "breaked" too much already. Cuso saw his point. What kind of "referees" could expect to do their job without respect?

"He thinks Reisman's being too cautious," Cuso said. "Wants us to do a Freeman." It had slipped out before he had a chance to cage it. Cuso thought Freeman was great, had a naval aviator's daring.

"Oh, really?" replied the admiral caustically, his eyes still on the screen, *his* tone a measure of *his* frustration, the frustration of all battle group commanders who, despite a military man's instinct, know full well that they and their careers are under control of the top civilian executive of the United States. He turned sharply to face Cuso. "What do you want me to do, John? By doing a Freeman? Start shooting? Get us into a punch-up in the strait when we're already overextended, spread from Afghanistan to Korea, to the drug wars in Colombia, to the four-thousand-mile-long border with Canada? And in the Philippines? And never mind we're still in the Balkans and Japan. You talk about Freeman—I can't understand why the President is using an old warhorse like him anyhow. Should be pensioned off!"

Cuso said nothing. Freeman was being used by the White House precisely because Crowley was correct—the United States, its superpower status notwithstanding, was stretched dangerously thin throughout the dangerous world, at sea, on land, and in the air. All reserves in the three armed services had been called up, including Marine reserves. Everyone, including Freeman and his ex-SpecFor warriors, was needed.

They heard Johnny Reisman once more order his fighters to "break west," the twelve ChiCom Fulcrums jinxing yet again. Crowley saw an EWO officer at his console glance questioningly at another.

"Something wrong, Abrams?"

"No—no, sir."

"Then watch the screen."

On the ship's signals exploitation space intercom, the "boffins" informed CIC that the ChiCom Sukhoi-30 fighter bombers were still proceeding northward in air space above the Penghu island group.

"Thank you!" acknowledged Crowley, turning again to Cuso, his tone, though still edgy, more conciliatory. "We can see that on our own screen. They think we're blind in here or—" Crowley had suddenly divined what Reisman had realized a minute or so earlier. The ChiCom fighters were jinxing *McCain*'s squadron to protect their fighter-bombers heading for Penghu. The admiral snatched the mike from its cradle, his short stature requiring him to perform what the less charitable among *McCain*'s six thousand souls called his "tippy-toe" maneuver.

"Mother to Hummer One. Do you read me?"

"Loud and clear," came Reisman's response.

"Give bandits warning on two four three—repeat, two four three—that if they jinx again you will engage. Repeat—if they jinx again you will engage. Do you read me?"

"Roger that. Warn bandits on Guard Channel. If they jinx again we will—"

"Bogeys jinxing twenty miles!" It was Reisman's wingman. "Noses on, Angels Nine plus," which told *McCain*'s CIC that the carrier's twelve Hornets were at nine thousand feet and climbing out of the way. Instantly, Crowley gave his aviators "weapons-free independent decision authority." To *engage*, not *evade*.

"Roger that," began Reisman when Drummer Crouper, five miles ahead, his eyes on his Tomcat's vibrant green heads-up display, saw the flashing MASTER CAUTION light on his right side advisory panel. Master Caution was now replaced by the flashing black on yellow acronym AAM, an air-to-air missile, seen as a green tadpole symbol on Drummer's radar screen, the missile fired by a Fulcrum and closing fast on the green X that was Drummer's bird.

Drummer broke hard right, hit the afterburner, broke hard left, left again, piling on the G force, using his upgraded digital readout that was telling him the Chicom's AAM was a PLA air force R-77, NATO code AA-12 Adder radar-guided active terminal, range thirty-one miles, speed Mach 4, warhead sixty-six pounds, HE fragmentation. It was still closing. He hit the cat's afterburner, again broke hard left, left again, piling on more G's, then hard right. "Ready for chaff!" he yelled to his RIO.

"Ready."

Drummer looked for his wingman. He wasn't there. No one was there but gray stratus, his radar showing him that what had been the ordered formation of Hornets and his fellow Tomcats was now dispersed to hell and gone, Fulcrums swarming in to attack. In the background babble, Drummer could hear Crowley's voice ordering Reisman's Hornets to go after the Flankers. Crowley, then Cuso, had realized that the Flankers were not stopping to jinx. Their intention was obviously to keep flying farther north, the real purpose of the Russian-made fighter-bombers not to help the Fulcrums intercept returning ROC Falcons and Mirages, but to bomb Penghu Island prior to invading it, the Fulcrums providing a fighter umbrella. Penghu, lying only thirty-five miles from Taiwan, would provide the ChiComs with several thousand Taiwanese hostages and an invaluable air base less than two and a half minutes away by air from Taiwan, closer than Cuba was to the United States.

As Drummer used all the capabilities his avionics would provide, breaking fast to nine G's and dropping chaff in the hope that the cloud of frequency-length cut aluminum strips would confuse the ChiComs' radar-homing missile, he saw it closing. Eight seconds to impact. The sweet lady's warning voice would kick in at five seconds.

"Bogey's mileage?" he shouted.

"Thirty, twenty-five, twenty." The RIO could see its contrail streaking toward them in the mirror. It was almost on them. His G-suit was sticking like Saran Wrap, perspiration pouring down his face, steaming up his visor. Then suddenly Drummer went straight up on afterburner, the cat on its tail, then into a loop, the missile passing below unable to turn as acutely, its envelope of air swallowed in the Tomcat's turbulence.

"Nice job, Drum. Nice job. Son of a bitch! You ran his clock out."

Drummer knew it was fifty percent damn good flying and fifty percent good luck that he'd managed to twist and turn enough for the missile to use up its thirty-one-mile range. "Son of a bitch has bought time for the Flankers, though," he answered, sounding utterly drained, as was his RIO. "Let's go help the Hornets."

It had been the same all over, in and out of the blue-gray sky, Tomcats and Hornets defending themselves from AA missile attack, the Fulcrums, though outnumbered, losing three. The ChiComs pilots were brave, and their MiG-29s were among the fastest birds in the world, but the overwhelming superiority of the American fighter pilots lay in their number of hours aloft, five to ten times the number of sorties flown by their opponents.

And the ChiComs were still making the switch from dominant ground control to individual initiative.

The Flankers, however, hotly pursued by the Hornets, had not yet been caught because of the necessity of Johnny Reisman's aviators to first protect themselves from the Fulcrums that had dived wildly into their midst. Two Flankers had gone down, but ten were approaching Penghu Island. The Flanker fighter-bombers' specific target was postulated by *McCain*'s SSES to be Makung City on the island's west coast and Lintou Beach to the southeast. As a target, Makung, with only sixty thousand people and virtually no industry other than tourism and fishing, seemed to have been selected simply to terrorize the Penghu Islanders into not resisting the oncoming ChiCom invasion. Lintou Beach, however, as Reisman's RIO was able to call up on his compact target location file, made more military sense. In Makung, the ROC had stationed two battalions, about two thousand soldiers in all. The regular army's 1st Battalion and the 2nd Battalion's reservists manned batteries of U.S.-made M-48 Chaparral SAM missiles.

"Afterburners!" ordered Reisman, wanting to catch and keep the Flankers from bombing the island. He was aware that his Hornet's fuel consumption would put them beyond the point of no return, unable to return to the *McCain* without refueling from the S-3B Viking, which would be a high-risk proposition, given the swarm of MiG-29s still battling Drummer's Tomcats in the wild free-for-all. Switching off his afterburners, Reisman immediately felt the reduction in G forces, and was encouraged by his RIO advising him that a pair of Tomcats, having broken out of the supersonic killing zone, were hustling to assist the Hornets.

At twenty-six miles from Penghu, Drummer was about to go in at Mach 2.1 to attack the Flankers when he saw one of them break formation, coming at him nose-to-nose.

"Master arm on!" confirmed his RIO, fear and adrenaline marrying in the rush of excitement. "Am centering the T. Bandits jinxed sixteen miles. Centering dot. Fox one. Fox one." The Tomcat's AIM-7 Sparrow missile's detachment from the Tomcat, powered by its boost-sustained solid-fuel propellant, left its hard point in a sudden hiss, the sleek, twelve-foot-long Sparrow reaching Mach 4.2 only seconds after it shot out from its glove pylon. Drummer's RIO made sure the missile was receiving constant illumination from the Tomcat's fire-control triad of signal processor, radar, and updated responses computer.

"Eight miles!" cut in another Tomcat. "Fox one, Fox one." Then another, "Two for Lennox. Tally two! Tally two!" meaning Lennox had a visual of the red-eyed exhausts from a duo of Flankers. These two Sukhoi-30s with insufficient Fulcrum fighter cover had obviously decided they'd better take time to kill this Tomcat on their tail in order to have a successful bomb run on Makung and Lintou Beach.

"Five miles," said the Tomcat's RIO. "Select Fox *Two*." Then, "Four miles . . . Lock 'im up . . . lock 'im up. . . . Shoot Fox *Two*. Fox *Two*."

"Good kill! Good kill!" It was Lennox or some Tomcat pilot shouting his congratulations as they saw Drummer's Sparrow missile hit its target, or more accurately, when the Sparrow's big proximity-fused fragmentation warhead exploded several meters behind the Flanker, producing a massive shotgun effect, the Flanker's kerosene fuel tank vaporizing in an enormous orange-white bloom of fire. Two seconds before Drummer's kill shot, however, the Flanker's pilot had fired one of his R73s, or Russian-made A-11 Archer close-combat heat seekers, its contrail lost in a wisp of stratus, getting out of harm's way before Drummer's Sparrow struck the Flanker. The Archer missile was now tracking Aviator Lennox's Tomcat, which, at eleven thousand feet, had just fired its Sidewinder at the second of the two Flankers Lennox had spotted earlier.

Lennox's wingman, a short, wiry twenty-three-year-old from Waco, Texas, suddenly found himself the pursued. His Tomcat—glove vanes on the leading edges of the fixed wings extended to reduce the more than Mach 1 strain on the fighter's tail planes—made a tight right turn inside the Flanker's defensive right break. And so, in classic Red Baron style, Lennox was now immediately behind and in the Flanker's cone of vulnerability. When he saw the lime-green arc formed by his gun's computer impact line and gun sight's green circle move to the middle of his HUD image of the Flanker, he fired. The long stream of his Tomcat's six-barreled 20mm Vulcan, spewing out ninety rounds in less than a second, chopped up the Flanker's turbofans and right tail plane. A collision warning sounded in the Texan's cockpit, and he instinctively broke in the opposite direction, but didn't climb fast enough to avoid the wake of "dirty air" from the disintegration of the ChiCom fighter-bomber. The supersonic swarm of debris that had been the Flanker's nose radar and other white-hot debris thudded into the Tomcat's nacelle housing and was sucked into the huge, canted intakes of the F-14's left turbofan. The engine shut down immediately, and the Tomcat's cockpit was so badly pitted by blades from the Flanker's engines that Lennox's wingman lost all frontal vision through the HUD, the fighter's right intake struck by a piece of the Flanker's heavy and unexploded ordnance.

"Right engine's gone!" shouted his RIO.

"Eject," ordered the Texan.

"Roger!"

Plummeting seaward, their bird tumbling out of control, the Texan and his RIO, ever faithful to the aviator's code, still had full confidence in the efficacy of their plane's design, specifically in the reputation of the Martin-Baker seats. They had been so meticulously made that with the aircraft parked upon a tarmac, the zero-zero system would still eject the pilots high enough to have their chutes open and bring them safely down. Now, fighting the punishing G forces exerted on the tumbling Tomcat, the two men nevertheless managed to reach and pull their snakes. In a split second the explosive bolts fired, releasing the seat.

Both men's necks snapped like twigs, the canopy's fairing having been severely dented and thus locked by the impact of the Flanker's supersonic debris.

Lennox glimpsed the tumbling dot of the Tomcat on his green monitor, saw it swell into sudden luminescence as it smashed into the sea. But his attention was quickly hijacked by the tadpole shape streaking in on his radar, a missile fired from eight miles behind. Normally it would have taken the missile .8 seconds to reach him, but thanks to Typhoon Jane's headwinds, it took 1.2 seconds, time enough for Lennox's RIO to drop chaff and pop flares, hoping to confuse both the Archer's radar and infrared. The American ruse failed, however, the agility and maneuverability of the Russian-made missile so acute that despite Lennox's and his RIO's countermeasures, the ten-foot Archer was able to lock on via the ChiCom pilot's helmet-mounted sight, a full forty-two degrees off bore sight.

Lennox, his RIO, and their beloved machine disappeared from the FITCOMPRON's Prowler's radar.

This second explosion shocked the already stunned Combat Information Center in the *McCain*, the room so quiet that only the hum from the air conditioners' vents and the whir of the 24/7 digital disc recorder could be heard. Four men and a hundred million dollars lost in less than six seconds.

"Hope to hell our screen's working," opined a veteran chief petty officer, referring not to the CIC's blue board, but to the carrier's protective screen of Aegis cruisers, destroyers, frigates, and two attack subs whose sole reason for being there was to prevent a ChiCom "box" or missiles getting through to the heart of the CVBG.

In *McCain*'s SSES, the chief boffin called Admiral Crowley with more bad news. Seven, possibly eight, of the ChiCom Flankers had reached Penghu Island, penetrating its defensive ring of Chaparral SAM sites. In fact, five-man Chaparral crews—each made up of commander, driver, gunner, and two loaders—belonging to the reservists' battalion on Penghu, were still frantically launching Chaparrals. The fiery backblasts from quads of the eleven-ton U.S. missiles were clearly visible to the ChiComs' seven remaining Sukhoi fighter-bomber pilots. Quickly going to their Lyulka afterburners, they rapidly climbed to eleven thousand feet, placing themselves a thousand feet beyond the Chaparrals' maximum altitude.

From this high ground they fired a rain of air-to-surface TV-guided missiles at Penghu installations, and dropped seven 1,100-pound bombs, knocking out six of the quad Chaparral launchers in a series of head-thudding explosions whose gases created a dust storm that swept across the island before being blown leeward by gusts heralding Typhoon Jane's approach. The hurricane of shrapnel from the bombs, however, was not so readily dispersed, scything through the reservists, who, unlike the regular ROC troops in the 1st Battalion, had failed to dig enough slit trenches along Lintou Beach. Instead, the reservists had clumped together in the tactically futile but psychologically understandable belief that protection lay in numbers.

In Makung, panic reigned in the fish markets and town itself, clustered about the picturesque harbor, and families who would normally have fled down to fishing boats to make good their escape from any man-made assault on their small island were afraid to do battle with the huge seas stirred up by Jane. Taipei radio had now upgraded Jane to supertyphoon, the winds off Taiwan's east coast reportedly reaching 140 miles per hour with gusts to 180. It meant that even if the families of Makung, their town ablaze from the ChiCom bombing and strafing, managed to escape the wind-fanned inferno and reach their boats, their Taiwanese navy could not help them, the wind-whipped seas drowning all hope of rescue. Meanwhile, the Americans could not help much, their Rules of Engagement requiring them to hold their fire for fear of overshooting the enemy planes and killing Taiwanese civilians. Penghu's sacred banyan tree was also destroyed, having been used by the ChiCom bombers as their initial aiming point.

"Damn!" said Johnny Reisman. "Can't do a damn thing!"

Crowley and Cuso heard and shared their FITCOMPRON leader's frustration, his voice remarkably clear through the crackle and labored breathing of an aviator who had just overseen the worst aerial defeat of American arms in the last quarter century.

Within minutes of the ROC 1st Battalion on Penghu sounding the air raid warning, 350 presumed tourists trapped on the island had quickly sought refuge from the Flanker blitz by taking cover in and around the popular Fengkuei cave on the rocky southwestern isthmus of the island. When the air raid finally ended, these "tourists" emerged from their ad hoc shelter, heading toward the fiercely crackling ruins of Makung, armed with Kalashnikov 47s, bandoliers of 7.6mm ammunition, grenades,

and light but deadly 60mm mortars. The arms had been planted
months earlier by PLA navy commandos during clandestine
landings by diesel-electric subs that had come in close to
Penghu during stormy weather, the rough seas having sub-
sumed the already quiet running of the subs' battery-power
propulsion, making the ChiCom presence in the strait undetectable by even the best Taiwanese sonar.

The island was now hostage to the PLA.

CHAPTER TWENTY-EIGHT

"SO," PRONOUNCED CHOIR Williams, as the SpecFor
group watched CNN's Marte Price reporting the Chinese-U.S.
conflict in the Taiwan Straits. "Looks like we don't need to wait
for *Petrel*'s water sample results after all, me boyos. It's the
Chinese!"

Salvini nodded in agreement.

"Choir!" Aussie announced triumphantly. "I think you just
lost a bet, boyo." His tone, however, was devoid of the usual
follow-up jabs that characterized the relationship between Freeman's Special Forces team. The bloody animal and human carnage they had seen in the waters of *their* strait disallowed the
usual spirited repartee—at least for now.

"What d'you think, General?" Aussie asked.

Freeman's attention had shifted from Marte Price to the TV
screen's sidebar weather map of Typhoon Jane. "Doesn't make
sense," he concluded. "Starting a war on *two* fronts. Fundamen-
tal. Even for a superpower. Beijing attacking Taiwan and us at
the same time? Anyway, if they were going to do that, why one
offensive in the open, the other not?"

"Maybe," suggested Aussie, "their planned invasion of Taiwan—which we know they've always had on the shelf—was triggered prematurely by the Taiwanese firing the first shot. ChiComs had to react?"

"I think so," agreed Freeman, "and I'll tell you why. It's that damned typhoon. No planned offensive by Beijing would willingly battle that bitch and the Taiwanese armed forces at the same time."

"So you think Taipei did fire first?" asked Salvini.

"Don't know, Sal," answered Freeman. "Sometimes we never know who fired the first shot." He paused. "'Bout ourselves, war, or anything else. I don't know if the ChiComs started it, but something—don't ask me what—tells me they're not the ones sinking our ships here in Juan de Fuca." He glanced across at Choir. "I wouldn't claim that wager with Aussie just yet."

"Then who is it, General?" pressed Choir.

Before Freeman could answer, the phone rang with the Coast Guard's IMU test. The Darkstar-detected anomaly was positive. Definitely isotope-tagged. There was a problem, however, in that the isotope match-up was for the oil used by a Caribbean Panama-registered cruise ship, *Bermuda Star*. Obviously, it had illegally jettisoned or leaked it en route to either Vancouver or Seattle, the two major Northwest cruise ship ports.

"Shit a brick!" said Aussie, crushing the plastic water bottle from which he'd been drinking and throwing it violently into the wastebasket, the mood of the other three no different. For a few seconds no one spoke. But if Choir, Salvini, and Aussie's silence was a measure of their bitter disappointment in having failed to narrow the search for the killer sub whose sheer audacity Freeman couldn't help but grudgingly admire for the utter chaos and humiliation such a small gutsy force had brought about—as his own team had in the past—the silence afforded the general a moment to think, uninterrupted by the others' theories.

He switched off the TV and tossed the remote on his bed, which he'd remade after the maid service had been in—the blankets now so tightly tucked that a tossed quarter bounced off it—testimony to the fact that as much as he was an original maverick thinker in the armed forces, he also valued the small but valuable drills that reinforced respect for tradition. He knew that some of the old ideas "in the box" could still serve well in times of personal and national crisis. Going back to the box of boring procedures for a moment, he asked Salvini to go online and into Google, to do a search on the Net for cruise ships' arrivals and departures. In a minute Salvini saw that the *Bermuda Star* had been scheduled to arrive in Seattle a week before, that is, *before the sinkings*. But the entry was flagged with a red asterisk.

"Queer," observed the general, explaining his comment by pointing out that Seattle Port Authority showed *Bermuda Star* as "delayed." Having departed Lahaina, Maui, for Seattle two weeks ago, the cruise ship had been compelled to return to Hawaii due to an outbreak of a virulent SARS-like bronchial virus, over a dozen passengers removed to the Kaiser Foundation Hospital in Honolulu. And the ship had been quarantined.

"So it didn't get to Seattle," said Freeman, his earlier fatigue replaced by a surge of energy.

"I don't get it," confessed Sal.

"The sub got hold of however many barrels it needed," said Freeman, "from *Bermuda Star*. So if the sub sprang a leak, from its hydraulics, whatever—"

"And we took a sample of the leak," cut in Aussie, "we'd think it was from this *Bermuda Star*. Only our terrorists," he elaborated, "didn't figure on the cruise ship coming down with a bug, having to stay quarantined in Hawaii."

Freeman was on the phone to the Coast Guard station at Port Townsend, which was known to have the best supply of rigid inflatables. He wanted a twenty-four-man RIB for his team and any available Coast Guard divers.

"General," the duty officer told him, "we've had to prioritize. This war's being fought on so many fronts. The best we can do is a sixteen-footer. And we haven't got any spare divers."

"*Prioritize!* We've found the sub!—well, at least where it's been. If we can trace the tail on that tadpole spill before it's sucked out or chopped up by the tides, we may be able to backtrack it to the bastards' operating base."

"General, I'm following orders," said the duty officer. "You find a sub base and I'll request antisub aircraft from Whidbey."

"That's no damn good if it's a cave. Can't drop depth charges into a cave. I need more divers—SpecFor guys like mine. I've only got three,'sides myself. If you can—"

"Hold on, General."

Freeman could hear someone interrupting in the background, then the Coast Guard DO came on again. "Young Peter wants to go with you."

"Peter—"

"Dixon," said the DO. "We'll send him over with an RIB. Sixteen-footer."

"Fine," said Freeman, who knew the duty officer was right. Everyone *was* spread thin.

It was obvious to Aussie, Choir, and Sal that the general, for all his prodigious memory, didn't recognize Dixon's name.

"Dixon's the swim buddy of that guy Albinski," said Aussie. "Albinski was the one they winched up on *Petrel*, smothered in kelp."

"Good," said Freeman. "He'll be keen to smoke those bastards out."

"How 'bout David?" asked Aussie. "Maybe he can help."

Choir and Sal looked uneasily at the general. They were glad it was his decision, not theirs.

He surprised them, however, by asking, "What d'you boys think?"

"Well . . ." Sal began awkwardly, becoming tongue-tied.

He deferred to Choir, the Welshman's shrug, like Sal's silence, also a diplomatic abstention.

"Aussie?" the general pressed. "You know the answer, same as these two ninnies. Don't you?" He said "ninnies" with the rough affection born of long team membership.

"He could be a liability," said Aussie quietly.

Freeman nodded, then looked at Salvini. "You asked from loyalty, Sal. I understand that. I admire that, but we all know that David's gammy right arm can barely hold the Bullpup he's been struggling with. Handling an RIB in this sea would be a hell of a lot more difficult than that." He paused. "Brentwood would make the same decision."

The three others agreed, but Aussie wasn't so sure. David

Brentwood was the kind of leader who, probably to a fault, would take a chance, having great faith in the power of will. He had often cited the extraordinary determination of the Vietnamese against all odds. Morale might not move mountains, as Freeman himself was often wont to say, but "it can sure as hell climb them." Then again, the general's responsibility was to the team, not any one individual.

"Call him, Aussie," Freeman said. "He'll be back at Fort Lewis by now. Tell him to sign out an antitank launcher with HE rounds—just in case we bump into the bastards. It'll give him a sense of lending a hand—well, at least doing something."

"I'm on to it," said Aussie, dialing Brentwood's cell. He hoped he wouldn't answer. Who wanted to be a gofer?

"Might piss him off," said Salvini.

"Oh, thanks for that, Sal. That really helps."

"We'll see," said Choir, all of which left Aussie wondering why Freeman wasn't calling his protégé.

To Aussie's relief, David didn't answer, so Lewis left him a quick but succinct message to bring them the antitank launcher from Fort Lewis.

CHAPTER TWENTY-NINE

DESPITE THE ASSISTANCE rendered by a Coast Guardsman who volunteered, on his own time, to accompany him to satisfy U.S. Coast Guard regulations, Dixon had trouble getting the RIB out of Port Townsend harbor on his way to pick up Freeman's team at Port Angeles.

It wasn't so much the gut-slamming chop created by the incoming tide that delayed the RIB's departure, but the disturbing number of oil-matted seabirds that had been washed into the harbor. Dixon had seen enough dead wildlife, and the possibility that some of the gulls, cormorants, and other birds might still be alive haunted him. Accordingly, he slowed down to no more than two knots, while the Coast Guard volunteer filled the time by double-checking what few provisions he'd been able to second from the already drained USCG quartermaster's supplies and the antitank launcher that Captain Brentwood had dutifully brought up from Fort Lewis.

Unaware of Brentwood's injury, Dixon had been about to ask David, whom he'd seen on CNN touring the hospital, if he'd like to come along on the investigation of Darkstar's anomaly when Dixon noticed the difficulty the Medal of Honor winner had lifting the relatively light fifteen-pound AT-4 rocket launcher unit.

As if reading young Dixon's mind, David had stayed to help push the sixteen-foot-long Bruiser off from shore, but his Vibram boot slipped on an oil-slicked rock, throwing him off balance. His immobile right arm instinctively flew out to regain balance, but instead he went, as Aussie Lewis would have said, "A over tit," and fell into the oily muck at the water's edge, able to use only his left hand to push himself to the kneeling position. The injured right arm that had failed him with the new ambidextrous Bullpup was draped in oil-slicked kelp washing ashore amid an offal of other diesel-soaked detritus. Out of respect, an embarrassed Dixon and the Guardsman had looked quickly away.

"What's wrong with him?" the Coast Guard man inquired, looking back.

"Dunno," Dixon replied, his attention arrested by the realization that the antitank launcher Brentwood had brought to the Bruiser was a Swedish disposable launcher/rocket. Once you fired it, that was it.

"Scuttlebutt," said the Coast Guard crewman, "is that he screwed up on some gig in 'Ghanistan?"

Dixon took offense at the green crewman adopting "'Ghanistan" instead of "Afghanistan." That was the right of warriors who had *been* there—or was he simply overreacting under the stress of the situation and the nagging doubt that *he* had somehow screwed up in failing to look out for Rafe Albinski, his swim buddy who'd literally had the life squeezed out of him? The bloody toothpastelike ooze had been so repellant that Frank Hall, after talking with Albinski's wife, had the diver's remains cremated at Port Townsend's hospital and scattered in a quick burial at sea from *Petrel*'s stern.

Freeman, Aussie, Salvini, and Choir were waiting at the Port Angeles wharf, loaded for bear. By the time Dixon arrived, they were already in their wet suits, with Draeger rebreathers and extra pouches of ammunition for Freeman, and Aussie's grenade-launcher-equipped Heckler & Koch submachine guns, as well as Kevlar vests, stun, smoke, and HE grenades, "7" flashlight— with its right-angle shape—Dakine hydrater camelback, plus night vision goggles with flip-down infrared visor, and what they called "other assorted goodies."

For Salvini, the weapon of choice was a waterproofed stripped-down lightweight "crap tolerant" laser dot, night-scoped M-16, and a hip-holstered sawed-off shotgun. In the unlikely event of an enemy in the distance, a trawler perhaps, this customized M-16 would give the team of six men, which included Dixon and the Coast Guard crewman, a reach far beyond the shorter but lethal HK submachine guns packed by the general and Aussie. And Choir, with his pistol-grip, Mossberg twelve-gauge shotgun, its pump-action mag loaded with alternate, double-ought and steel/flechette dart rounds, would provide additional firepower.

Freeman knew it was probably too much to expect that they would actually make visible contact with the midget sub. Then again, he remembered the astronomically high odds against the winning numbers of the New York lottery being 911 exactly a year after 9/11. All he could reasonably hope for was to find the general area from which the midget sub was operating and then call in for one of the 170-foot Mk IV Hurricane B class Coastal Patrol ships. These had a dash speed of 35 knots and bristled with heavy machine guns, chain guns, and pedestals for Stinger SAMs, plus a 30mm Gatling canon with the same armor-piercing power as the famously ugly and deadly A-10 Thunderbolt. The latter was a high-set, twin-engined tank buster that wiped the grins of derision from its uppity fighter cousins when it virtually destroyed Saddam Hussein's tank corps and anything else that moved in the Iraqi desert in the war of 2003. But when he'd suggested to Coast Guard HQ in Seattle that they keep a Hurricane craft on standby to assist his team should they find any signs of the midget sub's base of operations, the reply was polite but firm. Like all Coast Guard stations, they were swamped, and the Coast Guard admiral took the opportunity to get a load off his chest.

"General, there's no way I can release a CP ship. We've only three in the whole Puget Sound area, and we're using them with everything else we've got to try to bring some sort of minimal control—and I emphasize *minimal*—in every marina from Seattle to the San Juans. It's sheer unmitigated panic out there. Do you have any idea how many marinas there are in the Puget Sound, the San Juan Islands, and Juan de Fuca Strait area?"

"Yes, I under—" began Freeman, trying to get into the one-way conversation, but he realized the Coast Guard admiral was as much an ear-basher as himself.

"Over six hundred," the admiral went on, giving Freeman no time to reply. "And it's a mob scene at each one. Our refugees aren't listening to our assurances about tolerable levels of radiation, and are bidding like crazy for transport across the sound to the safety of Interstate 5. They want out—south to Oregon, Idaho, Nevada, Utah—as long as it's away from the Strait of Juan de Fuca. Local cops are overwhelmed. Washington, D.C., is trying to get the National Guard in to maintain order, but the arteries are jammed solid. Besides, Washington doesn't understand that the Northwest is waterways. We need *coast* guards more than the *National* Guards. Add to that the fact that the Pentagon is calling up reserves all over."

"But dammit, Admiral, the White House surely wants me to—"

"General, we've been caught with our pants down. We're getting hit on three fronts. There's a resurgence of terrorism in Afghanistan, terrorism in our own swimming pool here, and now we're on a knife edge with this Taiwan-ChiCom shit. We've got a new kind of world war on *three* fronts, General.

Have you seen CNN—they're calling the refugees in the North-west 'America on the Run'!"

"How about the NR-1B?" cut in Freeman. "It should be here by now, and—"

"There you're in luck, General. My 2IC tells me it's arrived on Whidbey, only five to six miles from the Keystone ferry ramp. Its crew'll be the next flight in. I'm sure Admiral Jensen'll get it launched as quickly as possible and send it out to you the moment the crew's aboard."

Keystone, Freeman knew, was approximately sixty miles to the east, on Whidbey Island. He also knew that, despite the wondrous gizmology of the relatively small 146-by-12.5-foot-diameter, nuclear-powered sub run by a crew of only two officers, three enlisted men, and two scientists, its maximum speed was said to be no more than eight knots on the surface and ten knots submerged. The general had learned from his contacts, however, that for the NR-1B it was closer to 25 knots surface speed, thirty submerged.

Even so, that would mean at least a two-hour wait, if all went well, before it could reach his SpecFor team.

"Do we go on or wait?" he asked the team.

"I say go," said Dixon, who'd remained silent to this point, somewhat overawed by the general's reputation, though less so now that he was seeing him in his wet suit, a little paunchier than the rest of them. Dixon was also surprised by the fact that a general would put an operational decision to a vote, the young SEAL making the mistake of so many who didn't understand that supremely confident leadership was unafraid to put it to a vote if time allowed, and that it was only the insecure machos who needed to be making unilateral decisions all the time.

"If we wait," said Aussie, "that oil tail could disappear, dispersed to hell and gone by the riptide. Then we'll have bugger all to show the NR-1B and all its superduper sensors!"

"Choir, Sal?" asked the general, who then turned to the Coast Guard crewman and Dixon. "Lieutenant Dixon, Jorge?"

Jorge Alvaro was astonished that his opinion—that of an ordinary seaman—was being sought by none other than the legendary "George C. Scott." Nobody, including his wife, asked him his opinion. Everyone, from his mother-in-law to USCG brass, was always *telling* him what to do. He heard the Welshman, Choir Williams, and the guy from Brooklyn—Salvatore, or something like that—say they might as well wait for the NR-1B, and the guy they called Aussie and his USCG comrade, Dixon, still arguing that they might save time by pursuing the oil spill now. The general wasn't saying anything, Jorge realizing that for once his opinion was not only being sought, but that Jorge Alvaro, the son of migrant Mexican farm laborers, held the deciding vote. He didn't want to court danger, but it was unlikely they'd see the sub. They'd just trace the spill, then call in the NR-1B. Besides, what if the midget struck again—this morning—and it became known he and the others had been bobbing around, waiting for the NR-1B?

"I say we go look for where that oil came from."

It was obviously what Freeman wanted. "All right, coxswain," he told Alvaro. "Get this RIB moving."

In seconds the sixteen-foot rigid inflatable's twin caterpillar diesels roared to 830 horsepower, the twin water jets thrusting the boat forward against the wind, the console's speedometer needle shaking at 28 knots. Every one of the six-man team, except Coxswain Alvaro, who stood at the Perspex-shielded control panel, was sitting on the fiberglass seats, one hand firmly gripping the aluminum steady bar, their weapons, stocks first, in the quick-release gun rack beside them. Freeman felt the painful arthritic jab in his left knee, an old war wound aggravated by the intense cold of the strait, and Peter Dixon had an uncomfortable sense of déjà vu.

"They're Chinese!" Aussie shouted into the breath-robbing wind. "Five bucks, Choir."

"Big spender!" retorted Choir, immediately drenched by a five-footer slamming hard amidships.

"All right!" Aussie yelled back. "Ten bucks!"

Choir seemed to nod, but in the kidney-whacking ride, Aussie couldn't be sure.

"You hear me, you little Welsh bastard?"

"Ten dollars!" confirmed Choir.

"Ooh, lah de bloody lah! Ten *dollars*! Anyone else?"

"Al Qaeda!" shouted Salvini.
"You're on, Brooklyn!"

Reboarding the Kiowa Scout for the early morning hop back
to Fort Lewis, David Brentwood was shivering so badly from
his dunking in the oily scum of Port Angeles that the pilot, a
quiet young redhead who obviously felt sorry for him, could
hear his teeth chattering. She tried some small talk as they
gained height above the waters of the strait and the wide slab of
Admiralty Inlet, but David, clutching an Army-issue blanket
about his oil-reeking body, had closed his eyes, the bunker-C
fuel absorbed by the blanket stinging them, his anger at the human and environmental havoc caused by the terrorists inflamed
by his inability to join his life-long buddies in striking back. The
David he knew was not with him; instead it was a morose, uncharacteristically sullen Brentwood who curtly thanked the pilot and ducked beneath the Kiowa's still-whirling blades,
scurrying away like some bedeviled pilgrim for whom the storm
had proved too much, and hating himself for his sullenness and
self-pity.

CHAPTER THIRTY

A QUARTER MILE from the Keystone ferry, from which the
NR-1B would slide into the strait where its somewhat
cumbersome-looking conning tower and bow would come into
their own, the advance outriders heard a rushing sound. It was
as if, one said, a stream of water from a hose had struck a pile of
fallen leaves. It was a fuse.

The blacktop erupted with such a bang that the sound reverberated through the NR-1B on its trailer as if it had been struck

with some enormous sledgehammer, the "singing" of the metal continuing for several seconds after the last of the black pebble-encrusted bitumen had fallen back down on and about the road, one lump felling an outrider, another two blown off their motor-cycles.

Admiral Jensen had already said, "Jesus!" at least five times, this followed by an incoherent rage of profanity as, leaping from his Humvee, he raced towards the NR-1B against the advice of his traumatized driver. The Marine escorts fanned out speedily in U formation toward the launch point, laying down a hail of automatic fire that after six seconds all but denuded the surrounding salmonberry and blackberry bushes, only a leaf or two remaining after the savage onslaught of the Marines' small arms fire.

There were no bodies to be found, only the bullet-flayed remains of the detonation cord that had been craftily buried, running from the salmonberry bushes through the sodden earth to the road. The long slit in which the det cord had been buried was patched and dusted in places with crushed gravel to make it look indistinguishable from a thousand other cracks on Highway 20.

"No one there, sir," the Marine CO told Admiral Jensen, who was fighting to regain self-control as several Marines, rushing from the Humvee with its fire extinguisher, doused some small fires on the sub's wooden trailer frame.

"No one?" said Jensen.

"No, sir. Must have been a remote detonation." The Marine swept his M-16 across the panorama of gently rolling hills north of the ferry landing that they could now see. The big metal stanchions bracing the docking area were turning golden in the early morning sun that was burning off the mist that had crept inland across the fields and cranberry bogs. "Somewhere up there, probably," said the Marine CO, now signaling his heavily armed men to secure the quarter mile of road that curved gently ahead to the deserted ferry terminal, the small waiting room, washrooms, and chained red pop machine appearing particularly forlorn.

A Marine corporal took his squad to make sure the building wasn't occupied or booby-trapped, everyone shaken, whether they showed it or not, by the sabotaged road. The admiral was confused, because the Marines were proceeding as if the explosion hadn't damaged the NR-1B, until, in a joyous moment, he saw that, despite the sandy soil and lumps of straw-colored passpalum grass that partially covered the sub's nose and the elongated conning tower, there was no hole or even a dent evident. But he knew that if even a hairline fracture was discovered, it would mean the integrity of the vessel would be violated. This would prevent the Navy's state-of-the-art research sub, capable of going to three thousand feet, from diving to even a few feet below the surface.

Feeling as if his heart was pushing an obstruction up into his throat, his breathing becoming increasingly difficult, Jensen approached the craft in a state of incipient panic. With the help of four Marines and his driver, he began brushing off the dirt, sand, and passpalum. "Look carefully," he enjoined them. "Each of us take a section and go over it with—" He paused, his breathing shallow and rapid. "Carefully," he said.

"You all right, sir?" asked the Marine CO.

"Carefully," Jensen repeated.

"Pricks made a hash of it, sir," said the Marine. "Looks fine. They didn't use enough C-4. Beat up the truck cabin and the trailer some. But everything else looks hunky dory."

The admiral heard him but didn't answer, as if any positive response would jinx his inspection of the one vessel that might find the midget sub and salvage his reputation. He closed his eyes for a moment, the Marine CO thinking he was in pain when in fact he was praying. He remembered what his mother had told him: "Never ask God for anything for selfish reasons—ask that *His* will be done, not yours." Jensen prayed that the NR-1B's structural integrity remained sound. There was no gash in the nose or nacelle that housed the sophisticated side-scan array sonar. No sign of damage on the small conning tower or the mast array housing. "Thank Christ," he murmured. "Amen."

"You morons!" Jensen's driver shouted at the amphitheater of fields and hills to the north. "You screwed up, you al Qaeda bastards!" The admiral felt duty bound to tell him to be quiet, but said nothing. The truth was, his driver was expressing the same surge of relief that the admiral and his Marine escort were now feeling: a release from the pent-up tension wrought by the slow, painstaking drive down from the Naval Air Station near Oak Bay toward the ferry.

Jensen, however, was too experienced a commander to leave anything to chance. He didn't ream out the Marines as he'd wanted to do when he heard the road explode under the vessel— it would have been virtually impossible to detect the fake road repair that had allowed the saboteurs to feed the det cord and C4 under the bitumen's surface. Instead he simply told the Marine commander to secure the small ferry terminal, and now decided that he'd send a dive pair down to check the water in and around the dock. For all they knew, the road explosion could be a cover to divert the Marines' attention away from the dock, where ear-muff charges could be placed on the pilings and exploded once the NR-1B was in the water. High-temperature oxyacetylene-like cuts from muff charges could easily sever H-shaped dock pilings and supports, causing them to come crashing down onto the superstructure of the 146-foot-long sub.

Unfortunately, his call to the Coast Guard ended in frustration. The last of their standby divers, Peter Dixon, was with General Freeman, and like all other divers in the strait, Puget Sound, and adjacent waters, he was doing triple time, trying to cope with the most pressing of the myriad diving tasks created by the recent rash of sinkings, including that of the *Georgia Queen*, most of whose passengers had died. The other thing that frustrated Jensen was the news that apparently Douglas Freeman had gone out without assist from the NR-1B. "I'd've thought Freeman would've waited for the NR-1B," Jensen told the USCG admiral in Seattle.

"Maybe, Walt, but you know how Doug Freeman is. Charge!"

Jensen held his tongue. Freeman was a glory hound, but he was also the one who had told Marte Price that it was his—Admiral Jensen's—idea to send out Darkstar for a "close-in" run along the reverse seven of the Olympic peninsula's northern Juan de Fuca shore and down south from Cape Flattery to the national wildlife refuge. It had been an unselfish act, Jensen

knew, on Freeman's part to help a disgraced admiral regain
something of his reputation after the disastrous loss of the *Utah*.

"Any of you fellas swim?" Jensen asked the Marines, his
question clearly a request for volunteers.

Four Marines immediately stepped forward.

"Just in for a few minutes, guys—long enough to check the
pilings. Okay?"

The four men stripped to their skivvies, taunted good-
naturedly by their comrades, "Brass monkey balls in there! You
won't last more'n three minutes, cowboy!"

The remaining Marines used their compact field glasses to
zoom in on the pilings and launch ramp, seeing nothing suspicious, while the four ad hoc divers plunged in. They were immediately struck by the extraordinary clarity of these Northwest
waters. They saw thick clumps of barnacles, oysters, and other
marine crustaceans, any of which could hide explosive, which
was infamously easy to camouflage. Still, they could see no
wires, no det cord. The four Marines' lips were soon dark blue,
bodies shivering as uncontrollably as David Brentwood's had
the previous evening at Port Angeles.

"Looks clear, sir," the Marine CO informed the admiral,
adding a caveat for his own protection. " 'Course, you never
know."

Jensen hesitated, wondered and worried. Apart from anything
else, this was a billion-dollar machine in his charge.

"What's that?" asked one of the Marines, pointing to a dot,
obviously some kind of vessel, coming from the direction of
Port Townsend, ten miles southwest across Admiralty Inlet.

The dot on the inlet's cobalt blue was Washington State's
Port Townsend–Keystone ferry, due to arrive at Keystone in
twenty-five minutes.

"What the hell's it doin'?" asked a gum-chewing Marine.

It was the question on everyone's mind. Surely the carnage
unleashed in the last seventy-six hours argued against any resumption of normal ferry traffic.

"What if they've taken over the ferry, Admiral?" the Marine
CO asked.

"Using it to stop our launch," said the admiral, "now that they've seen their road mining didn't work."

No one knew who "they" might be, but the sinking of billions of dollars of U.S. naval ships clearly had been done with the aid of damn good intelligence. They'd known precisely where the ships would be and *when*. And it was more than likely that the same HUMINT who had informed the terrorists of this would know the "road-blow" had failed to perforate the high-tensile steel of the NR-1B.

Jensen wasted no time and ordered one of his COMSUBPAC-9's two 170-foot Coastal Patrol ships that normally serviced Hood Canal and Puget Sound to intercept the suspect Townsend-Keystone ferry with all possible haste, to stop the ferry and have a boarding party investigate.

"Any resistance," Jensen instructed the Coastal Patrol ship's captain and thirty-two-man crew, "is to be met with deadly force. I say again, deadly force."

The two Hurricane-class Coastal Patrol Ships, unlike the three Hurricanes commanded by USCG Seattle, were on picket duty in Hood Canal, their sole responsibility to guard the entrance to Admiralty Inlet and the waters north and south of the Hood Canal bridge. It was through the Hood Canal's retractable section that Jensen's U.S. Hunter Killer and Boomer ballistic missile subs had to pass during their egress from Bangor Base, through the strait, on their way to open, rolling ocean west of Cape Flattery. While one of COMSUBPAC-GRU-9's two Hurricanes remained on station at the sabotage-susceptible bridge, the other, the USS *Skate*, primarily responsible for the waters north of the bridge, set off immediately into the Prussian blue stretch of Admiralty Inlet, toward the suspect ferry eighteen miles to the north.

With a fuel-guzzling "dash" speed of 35 knots, the *Skate*'s estimated time of interdiction with the ferry was fourteen minutes, at a point plus or minus three miles from Keystone. The *Skate*'s captain and third officer, their binoculars glued to them, devoutly hoped that there would be no more "floaters," whom they'd feel they should stop to pick up. The best the *Skate*'s skipper could do, similar to what Frank Hall had done on *Petrel*, was to have one of their two inflatables ready with a paramedic and three other able seamen standing by.

"Anything, lookouts?" called the captain.

"No, sir," came the answer from starboard and port. "Just a lot o' dead fish. They smell somethin'—"

"Very good. Keep sharp."

"Twelve minutes fourteen seconds till ETI," responded the third mate.

"Very good."

By now the *Skate*'s radio officer, like Jensen's Marine guard contingent, was trying unsuccessfully to make contact with the ferry. No response.

"Something's wrong," opined the patrol ship's mate. "Twelve minutes ETI."

Every skipper in the Northwest was on edge, to put it mildly, and the *Skate*'s captain sounded Action Stations.

Suddenly the ship came alive with dozens of crew who only minutes before had been comfortably in the rhythm of their watch. They were now running along with off-watch personnel, pulling on helmets and flak jackets, manning their stations from the stern's Mk 38 gun and Stinger launcher pedestal to the ship's two .50 caliber machine guns, its two 7.6mm machine guns, grenade launchers, and, up forward, another Mk 38 25mm chain gun.

Yet despite all this armament, many of the *Skate*'s crew felt uncomfortably vulnerable. The 170-foot-long, twenty-five-foot-wide ship was, in their view, grossly undergunned for its size, and presented a big enough target for surface-to-surface or air-launched missiles of the kind that had killed the night watchman at Cherry Point and set the whole complex ablaze.

"Don't sweat it," a petty officer assured the young chain gunner. "It's only a friggin' ferry we're coming to. People and cars, ol' buddy. That's all."

"Yeah, but what nut would take a ferry out when there's a midget sub still around?" He was thinking of the Canadian ferry *Georgia Queen*.

The petty officer shrugged. "Ah, he's probably taking stores over for Whidbey's Naval Air Station."

"Without an escort? Gimme a break!"

"ETI nine minutes thirty seconds," the captain's voice boomed out. "Stay focused. Stay alert. ROE—no firing unless I give the word. I say again, no firing unless I give the word."

"Yeah yeah," said one of the gunners. "I get it." But the captain would repeat his order, knowing that, given the ongoing trauma of the past few days, everyone was on edge. No one on *Skate* had been sleeping well. It was also a common complaint ashore.

"ETI nine minutes."

CHAPTER THIRTY-ONE

WHEN WU LING heard the knock on her door in Beijing's Haidan District, it was near midnight, and she feared it was the Gong An Bu. Instead it was a neighbor, an elderly woman who had lost a son in the fighting against the terrorists in Kazakhstan. A member of the PLA Corrections Service, she came to Wu Ling in civilian clothes and gave her a well-worn postcard. The card, Wu Ling thought, looked as if it had been carried around for some time, an assumption borne out by the fact it had been postmarked two weeks earlier. Wu Ling gave the uninspiring picture of one of the Forbidden City's 9,999 rooms only a cursory glance.

The corrections officer left quickly, disappearing into one of the maze of *hutongs*.

The note from Chang wasn't long: twelve lines. He wrote that he was fine, the prison food bad, and the Central Committee blaming him for the setbacks the army was experiencing in

Kazakhstan. Li Kuan's terrorists had more sophisticated weapons than anyone had anticipated. He missed her, but he had friends, "and tell as many of them as you can what's happened to me." He was sure his 12th Army and the other PLA divisions would soon regain the offensive, and then they'd have to let him out of jail. He missed her and "bamboo in the wind," the last a sexual reference to something he'd taught her when she first became his concubine, then his lover.

It was his writing, all right. She made a photocopy and sent it to Charlie Riser, Cultural Attaché, U.S. Embassy, Xiu Shui Bei Jie 3, Chaoyang District, Beijing. Maybe Mandy's father could use the information to embarrass Beijing and the Nanjing Military District into admitting the ridiculous lie that her lover and protector wasn't in perpetual conference but was being used as a "scapegoat"—she remembered the word from Mr. Riser—for Beijing's failures in Kazakhstan. She wasn't a fool—she also sent copies of the postcard, in good quality, opaque envelopes, to those who were still General Chang's friends in the Politburo.

Riser took his copy straight to the military attaché, Bill Heinz. "Bill, I *knew* they were lying," he said. "Look at this."

Heinz didn't immediately look, preoccupied as he was with the two-China war. It still wasn't possible to nail it down—who'd actually started it. Not that it mattered now that the typhoon's atrocious weather put pay to the idea of any ChiCom invasion of Taiwan, at least for the foreseeable future. But Beijing now had a foothold on Penghu as well as Matsu, a fact that for now the United States, preoccupied as it was with the catastrophe in its own waters, wasn't disposed to remedy. The home front had priority.

Finally he looked at Riser's copy of the postcard sent to Wu Ling. "So?"

"Well, it proves I was right. Chang is in jail. And if I can see him—I mean he talks about Li Kuan being in Kazakhstan—and get more details about—"

"You want me to use my connections to find out what prison he's in."

"Yes."

"We've got to use our informants sparingly, Charlie. It's like capital. You can't spend it on—"

"You think it's frivolous?"

"No, no, no. Hell, no. But right now we've just had a war across the strait."

"Which one?"

"Exactly. I've got orders from Washington to spend 24/7 on future PRC-ROC relations. Nothing else."

"You won't help?"

"Of course I will, Charlie; but it's gonna have to be on the fly. Can't promise more than that. I can ask questions about Kazakhstan." There was an awkward pause. He knew Riser was still hurting over Mandy, but Riser would always be hurting, and the reality was, Riser would never see Li Kuan. Never get near him.

"I'll ask questions," he told Riser. "Something might come up."

But Riser could tell his embassy colleague held no hope, and the truth was, despite his own resolve to see Li Kuan brought to justice, he felt hopeless too.

CHAPTER THIRTY-TWO

"ETI THREE MINUTES," advised the *Skate*'s third mate.

The Port Townsend–Keystone ferry was five miles from the Keystone dock. "Still no radio response, Admiral," *Skate*'s captain reported to Jensen. "We're going to siglamp."

"Very well."

Only a handful of *Skate*'s thirty-five officers and crew had ever seen a signal lamp in action, the brisk, sharp, louvered flashes of light in Morse alien and amusingly old-fashioned in their nanotech computer age. Still, a young able seaman who'd volunteered for the course in signal lamp communication—or "dinosaur blinking," as it was derisively referred to by Navy nerds—suddenly found himself the center of attention on *Skate*. If the ferry skipper—they were almost always retired Coast Guard captains—understood the "dinosaur blinker" and hove to as he was being ordered, it might prevent some ugly stuff.

As *Skate*'s signal lamp flashed golden above the blue of Admiralty Inlet and the patrol ship drew closer, only a quarter mile from the ferry, several gunners checking their laser-aiming point boxes were surprised to see that there were no vehicles on any of the ferry's three decks. And no one on deck.

"Damn ghost ship!" said a starboard gunner.

"On autopilot," suggested an increasingly nervous second mate, the third mate organizing the boarding party.

"Damn peculiar!" conceded *Skate*'s captain. "Slow to twelve knots."

"Slow to twelve knots, aye, sir."

The sudden decrease from dash speed to twelve knots created a surge of water from the stern that broached the afterdeck. But there was none of the gusto of a wave breaking over the bow, exiting quickly, foaming through the scuppers. Instead, the water sloshing against *Skate* from astern seemed markedly lethargic.

The starboard door of the ferry's bridge flew open and a heavy, bearded individual stepped out, bullhorn in hand. "What in hell are you doin'?"

"What is your cargo?" asked *Skate*'s captain.

"Classified," came the reply. "Headed for Keystone."

"Stop your engines and prepare to receive a boarding party from USS *Skate*."

"What in hell for?"

"Prepare for boarding," *Skate*'s captain instructed the first officer, who gave the winch man the signal to lower the RIB.

Few reporters had qualms about using their sex appeal and charm to get a story, but Marte Price did it better than most. She had even bedded the formidable Freeman once because, she'd confided to a friend, she liked his gruff intelligence and manly disposition, so much more attractive than the petty, self-indulgent young studs of the entertainment world. Most were more interested in their coiffed hair and makeup than what was going on in the real world, where men like Freeman and his Spec Ops warriors were at the sharp end of things. So that Bel Air brats could pout over multimillion-dollar contracts, she thought, and America's kids could go to school without living in the perpetual chaos of hatred that marked the totalitarianism of much of the non-Western world.

Compared to Douglas Freeman, the fiftyish captain of the Port Townsend–Keystone ferry was a pushover for her. He redirected his stare from the tightly sheathed orbs of her Angora sweater to his radar, amusing the third mate, who, standing behind Marte as the *Skate* first hailed them, gazed without embarrassment at her curvaceous derriere enveloped in a pair of tan microfiber pants that seemed no thicker than Saran Wrap. The ferry's captain, annoyed that the *Skate* was making such a "big deal" of his radio being out, reverting to a signal lamp, lifted his bullhorn again and told the *Skate* he was on a tight schedule. "I'm transporting highly classified personnel to Keystone."

"Who are they?"

"None of your business."

This retort snapped the ferry's third mate out of his reverie with Marte Price's anatomy. Aware of the guns bristling all over the *Skate*, he dared suggest to his captain that he should welcome the boarding party, which was now bobbing up and down in their RIB immediately aft of the *Skate*.

"I was specifically told by Washington," the ferry captain told his mate, "not to allow anyone on board other than the NR-1B's scientific party and Ms. Price's assistants, and she is only permitted a camera interview with them for later broadcast, subject to the military censors and—"

"We're coming aboard! Stand by to assist!"

Admiral Jensen, watching through his binoculars from the Keystone ramp, was as perplexed by the boarding party as Marte Price aboard the ferry. But to the Marines, there was nothing perplexing about it—it was FUBAR, situation normal, fucked up beyond all recognition, a classic case, the age of electronic wizardry notwithstanding, of one branch of the government not knowing what another was doing. In this case, someone, somewhere, had failed to notify the admiral that the military airlift flight scheduled to deliver NR-1B's two scientists and their crew from the east coast to NAS Whidbey had been canceled due to anonymous but "credible" bomb threats. Instead of having the NR-1B's personnel from out of Newport en route to Keystone, the new delivery point selected was Port Townsend.

As the *Skate*'s RIB approached, the bellicose ferry captain, reverting to his high school macho in front of Marte Price, was about to call up the four heavily armed military police who had been assigned to guard the NR-1B team on the cafeteria deck.

Marte, quick to see the possibility of tragedy and brushing her hair back, its sheen enhanced by the early morning sun, said, "Captain, you're handling this superbly. I wonder, though, if it wouldn't be just as well to lend them a hand. You know, everyone's so jittery these days. Besides, I was wondering if I could get a shot of you welcoming the Navy aboard. Brothers in arms, you know. I think the American people need to see that sort of thing. What d'you think?" Her smile could have launched a thousand RIBs.

"Er, well—" began the captain.

Marte was hurrying the cameraman. "You think you could put on your cap?" she asked the ferry skipper. "I think that would give us just the right air of authority."

"What—my cap?"

"Yes."

"Huh—I guess, if you think—"

The *Skate*'s mate snapped him a salute from the RIB. That did it. Marte heard an intake of air, the captain's chest visibly expanding, his waist morphing from a generous 44 to an alarmingly fit 36, possibly even a 34. The captain barked at a deckhand, "Look lively!" and brusquely indicated that the RIB party be given prompt assistance up the rope ladder. Another deckhand, hastily unfurling the wooden-slatted ladder against the ferry's side, all but knocked the *Skate*'s mate out of the RIB.

"Steady on, man!" barked the captain with the authority of a Royal Navy chief.

"They're aboard, sir," the *Skate*'s OOD informed the gunship's captain via his walkie-talkie.

"I can see that, Rolston! Who's he got on board?"

Freeman's RIB was taking punishment, Alvaro, at the console, doing all he could to cross the ocean swells that had rolled in through the choke point between Vancouver Island and the Olympic peninsula. Because of the rain that periodically poured down on the Olympic peninsula—up to twelve feet a year on Mount Olympus itself—hundreds of waterfalls cascaded here and there over rock cliffs into the sea, new falls born overnight as the Pacific-bred storms caused fresh erosion of the peninsula. To the bitter disappointment of Freeman's six-man recon team, when they reached the position, the isotope anomaly had disappeared.

"Probably sucked out in the high tide's drain-off from the strait," said Sal, his voice all but drowned out.

"Either that," shouted Aussie over the crashing of the nearby surf against the rugged sea-stack shoreline, "or the spill's faded because the sub's turned into some supply cove or something."

No one else commented. Everyone, including Aussie and Sal, were gripping hard on the handrails midships of the inflatable, its fiberglass keel smacking hard into swells, over unbroken crests, then sliding fast into the troughs. Had it not been for Alvaro's seamanship, the RIB would have capsized in a backflip several times over. The Mexican-American saw that one of the SpecFor warriors, the Welsh-American they called Choir Williams, was turning a faint yet distinct shade of green, made even more sickly looking by the drizzle of rain that continuously leaked from the gray status along the coast and the dreary mist, which, unlike the cloud cover sixty miles to the east, around Whidbey, had not yet been burned off by the pale disk of autumn sun.

"We'll go in the quieter water, wait till this rain passes," Alvaro assured Choir, indicating a natural rock-strewn, crescent-shaped harbor off to their left on the port quarter. The harbor, about a half mile across and several hundred yards deep, was fed by a massive, flood-controlled waterfall, about fifty feet high and three hundred feet wide, plunging precipitously from the hundred-foot-high cliffs that ran the whole curve of the beach, forming a vine- and bush-covered amphitheater. It looked as if the side of a volcanic seamount had been blown out eons before.

Choir raised one hand in thanks to Alvaro as the RIB passed through the pummeling surf, his other hand still white from gripping the roll bar. The rough forty-three-mile trip out from Port Angeles had convinced Freeman even more how difficult and, frankly, how useless David Brentwood would have been in the rough weather.

In less than four minutes the RIB's shallow draft keel passed over a sandbar covered in a foot or so of water, and the six men immediately felt the change, their grips on the hold bars relaxing, the roar of the cataracts plunging all along the cliffs a welcome sound after the constant, bullying roar and buffeting of the open sea. Aussie became excited for a moment, pointing to something man-sized in one of the many channels that ran out from under the heavily vegetated cliffs in the area. A second later he saw the figure reappearing from behind the curtain of the waterfall into one of the water channels.

"Seal!" said Salvini.

"Sea lion," Aussie corrected him.

Freeman took his cell phone from its double Ziploc bag and called Admiral Jensen at Keystone, the much-relieved COMSUBPAC-GRU-9 commander telling the general that the NR-1B's two scientists, two officers, and three enlisted men had just arrived at Keystone. Jensen didn't bother to bore the general with the "screw-up," as the Marine CO had succinctly described the fracas between the Navy's *Skate* and the Washington Ferry Corporation's captain.

Now that he'd found nothing after having put a "rush" on the NR-1B, Freeman felt a rare of case of embarrassment. For his part, Jensen was annoyed, to put it mildly—after all the trouble he'd gone to get the research sub to the West Coast. Then again, Freeman had been the only one who'd offered to help him when he was getting flak from everyone for not having assured a "mine free" strait. And it was Freeman, Jensen knew, who'd given him credit, via CNN, for the fifty-seven-mile coast rerun by Darkstar. So the admiral said nothing, other than to tell Freeman that the NR-1B would be ready if and when Freeman found anything. Besides, there was still a lot the NR-1B could do, the consensus in the Pentagon being that it was the craft best suited to hunt down another small sub.

Freeman glimpsed the sparkle of light beyond the lacy edge of the mammoth waterfall. The nanosecond of recognition was followed by his shouted warning to the other five on the RIB. Whether Aussie, Choir, Salvini, and the diver, Peter Dixon, like the general himself, had reacted more quickly than coxswain Alvaro because of their long combat experience was impossible to discern. Perhaps it was because Alvaro was the most visible, standing up at the RIB's steering console. In any event, it was Jorge who took the full burst of machine-gun fire, its sparkle of one-in-four tracer now long white darts shattering the console's Perspex and knocking the young man overboard, the bloody cavity that a second before had been his chest, awash in the wake of the RIB.

The inflatable, with no one at its console, spun out of control, slicing through the smaller but still powerful chop in the bay at such an acute angle that it teetered and would have capsized had Choir not quickly moved from his hunkered-down position behind the roll bar and grabbed the wheel. He brought the sixteen-footer about smartly, cutting through the RIB's earlier wake and, with his comrades gripping the two hold bars, shoved the throttle to full power, enabling the RIB to surge well away from the waterfall. Choir then just as quickly cut power at the water curtain's halfway point, where the waterfall was so voluminous that whoever had fired the burst at the RIB would no longer be able to see it.

"Rocky island, one o'clock!" Freeman shouted at Choir. "Take us there. Aussie, Dixon, grab your Draeger, recon beyond the falls. See what we're up against. Sal and I will man the island with the M-60 and A.T. anchor."

Aussie, using his legs in a scissor hold around the left stanchion of the roll bar, had his arms free to check and put on his

Draeger rebreather. Dixon, with more recent practice, was already "in suit," the fright he'd experienced from the burst of fire replaced with a surge of anger. It was the first time he'd been shot at, and he was surprised how quickly his outrage had evicted fear. Now he wanted to shoot back. Freeman was on the radio, calling Jensen at Keystone. No response, not even the sound of static.

"Shot to ratshit!" Aussie informed him, indicating the console, the radio's innards a mess of shattered circuit boards and wiring on the RIB's deck. With that, Freeman unclipped his Ziploc-encased cell phone. But Murphy's Law was at large, solar flare activity knocking out all satellite bounce-off signals in the ionosphere high above his fog-bound environs.

Cursing but undeterred, the general grabbed one of the RIB's three marker buoys, switched on its flasher light and pulse signal locator, and tossed it overboard. Hopefully the NR-1B now had its scientists and crew aboard and was already under way, en route to assist his team.

Choir geared the RIB down to quarter speed and made for what Freeman had hurriedly described as a "rocky island."

As the RIB approached it, however, the SpecFor team could see it was in fact no more than a stack of granite thrusting out of the bay—an islet thirty feet in diameter, its highest, westernmost half a serrated wall four or five feet above sea level. Its eastern half, closest to the approaching RIB, seemed to be awash in choppy water, the result of turbulence radiating out from the waterfall-sea interface as the falls tumbled from a wide slit halfway up the heavily vegetated cliff face.

"We should be out of sight of that shooter once we get to these rocks," said Freeman.

"Providing he doesn't move farther around the bay," replied Choir, raising his voice above the ear-dunning roar of the three-hundred-foot-wide wall of white water pouring into the crescent-shaped bay with the unyielding power of a dam whose spill gates were opened for maximum runoff. Fire support for Dixon and Aussie, should they call for it, would be blind, Freeman, Choir, and Sal realizing that the best they could do would be to fire a "banana" arc through the fall in hopes of keeping any shooter's head down. There was a sudden series of crashes as dark branches and clumps of earth plummeted down in the otherwise pristine curtain of water.

"Son of a bitch!" said Sal. "With our radio kaput, Aussie and Dixon won't be able to call us."

"No sweat, Brooklyn," Freeman assured him, with more confidence than he felt. "We'll do it the old-fashioned way. Wait for 'em to swim back and report."

"Why the hell would a shooter have just opened up on us like that?"

"You been smoking something, Sal?" asked the general, Choir answering the question as he coaxed the RIB alongside the islet on the off, protective seaward side. "Because he thought we saw something."

"Jesus—the midget sub?"

"A perfect hide," said the general. "Falls are a perfect curtain—cold water to throw off any infrared snooping UAV."

"Don't fancy those whirlpools, General," opined Choir, looking toward the falls.

"They can swim," said Freeman tersely. " 'Sides, they can pull their rip cords if they have to." He meant that Aussie and Dixon could activate their Mae West inflatables.

Choir nudged the islet's side with the RIB and, despite the foamy, choppy water, could see a protruding ledge three feet below. If there was a sudden suck-down, the RIB's fiberglass keel could find itself on the ledge and tip.

"Piece o' cake," Sal told him, Salvini sensing Choir was worried about what could be a tricky docking in the chop.

"You ready with that line?" Choir asked Sal.

"Good to go, Mr. Williams."

"When I say go—right?"

"Right."

CHAPTER THIRTY-THREE

THE ROC F-16 WAS escorted by two of *McCain*'s F-18 Super Hornets, one of which was piloted by Chipper Armstrong and his RIO Evans, the other by Manowski and his RIO. Evans was still smarting from having been left out the dogfight against the ChiComs, and Manowski's RIO was in no better mood as the pair of Super Hornets continued to escort the "Bizarro" Taiwanese Falcon toward the carrier battle group.

Admiral Crowley, though still in shock over his squadrons' failure to prevent the bombing of Penghu, nevertheless had to force himself to concentrate on the Bizarro situation. His position about not allowing the Falcon to land still stood. For one thing, the Taiwanese Falcon, not being a carrier aircraft, did not have sufficient underbelly strength to make a hard carrier landing; hence the nickname "Jelly Dick," by which "Hard Dick" Navy aviators condescendingly referred to Air Force fighters. An F-16 pilot, at his best, trying to minimize the shock of hitting the carrier deck, would probably collapse his landing gear, the fighter skidding and cartwheeling and either crashing into billions of dollars of *McCain*'s parked aircraft or slamming into the base of the island. In either case, there would be massive fire wreckage, which would mean Crowley couldn't bring in his low-on-gas squadrons coming back from Penghu. It was a nightmare scenario. The rescue of one pilot, Taiwanese or American, wasn't worth the risk to the *McCain* and those who worked on her.

"We could put out a net," Cuso suggested, but Crowley shook his head; the idea of using "Badminton"—a big net stretched across the deck—to break the touchdown of a plane so low on gas that it didn't have enough fuel left for a "go-around," or was in some other way incapacitated, still ran the risk of the Falcon crashing into *McCain*'s superstructure—the carrier's island—before it reached the net.

"No," said Crowley with an air of finality. "He'll have to ditch. Have our chopper pick him up."

Cuso nodded assent, but felt compelled, no doubt because he'd been an aviator himself, to add, "Chipper says the pilot's shot up pretty bad. Ejection might not be an option."

"Life's tough!" Crowley said brusquely. "If he can't eject, maybe he can ditch—stay afloat long enough for our helo to snatch him."

Cuso said nothing. They both knew that if the pilot was so badly wounded that he couldn't reach down to grab the snake—the F-16's ejection pull loop—then he almost certainly didn't have the strength required to boss the controls to pancake long enough for the Jolly Green Giant helicopter reach him.

Crowley conveyed his decision to the rescue helo, Chipper Armstrong, and Manowski.

"Thrilling mission, Chip," came the wry voice from his back-seat.

"Well, look at it this way, Eagle," said Chipper. "Maybe Bizarro is the son of one of those super-rich Taiwanese industrialists, and when he gets home, Daddy's gonna be so grateful, you and I get a big, fat envelope—reward for fishing Junior out of the chuck."

"Your oxygen feed must have dropped below twenty, right?"

"Maybe," Chipper answered, his voice tired but, not surprisingly, no longer as tense as when FITCOMPRON took off. The sight of the carrier, and the focus needed for landing on a "postage stamp," was always a pick-me-up. The only problem remaining, given that the Taiwanese fighter's radio was out, was that either Armstrong or Manowski would have to make it clear to Bizarro that he or she wouldn't be allowed to land on the carrier and would have to eject or ditch. Eagle Evans, however, already had the potential problem solved. Using his navigation highlighter, on the inside of his cockpit he'd drawn a rough, simple diagram of an L-shaped pilot's seat inclined backward, showing an arrow curving up and out from it, his large drawing clearly visible to the pilot of the shot-up Falcon.

"Outstanding, Eagle," said Manowski on the far right side of the Falcon. "I can make that out from here. If Bizarro can't see that, man, he's blind."

Chipper brought the Hornet in closer to the Falcon, his thumb gesticulating to Evans's ad hoc poster, which Chipper now knew would pass into the folklore of the "boat," along with the sadness of having lost so many good aviators in the miscalculation of the ChiComs' intentions over Penghu.

"He sees it," Manowski said, the wingman glimpsing the Falcon's driver, who, though grimacing in pain, slowly raised his hand from the control stick and pointed a bloodied thumb. "He's gonna do it," Chipper advised *McCain*'s CIC. "He's gonna eject."

"Roger that," came CIC's recognition. "Put yourselves between him and the boat, just to be sure. Repeat—you and Manowski get between him and the boat."

McCain's two Super Hornets did so, Chipper speeding a quarter mile ahead, Manowski neatly executing a sideslip left, over the Falcon and into what had been Chipper's position. Both Hornets were in a shallow low left turn at three thousand feet toward the *McCain*, leveling out two miles from the carrier. The three planes, now down to 200 knots, had been given clearance to pass through the carrier battle group's usual no-fly zone. *McCain*'s Jolly Green Giant was already aloft, its swimmers checking their gear as the chopper's pilot, *McCain*'s CIC, Armstrong, and Manowski verified that everyone was on the same page vis-à-vis the precise GPS spot near which they'd like the pilot to ditch.

"Can Leonardo draw another billboard?" inquired John Cuso, with an unmistakable tone of admiration for RIO Evans's initiative.

"Can do," confirmed Eagle, quickly slipping pages out of his knee pad to write out the GPS numbers. The three jets were aft of *McCain*, beginning a slow, wide U-turn left, the Falcon pilot obediently pulling to the outside so the two Super Hornets were again between it and the carrier, now a mile to the west. Suddenly, the Falcon pilot began pointing down at his digital control panel with such urgency that the four Americans could see he was plainly alarmed.

"He's out of gas," proffered Manowski's RIO, "and too low for him to eject. Damn!"

"I don't—" began Manowski. Then they saw the pilot's thumb jabbing down again, this time toward the sea.

"Give him room!" ordered Cuso, who then advised the helo, "Go get him, but keep clear of debris till he's settled. Chipper, Manowski, stand by to enter glide path."

The Falcon was trying to go into as shallow a dive as possible toward the sea, but Chipper and Manowski could see there'd be no pancake landing, but a pelican crash—a nosedive that would drive the Falcon into the ocean with such impact, there would be little chance of rescue.

"God, he almost made it," cut in Evans. "Only a mile out and—"

At a thousand feet the Falcon made an astonishing recovery, the pilot managing to pull it out of the dive. Chipper's HUD showed it leveling off at three hundred feet at 400 knots. It was Eagle-eyed Evans who, despite the obtuse angle of the Hornets' aviators to the Falcon, spotted the twin red dime-sized glows, the Falcon going to afterburner, its blip on both Hornets' radar moving rapidly from 400 knots to 950, breaking hard right, hard left, hard right, from the beginning of what was expected to be its crash landing on the *McCain* but in fact was a crash dive.

Striking the carrier's deck, it sent a huge, rolling fireball that engulfed the center island, incinerating three men on Vulture's Row, colored jackets running for their lives. The flight deck was penetrated by a jagged fourteen-foot-diameter crater, the high explosive bomb that had been built into the Falcon's radar-gutted nose ripping open the rubberized deck with such force that would-be rescuers were burned and blown violently about the mangled deck or over the side. Many, their clothes afire, were scalded raw before they hit the water, the bleeding mass of wounds immediately attracting the sharks of the strait's relatively warm waters.

Everyone was stunned by the sheer fury and unbelievable speed of what was the most successful kamikaze attack on an American carrier since World War II.

The two Super Hornets' pilots, already low on gas, realized there was nowhere to land for either them or the two badly mauled squadrons of Tomcats and Hornets returning from Penghu.

Armstrong and Manowski had six minutes' fuel remaining. And Admiral Crowley had a monumental problem on his hands. The five hundred feet of the designated launching area of the carrier, from the rearmost of the four arresting wires to the stopping area three hundred feet farther down the deck, at approximately midships, had been shortened to 260 feet because of the huge and still smoldering crater caused by the impact of the suicidal Falcon. Somehow, with Armstrong and Manowski making pattern in the four-by-one-mile oval-shaped fly zone off the carrier's port side, and the twenty-two returning planes of *McCain*'s FITCOMPRON only twenty minutes away to the northeast, Crowley, Cuso, and their staff in the carrier's air traffic control center had to figure out how to bring their pilots and their billion-dollar birds home.

If the planes' tail hooks could catch the first wire, rather than the third one, which exerted the least strain on a plane's body, or the fourth wire farther down, they could buy themselves 150 vital extra feet. And with the hydraulic braking cylinder below deck jacked up as much as possible, without risking the tension in the arresting wire literally tearing the tail section off the plane, Crowley figured he might just conceivably get them all down. The net barrier could also be rigged to try to stop those aircraft that failed to be snagged by any of the arresting cables. The difficulty with the net, however, was that it was time consuming. The aircraft had to be disentangled from the elasticized net and a blue shirt had to direct the aviator out of the landing zone before the tractor hooked up and pulled the aircraft away to the designated parking areas along either side of the deck or below, into the hangar. And the whole enterprise depended on the hydraulic cylinders under the flight deck.

If the two cylinders had been damaged by the white heat from the crash's fires, would they be able to provide the counterforce needed against the tremendous pull exerted by a landing aircraft's tail hook? On inspection, immediately after the deck fire was doused, it was discovered that the explosion of the suicidal F-16, obviously one of the ROC jets captured on Kinmen by the ChiComs, had produced such intense temperatures that the hydraulic cylinders on the gallery deck for the fourth and the third wire, though aft of the crater, were bleeding, and that therefore the integrity of both cables and their spools was in question. Cuso's conclusion, with which the flight director concurred, was that only the first and second wires could be trusted to trap the incoming planes successfully, bringing them to a stop from 150 mph in seconds. This did not eliminate the always clear and present danger of a plane's tail hook failing to snag either of those wires. For this reason, the incoming pilots, as usual, would push their throttles to full power at the moment of touchdown, should they have to "bolter" down the fourteen-degree-angled deck, taking off to rejoin traffic for another attempt.

With the squadrons' Tomcats and Hornets now only eleven minutes away, John Cuso quickly phoned the landing signals officer on the tiny forward portside platform. "LSO, it's Cuso here. Give me your greenie board list." Normally, this score list of the pilots' carrier landing ability was kept in the relevant squadron's Ready Room below the "roof," but Cuso wanted a computer readout. Armstrong's and Manowski's Super Hornets, being so close to the boat, would be first in, but for the remainder of FITCOMPRON, now only ten minutes off, Admiral Crowley wanted the Hornets and Tomcats stacked in greenie board order. This meant that the best aviators in the squadrons would be given priority in the wait zone, since their previous "traps" record indicated that they would have the best chance of being able to hook the 1 wire on a first attempt. This would allow the colored shirts to clear the deck quickly for the next incoming plane.

And so the normal, nerve-wracking pressure with which *McCain*'s aviators had to contend during carrier landings increased exponentially, each battle-fatigued pilot knowing there was not the slightest margin for error on the crater-shortened flight deck.

"FITCOMPRON ETA eight minutes."

McCain's landing signals officer switched on the lenses, an arrangement of green, red, and orange lights to guide in the pilots, the first, in this case, being Chipper Armstrong. He'd made the break from the holding pattern, coming in downwind of the stamp-sized carrier deck ahead of him. His fuel level was critical, since his Super Hornet hadn't been topped up from the usual standby airborne tanker, which was prevented from taking off from the carrier because the tanker's props had been demolished by the Falcon's suicide attack.

The landing signals officer watched Armstrong's Hornet lowering its tail hook, landing gear, and flaps. "Call the ball!" he radioed Chipper.

In the Hornet's back seat, Eagle was straining his neck, willing Chipper, as if by mental telepathy, to see the orange blob of the "meatball," to make sure they were on the right line of approach.

"Call the ball," came the LSO's voice, his tone more demanding now. An ex-aviator himself, the LSO was both more and less forgiving of his charges, his eyes glued to the approaching speck in the leaden sky. "Snag it!" he told Armstrong.

It was critical, and every man and woman aboard the boat knew it, the LSO eschewing normal emissions control procedures, in which light signals only were used to avoid employing enemy-alerting radio.

"Call the ball!" the LSO barked.

"Doing my best," Armstrong assured him.

"Best isn't good enough! You're a naval aviator. Snag it!"

"Roger ball!" said Chipper, confirming he had the amber light and row of green okay lights below it in his line of sight. It was a technique pioneered by a British official in Whitehall who had his secretary sight his desk as if it were a British carrier, telling her to keep a ball in sight. It required her to lower her torso comically, like someone forced to keep walking with some invisible weight on her head, pressing her down farther and farther as she came nearer to the desktop.

In the next nine seconds aviator Armstrong, Eagle Evans behind him in silent prayer, dropped the Super Hornet to thirty-five feet above the wounded carrier's fantail, the fighter-bomber, its nose up, approaching at 143 knots, or approximately 158 mph.

"Bit too fast," said someone in Air Traffic Control, "considering the crosswinds."

Armstrong raised the nose a fraction higher, his tail hook lowering. Hitting the deck at 160 mph, he immediately gunned the twin turbofan-enhanced performance engines to full power, the scream of the turbofans and the thud of the landing or "controlled crash" deafening several off-duty sailors up on Vulture's Row.

Armstrong and Evans were thrust forward with such violence by the stopping force of the first wire jerking out its cable from the hydraulically reined spools on the gallery deck below that Evans would have bruise strips down both pectorals.

In milliseconds the "colors" swarmed the Super Hornet, the green-vested "hook-runner" and blue-shirted "handlers" the first in action, the latter guiding Armstrong away from the crater area to the second elevator forward of the island.

"Get 'er down!" hollered the blue shirt boss. "Manowski's about to break."

Armstrong's wingman was in fact already beginning his approach, his fuel alarm blinking an urgent warning, delivered verbally in the dulcet tone of a woman calmly telling him he was rapidly approaching empty. "I know it, sweetheart. Dammit," said Manowski, who, during long missions, was more disposed than usual to what the battle group's senior surgeon called "politician gut." The agony of his gaseous condition was not helped now by his mounting anxiety about the tiny slab of holed blacktop rushing up at him. It felt as if his politician gut was about to explode against the restraint of his seat harness, the prospect of the sudden negative G upon landing more frightening than the approach of any bogey. Dammit, all he needed was to fart—but no, that'd be too helpful, and that bastard Murphy was clearly determined to make him suffer.

CHAPTER THIRTY-FOUR

ADMIRAL JENSEN WAS happy to hand over the NR-1B to its two scientists and crew. He'd issued a huge sigh of relief as he watched the research sub slide off its badly singed but still functional trailer under the watchful eyes of the Marine guard. Inside the small waiting room, one of the two scientists, a Brit, grateful to the four Marines who'd risked hypothermia to check the waters about the ramp, now produced a flask of brandy, handing it to the Marines, who were warming themselves up. "I think I'll partake of the medicinal elixir myself," he told them, his nerves, he added, "still rather fragile" following the terrifyingly near fatal confrontation between the ferry's captain and the gun-festooned USS *Skate*.

Outside the waiting room, Jensen, standing with the Marine captain, watched as the other scientist, about to descend the conning tower's ladder, his eyes shaded from the sunlit-mirrored water, glanced back at the singed and partly splintered wood of the sub's trailer. This oceanographer, a white-bearded man in his mid-fifties—onetime mentor to Alicia Mayne, who had been so badly burned in the attack on the *Utah*—shifted his gaze from the trailer to the NR-1B's superstructure and ninety-six-foot-long pressure hull.

"The blast didn't damage the hull," Jensen called out to reassure him. "We went over it with a fine-tooth comb. Not even a hairline fracture."

The oceanographer, whom the Marine captain had already dubbed "Santa" because of his long white beard, waved and took a pen-size flashlight out of the pocket of his sky-blue coveralls, the latter bearing the proud sailing-ship insignia of Woods Hole Oceanographic Institute. "We'll take a look anyway," he told the admiral. With that, he and two crew members, one a female naval officer with a distinctly mannish haircut and serious demeanor, disappeared down into the super high-tech research sub whose side-scan sonar, the most sensitive in the world, was capable, according to one Marine, of detecting a safety pin on the sea bottom.

The Marine captain asked Jensen about this claim. "Is that true, sir?"

"No," replied Jensen, the admiral's response accompanied by a smile. "It's like those satellites that are supposed to be able to read a newspaper in Red Square. It can spot the newspaper—not the print. Maybe a four-inch headline or a big photo, but not—"

Santa reappeared, standing waist-high in the small conning tower. "It's buggered!"

"What d'you mean, buggered?" shot back Jensen, but he knew well enough. What the scientist was telling him was that the NR-1B was out of commission.

"The nacelle," said the scientist, by which he meant the nose section of the sub, "has been spalled."

Surprisingly, at least to the Marine captain, the admiral didn't seem to understand what Santa meant by "spalled"—that while the terrorists' explosion of C4 beneath the bitumen road hadn't so much as scratched the NR-1B externally, the tremendous concussion of the explosive against the NR-1B's three-inch-thick high-tensile steel had been akin to someone striking a forty-four-gallon drum with a rubber-headed sledgehammer. Minute flakes of rust from the inside wall of the drum or, in this case, flecks of paint on the inside wall of the sub's nose cone, had broken free at supersonic speed from the impact. This spalling, red-hot, paint-flaked shrapnel had sprayed the delicate if firmly housed electronic array that was the research sub's prized sonar.

In effect, the eyes of the NR-1B, which had so successfully searched for and recovered vital parts of the '86 space shuttle *Challenger* wreckage, an Air Force Tomcat that had gone down in the sea off North Carolina, and, among its most glorious military and civilian exploits, discovered no less than twenty-six shipwrecks in twelve hours, were now blind and of no use to Freeman and his team, or to anyone else.

"Can we replace it?" Jensen called out, on realizing the damage. "The sonar?"

"Yes," said the oceanographer.

"When?"

"Two weeks—maybe less. Then we'd need sea trials to calibrate the—"

Jensen had his hands over his face—hiding sheer frustration, or tears, or both—the Marine captain wasn't sure.

"Same thing when a tank's hit," said the Marine, by way of relieving the gloomy silence that had descended like sudden rain over the sun-glinting sea. "Doesn't matter if the round penetrates, force of the hit fills the air inside with tiny white-hot metal fragments. Like a swarm of—"

"Why the hell didn't you think of that before?" Jensen cut in, as if it would have made a difference. The fact was, the NR-1B was effectively a write-off until the Navy and its civilian contractor could rush in a replacement sonar. And even then, the job of extracting the ruined components from the NR-1B would be a singularly time-consuming task of negotiating awkward angles in confined spaces. The tiny NR-1B, unlike Rorke's former Virginia-class sub, did not have the advantage of add-on, take-off modular architecture, whereby whole remotely controlled or man-crewed submersible modules could easily be added or removed as needed for special missions.

"Freeman's on his own," Jensen said disconsolately, overwhelmed by the bitter irony that the very man who had given him the reputation-salvaging chance of helping to zero in on the cause of the U.S. Navy's catastrophe in the Juan de Fuca Strait was now denied the assistance of the NR-1B because he—Jensen—had failed to deliver the boat safely to the Keystone dock.

"They'll call me the 'Keystone admiral'!" Jensen told the Marine captain bitterly. But the officer, of a younger generation, failed to get the analogy to the infamously incompetent Keystone Kops of celluloid screen.

"You could send the *Skate*," suggested the Marine captain.

"Yes," agreed Jensen, wracked by indecision. He knew that to dispatch the patrol craft would leave only one to guard the Hood Canal bridge, and thus the egress of any submarine out of Bangor, which could invite further disaster.

Aussie was glad that the waterfall and environs were shrouded in fog and sea mist. He had heard about the supposed extraordinary clarity of the cold Northwest waters but had put all the reports in what he called his "Fifty PBS"—fifty percent BS—file. Even with the fog hanging over the surface above him, the water's transparence was a shock to him, and with every breast stroke he took twenty feet down he feared being spotted by anyone high on the cliff beyond the waterfall, or, for that matter, by anyone on what was probably an apron of rocks and sand behind the crescent bay's falls.

Peter Dixon, only a few feet away on Aussie's right, was more comfortable, because of the frequent shower of rain that peppered the surface and the surface disturbance created by the local whirlpools from the turbulence of the waterfall. He knew that all of this would make it difficult for anyone swimming on the surface to see more than several feet below them. Once he was through the thunder and caldronlike fury of the falls churning beneath the surface, Dixon indicated they go up to recon. Aussie was unable to see his swim buddy's arm signal at first, blocked as it was by the effusion of bubbles that momentarily rendered their bubbleless Draeger units redundant. Dixon's signal had also been hidden by a silvery gray school of Chinook salmon, their fluid beauty pocked here and there by grumpy-mouthed rockfish who refused to move out of the way of their more numerous and streamlined cousins.

By the time Aussie saw the second signal from Dixon, whose thumbs were jerking impatiently upward, Dixon was already four or five feet above him. He broke surface first, deafened by the thundering of the waterfall about ten feet directly behind him. When Aussie surfaced, he found himself amid such a profusion of bubbles and the mist they created, it took him, like Dixon, ahead of him, a while to adjust his vision. It was as if they'd moved from a dull, winter-lit room to an even dimmer one, the water behind the falls significantly darker because of the overhang of the cliff's face, the waterfall's effervescent mist also "blooming" out their infrared lenses. Still, in the gloomy light between the falls and the edge of the bay, Dixon saw something few men had ever seen. Seeing it too, Lewis actually gasped in surprise.

It was a midget sub, docked a hundred feet in from them by a natural rock wall that formed part of the crescent bay and was curtained by the falls. Dixon counted four guards, two at the bow and two at the sub's stern.

In his mind's eye, Aussie had thought of this midget sub, first reported by Dixon's deceased swim buddy, as being like the Japanese navy's small midget sub, three of which had slipped through Sydney Harbor's defenses in May 1942, torpedoing the ferry *Kuttabul* and killing nineteen. But what he was looking at now was considerably bigger—a long cigar shape, over a hundred feet in length, its diameter about twelve feet, and the conning tower around eight feet high. But after he and Dixon swam back underneath the turbulent cover of the sea-waterfall interface to reach the rocky islet a hundred yards away, their descriptions of the midget differed. Dixon, his weathered, war-painted face grimacing with the effort of shucking off the weight of his Draeger rebreather, flippers, and other kit, thought that the bow was not so much spherical, but a tad wider than it was high.

"Maybe it *is* a *tad* wider," riposted Aussie. "So what? Must be only a difference of a few inches, at that."

"If it's spherical," said Freeman, "it could be nuclear. That's the difference, Aussie."

Choir raised his eyebrows, but Sal gave no indication that he'd heard the general, concentrating on checking his M-16, one cartridge in the chamber, his finger resting on the safety. If anyone so much as poked their snout around the western edge of the falls, he told Choir, "I'll take their fuckin' head off!" The "boy from Brooklyn," as Aussie often called him, had no intention of ending up like the once valiant Medal of Honor winner, one arm as useless as "a spent dick," to be left dangling by his side for the rest of his life.

For Salvini, the shock of what had purportedly happened during the ODA mission to take out terrorist chief Li Kuan troubled him nightly, like his persistent dream of not having passed his high school exams, which tormented him with the endlessly recurring scene in which he was barred from entering the final examination room—American history—because he was late, having wasted time at a crosswalk, bending down while the rest of his buddies caught the light and crossed the street. By the time he'd tied up the lace of his Nike "Just Do It" sneaker, the pedestrian signal had changed back to "Don't Walk," the red signal's blink morphing into a stream of paralysis-inducing red tracer.

"So what if it's nuclear-powered?" Aussie challenged the general in a tone that surprised Dixon, who, used to the "Yes sir, no sir" exchanges between officers and men, was taken aback by the lively sense of equality in Freeman's team.

"Because," Freeman answered Aussie patiently, "if it's nuclear powered, what's it doing needing a dock? A nuclear boat doesn't need recharging for fifteen to twenty years."

"Needs rearming though," said Aussie matter-of-factly, seeing the point and adding, "Nukes can also go a long time without replenishing freeze-dried food—but not munitions, not at the rate this sucker's been sinking our boats."

Aussie's comment made such an obvious yet important point that the general realized just how sleep deprived he was. With that, Freeman did something he normally tried to avoid. From his load vest he pulled out a small, watertight Ziploc bag of dark chocolate-covered roasted coffee beans, took four by way of example, and offered the rest to the team.

Without looking up, Sal said, "Two for me, sir." Aussie also took two, Choir and Dixon declining. The frigid water had been more than sufficient to wake them up.

"How many guards?" Freeman asked Aussie and Dixon.

"Four that I saw," said Dixon. "But I couldn't see shit in there for a while—water fogged my IR."

"Aussie?"

"Four. And that doesn't make any sense. Where's everybody else? No sign of a crew."

"Aboard the sub," suggested Choir.

"Fine," acknowledged Aussie. "But where are the supply donkeys?"

Dixon mentioned that he'd seen something that looked a bit like a dark canvas awning extending back from the sub's conning tower to the base of the cliff. "But maybe it only covered a gangway that went as far as the rock landing. It was so damned gloomy."

"I never saw it," answered Aussie. "Probably 'cause I broke surface at right angles to the conning tower. Could have been a stream of guys coming and going under a tarp and I wouldn't have seen 'em."

"Would've thought they'd be out in force," Choir said. "After that bugger took a shot at us?"

"Damn!" began the general.

Had the caffeine from the chocolate-coated java beans jolted him that fast? wondered Choir.

"That's why we didn't see a crowd," Freeman continued. "Bastards are frantically loading the whore so it can cast off and run riot again in the strait. We're going in!"

Aussie Lewis had known, ever since he was a small boy, that he was brave—always ready to "stand on his dig," as the Australian prospectors used to call it, refusing to give up their claim in the gold field. But refusing to give ground and dashing off half cocked were two different things.

"General," countered Aussie, "the moment our RIB pokes its nose around either end of the friggin' waterfall, those lookouts are gonna have us cold, dead in their sights from either end of the sub. And they'll be firing from solid ground. If we do get a chance of return fire, we'll be bobbing around like a cork. Brooklyn here couldn't even hit 'em with his scatter gun." Aussie took a breath and said something SpecFor warriors seldom say. "It's too risky. They'll take us all out, and then what? No one knows where we are. No backup. Nada. And we're out of radio contact—no cavalry."

"NR-1B should be on its way," said Choir.

"So's Christmas!" retorted Aussie. " 'Sides, all that Jensen has is our general area."

"Air strike possible?" asked Dixon, his own question answered as he looked about at the sea mist and fog hugging the coast like a coat, not a single tree visible atop the cliff from which the falls cascaded.

"Weather's socked us in," said Freeman, raising his voice again over the sound of the falls. "Anyway, by the time Whidbey got any ASW birds airborne, the sub'd be outta here."

For several moments no one spoke, and in the dreary gray world that had enveloped the crescent bay and surrounding coastline, all they could hear was the continuing thunder of the falls and the ocean's unceasing attack against their rocky islet. Freeman's mind was racing like a computer, drawing on all his past experiences—from the steamy jungles of Southeast Asia to the bone-cold engagements on the north German plain and the forays of his SpecFor teams in the snow-packed mountains of the Pacific Northwest itself, where he, Choir, Aussie, Sal, and David Brentwood had gone toe-to-toe against white supremacist militias.

"There is one way," Freeman announced, his eyes fixed on Aussie Lewis.

"Damn," said Lewis. "I think you want me to get wet again, General."

Freeman's weathered face turned to Dixon. "How 'bout you and Aussie strap on those Draegers and go under the falls again—only this time come up shooting. It'll be the last thing they'll expect."

Dixon nodded, slowly, either from a distinct lack of enthusiasm or because of his failure to envision the whole plan. "You want us to pin them down?"

"No," said Freeman. "I want you to kill them."

"While you three make an end run around the end of the falls in the RIB," Aussie said. "Right?"

"No," said Freeman. "We three'll do something else they won't expect."

"You're going to attack *through* the falls," said Aussie.

"Affirmative," confirmed Freeman. "Full bore through the middle." The general slapped Choir on the shoulder. "Think you can handle that, my friend?"

"Piece o' cake," said Choir.

"Jesus!" put in Sal. "Those falls'll sink us."

"Not if we hit 'em at full power," the general assured them, with more confidence than he felt. True, the falls were no more than three or four feet through, but with the tumbling force of thousands of gallons a second, the impact would be tremendous. It would be, in the parlance of his British SpecFor compatriots, "a close run thing." If Choir couldn't master the wheel in the crushing wall of water, if the good Welshman allowed the inflatable to veer slightly one way or the other away from a right angle impact, the skew torque, as Aussie Lewis so eloquently warned them, would send the RIB "ass over tit," upending it, dumping the legendary general, Salvini, and coxswain Choir into the swirling water moat between the falls and the midget sub.

"Sitting ducks," Aussie told them.

"Thank you," riposted Choir, "for your vote of confidence."

"Biggest thing you've steered," said Aussie, "is one of those dorky piss pots you Welsh paddle across a creek!" He was referring to a Welsh coracle, the ancient basketlike and portable one-man boat made from the small branches of shrubs and trees and still used by quiet water fishermen.

"Hurry up with those Draegers," the general told Aussie and Dixon, "before they cast off."

Dixon easily put the Draeger on, he and Albinski having gotten used to donning their rebreather units with the same ease and confidence of long practice with which Aussie Lewis handled his Heckler & Koch MP submachine gun. "These weapons are waterproof, right?" Dixon asked Lewis.

"Well," began Aussie, "if you—"

"Quiet!" It was Salvini, his concentration so focused that he was the first to hear the sound. A faint but distinct rumbling.

"A diesel?" proffered Dixon anxiously. "So much for it being nuclear powered."

"Synchronize watches," ordered Freeman. "We hit the falls at 0814, in five minutes."

"Five minutes, at 0814," acknowledged Dixon, followed by Aussie, who, like Dixon, was spitting into his face mask, quickly rubbing the saliva about to guard against condensation. It reminded Dixon of his dives with Rafe Albinski.

"Go!" Freeman ordered, and both Aussie and Dixon dropped backward into the sea.

"Into the RIB," Freeman told Choir and Salvini. "Lash the tarp tight over the gear."

Choir was already priming the outboard's gas pump, while Salvini, anticipating the interval between the rise and fall of the Bruiser, adroitly jumped to the inflatable and immediately began securing the weapons, ammo, and other equipment.

Freeman quickly handed his HK submachine gun down to Sal to have it clipped into its rack. It was a race before the midget sub cast off and submerged, free to resume its unseen control of the strait's choke point.

Freeman's gung-ho body language exuded confidence, and the instant he was on the prow of the boat, he was taken back to the exact moment in which his desire to be a leader had crystallized, the moment when, as a young boy, he'd first gazed upon Emmanuel Leutze's famous painting of Washington crossing the ice-floe-choked Delaware, the revolutionary general standing proudly in the boat's prow.

Freeman's confidence, however, was qualified by his own surprise at the terrorists not having already followed up on the burst of fire by their lookout, whose vigilance had unwittingly given away their position. It had only been fifteen minutes ago, but Freeman knew that if he'd been in command on the other side of the falls, he would already have had his men launch some kind of follow-up attack against the five Americans. Why hadn't the enemy done so?

CHAPTER THIRTY-FIVE

AS FREEMAN TRIED using his satellite phone, to no avail—the atmospherics still dominated by the frying-fish sound of interference in the ionosphere—he caught sight of Aussie Lewis's flippers. Aussie had momentarily surfaced to get his bearings before making a deep tumble dive to get well below the underwater turbulence of the falls before swimming the hundred feet or so to the sub. The fact that the general, Choir, and Sal all agreed it was Aussie, although his gear was exactly the same as Dixon's, bore testimony to how closely they had worked over the years. They were like friends distinguishing each other from a crowd not by physical features, but merely by the way they moved, reading one another's body language with an unconscious certainty that amazed Dixon, the newcomer.

The Coast Guard diver, having more experience in the strait than Aussie Lewis, had not felt the need to surface to make sure of his bearings. Now, he was waiting on the other, landward, side of the falls, in the darker water that served as a moat between the falls' deafening torrent and the sub—whose type, other than it being a midget, was still a matter of speculation. Not even the identity of the balaclava-masked terrorist he and Aussie had spotted earlier was known, though Dixon was confident that he and the rest of the SpecFor team would soon find out. It was three minutes since he and Aussie had left the islet. Another two minutes and Freeman, Choir, and Sal should come through the falls like gangbusters, and then the five of them would open up.

Aussie, for his part, estimated that Freeman, Sal, and Choir should reach the sub in short order. A couple of HE grenades down the hatch from either Sal or the general would do nicely, he thought, certainly enough to delay the bastards until either the NR-1B or a Coast Guard gunboat could arrive for the coup de grace. Relying on the waterfall's turbulence, now a mere fifty feet behind them, neither Aussie nor Dixon anticipated any problem surfacing.

Any anxiety Freeman might have had about the fog rolling in, now completely obscuring the falls, was not evident in his brisk, eager preparations. He assisted Sal in mounting the stripped-down SEAL version M-60 on the bow's pivot mount as the noise of the falls smothered all sounds save the deep, pulsating rumble that he and the other four men assumed was the sub's diesel-electric warming up, readying for imminent departure.

"Two minutes!" shouted Choir, keeping the RIB's Volvo Penta inboard purring, while Sal, the M-60 now secure, took the fourteen-foot spiked pike from its quick-release rack that ran along the port side, pushing the pole against the islet to keep the RIB clear of the dangerous, barnacle-clad projection of rock that appeared and disappeared threateningly with each suck and surge of the sea.

For Sal, the kind of vigilance needed to keep the sixteen-foot boat from being tipped over through contact with the protruding ledge proved more stressful than combat, and he remembered that for David Brentwood, the most trying part of a mission had always been going over the Rules of Engagement. The Medal of Honor winner was always concerned that he might commit a blue on blue—an attack on his own forces. Sal knew it was a different source of tension than he felt, but the effect was the same: They almost welcomed combat as a release, not only from the immediate anxiety of the situation, but from the tension of life itself.

As Choir gave the RIB engine its head, the waterfall speeding toward them, Sal quickly left his roll bar position to reach the bow-mounted M-60. "Hold on and duck!" yelled Choir. The RIB struck the waterfall at thirty-five miles an hour, all three men fighting against instinctively closing their eyes, the ice-white thunder collapsing all around, slamming them into the swirling maelstrom of foam on the deck. Then they were through.

Freeman heard the unmistakable rip of Kalashnikov bullets peppering the whirlpools about the RIB, the craft's series of neoprene inflatable cells along the starboard midships section exploding like popcorn. Choir, seeing the team's hoped-for surprise popped along with the inflatable cells, opened up the Volvo Penta, the RIB's bow fairly leaping out of the salt chuck, hitting 35 knots as it sped past the sun-sparkling curtain of falls, with only ninety feet to go to the sub.

"Turning!" Choir yelled, then, "Hard right!" so loudly there was no possibility of either Freeman or Sal not hearing him, despite the rip of the M-60's one-in-three tracer, almost a red line at that close range.

With barely forty feet to go, Sal's M-60 fire was wild and unavoidably inaccurate in the RIB's hard, brain-pummeling progress against the relatively calmer but still rough water between the RIB and the sub. Choir dropped the speed to twenty knots, simultaneously wrenching the wheel astarboard, further confounding the enemy's aim. Salvini, given forewarning of the turn and having seen that his previous M-60 bursts were too high, dropped the barrel down an inch or so and raked the upper lip of a dark, thirty-foot-wide cave mouth he could now discern immediately behind the docked sub. He also raked the long, black "floating log" of a sub. The midget's ten-foot-long sail, or conning tower, was a black lump that sparked with the fiery orange hits of his sustained burst, which was completely ineffective, as Sal knew it would be, against the high-tensile steel. But his firing had at least forced the sub's AK-47-armed lookouts to run for cover.

Two of them were hit as they raced from the sub's bow along its deck, heading for the narrow, covered walkway that led inshore from the sub's sail toward the cave. Salvini's M-60 rounds kept coming, and he cut them down, one man toppling into the water, thrashing about in an agony that ceased with a quick burst from Freeman's HK, the other one up and running again until the general's 9mm bullets finished his desperate sprint. Normally, the parabellum rounds he'd just fired had less stopping power, particularly when sprayed at obtuse angles, but the general had fired a tight group of three rounds more or less straight in over the forty-foot range. The other reason the bullets had proved so deadly and weren't "bee stings," as Freeman was wont to say, was that—in direct contravention of the Geneva Accords—he'd used HydroShok ammo rather than legal "hard ball." The frangible head of the HydroShok expanded inside the recipient's body the nanosecond he was struck.

"Where the hell are our swimmers?" Sal shouted.

"Underwater!" replied Freeman. "Where I'd be with all this crap flying—" His sentence went unfinished as Choir drove the RIB through a dangerously unstable S pattern, which further confounded the enemy's aim and forced Freeman to grab the roll bar, letting forth a burst of obscenities which only a long-shoreman and Aussie Lewis, if he was still alive, could have fully interpreted.

At the moment, however, Aussie Lewis and Dixon were fighting for their lives. They'd seen two dark shapes diving from the sub's deck, both bearing knives—not the standard K-bar blades or expensive Randalls, but eighteen-inch bayonets that would pass right through a man, with steel to spare. Alarmed, Dixon glanced across at Aussie, who pointed down and drew his hand across his throat, a move that caused Dixon to gulp and swallow a huge bubble from the fierce "wash cycle" churned up by Choir's effective but bone-busting evasive antics. The Welshman's "crazy pattern" wake all but covered the moat area with bubbles, which temporarily kept both pairs of divers from each other as well as from their respective surface combatants.

The RIB, careening successfully at first, crisscrossing the moat behind the falls and sub, now came under steady and heavy automated fire from the cave behind the sub. Below, the two pairs of divers engaged, without circling each other or using any of the fancy energy-wasting tricks and turns imagined by some who have never been swimming for their lives. In the sand-stirred undersea world bounded by the falls and the submarine, the soft sound of rubber fins was obliterated by the high whine of the RIB's engine and the increasing rumble of the sub's diesel.

Aussie, intending to take the initiative, closed with his opposite number, who kicked hard in a burst of speed, trying to drive home the overreach of his bayonet through Lewis's chest. Aussie slowed, trading speed for accuracy of impact. The enemy's first right-handed bayonet thrust was short, a feint that drew in Aussie's K-bar, which Aussie's opponent smartly deflected with a smaller blade that had suddenly materialized in his left hand. Aussie, against all logic, released his grip on his parried right hand, gripping the enemy's knife wrist instead, the enemy diver driving his bayonet in a flurry of effervesced water hard toward Aussie's chest. Aussie twisted, the bayonet slicing clean through his Draeger's left-side hose and ricocheting off the Draeger's chest-mounted housing. Then Aussie kicked once, bringing up his free left hand, thrusting hard, striking the other swimmer's mask with such force it was knocked away from the man's face, the expelled air momentarily blinding both him and Aussie. But with his mask still on, Aussie had the better of it. When his opponent turned frantically to retrieve his own mask, Aussie brought his right knee up hard into the man's scrotum. The man's mouth agape with the shock of the hit, he involuntarily gulped in seawater, which Lewis knew would drown all discipline and training his opponent might have.

In an intuitive act of survival, Aussie's opponent rose quickly toward the surface for air. Any breath his lungs might have had in reserve was now depleted, the bubbles rising from his transit to the surface joining those coming from Aussie's left hand as Lewis grabbed the man's right leg as it passed in front of him and, with one savage slash of his K-bar's blue steel, sliced through the man's neoprene sheath with such fury that it cut to the bone. A cloud of cherry-red blood obscured Aussie's view before it was quickly diluted to a watermelon pink, through which Aussie glimpsed the tail end of a school of salmon, which he now realized had been all around them and were fleeing—perhaps, Aussie thought, because of approaching sharks. He kicked with all the energy he had, his fins propelling him fast toward the surface, the whine of the RIB engine piercing his eardrums as he crashed into the frenzied body of his opponent at the surface. The wounded man, gulping in the icy, pristine air above the roiling blue, had realized he was no longer able to swim.

To Aussie's astonishment, he and his opponent were no more than twenty feet away from an enormous floating log, which Lewis quickly realized was the midget sub. His vision impaired by the turmoil created by the other man's panic, Aussie grabbed at a black orb that was his opponent's head, stabbing it repeatedly with his K-bar. Aussie's enemy, meanwhile, charged with fear and adrenaline, was like a writhing swordfish and still dangerous. So instead of going for his heart, as ancient Greek warriors had—and would have been his preference—Aussie did it the most effective if messy way—puncturing him wherever contact could be made. He dragged his opponent under and stabbed him repeatedly, until the man's body went limp. Exhausted, Aussie then released him, the only sound he could hear, apart from the falls, being the rapid fire of machine guns.

He'd seen a dozen or so men casting off lines from stakes that had been driven into crevices along the rock shelf in front of the cave and here and there in a crushed-shell beach just east of the rock ledge. But he couldn't contact the RIB. He looked around for Dixon, but all he could see was the sub moving out, and beyond it, on the rocky ledge in front of the cave, a pile of discarded cardboard boxes, large sheets of torn paper, plastic wrap and assorted rubbish littering the beach, the paper alternately billowing and collapsing from phantom breezes that seemed to be coming out of the cave.

Freeman, Sal, and Choir had returned to the islet, ignobly but sensibly taking cover behind the small, jagged six-foot-long, five-foot-high rock wall. The guano that had remained undisturbed atop the wall now rose like chalk dust as the sub's defenders—"About fourteen of 'em," Sal told Freeman—continued to rake the rock with light and heavy machine-gun fire.

"Where the—" began Sal, his words drowned out by such an enfilade of heavy caliber and light machine-gun fire that the salt air above the small islet sang with the discordant noise of ricocheting rounds which, had it not been for the small rock wall, would have literally chopped the general and his two compatriots to pieces.

"You see Dixon or Aussie?" It was Choir, his Welsh accent always more pronounced in the taut, crackling air of a firefight.

"I don't like this," said Sal, in one of his more memorable understatements. "I don't like it at all."

Choir, crawling along on his belly, ignominiously peeked an inch or two around the end of the rock wall. "*Shite!* The sub's moving."

"Goddammit, Sal!" bellowed Freeman, pointing to the lashed-down hump of equipment in the RIB, which slapped noisily and annoyingly against the protected sea side of the islet. "Gimme that AT!"

"Won't stop it with that, General!" Sal said as he passed the one-shot, self-contained antitank launcher Freeman had eschewed using earlier from the islet because it would have been a wasted shot, given the impediment to his line of sight formed by the falls. He'd also known that had he tried a blind shot, the Swedish-built rocket would have exploded in transit the second its warhead struck the water wall. But now the sub's fifty-foot-long forward section from sail to bow was nosing out beyond the edge of the waterfall.

"Got that AT round ready?" Freeman shouted, answering Salvini's skepticism about being able to hit anything worthwhile, given the impediment of the sub. "Countdown from ten to fire!" he told Salvini and Choir.

"Ten to fire," confirmed Sal, ready to heave up the stripped-down but still substantial M-60, the terrorists' fire increasing, as if they had divined Freeman's intentions. The general, his left side hugging the western edge of the islet's rock wall, was ready to swing the AT-4 launcher around as Choir and Sal prepared, at great risk, to lay down covering fire, the enemy's enfilade whacking loudly into the islet's protective rock wall and surrounding water, other rounds whistling ominously overhead.

"Ten," Freeman began, "nine, eight, seven—son of a—hold it!"

Sal, crouched, poised to come up with the M-60 firing before its folded bi-pod even had time to rest on the top of the islet's protective wall, gave a snort of suppressed laughter. Despite the precariousness of their situation, the sub nosing out from its cliff-bottom berth behind the waterfall, and despite the worrisome fact that none of the three had seen any sign of Aussie or Dixon since the two divers had disappeared under the fall, the fact that in the middle of this murderous encounter Freeman should be so conditioned by modern technology that he stopped his countdown because his cell phone's vibration had put him off his count struck Sal as singularly hilarious. Yet part of the reason Freeman answered the cell so promptly was that it was obviously working now, the atmospherics having improved sufficiently for communication to be reestablished.

"It might be Jensen," said Choir, hoping the NR-1B was en route.

That the news wasn't good from Jensen's end was evidenced by Freeman cursing above the sound of the terrorists' fire and the increasing bass of the midget sub's diesel engine. "The goddamned NR-1B's *kaput!*" he yelled.

"The only thing that might be available," Jensen had told him, "is the patrol craft," adding, "What's all that noise?"

"A damned firefight!" Freeman bellowed, his voice whipped away by gusts that were turning the previously calm blue bay into a spindrift-veined caldron. "We've found the goddamned midget sub—only it's not such a midget after all. Better send your patrol boat, send anything you've got—fast as you can, Admiral!" With that, Freeman gave Jensen the GPS coordinates on his cell.

"Sub's coming through the falls, General," Sal warned. "Bow at eleven o'clock."

It told Freeman, still holding the AT launcher, that the bow had now moved away from its earlier two o'clock berth position to a point a hundred yards left of the islet. Which in turn told him that if he didn't fire soon, the sub would be through, past the falls, and heading unhindered out to sea. And that the protected space behind the islet's six-foot-high wall would then be exposed to unhindered lateral fire from the sub at virtually point-blank range.

Freeman shouldered the launcher. "Ten, nine, eight, seven, six, five, four, three, two, one . . ." A vicious gust punched the islet, combining with the ferocious backblast of the rocket motor as the cone-shaped 84mm warhead shot out from its fiberglass tube at sixty-four miles an hour.

Metal whacked metal, the sub's progress so inhibited by the

buckled steel basket around its prop that Freeman estimated its speed at no more than a knot. With its steering likewise affected, it was crabbing toward the eastern sandbank of a twenty-foot-wide exit channel. Choir, reading the situation as clearly as Freeman and Sal, was already in the RIB, the three warriors anticipating the consternation in the sub and preferring to take their chances in the RIB as a fast, mobile target rather than remaining on the islet. Freeman's shot disabling the sub, ironically, had also exposed the islet as a target, should any of the terrorists mount the midget sub's sail to pay back the Americans for their audacity.

"Where the hell's Aussie and Dixon?" called Sal as Choir gunned the RIB, calling on all its horsepower.

"I see Dixon," yelled Choir. "He's stuck on that sea stack over there." Choir indicated a stubby, Dumpster-sized, starfish-cluttered sea stack fifty yards west of them. The SEAL diver, having clung to the sea side of the stack, had now inched his way farther around it. While it didn't afford any flat areas upon which he might rest, it was nevertheless scabrous enough with crustaceans that he had no difficulty hanging on to it out of the sub's line of fire.

Heading for him, the RIB began taking fire from a dozen or so of the hooded terrorists who positioned themselves along the "dock"—a crescent of crushed shell and sand to the left of the cave. Inaccurate though it was, given the fast-moving RIB, neither Freeman, Sal, nor Choir had much more success at hitting their terrorist targets once they'd "looped" Dixon aboard. One second they were firing from atop a four-foot chop, the next they were shooting on the downslide, the loud, crackling firefight coming from both sides unable to exact any serious punishment. Then Aussie, having successfully sought the turbulence of the waterfall-sea interface to hide in, saw the sail of the midget, which had appeared much larger from the water, coming alive with men wearing black balaclavas and overalls.

Like soldier ants erupting from their hive, half a dozen of the terrorists were already on deck, another cramped four remaining in the sail. Two of the latter, Aussie could see, were a machine gunner and his feeder. Of the other duo, one was obviously what

U.S. military attachés around the world colloquially called the TIC—terrorist in charge—his authority evident as he directed a work party hurriedly toward the stern. The other man held an AK-47.

While the TIC continued to instruct his minions aft via what Aussie guessed must be a throat mike, two of the six soldier ants opened up with Kalashnikovs, the sound augmenting the tarpaper-ripping noise of the sail's heavy .50 caliber machine gun, whose fan-shaped sweep of fire moved unhurriedly but with relentless intensity through a seventy-to-ninety degree arc, from the RIB that had picked up Dixon across to the interface of the waterfall and the open sea. It was as if the TIC had anticipated that the remaining American diver—Aussie—possibly wounded, would seek the camouflage of the falls, perhaps using its noise as a cover in the event that he was so badly hurt he could not silence his pain.

Freeman, unable to see Aussie Lewis, nevertheless refused to risk losing the RIB in looking for him. He knew Aussie would have made the same decision—no point going after one man when it was critical that the RIB, by using the sea stack and islet as protection, could continue to harass the sub to buy time until Jensen's patrol craft and/or aircraft could arrive. And should the sub, despite the violent cavitation of its shaft, somehow manage to get to deep water and dive, Freeman knew it was imperative that he, Choir, Sal, and now Dixon mark its position for the massive antisub attack that would be launched. In any event, even if it managed to maintain a knot—or more, should the soldier ants repair the prop's basket—the four Americans seriously doubted that the sub would get beyond the main channel.

Freeman, Choir, and Salvini also understood that despite their RIB's maneuverability and firepower, now that they'd expended the AT-4 launcher, their collective small arms fire would be no match for the sub. Though a midget, it nevertheless dwarfed and outgunned them with the big .50 mounted on the sail.

Aussie, his strength waning as he trod water in the sunlit mist of the falls, also understood the necessity of the RIB biding its time, now using the protection of what would afterward be known as "Dixon's sea stack." Aussie further understood something his four companions couldn't because their line of sight was obscured by the waterfall's mist and the islet east of them: A work party of four of the black-clad submariners was already busy with monkey wrenches, a man with a sledgehammer standing by. The four men were obviously trying to unscrew the four bolts that held the prop's protective basket in place, one of the two starboard bolts already undone. If they managed to remove and jettison the protective basket in time, the prop's shaft, free of the warped basket, could surge to full power. Then the sub, even at six or eight knots, would be out and crash diving in minutes.

Aussie knew that even if the general had reestablished contact with Admiral Jensen, and COMSUBPAC-GRU-9 had dispatched the cavalry, it was highly doubtful they'd detect the midget, because the sub was sheathed entirely in a kind of sound-absorbing anechoic tile he'd never seen before, the tiles so barnacle-free that Aussie guessed they must be virtually brand new and impermeable to antisub sonar. Added to this was the one great advantage the diesel-electric subs had over the nuclear super subs, such as Captain Rorke's late Virginia-class *Utah*: The old-fashioned diesel electrics were able to shut down completely, able to sit somewhere on the vast ocean bottom in absolute silence, while the nukes, for all their noise-dampening independently suspended compartment technology, could never be totally noise-free because of the necessity of keeping the reactor's cooling pump going at all times, the giveaway heartbeat, however faint, of every nuclear navy.

Aussie intuitively flinched as another long burst of the sub's heavy caliber machine gun raked Dixon's sea stack, the .50 rounds zinging off the basalt rock, sending beehive-humming fragments of starfish and crustaceans into the air. Perhaps, Aussie thought, if he could muster enough energy to dive and swim to the sub, coming in on its eastern flank, where the terrorists were least likely to expect an attack, he could toss two or three of his HE and flash-bang grenades and take out the .50, allowing the RIB to speed in and unload all the ordnance it had on the work party.

As if his comrades two hundred yards off to the west behind the sea stack had the same intent in mind, Sal, Dixon, and Freeman—Choir steering the RIB as it darted out from behind the stack—opened fire. Sal was on the bow-mounted M-60, Dixon feeding its belt, and the general was firing his MP5. Thin, high plumes of water were leaping up about the sub's stern from the fusilade. One of the terrorists' four-man work party dropped away from the prop's basket, his body spurting blood as gulls screeched in alarm and expectation above the sub, whose sail seemed to explode in an outrage of return fire that sent the RIB in a tight U-turn back behind the stack. What gave Aussie pause for thought was the extraordinary bravery of the work party—only one of the remaining three flinching under the RIB's attack. Even so, there was no pause in their work, none of them deigning to turn around, the only visible sign of their concern being the increased activity around the basket, their remarkable concentration projecting an air of contempt for the nuisance Americans.

Seeing the same insouciance, the general admiringly muttered, "By God," as he helped Sal and Dixon secure the RIB to the stack's barnacle-crusted hide. "I'd decorate those sons of bitches—every one of them!"

"I'd rather shoot 'em, General," said Sal.

The general slapped Salvini heartily on the shoulder. "So would I, Brooklyn, so would I. But all we have to do is worry them for another ten minutes—then we should have close air support. Sink the bastards!"

"That's for me," said Choir.

Dixon said nothing, the delayed shock of his underwater fight now hitting him full force, leaving him unable to join in the banter that seemed to come so naturally to these combat-hardened warriors. The loss, too, of his mentor and friend Albinski was still too recent, along with the scenes of floating, often eviscerated dead he'd seen littering the strait east of the U.S.-Canadian choke point. And the *smell* of the dead, something that none of the training films or movies had managed to convey, a stink that evoked feelings of revulsion, then guilt for feeling such revulsion. All this had at once frightened and confused him. If only he had the guts to dive, he thought, to swim out and pop up close enough to the sub's stern.

"Dixon," Freeman said, the general's left hand acting as a pike for the RIB against the stack.

"Sir?"

"You see what nationality the guy was?"

"No, sir. Was all I could do to stop the bastard from killing—"

They both instinctively ducked, together with Choir and Salvini, the sub's machine gun punching its heavy caliber rounds into the stack. The wind behind them made their impact so loud, it sounded as if they were going to come straight through the rock. The ricochets went every which way, one of them clipping the RIB's defunct radio mast, which the man on the sub could see now and then as the inflatable rode up and down in the chop.

"Nothing particular about his weapons?" Freeman asked Dixon, the general's cool under fire remarkable to Dixon, whose first kill had happened only a half hour or so before.

"Nothing particular that I saw on him, General."

"Knife?" Freeman pressed.

"Son of a—" began Dixon in surprise, when another of the .50's bursts found its target, keeping the Americans' heads down, buying time.

"What was it you saw?" demanded Freeman.

"It was a TAK—ten-inch blade, with a—yeah, a drop point. I recognized it because some of the Canuck JTF-9 guys use 'em." JTF-9 was the Canadians' select antiterrorist commando force. "Canvaslike grip," continued Dixon. "A cutting edge—I dunno—about four or five inches."

"I know it," said Freeman.

"What we *need* to know," said Choir, "is what kind of sub it is."

"Oh, I know that," said Freeman. "It's a midget!"

"Shit," said Sal, shaking his head.

This time the three veterans' laughter was joined by Dixon's. He liked these guys. A hell of a situation they were in, unable to stop what might have been the biggest threat to American security in the history of the republic, and these guys could crack a joke—a weak joke, sure, but a joke. This, he thought, was what the drill instructors meant about "staying calm under fire."

"For my money," said Freeman, still talking about the TAK knife, "it means this damned sub might be supplied locally from across the line. From terrorists in Canada. Not the sub's ordnance—that's been dropped off. Probably the same freighter that dropped off the midget in the first place."

"So?" pressed Sal, his tone of cheeky informality still capable of surprising Dixon, the outsider; a welcome one, but an outsider nevertheless.

"Whoever those bastards are on the sub," Freeman said to Dixon, "you think you could get close enough to delay them a bit longer?"

The general's question was just that—a question, not a command. The sub's .50 paused for a moment. "Barrel probably getting too hot!" said Freeman, adding, "Remember, son, *l'audace, l'audace, toujours l'audace*!"

"It means—" began Sal.

"I know what it means, goddamn it!" replied Dixon hotly. "Yeah, I might get close enough with a swim buddy, but I haven't seen Aussie. Have you?"

None of them had.

"Yeah," said Sal, keeping his head low, "you're right, Pete. It'd be pretty dicey. That'd be just what they'd be looking for."

Two hundred yards away, Aussie cinched the strap on his flippers and, descending below the undulating and sunlit surface beneath the falls, went deeper, but not so deep that he couldn't see his HE and flash-bang grenades and his MP5. He swung the submachine gun around to his front and loosened the sling so if they spotted him as he surfaced, he could squeeze off a burst— get the bastards' heads down long enough for him to toss a couple of the grenades at the work party.

By now he'd seen that they had two of the bolts off the prop's basket, one of the terrorists working so hard and fast he'd slipped on one of the anechoic tiles and into the sea. He was quickly jerked back up to the deck, monkey wrench still in hand, resuming work in seconds.

The next deep thumping sounds of the sub's machine gun and the crackle of lighter AK-47 fire echoed off the stack, the base of which absorbed several hits. Fist-sized chunks flew off, some smacking loudly into the water, other fragments tearing into the RIB's stern, which, despite Choir's best efforts, had been caught in the constant wash behind the stack and sucked out from it long enough to make it at times a clearly visible target. Rock fragments from the stack had already taken out three or four feet of the inflatable flotation cells, and the resulting holes immediately flooded with seawater.

Then Freeman was knocked back into the stern and Sal crashed into Choir. The general, temporarily underwater, was spluttering obscenities as he surfaced. "Goddammit—that's enough! Dixon!"

There was no answer.

"Dixon?"

"He's gone," said Sal, nodding in the direction of ten o'clock, at a point about twenty feet out. "He's under, General. He slipped under during our scramble."

Freeman was dragging himself aboard. "Can you still see him, Sal?"

"No."

"Was he hit?"

Sal and Choir considered the question. They realized they didn't know. Maybe he hadn't dived in at all.

"Son of a—goddammit!" It was the general holding pieces of what used to be a functioning cell phone. "Goddamn it, that's unreasonable!"

Sal was checking Dixon's gear bag to see if there was any blood on it. There wasn't, but he saw that the bag contained what was immediately recognizable as a three-foot-long spear gun. Collapsible.

"So," put in Choir, "that's how the laddie took care of his underwater nemesis. Never said a word, did he?"

"No," said Sal. "He didn't. Where the hell's Aussie?"

CHAPTER THIRTY-SIX

CHARLES RISER WAS going home. Sent home by Ambassador Rogers, who had been his staunch defender at the embassy, more willing than most to "cut Charlie some slack," as he put it, after the tragedy of Mandy Riser's murder by Li Kuan's terrorists in Suzhou. It wasn't so much Charles's behavior at the embassy in Beijing, but his unauthorized forays into Chinese officialdom, such as his pestering General Chang, which had resulted in a plethora of complaints from the Chinese. Beijing used the complaints to deflect the U.S. ambassador's enquiries about why the PLA air force, under the guise of Red-Cross-flagged ships supposedly supplying the people of Penghu with urgently needed food supplies and rebuilding materials, had in fact been unloading more crates of MiG-29s Sukhoi 30 Flanker fighter-bombers.

Charlie was fuming, but in those rare moments of objectivity he forced upon his grieving soul, he knew that the ambassador had made the correct decision for the embassy as a whole.

While waiting for the China Air flight to Seattle via Narita, he took the photograph of Amanda from his wallet. There was something important about actually holding it. Merely looking at framed pictures of her had never been enough. Intellectually absurd, he told himself, but nevertheless it somehow drew her closer. The only photo of her that he kept in his wallet was one of her with their chocolate-colored spaniel. Mandy had called him "Truffles," because of the dog's ears. Truffle had habitually refused to surrender a grungy old rag Charlie's wife had used to wipe the dog down when he'd rolled ecstatically in the piles of

277

bitch-scented fall leaves from the border collie next door. Everyone said it was because of the collie's scent that Truffles had refused to give up the disgusting old rag, but Charlie knew it was because of the dog's memory of his wife. Truffles had held on to that rag until the day he died of grand old age, everyone fondly remembering the faint deathbed growl as the vet tried to move it during his final examination. The family, in fact, had erupted in laughter, and it had smoothed the beloved pet's passing.

But nothing could ease Mandy's passing in his mind. There was never so-called "closure," but at least he'd hoped and prayed for the possibility of justice. And now even that seemed lost.

It was meager solace, but Charles Riser had treated himself, paying the substantial difference between the embassy's economy allowance and first class. It didn't make being sent home to the doghouse any easier, but at least it allowed him to be miserable in comfort. He did not mind airline food, though as a cultural attaché in the foreign enclave of Beijing, it was mandatory for him to voice detestation of airline—and especially American—fast food, particularly at a French-hosted soiree. In fact, it was mandatory for cultural attachés never to offend any other culture. But going home had its compensations.

To hell with the French, he thought now, and their pompous posing as the moral arbiter of European interests. They'd sell their mother for a sou as quickly as Pétain caved in to the Nazis. To hell with the whole anti-American lobby and their "root causes" aid and comfort to the terrorists. Only the British and the Aussies had immediately allied themselves with America in Iraq. Even Canada, once America's dependable ally, had degenerated under what he considered an unbelievably incompetent and fence-sitting anti-American government into one of the undependables, all the time secure under the protective American umbrella. What was it Barzun had said so well? "Democratic civilization is the first in history to blame itself because another power is trying to destroy it." Well, to hell with them. All that mattered now in his life was seeing Li Kuan and his terrorist legions, who had murdered Amanda, who were attacking America right now, punished.

On China Air's screens, however, CNN's "War in America" held little hope, the updates from Homeland Defense Director Hawthorne admitting they still hadn't found the terrorist submarine. The department had received so many false reports and predictions of the sub's whereabouts from rumor-rife refugees that, Hawthorne said—sensibly, thought Riser—the only "updates" about the midget sub from now on would be of its "confirmed demise." Clever, too, Charlie acknowledged as he washed down another of the cerulean-blue Zopiclone pills that would take him out of the savage world, at least for the duration of the flight, back to the happy world of his sweet Mandy.

His recurring image was of her shrieking with delight as he took her on a horse ride along the wide, white strand of Cannon Beach. The breeze in their faces, the white-slashed blue of the Oregon surf pounding down, exhausting itself in floods of lacy foam that swirled about his feet, the gulls screeching, were so real, he believed he could smell the sea as Mandy laughed, urging him on, "C'mon, Daddy, giddy-up, fast twot, faster!"

By the time the flight attendant had begun to distribute the first-class section's meal, Charles was asleep, smiling, to the unspoken amusement of the attendant who switched off his TV console, the faces of wanted terrorists gone in an instant.

"If only it was that easy," said the passenger in the seat adjacent Riser's.

"Pardon?" said the attendant.

The passenger pointed at the blank screen. "If only we could get rid of those bastards so easily."

It was a strict government policy, adopted by all the airline and other industries these days, that employees not become involved in any "dialogue that might offend specific religious, political, and/or minority groups."

The flight attendant looked at the passenger. "I'm afraid I can't comment, sir. Have you ever heard of Cofer Black?"

"No, who's he?"

"Used to be one of George Bush's inner circle at the White House, and he said when we're finished with those terrorists, they're gonna have flies walking across their eyeballs."

"I *like* it!" said the passenger, passing his menu back to her.

"I should tell you," she said, "it's not on the menu, but if you prefer we have a vegetarian casserole."

"Fuck the vegetarian. I'll have the steak. Where's it from?"

"Nebraska. U.S. First grade."

"There you go!"

As Charles Riser was heading back to the United States, Commander John Rorke was leaving it on a military transport, not a commercial airline, his thoughts for the moment not on the coming mission but on Alicia Mayne, whom he decided to write.

> Dear Alicia,
>
> I hope you're feeling a lot better than when I visited you in the hospital. I feel a terrible sense of responsibility for what happened to you, wracking my brains for what I could have done differently. My mom and dad were fond of saying, "Everything works out for the best." Can't say I feel that way—sure as heck don't feel that way after the last little while. Seems like the roof has fallen in on us. My uncle Leroi in Panama City (the city in Florida) called the other night on my way to L.A. and said he was a boy when the Japanese attacked Pearl Harbor, and after that he grew up thinking nothing worse could happen to America! I guess I'll never get over the shock of what's happened since 9/11—so many good men and women lost—and then what's happened to you. One thing it's taught me, Alicia, and I guess a lot of others, is that life really is short, and we shouldn't put things off till tomorrow and should tell people who mean a lot to us just how much they mean to us, before it's too late.
>
> Which brings me to thinking about you. Truth is, I've been thinking about you all the time. I love you. There, I've said it. I used to laugh at those guys who said they knew it right away—the moment they saw her, etc. Well, I knew it the day you set foot on the boat. I'd heard about this knockout woman scientist we were going to have to take aboard, and at first I thought, "Right, that's all I need, a boatful of horny guys and a good-looking woman—I'll have to walk around with a

bucket of water." And then, like the old Beatle song says, "When I saw her standing there." Sounds corny, I know, but I hope you can make allowances. I'm trained to run a boat, not write love letters, but I guess that's what this is—a love letter. I've never written one before—I guess that shows—but I wanted to get this down before I get to my new posting. You'll understand I can't tell you where it is—except it's out of the States. Big clue!

I've got to hurry this up—we're about to land and, knowing the Navy, I'll be expected to get right to my job. It's true, Alicia. I've never written anyone like this in my life. Okay, I've had a few girlfriends, some pretty serious, I guess, but you're the one. I love you, and if you'll have me, I want to tie the knot. How original is that (!), but I'm rushed at the moment and I have to submit this to the unit censor, it being wartime and all, so I really can't tell you about where or when we'll see each other again, honey, but hold tight—God willing, I'll be back.

All my love, John

P.S. Maybe my mom and dad were right—at least for me.

Love, John

He read over it quickly—damn, too many "I guesses," he thought. It made him sound like an "aw shucks" grade school kid. But at least he'd told her. Before leaving the States he had wrestled with the idea of telling Alicia that her burns would heal, that he'd be there for her, that it truly didn't matter to him—and it didn't. But he'd decided against it. It would have sounded as if he was loving her out of pity, out of a sense of responsibility for her terrible ordeal.

As the military transport Hercules landed under fighter escort in Okinawa, John Rorke looked out of the window to see if he could locate the sub base, but the Perspex was streaked with rain, the lush fields of the Japanese island a dark, greenish smudge. The roar of the Herk's engines was so loud he wondered how the bus drivers could stand it. Much better, whatever the danger, to be on the standoff weapons platform, the USS *Encino* he'd been ordered to. The Los Angeles sub's mission was to position itself in the Bashi Strait between the Philippines and Taiwan, well off the *McCain*'s carrier group's eastern flank, which was coming out of the South China Sea.

It was only after he'd submitted the letter to the base censor, confident that the censor would not see any indication of where one of the U.S.'s supreme weapons platforms had been posted, that Rorke realized Alicia probably wouldn't be able to read it without someone holding it for her, since her hands, like her entire upper torso, were swathed in bandages. Well, he thought, so what if someone had to read it to her? Better to have said it than not. If she didn't feel the same about him . . . Better to have loved and lost than never to have loved at all. He could see people saying he wanted to marry her out of pity, and how could a man want a woman who was so—well, disfigured? But all he knew was what he felt. He loved her. Now, all he had to do was survive.

CHAPTER THIRTY-SEVEN

IF THE SUB'S diesel-electric capability of attaining absolute silence made for evasion of sonar signals amid the cacophony of competing ocean noise, the four terrorists banging and otherwise working at the sub's stern did exactly the opposite. Which was why the sub's captain continued to exhort his men to hurry. Aussie could see that at this rate, by the time the patrol craft out of Keystone or an antisub plane from Whidbey Island reached the sub, it would have jettisoned the basket.

But neither the sub captain nor Freeman, who was totally occupied by the dangerous business of staying alive long enough to delay the sub, had factored Frank Hall's *Petrel* into the equation. The moment his highly sensitive sensors, normally used to detect the whereabouts of dummy torpedoes fired on the test range, picked up the loud banging—vectoring in the sub's exact location—Hall had decided to investigate, to see if it was friend or foe. If the latter, he would "lend a hand," as he put it to his first mate and crew. Besides, as an ex-SEAL, Hall had a personal aversion to people who fired torpedoes at civilian vessels.

"Lend a hand?" asked the bosun hesitantly. "What exactly does that mean, Captain?"

"Don't know exactly. But I'm working on it," answered Frank, having already instructed the *Petrel*'s helmswoman to swing about, putting the vessel on a course for the banging noise that was still blipping as an amber dot on his sonar screen.

"It's close inshore," said the first mate. "Between Pillar and Slip Points."

"This is voluntary?" pursued the bosun, adding quickly, "I'll go, but some of the crew—"

"The crew's American, aren't they?" said Frank.

"Yes, but—"

"I want to be fair," answered Frank. "If any of the crew want out, I'll understand. They're free to go overboard."

"Into the RIB?" said the bosun.

"Five second fuses for the balloon-carried charges?" asked the first mate.

"No," Hall corrected him. "If this bogey's the terrorist sub—which I'm sure it is, given the location of that fish that was fired at us—we're going to need our RIB and our whirly bird in—" He glanced up at *Petrel*'s chronometer. "—in about ten minutes at full speed. So batten all hatches and get the helo ready to fly."

"Sir," interjected the mate, "Doppler scope shows fog moving in quickly along the coast."

Hall acknowledged the meteorological information. This time of year fog was always moving in, then out, then in. He turned back to the bosun. "I'll fill in the pilot on the GPS, et cetera. While I'm doing that, I want you, six crew, and the chief," by whom he meant *Petrel*'s chief engineer, a man of fertile imagination and outstanding mechanical aptitude, "to mold a dozen or so five-pound blocks of LOSHOK—five-second fuses—and jerry-rig four slingshots for them. Big slingshots. Got it?"

Before the bosun could respond, Hall turned to the first officer. "Mate, I want you to organize a few charges for our helo, about seven pounds apiece, then tell the pilot I want a word with him."

The bosun's earlier sense of excitement, gained from his skipper's infectious enthusiasm, was suddenly arrested. He wasn't concerned so much by the prospect of handling the packs of ammonia-dynamite cartridges, but by having to insert the fiddly, thumbnail-sized blasting caps used at the end of the fuse or primacord that would have to be attached to each LOSHOK's primary charge. He'd never seen anyone killed by an accident with cartridges of LOSHOK, but he knew a few ex-Marine geology seismic technicians who were missing fingers from having to handle the tiny blasting caps under this kind of time pressure.

"Cut five-second fuses for the five-pound slingshot packs," Frank told the bosun.

"How long for the helo packs?" asked the first mate.

"I don't know," said Frank. "We'll have to cut them to order, depending on the wind."

"No wind now," said the mate. "Doppler shows—"

"Fog!" shot back Frank. "Yeah, I know—you told me before. We'll just have to do the best we can."

The bosun and mate exchanged worried glances. It was the first time Hall had implicitly confirmed that he was playing all this by ear, that he wasn't at all sure that whatever he had in mind would work. Well, thought the bosun, he'll have to explain his general idea in a couple of minutes, at the most. Short, if not so sweet, because in another six minutes they'd be closing on the sonar's blip.

Hall grabbed the PA mike. "Attention all hands. This is the captain speaking . . ."

"A *slingshot*?" the chief engineer asked the bosun.

"Yeah," said the bosun, making a skeptical "I *know*" face to the clutch of oilers who'd also been summoned. To his surprise, however, the chief turned casually to his engine room watch, raising his voice to compete with the thunder of *Petrel*'s 1,500 horses while the normally "off-watch" engine room crew attended to the engines' glistening, oil-slicked pistons. They were pounding hard, to spin the prop to maximum revolution, the oceanographic vessel shaking so violently at fifteen knots that every rivet seemed on the verge of popping.

The chief was holding up two twelve-foot-long pieces of aluminum rod. "Take these to the pipe bender, guys. I want you to turn out four Y shapes. No soldering to get a single stem—haven't got time. Means you'll have a long, skinny U-handle for each slingshot. We'll use some of our quarter-inch rubber tubing for the slings. Okay?"

"Yeah, Chief, but what'd we use for that part—you know—that'll actually hold the LOSHOK as we pull it back?"

"For chrissake," retorted the chief. "I have to tell you everything? I dunno—use your initiative. Cut sections of leather from your belt." He pointed to "Tiny," *Petrel*'s big, overweight diesel mechanic. "Use Tiny's belt. Enough for twenty slingshots, right, Tiny?"

"Yeah, very funny!"

"Go!" commanded the chief. "I want you back in five. Fastest gets extra shore leave."

"Gimme that friggin' rod!" said one of his crew. A few seconds later he was spinning one of the vices' handles, the jaws opening like a gopher.

"Hurry up!" his helper, Jimmy, said, adding, "You're like an old woman."

"Up yours," retorted the other crewman, Malcolm, already having made the first bend in the pipe. "This sucker'll throw a baseball a hundred yards."

"You won't be throwing a ball," Jimmy said. "You take time winding up with that LOSHOK like you do at baseball, you'll blow your balls off!"

Malcolm didn't answer for a few seconds; he was already making the second bend in the aluminum rod, sweat pimpling his forehead, tongue squeezed hard between his teeth in concentration as he made the third bend. He then swung the four-foot unbent section wide, its end clipping Jimmy on the stomach. "*I* won't be firing the slingshot, Jimmy. *You'll* be."

"No way, José!"

Frank Hall's voice couldn't be heard on the PA system in the engine room, and so he sent down a crewman to tell them. *Petrel* was bucking the incoming tide, reducing the ship's speed by two to three knots. Even so, the ETA was about seven minutes.

"Can you finish in time?" inquired Frank's anxious messenger.

Neither Malcolm nor Jimmy bothered answering him. Not a second could be wasted in superfluous conversation. "Tiny!" yelled Jimmy. "We need your—"

But the big oiler had already taken off his leather belt, and cut four six-inch-long strips from it.

"Atta boy!" Next, Jimmy turned to Malcolm. "Tubing, Mal!"

Malcolm handed him the flexi quarter-inch rubber hosing.

Jimmy, his face now streaming with perspiration, could've kissed Tiny when he saw that the big mechanic had already punched holes at either end of the four six-inch sections of belt leather, because all he had to do was slip the rubber tubing through both holes and tie a knot. He gave the completed slingshot to Frank's messenger. "Try it out topside. *Lose* it and I'll—"

"I won't," said the messenger, scuttling up the grated stairway.

"Use somethin' that weighs about five pounds!" Jimmy hollered after him.

Meanwhile, Malcolm was halfway through the series of bends required for the second slingshot, his job made easier because a crewman had already cut the second twelve-foot rod into the required lengths.

Ten feet below the surface of the crescent bay and six feet ahead of him, in what would normally have been the crystal clear water of the bay, Peter Dixon saw a huge inky stain in the dull, fog-filtered light. Unlike an oil spill, it swayed back and forth in an underwater ballet. It was kelp, he realized, extending left and right of him as far as he could see. He couldn't help but recall the bloody ooze that had once been Albinski, his swim buddy, and momentarily he panicked, turning to go back to the stack to rejoin Freeman, Sal, and Choir. Then he saw that an arm of the kelp had moved around in back of him. He might have to surface right here, at what he guessed was about fifty yards from the sub, and take his chances, knowing the MP5's maximum effective range was fifty yards. Surface or run?

By feel alone, Dixon switched the safety off, selecting the automatic position, and pulled the cord on his CO_2 cartridge to inflate his flotation vest, to relieve him of the necessity to tread water in the chop as he fired.

The moment he surfaced, the gunner's feeder on the sub spotted him, the dark green kelp—black in the fog—having drawn his attention. What saved Dixon from the first burst was the height of the gunner. He was short, and the few seconds it took for the gunner to up his hand grips to sustain close-range fire, Dixon got off two three-round bursts. The 9mm thudded into the work party, two of the men splashing into the water. Dixon waited in a trough in the bay's chop before firing again, and hit a third terrorist.

Freeman, manning the RIB's bow-mounted M-60 as it now shot out from the sea stack's protection to assist, opened up with one-in-five tracer, the white streaks flying high over the sail before he heard his rounds striking, sparking, on the sail's port side. The M-60 failed to penetrate the high-tensile steel, but the tracer was worrying the sub's gunner and his feeder, who pushed the ammunition belt so high above his head while ducking to avoid being hit that Freeman thought his gun would jam. It didn't, the next burst from the .50 "cracking" in the air, missing Dixon but raking the peaked bow of the RIB another fifty yards to the west. It splintered the inflatable's fiberglass keel, the disintegration at a chop-pounding thirty knots sounding like the multiple splitting of thawing spring lakes. Rather than chunks of ice disintegrating, however, the fiberglass came apart in lumps that bore an uncanny resemblance to cotton candy.

The RIB was sinking, but Freeman doggedly squeezed off a three-second burst even as the inflatable sank nose down into the choppy sea. The burst was so long that the M-60's barrel turned dull red, as it was wont to do after a quick hundred rounds. Sal was convinced that if he'd been able, the general would have snatched and fired his MP5 or thrown a couple of his grenades at the sub, except for the fact that he was sinking.

"C'mon, General!" Sal shouted. "Head for the falls—three o'clock!" As the overheated barrel sizzled, releasing vapor into a fog that was quickly growing thicker, obscuring the sub, Choir and Sal saw the general with his hands still on the M-60, seawater spurting up through the multiholed deck. As Freeman was obscured from sight, the fog was pierced by tracer, which, given the RIB's acute angle, had no possible chance of hitting the sub.

Aussie Lewis, hearing the noise of the firefight, along with the surge of the RIB's prop as it raced through the water, dived and kicked furiously to clear the turbulence of the falls. Submerged and without an attack board, he was keeping the distance count in his head—usually a simple enough task, but under fire, demanding. When he judged he was within range, his vision blocked by the inky droop of what had become a bay-wide blanket of kelp, he came up, wiping kelp off his mask, glancing quickly to see whether Sal, Choir, Freeman, or Dixon was in his line of fire.

He saw nothing but fog and the dark stain of kelp off to his left, beyond which he then spotted his four SpecFor buddies. They were swimming toward the now deserted beach where discarded boxes and drums were afire, suffusing the fog with an orange glow. The fierce crackling noise of knotted pine packing cases going up in flames made it sound as if a distant firefight was in progress, when in fact no one could be seen in the cave or along the sand and rocky shoreline.

Like the others still swimming toward the shore, Aussie had lost sight of the sub in the dense fog that kept rolling in. All he was aware of now was the soft whir of a helicopter that was already above him before he recognized its telltale, muffled engine sound. It was a two-seater Little Bird, PETREL II stenciled along its tail boom. The chopper swooped over Freeman, Choir, and Sal, as well as Dixon, who was in the process of joining his comrades, still about forty yards from the bay's shore. Aussie guessed, correctly, that the Little Bird's infrared homer had been drawn into the bay by the heat of the fires on the beach.

He dove again and kicked hard for the beach, making better

time submerged than his surface-borne comrades. He was slowed, however, by more kelp, and when he surfaced again, his ears were ringing from the noise of the two approaching ships that the others had also heard and also were as yet unable to see. As Aussie drew closer to the other four members of the team, he surfaced. His kelp-draped head startled the nerve-rattled Dixon, who was about to fire when he recognized the floppy SEAL hat above the mask of the "creature from the Black Lagoon," as Salvini would later call Lewis.

Now, however, Salvini, the general, and Choir were not watching Aussie, but the cliff face. Like a motorist seeing an onrushing car too late, everything had slowed to breath-stopping slow motion as the Little Bird pilot, his helmet visible despite the fog, realized the fire his infrared had detected was just that—a fire on a beach and not a burst of radiant heat from a fleeing sub. He took the Little Bird up sharply, avoiding the cave's mouth and most of the soaring green cliff face—but not its overhanging lip of vegetation-covered rock.

The helo's blades sliced into the hidden underside of the overhang then dropped, tail rotor first, plummeting down to the beach. Freeman's team involuntarily braced for the explosion they all expected, and it came a few seconds after impact, the flames belching upward, illuminating the cave mouth. For the first time, they saw an aluminum ladder, about twelve feet long, leading up from the beach to the cave, clearly visible as the heat of Little Bird's conflagration, which included the three packs of LOSHOK, melted the ladder's struts, the struts drooping like strips of spaghetti as the ladder collapsed into a whitish, stringy pile of molten metal.

While Freeman's swim team approached the beach, they could see the fiercely burning hulk of the helicopter, and two dead terrorists floating just out from the beach, their oil-slicked bodies reflecting the fiercely burning remains of the chopper. As the pilot's khaki-green uniform turned black, his stomach bursting, the general looked away. It wasn't squeamishness—he'd seen much worse. Rather, it was a habit adopted years before the war on terrorism when a suave young Grand Prix champion had been invited to address a NATO officers' mess in

Heidelberg. "Whenever there is the catastrophe on the circuit," he had told his American hosts, most of them officers from armored units, "you must never watch—you understand? You must watch your bottom, because in that moment when you are watching the catastrophe in front of you, the driver on your rear will take advantage of your lack in concentration and—voilà!— will attack from behind and win the race. Yes?" There had been a lot of Belgian beer drunk that night, and a lot of drunks, bored with the routine of guarding the Fulda Gap through which Soviet armor was expected to pour if the Communist Warsaw Pact attacked. No one had even heard of Jihad, bin Laden, or Li Kuan in those peaceful cold war days. But Douglas Freeman, then due for his "bird," his promotion to colonel, had remembered every word that the "Bottom Belgian," as he was called, had said. And now Freeman, though sorry for the pilot, watched his rear, turning seaward, and caught a glimpse of the sub as the thick fog in the bay momentarily thinned, burned off by the heat from the helo and beach fires.

Though Freeman, now swimming to catch up to the others, couldn't hear the sound of the prop yet, the sub seemed to be moving, perhaps using its battery power, not wanting to be heard leaving the bay.

"Sub's escaping!" he yelled. Yet he felt a surge of hope. The fact that the sub was still on the surface could only mean she hadn't yet reached water deep enough to submerge, and the fog was too thick to permit the terrorists to see the landmarks they'd used as channel markers.

By the time Freeman had called to his comrades above the noises of the beach inferno and crashing waves, the sub had vanished. No one except Dixon doubted him, the raw-nerved diver remembering, as Freeman did, something *he* had been told at the beginning of *his* career and seen verified by his own experience: that under high stress, combatants become powerfully predisposed to see what they expect. Perhaps Freeman had projected the image of the sub, in his mind's eye, out into the fog. After all, Dixon had seen two terrorist underwater swimmers in the kelp that turned out to be peripheral trails of submerged kelp.

"You sure, sir?" he called.

"Yes—"

"General!" It was Sal, hauling himself ashore. "On the beach, one o'clock."

It was a small, fifteen-foot aluminum boat, on pushcart wheels. A golf-cart-like handle stuck up from under the bow, a good-size cream-colored outboard was on the stern, and the paint was blistering from a combination of radiant heat from the fires to the left and from the Little Bird's crash. The helo's explosion had created a firebreak in the scattered line of burning debris, a break without which the aluminum boat, its wooden trailer already smoldering, would itself have been engulfed in flame.

"Time we got a friggin' break!" shouted Aussie, unconscious of his pun until after he'd said it. In any event, no one laughed, the pilot's torso now a cinder block toppling forward into the taffylike blob that had been the Little Bird's plexiglass bubble.

Salvini being closest to the beach, about ten yards off, and having deflated his Mae West, struck out in an Australian crawl toward the trailer and boat, his powerful strokes testimony to the superb training that Freeman insisted upon and was so proud of.

"Dixon!" the general commanded, between intakes of air. "Check out the beach. We still don't know where these bastards are. Choir, you, me, and Aussie into that tin boat."

CHAPTER THIRTY-EIGHT

SALVINI EMERGED FROM the sea in a tangle of kelp that had formed a wide, dark margin around the bay. Exhausted, running on adrenaline alone, he lumbered across a thin sliver of sand, up over a waist-high rock ledge, and across more sand to the aluminum boat. Cupping his hands, he then began dousing its trailer's flames with sand. He worked hard and fast and had the fire snuffed out in less than five minutes, by which time Choir, the general, the kelp-covered Aussie, and Peter Dixon had all reached the beach fifty yards east of Sal's superb one-man fire brigade.

Sal could feel his knees hot, about to buckle. As a distance runner in his off-duty hours, he knew this was a dangerous sign, realizing he'd have to stop for a few minutes and rehydrate, or he'd be of no use to anyone for the next twenty-four hours.

"Taking a little nap, are we?" Aussie asked him. "Brooklyn's bust!" Aussie told the general and Choir while leaning on the boat's gunwale to take a rest himself and eat some of the emergency rations they'd managed to salvage from the sinking RIB.

"All right," said Freeman, shifting the weight of his MP5. "Let's see if this outboard's still alive."

After just one pull of the Mercury's starter cord, the engine purred like a sweet old tabby, the most welcome sound the SpecFor warriors had heard since picking up the far-off sounds of the approaching *Petrel* from which Little Bird must have been launched.

The aluminum boat had become a junk drop for fishing tackle, used pop cans, paint cans and brushes, the latter's bristles now stiffened, the failure to have soaked them evidence of the haste with which the sub's quick patch-up jobs had been done, the minor repairs no doubt speeded up by the appearance of Freeman's team.

"Mother of God!" It was Choir, unusually profane, and all work stopped. The bundle of paint rags he'd just tossed out of the boat revealed a long, rough-edged gash in the bottom, about four inches wide and a foot long, as if an axe had been used to frantically sabotage the bottom of the boat.

"Tape!" shouted Freeman, intolerant of the slightest delay. "C'mon, move!"

Aussie's roll of the super-strong military-issue duct tape had been badly slashed by his fight with the underwater terrorists, but Sal, Choir, Dixon, and Freeman's waterproofed rolls were intact. "Cut rubber slices to fit off the trailer's tires," Freeman continued. "Stuff 'em into the gash and tape the whole lot, inside and outside the keel."

"Won't last more'n an hour," opined Dixon, whose hands were shaking from the cold, despite the insulation provided by his wet suit. He was retrieving the rags, tossing them on the beach fire to warm up the team.

"Half an hour's all we need," said Freeman.

Choir's K-bar made short work of the boat trailer's tires, the rubber still so hot from the beach fires' heat that it couldn't be handled with bare hands. "Get some water, Aussie," he said, Lewis heading down toward the line of kelp that fringed the fogbound beach. Choir cut the engine, and now they could hear the low, pulsating sound of a vessel three to four miles off in the fog. It was either the oceanographic vessel *Petrel*, Freeman told them, or the bigger and faster Hurricane-class patrol ship, the *Skate*, that Admiral Jensen had told him was being dispatched from its Keystone station. Despite having to travel almost twice the distance to the Darkstar anomaly, the 170-foot-long *Skate*'s speed of forty miles per hour against *Petrel*'s fifteen would mean they should both arrive around the same time.

"I heard two ships before," said Aussie, returning with water to cool the rubber tires.

"So did I," added Choir, who with Salvini's help had now sealed the gash inside the boat, Dixon and Freeman still working as fast as they could on the keel.

The combination of odors from fires in the cave and the pungent, now empty diesel drums, their hand pumps still attached, mixed with the sweeter smell of burning pine and the lingering odor of cordite and expended tracer casings to create a cloying mix that made Choir feel as if someone had stuffed his nostrils with cotton batting, forcing him to breathe through his mouth. And the warmer atmosphere on the beach that had pushed the fog offshore for a while was gradually disappearing, adding to the general discomfort of the team.

"Let's hurry this up, lad," Choir told Dixon. "Sooner I get some fresh air—"

"Hey!" shouted Dixon. "Get off my back!"

Aussie and Salvini's silence seemed to thunder up and down the beach. Peter Dixon *did* have an attitude.

"Anyone seen any weapons, ammo, lying about?" cut in Freeman.

"Saw an M-60," put in Aussie, "where I came ashore, but it's useless. They spiked it."

"So," said Freeman, "we make do with what we have."

Dixon scrambled out from under the trailer. "Finished."

"Outstanding," the general told him, slapping him on the shoulder. "You stay here and hold the beach in case we need a hand when we return."

"Right." Dixon nodded, grabbing his camelback and taking a long drink through its flexi tube.

"Let's go, SAC!" said the general, his acronym standing for Salvini, Aussie, and Choir.

It had once been BACS, but this was the first time Brentwood was missing from the roster, forced to stay behind at Fort Lewis, where Freeman knew that the only outlet for his frustration at not being with his old team—and for the guilt he felt over his failure to get Li Kuan in Afghanistan—was to spend hour after hour firing small arms on the practice range. But even then, Freeman guessed the ex-SpecFor warrior must be frustrated by the fact that his left hand couldn't master anything bigger than a handgun. At Fort Lewis, his proficiency with the Colt .45 and HK 9mm pistol was so good it had earned him the moniker "Wyatt Earp." But Brentwood, like Freeman, like everyone else in a modern army, knew that the day of the handgun was over in war—it was merely a backup piece rarely, if ever, used. In this world war against terrorism, sidearms were used only by pilots shot down behind enemy lines, if such a "line" could be found in a war marked by ever-shifting and remarkably fluid fronts.

As their aluminum boat glided over the kelp at the water's edge, Freeman, standing up in the bow, bracing himself against the chop, fixed his binoculars on the fogbound sea beyond the roar of the falls, helping Choir navigate past the sandbars they'd seen when first entering the bay.

"Think he saw the sub?" Sal asked Aussie, both of them kneeling behind the boat's midline.

"Got eyesight like a friggin' eagle, the old man has," said Aussie. "And ears. If he says he saw it, he saw it, mate."

"Hush!" said Choir, also straining to hear.

"Hush?" Sal whispered to Aussie. *"Hush!"*

"It's gone!" proclaimed Freeman.

"Maybe a chopper from that tub Jensen's sending?" proffered Aussie.

Freeman shook his head, and without turning around, said, "No. Hurricane class doesn't have a chopper. Could be a Navy chopper out of Whidbey, but they're all but useless in this pea soup."

No one answered. The fog was rolling in on them in huge banks of bone-chilling air, the warmer convection currents generated by the beach's fires replaced by colder sea air. For Choir it felt as if someone had opened the doors to a gargantuan freezer, the resulting wind chill factor evicting any residual warmth the SpecFor warriors had absorbed from the numerous small fires while on the beach.

"Can't hear those ships anymore," said Choir.

In fact, they hadn't heard the sub's quiet, electric-smooth exit from the bay, but had all heard the unmistakable underwater throb of two approaching vessels.

"Cut the Merc!" ordered Freeman. "I'll go over, have a listen."

He went in and sank beneath the surface. Then Sal, Choir, and Aussie waited anxiously to see whether the general, taking advantage of the speed of underwater sound propagation, could pick up the sound of the two vessels. After a while, the three veterans in the boat grew worried. The fogbound sea was calmer than before, and there were no whirlpools to be seen in the twenty-foot radius of visibility around the boat. Maybe it was just their fatigue, but it seemed that the general should have popped back up by now. You either heard something or you didn't.

"What now?" said Aussie disgustedly.

Sal, trying to see through the fog, shrugged. "That bastard Murphy again." Their string of mishaps and near misses had been no different than in any other war they'd been in. Victory wasn't a matter of "Rambos" going crazy, but of a team working through the screw-ups, having the will, equipment, and training—or "WET," as the general called it—to see it through.

Then Freeman's head popped up right beside Choir. "Jesus—" began the usually sanguine Welshman.

"Hide and seek," said the general, spitting out a fringe of kelp. "Sound vectors coming at you from every direction down there."

"Decoys?" suggested Aussie as he helped the general aboard.

"That's my read," replied Freeman. "Damn sub's dropped sonar 'sub' decoys along the way. Decoys are sending out sub engine noises all over. Our boys on *Petrel* and the *Skate* have obviously stopped and cut engines and are listening—trying to figure out which sub sound is the real one."

"How long do those decoy batteries last?" asked Salvini.

"Two, three weeks," said Choir.

"Oh shit! Meanwhile those Chinese are sitting all quiet and cozy on the bottom," said Aussie.

The others ignored Aussie's certainty that the terrorists were Chinese.

"They're not so cozy," said Freeman. "Their air'll run out sooner or later."

"But before the CO_2 scrubbers are exhausted," said Choir, "they could last what, three to four days?"

"Something like that," agreed the general.

"Oh shit!"

"Wish you'd stop saying that, boyo," said Choir.

"Oh *hush*!" said Aussie.

"Yeah," joined in Sal. "*Hush*, you little Welsh—"

"Knock it off," the general ordered, which he rarely did. But even among the most resistant SpecFor teams, nerves could get frayed, fatigue and cold misconstruing friendly abuse. "Let's head back to shore," Freeman added. "I'd hoped we could tag that bastard midget, but we're only spinning our wheels out here."

As they returned through the ever-thickening fog, no one could see Dixon, not even when they were practically at the beach.

"He's drying out," said Aussie, "by one of the fires."

"I can't see him," said Sal.

"Shouldn't have left him alone," said the general.

"He's a big boy," Sal assured him.

Choir said nothing, but, remembering how Dixon had been shaking so badly, feared what no SpecFor ever wanted to contemplate: that Dixon's hand-to-hand combat had undone him; that, spooked by the beach, he'd decided to bolt instead of doing what Freeman had ordered—stay on the beach to lend a hand to his comrades upon their return. Choir, who'd seen it happen a few times before on special operations, was pretty sure Dixon was hiding somewhere in the cave, shivering uncontrollably from the twin demons of a combat swimmer's lot—cold and unspeakable terror. The one thing you always remembered was the blood in the water, engulfing you in your sin as much as it did your dead foe, haunting some men for the rest of their lives.

Circumventing the floating kelp bed, Choir almost ran aground on a sandbar. Along the shoreline, an army of wine-dark kelp crabs moved en masse, ready to swarm any detritus trapped by the kelp. It was one of the ugliest things Choir had ever seen.

Choir was right. Dixon was in the cave. There were no distinctive footprints to guide the SpecFor team. The sandy apron below the cave had obviously been "Main Street," as the team habitually referred to the main trail or thoroughfare used by the enemy—in this case, by the terrorists to hurriedly replenish the sub. Dixon's eyes widened when he saw Choir, who had followed the speckled trail of blood from the beach, and his intake of air made an annoying, laborious sound, as if he were inhaling through straw. What neither Choir nor his three comrades had seen in the cave's dripping gloom was the duct tape across Dixon's mouth, which they now saw while approaching.

"This'll hurt, boyo!" Choir told him as the Welshman, resting his HK against the nearby boulder, knelt down to unbind Dixon. Freeman, Aussie, and Salvini, as if by instinct rather than training, formed a protective C around them.

"Mother of God!" It was Choir, in shock, realizing that Dixon's strained breath had been his last, that the damp sand the

Welshman was kneeling in was wet with blood. "Boys," Choir said softly in a tone of a sadness that physically seemed heavier than his pack.

"What's up?" asked Aussie, eyes still to the front. There was no answer from Choir, and Aussie glanced back, froze, then looked away—at anything rather than the young swimmer whose mouth had been stuffed with what remained of his blood-sodden genitals.

He had choked to death. Aussie, who would later chastise himself for his morbid curiosity—or had it been the simple human need to confirm what he thought he'd seen?—looked down in the gloom at the dead man's groin area. Jesus . . . Dixon's corpse voided, the stench vile. Even Freeman, who'd seen his share of death, felt as if he would throw up. But as usual, he maintained command and control of himself, and before he gave any order to the others, turned and, steeling himself, went over to the dead American, and took off the warrior's dog tags. "Sal, you and Aussie wrap him up. Place him on one of the beach fires. No one should see their loved one like this."

Sal, being Catholic, had an aversion to cremation, and funeral pyres in particular, but right here, right now, he agreed with the other three.

"Those bastards!" said Aussie. "That's pure evil."

No one disagreed, and as Freeman led them in a short prayer, they piled the fire with any other wood they could find from what had obviously been torpedo crates.

For several minutes afterward no one spoke, each counseled by his own thoughts as they desultorily checked the splintered wood on the pyre. But each of the four were ready to exact revenge. The general was standing at the water's edge, listening. He heard no sound of ships moving or the earlier chopper. He looked up into the gray sky and saw and heard nothing but the continuing roar of the bisected falls in front of them.

"Sal, you and Choir stay by the boat," he finally said, breaking the silence. "Whoever was here has probably gone by now, but keep a sharp eye. Aussie, you and I'll recon the beach."

Halfway along the rock and crushed-shell shore, Freeman

stopped several times to stare up into the fog and around the bay.

"Hear something, General?" asked Aussie, whose tone still conveyed his anger over what had happened to young Dixon.

"No," answered the general, and stopped walking. "You ever been to San Francisco?"

"One summer," answered Aussie, his dark mood momentarily arrested by Freeman's inquiring tone, a giveaway to those who had fought with him that he was mentally flicking through the thumb-worn codes, the precomputer card index files that held his vast repository of what sometimes seemed to others useless and unrelated information.

"I lived down by the bay for a few years," Freeman continued. "Sometimes the fog would come in like this, roll in and lie there for hours in a layer right across the bay. It was so layered you could drive right over it on the bridge."

"Well, General, there's no bridge here we can drive—oh, you mean the fog mightn't be as high as we think."

Freeman had turned around, craning his neck to look up at the dark-green-sheathed cliff face, veiled in an ever-changing curtain of fog and fire smoke. A lost world, a remote enough part of America in normal times, but now even more so as a result of the panicky evacuation of entire populations in the Northwest to all points south. Fog, cold and lonely. "See that line, kind of an S shape about eleven o'clock?"

Aussie looked to the left and saw the trail winding up the eastern end of the cliff, away from the falls and about two hundred feet east of where the Little Bird had come down, pieces of its tail rotor assembly faintly visible in the ghostly fog that rolled down over the cliff face.

"You want me to have a go?" said Aussie.

"I'll go," Freeman said.

"Ah, I'm still stiff as a prick from crouching in that damn tin boat. I could do with a stretch."

"Think I'm past it?" Freeman said challengingly. "I can still press two hundred and—"

"Hell, General, you're in better shape than anyone here." It was close to the truth. "Like I said, I need the stretch."

"Very well. Watch for mines, though I would think the last thing the terrorists would do is plant mines around—have some wild goat wandering about, getting blown up and drawing attention to the place."

Aussie took off his pack, tightened the HK's sling on his back, and put on his gloves.

Freeman glanced at his watch. "Thirty minutes?"

"Thirty minutes," confirmed Lewis, and set off.

The last he saw of the general, the legend was busy, one hand on his hip, the other directing a steaming thin stream into the kelp.

CHAPTER THIRTY-NINE

CHARLES RISER AWOKE from his Zopiclone-induced sleep to the nerve-slicing screams of children, the Boeing Jumbo having plunged two hundred feet in the worst turbulence the airline's pilots had experienced in a decade of carrying passengers over the Pacific. Riser felt faintly queasy, but in his semisomnolent state he truly didn't care whether the aircraft crashed. Death would be virtually instantaneous, and a shutter would slam down on the window of his grief- and hate-filled life. He knew he never used to hate like this, and he despised himself for it. He'd had always taken the high road, the one supposedly traveled by the cultured, educated elite who disdained the vulgarity and eschewed the banalities of the masses, for whom an eye for an eye was the guiding principle of justice, for whom rehabilitation of criminals was despised as the philosophy of effete academics who worked in tenured castles and lived on the safer side of town. It was a shock for Charles to discover that he was at one with the masses in the matter of murder.

The seat belt signs stayed on for the remainder of the flight to Seattle, some parents complaining that the CNN newscasts of the terrible situation in the U.S. Northwest should not be shown.

"We can't censor the news," the plane's purser told one of the angry mothers. "We just bring in the signals."

"Then send them back."

"Ma'am, some of the other passengers want to see it. They have loved ones in the Northwest. Besides, all you have to do is change channels or turn it off."

"It's no good turning it off," retorted the woman. "The children can see it on all the other screens in the plane."

"There's a cartoon channel."

"Cartoons!" snorted the mother. "Have you *seen* the cartoons? They're not funny. They're full of violence."

"Have they got Li Kuan?" Charles asked the man next to him.

"No. They say he's left that Kazak—"

"Kazakhstan," said Charles.

"Whatever. Some guy on PBS reckons that seeing as how Beijing couldn't beat the terrorists in that Kazak place that Beijing's done a deal with that bastard."

"They're gonna split the oil," put in the man across the aisle.

"I want to speak to the captain," the woman demanded.

"Ah, ma'am, he's kind of busy right now. We're approaching SeaTac." Then the purser said something he knew he should not have, but it had been a long, rough trip from Beijing, with long, hot stopovers at Shanghai, Narita, and Honolulu. "Ma'am, the cockpit's on total alert during approach. You know terrorists have been firing hand-held SAMs at U.S. carriers?"

"What's a SAM?" blurted out one of the kids. "Are the terrorists gonna kill us, Mom? Are the—"

"See," snapped the woman. "See what you've done?"

"I'm sorry," the purser said, and excused himself, the woman threatening massive lawsuits against the airline.

"Y'hear that?" Riser's companion asked. "Guy says the cockpit's on *total alert* during approach. What the hell they doin' the rest of the time? On half alert?"

"Too many damn computers," said another passenger. "That's

the problem. Meanwhile, one of those Arab bastards can shoot and scoot. What's Homeland Defense's computers gonna do about that? We need men on the ground."

"We've *got* men on the ground," said Charlie Riser, surprising himself with his vehemence.

"Yeah, well, what the hell are they doin'?" the other passenger pressed.

Riser didn't answer. He knew what they were doing. Bill at the embassy had kept him up to date about that, had even told him that the unconventional General Freeman had been called in to see what he could do. And the first thing Riser intended to do was contact the general—even see him if he could—tell him about Chang's imprisonment, explain that Chang, as well as being blamed for the Chinese military defeat against the terrorists, had probably heard about a deal with Li Kuan, and now Beijing wanted to keep him quiet. He mused about what kind of oil split Beijing might have offered the Muslim fundamentalists who were fighting the PLA, who were no doubt urgently needed for an invasion of Taiwan.

Riser sat back and closed his eyes again, not in repose—these days he was never naturally relaxed, only artificially with the Zopiclone at night and the antidepressant Celexa during the day. He'd closed his eyes to shut out any distraction, milking his memory for anything the distraught Wu Ling had told him at the airport. Nothing more came to mind. He hoped he might get a postcard from her, indicating where the general had been taken. All he needed was a single word, a phrase, so he could tell Washington where Chang was, so a SpecOps team could execute what Bill Heinz dryly called a "snatch and grab over the fence"—a blatant violation of another country's sovereign territory. It would be a snatch to either rescue the general and find out if he knew where Li Kuan was, or a snatch and grab to kill Li Kuan on the spot. Better yet, a snatch and grab to *capture* Li Kuan, unlike the botched Afghanistan attempt led by that Medal of Honor winner David Drentwood . . . or was it *Brent*wood? Charles couldn't remember. A snatch and grab to get Li Kuan and then torture him, put his feet to a fire, cut off his penis— Mandy had been raped—see if the seventy-two virgins in Islamic heaven would want him then. And do it slowly—make the scumbag scream. Take hours and hours and then lock him up with starving rats and—

"You okay?" the other passenger asked. "You're shaking."

Riser wasn't actually shaking, but he was grasping his armrests so tightly his hands were white, his hatred having drained the life out of them. "I'm fine," he lied. "Thank you."

"Ah, don't sweat it. We'll be down in a few minutes. Listen, I used to be a white-knuckle flier. Then I took this course called 'Who *Am* I?'" The man was fishing in his wallet for a card for the New Age guru who had a Ph.D. in Wellness from a California institute and who'd studied in India for two years at Canada's Peace and Wellness University. "Yoga guru and exposure therapy. Worked great. You oughta try it."

"Uh-huh," replied Charles.

As the stream of tired passengers entered SeaTac Customs and Immigration, Riser walked toward the quick-exit consular gate and was met by a junior State Department official, her greeting polite rather than warm. She told him that the information he had requested through his e-mail from Beijing—namely, Freeman's private cell number—was not available.

Riser smiled wearily at the tall, gangly young woman who wore a gray suit and printed scarf. Buttoned down. State Department intern, he thought, full of nervous enthusiasm and willing to lie for Foggy Bottom, as she'd just done about Freeman's cell number. How could State not know his number? He wasn't important enough to be on the "not listed" disk.

"I heard Li Kuan's organization might have penetrated the States," he said.

"Ah—yes, I've heard that rumor too."

"The department doesn't want me to contact General Freeman," he said bluntly. "Correct?"

"We don't have his number, sir."

"Did you try information?"

She laughed awkwardly.

"I don't need to see him personally," Charles told her, and could see the relief in her face, her shoulders visibly dropping.

"Well, of course we wouldn't know exactly where he is at this moment."

"How 'bout *somewhere* at this moment—like the Northwest?"

"I wouldn't know. Ah, do you have much luggage?"

"No."

"We have you booked in at the Four Seasons."

"Fine."

The situation at the hotel shocked him. It was so foreign, so choked with *refugees* pouring in from the Olympic peninsula, that for several moments he expected to hear some movie person instructing the mass of extras on how to prepare for the next shot. Only this was no film rehearsal, but the reality of frightened begging and pleading people, some waving wads of cash. Good Lord, it was like the airport at Nanjing—better dressed, but reeking of body odor. And fear.

Charles and the intern managed to get the attention of the harried, sweating concierge by holding up their State Department badges, which Charles hated to do among fellow Americans. But he'd been too long in China, where push, shove, and VIP status always won the day. By way of atonement for pulling rank, he offered to share his room with three of the refugees, his assigned room having one queen-size bed and a pull-out.

"That's very nice of you," the intern commented. It was the first genuine thing she'd said.

Charles shrugged nonchalantly. "Another point with the man upstairs!" It's what Amanda used to say. The intern was nonplused, not knowing who "the man upstairs" was.

A grateful young family of three accepted Charles's offer, and while they were getting settled, he excused himself, went to the bathroom, overloaded the toilet with toilet paper and depressed the flush button, immediately clogging the drain. He called the front desk, reported that his toilet was backed up and he'd need another room. Right now. This was unacceptable, he told them. No, he couldn't wait, he was exhausted—in the air for twenty hours.

A desk clerk, looking as harassed as the concierge, and miffed into the bargain, told Mr. Riser they had a single room, without a view, single bed only, by the elevator. "Best we can do, sir."

"Fine," said Charles, and when he got to the new room, immediately dialed CNN Atlanta. The toilet-stuffing ploy for a new room had been an old China hand's trick to escape the electronic bug that the authorities—in this case from either Homeland Defense and/or Ashcroft-trained FBI agents—had no doubt planted to listen in on phone calls.

The friendly young woman's voice in Atlanta told him that Marte Price was on assignment. Would he like to leave a voice mail? No, he wouldn't. "Tell her I have a good story vis-à-vis the PLA's General Chang, that Chang may have stumbled upon a deal between Beijing and Li Kuan."

"What was that about a visa, sir?"

"Visa?" asked Riser.

"Yes, sir. You said you had a good story—" Riser could hear the shuffling of paper on the other end, then the voice came on again. "Yes, something about a *visa*. You mean a travel document, sir, or a credit card? A credit card scam?"

Riser rubbed his forehead in frustration. "No, that was *vis-à-vis*—it means with regard to—a story about General Chang being important because he found out about—Look, would you please call her, give her this number." He read it out slowly, adding, "It's urgent. If I don't hear from her in an hour I'll call Fox. Point is, if she hears later that I called and it's been on another network she'll be totally freaked!"

"I understand, sir."

Riser hoped so.

"Mr. Riser?"

"Yes."

"Charles Riser, cultural attaché?"

"Yes. Is this Marte Price?"

"It is. Returning your call. I'm actually not that far away—in Port Townsend covering, or rather trying to—"

"Can we meet?"

"Ah, can you tell me on the phone? E-mail?"

Riser laughed, uncharacteristically rude. "Are you serious?"

"It's difficult for me at the moment to drive down to Seattle. The roads are clogged with people, traffic jams. No flights either. The fog is—well, very bad."

"Then how am I supposed to tell you? Beam myself up there?"

Marte Price was a tough veteran of the media, but she was taken aback by the man's aggressiveness. Her assistant at CNN had said he'd been "pleasant enough," actually a rather timid-sounding man. Not this guy. "Mr. Riser, there are no civilian helo charters up here, but in a city the size of Seattle I'm sure you could get some local pilot who knows the terrain well enough for the right price." She paused. "How about this: CNN'll pay half the charter, and if the story's as important as you say it is, we'll spring for the whole lot?"

Charles was gazing at the plum-colored brick wall opposite his hotel, the wall festooned with spiderwebs, moths trapped in many of them, some still alive. He turned away, looking instead at his "single" room's flickering TV, its ribbon report giving details of an American battle group, its carrier, *McCain*, having been attacked. Typically, the first reports of the carrier having been bombed or attacked by missiles were being corrected by updates. It seemed that only one plane had been involved. "Extensive damage," CNN reported, but no pictures as yet.

"Mr. Riser," came Marte Price's voice. "Are you still there?"

"I'm not worried about the money," Charles told her. "I'll find a local and come up."

"Good." They arranged to meet at a Port Townsend hotel.

"One thing more, Mr. Riser. Why did you insist on seeing *me*—why not call the local CNN affiliate or—"

"Everyone watches you."

"Well, thank you. I look forward to seeing—" But all she could hear now was a dial tone.

"What a rude bastard!" she announced to her cameraman, slamming down her phone.

Riser's truculence had come out of a bottle of Jack Daniel's. Used to neither spirits in general nor forty-proof whiskey in particular, and given Mandy's murder, the terrible state his homeland was in, and being recalled—like a "loser," as he'd heard an embassy colleague refer to him in the final days—had all proven too much. He'd begun drinking heavily, which, to his surprise, had not relieved his acute anxiety and depression. Instead, it had brought out the worst in him, behavior he was thoroughly ashamed of a few hours later at SeaTac as he strapped himself into the chartered helo, then put his head back, staring at the surly gray fog outside.

"Don't worry," said the hefty, bearded pilot cheerily. "I've been instrument-flying in this soup. Hell, in 'Nam—"

"Excuse me," said Charles, gently massaging his throbbing temple with an ice pack he'd gotten from the hotel. "I don't mean to be rude, but would you mind not talking? I'm feeling kind of—"

"Tie one on, did you?" replied the pilot, grinning. "Know how it feels, buddy."

"Yes," said Charles, whose senses were suddenly assaulted by a blast of rap noise.

"Do you, can you—please turn that off!"

The pilot's face was close to shock. "Don't like music?"

Charles's eyes closed.

"Okay, you're payin' for it."

"Have you any water?" Charles asked.

"You betcha!" the pilot said, though the frown of mystification remained on his face.

Charles took two more aspirin.

It turned out to be a surprisingly smooth ride, compared to the violent last leg of the flight from China, the pilot yelling only twice, first to tell Charles that he was following the line of Puget Sound—"God's country! 'Course, can't see a friggin' thing today"—and later to announce, "Be down in about fifteen."

Charles merely nodded, the aspirin he'd taken causing the headache to abate but now making him feel nauseated. His hands were shaking.

CHAPTER FORTY

AUSSIE'S SPECIAL FORCES training had instilled in him a love of climbing *up* things but a fervent dislike of going *down* them, finding the restraint his muscles had to exert during descent often was more taxing than when he was ascending.

"I like going down," Sal had once quipped, "if she's good looking."

Aussie had affected such an air of propriety and shock that even David Brentwood, who ignored sexual ribaldry, had joined in the team's laughter at Aussie's performance. But now there was no humor in Aussie as he ran back down the precarious S-shaped path on the side of the cliff, his Vibram boots gripping and braking hard in the damp, loamy soil. His gloved hands did their part as he slid on his backside here and there and grabbed, released, and grabbed again at the thick vegetation to brake his rapid descent. Freeman, seeing Aussie's fast, controlled descent, wondered if he could have done it as speedily. In the final segment of the S curve, Aussie came off the cliff as if from a short, steep waterslide, his boots sending warm ash from the edge of the fires into the air like gray talc.

"Fog and more fog, correct?" said Freeman, handing Aussie his canteen.

"No," answered Aussie, his macho streak trying but failing to contain his excitement. "You were right, General. Fog's layered—tip of a high radio mast spiking through it. Not all the time, but I spotted it twice."

"You get a GPS?"

Aussie took off his left glove, having written the latitude and longitude on his hand.

Sal and Choir could tell something was up as Freeman and Aussie ran toward them. "We go!" the general called out. With that, the two, grateful for the relief from the outrage and help-lessness they'd been feeling since discovering Dixon's muti-lated body in the cave, quickly pushed the aluminum boat on the wobbly trailer to the kelp line. Choir pulled the Mercury's cord rather than use up the starter motor's juice as he and his three comrades-at-arms got aboard, heading out to the mast's posi-tion. Was it the *Skate* or the *Petrel*? The position of the mast that Aussie had pinpointed by the GPS was 2.3 miles due north—well and truly out in the strait.

"Keep your eyes peeled," Freeman told them.

"We're not gonna miss her, General," Sal assured him.

"I know that," Freeman replied, "but keep your eyes on the water as well—see if that sub jettisoned anything. Remember we hit her quite a few times. Nothing substantial other than buckling the prop basket, I agree, but we sure as hell chipped her paint and tiles—stuff that'd float."

Aussie shook his head, smiling to himself in sheer admiration of the general's attention to tactical detail, which he'd fused to his philosophy of audacious strategy.

The *Petrel* was proceeding so slowly that her props barely created a wake, all her off-duty crew out on deck. Frank Hall was on the bridge, the oceanographic ship's two side-scan sonar technicians in the aft dry lab two decks below. The side scan's pictures did not come in via the clear color TV screens so beloved by Hollywood producers to make them more visual, and more believable, but rather in a dull, monochromatic series of dark gray lines on lighter grayish-white paper. Each line recorded the depth of the sea bottom, which at times was flat and at other times creviced by canyons formed millions of years ago. The end result was a two-dimensional view of the sea bot-tom, as if someone with a very sharp pencil—in this case the recorder's stylus—had drawn a look-down sketch of the strait's seabed.

Nothing but seabed was turning up on the return *pings*, the echoes of the sound strikes sent down from the electrically buckled plates in *Petrel*'s "fish"—a squashed and single-finned, tear-shaped transponder towed astern, its fin barely visible in the huge breaths of sea fog that one second seemed to swallow the *Petrel*, only to release her moments later. Cookie, the cook's helper, en route to delivering a late lunch sandwich to Jimmy and Tiny on the stern deck, sneaked into the aft dry lab, manned by the two sonar technicians, to take a peek at the side-scan profile. "Any sub, guys?"

"Six so far," one of the technicians replied dryly. "How 'bout bringing us some coffee 'stead of asking us dumb questions?"

Cookie sullenly retreated.

"Shouldn't piss him off," the other technician told his colleague.

"He's a dumb ass."

"I don't care. You get on the wrong side of these guys, they can make you sick—piss in your coffee. I know one skipper—grumpy old bastard—all he did was criticize, so one day when Cook was making custard, this kid grabbed a *Playboy* center-fold, took the old man's bowl, and went to—"

"Hey!"

"What?"

"You see what I see?" His colleague watched the stylus racing back and forth with the speed of a weaving machine's shuttle, giving them a profile from thirty-two fathoms—180 feet. Stuck in the background of a mud slope and looking like a blurred double exposure was an outline of what could conceivably be a slab of metal—either that or a slab of rock.

One of the "techies" called the bridge. "Captain, you better come down and see this."

Frank Hall walked in less than a minute later, took one look at the profile, and told the technicians, "Zoom in. High resolution." The zoom made it bigger, but not as sharp as they'd hoped.

"There's no base to it, sir. I mean, it looks like it's a slab sticking up from the mud. Maybe an old bulkhead—a wreck?"

Hall thought that the technician was right; the Strait of Juan de Fuca was littered with the metallic skeletons of marine disasters from long ago. And it would be much worse if Navy salvage and retrieval ships such as the *Petrel* didn't clear the massive hulks of the ships sunken by the terrorist sub.

"Its base could be a sub," proffered Frank, looking at the slab profile. "Some anechoic tiles could have fallen off the sub's sail. Water flow is powerful at that depth—at any depth in the strait. If the tiles on the rest of the hull are still intact, sucking up our sonar signals, we wouldn't see the base of this slab."

The recorder's stylus never ceased, but the machine's amber light was flashing, the roll of paper almost used up.

"Not *now*!" said one of the technicians, his exasperation echoed by his colleague, who ran toward the lab's paper locker situated high up to avoid any possibility of water damage, in the event of the ship's scuppers overflowing on deck and flooding over the dry lab's sill and into the lower cabinets.

Frank said nothing, calmly watching the stylus keeping up its busy work, dashing from one side of the recorder to the other like some frenzied, animate being. Sometimes it had made him smile, like the busy little "office assistant" in the corner of his computer. But the oceanographer wasn't amused now, his eyes focused on the profile, his heart punching the wall of his chest. "What are the dimensions of that slab?" he asked the attending technician, who quickly worked the recorder's control panel.

"It's about the size of a garage door. Not very big, Captain. For a sub, I mean."

"No," Frank agreed, hands behind his back in what the crew, he knew, referred to as his "Horatio Nelson" bit. "Slab isn't big for a *full-sized* sub."

The truth was, neither of them knew how big the sail of a midget sub would be. They'd never seen one up close. Few people had.

"Where's that friggin' paper?" the technician called out. "We're almost out here!"

"Easy," said Frank. "Let's not get excited." That's what Nelson would have said, he knew, but like the two technicians, he knew too that when they changed the paper, which had only about four inches of lateral scroll remaining, they would have no picture at all for ten to fifteen seconds. Frank calmly sum-

moned the bosun, telling him to cut a length of fuse for a
hundred-pound pack of LOSHOK set to detonate at thirty-two
fathoms.

"Sheesh, Skipper, that's about all we have on the ship!"

It had been a measure of the men's discipline, and perhaps
their distance from Little Bird's demise, that it had not preyed
on their minds. Instead, they'd done what they were supposed to
do without either protest or second-guessing the captain. Even
so, now was not the time for the bosun to point out what he must
know the captain already knew: that a hundred-pound charge
would just about exhaust their supply of the explosive. And so,
instead of commenting either verbally or by facial expression,
Frank maintained his steady gaze on the stylus. It helped that the
stylus had a mesmerizing effect, like watching highway lane re-
flectors at night.

" 'Bout two minutes of paper to go, Captain," said the technician next to him.

"When the amber goes to red," Frank instructed quietly, his
voice barely audible above the *sherp, sherp* of the stylus.

"Amber to red," said the technician, "right," his lips so dry
that not even the moisture of the ghostly invasions of fog could
prevent them from cracking, the faint metallic taste of blood in
his mouth.

"Captain?" It was the mate on *Petrel*'s bridge, looking
quickly from the radar out into the late evening fog and calling
down to the aft dry lab. "We have a *surface* blip—small, no bigger'n a dory. Coming in on the starboard aft quarter, five
o'clock."

At that moment, Frank saw the side-scan recorder's light go
from amber to red, the machine emitting a piercing squeal. It
was a sound some of the LOSHOK slingshot party outside the
dry lab hadn't heard before, and they momentarily thought it
might be a fire alarm.

"Fire flares! Starboard aft!" ordered Hall, his voice so loud
that it seemed to those on deck as if the whole world could hear,
including the crew of a submerged sub. "Have slingshot packs
ready to—" Damn, he remembered he'd told the bosun to pack
a hundred-pound charge for what might be the sub. The insis-

tent squeal of the recorder had panicked him, something he'd always believed his SEAL training would override. Admonishing himself to "get a grip," and, on the verge of telling the side-scan operator to "Hurry the fuck up" and finish changing the damn paper, he paused. Then, with a face suffused with self-assurance, he strode briskly to the lab door, hands behind his back.

"Bosun?" Hall said. "Have you made up that hundred-pound pack?"

"Just about finished, sir," the bosun replied, busy recounting the fuse length for the LOSHOK pack that would serve as an ad hoc depth charge to be dropped atop the sub—if it *was* the sub. "I made it about seventy pounds, Captain," the bosun added. "That leaves us with about half a dozen slingshot charges of—"

"Better call than mine, Bosun," cut in Frank. "Well done."

Hall's admission to the bosun impressed Jimmy, Malcolm, Tiny, and the other slingshot party on deck.

"Captain!" The side-scan's squealing had stopped, the stylus busy again converting *Petrel*'s *ping* echoes into more dull gray lines, the flat section that might either be a slab of sheared coastal rock or the midget sub's sail still standing alone, as if anchored in mud. There were no sound echoes that would signify anything else but ooze.

The thump of the flare gun made Tiny jump. "Did you fart?" Jimmy asked Malcolm.

But Malcolm was too wound up to see anything remotely humorous in Jimmy's comment. No doubt Jimmy wanted to appear cool, but he didn't mind voicing his fear of the boat, the radar's dot, coming in from the starboard aft position at about five o'clock. If the terrorist sub had been damaged by the SpecFor team, flooded maybe, and some terrorists were making a run for it in the sub's inflatable—well, everyone knew how fanatical terrorists were—fight to the end. And what terrorists would want to be captured by the Americans after what the CIA boys did to their al Qaeda prisoners at the U.S. Bagram base in Afghanistan? As the CIA guy had told Marte Price on CNN, "There was before 9/11, and after 9/11. After 9/11 the gloves came off."

The first parachute flare had deployed and was slowly descending, the fiercely burning flare suffusing the fog around the *Petrel* with a flickering orange light, the thump of the second flare making Tiny jump again. No jokes from Jimmy now, because the light from the second flare, allied with that of the first, had illuminated the approaching boat. Not a dory, as was thought, but a long, twenty-four-foot inflatable.

Up on *Petrel*'s bridge, Hall's first mate looked through his binoculars at the approaching craft and rang down to the dry lab, where Frank took the call.

"Captain," the first mate informed him, "it's an RIB, about three hundred yards off. Barely visible but looks like a landing party."

"Uniforms?" Hall asked.

"Greenish khaki."

"That's not Coast Guard."

"No. Could be that SpecFor team."

"They armed?"

"Like Pancho Villa," answered the mate. "Bandoliers."

"Can you make out their faces?"

"No, only war paint. Camouflage."

"Caucasian, Hispanic, what?" pressed Hall, knowing the moment he said it that it was a silly question. Canada and the United States were full of minorities, particularly in the Northwest. Racial features wouldn't prove a damn thing. But they sure as hell weren't SEALs. All that bandolier crap looked good for the media and in the movies, but was scorned by all Special Forces. Bandoliers in a firefight, as Hall's old buddy Aussie Lewis used to put it, were about as useless as "tits on a bull." By the time you unraveled the macho crisscross bandoliers to reload, you'd be meat.

"If they're ours," said the first mate, "why haven't they tried to radio us on sixteen? They're moving slowly."

"I'm coming up," Frank told the mate. He took the short route, straight up the ladder from *Petrel*'s stern deck to its Little Bird hangar deck, then up the four steps to the chart room immediately aft of the bridge.

"Doesn't add up," Frank told the mate, taking up the binoculars. "If they're terrorists and they don't know sixteen's the open channel in these waters, they haven't done their homework. But they've caused more damage to us since Pearl Harbor and 9/11, so they sure as hell *must* have done their homework."

"Well, who the hell—"

"They're within hailing distance now," cut in Frank. Snatching the megaphone's mike, he moved quickly to the bridge's starboard wing, the first flare now fizzling out in the fog. "Stop your vessel! Identify yourself!"

"Wanna bet they speak Arabic?" said the helmsman.

The megaphone response startled everyone on *Petrel*. "We're Coast Guard from the USS *Skate*. Stand by for boarding!"

"Screw you!" came the voice of one of *Petrel*'s crew, audible to Hall but probably not to the inflatable carrying what looked to be six or seven men.

"What are we going to do?" asked the first mate, then answered his own question with a nervous laugh. "Let 'em board, I suppose."

"Not yet," said Hall, whose great-grandfather had regaled him with tales of the awful Pacific war after Pearl, when American-educated Japanese who spoke American English had on more than one occasion duped gullible young GIs into coming out into the open. The Nazis had done the same thing even more effectively, since they were Caucasians, dressed up in American uniforms, penetrating the American perimeter in the fierce counterattack through the Ardennes in 1944.

All right, so Hall knew it would sound corny, but better safe than—

"Prepare to be boarded!" came the insistent voice from what was now 150 yards away, the RIB a black shadow in the fibrous fog.

"Screw you!" yelled one of *Petrel*'s crew.

Hall strode back to the stern edge of the hangar deck. "Shut up!" he warned his crew. "Get ready to fire those LOSHOKS when I give the word."

"Stand by to be—"

Hall raised his megaphone. "You come any further and we'll ram you!" To make the point, he ordered the chief to bring engines to full power, but as yet did not engage the prop, hoping the sudden rumble of the engines would produce the desired effect.

"Looks like they've stopped!" the mate said, unsure and wondering aloud what sort of trouble *Petrel* would be in afterward if it was a Coast Guard officer who'd hailed them, and not an English-speaking terrorist.

Frank brushed the mate's concern aside. "Navy trumps the Coast Guard!"

Frank pressed the megaphone's button and asked, "Who won the last World Series?"

There was silence from the stopped boat, and Frank uncharacteristically turned to the mate with a self-indulgent smile of victory, but the mate's puzzled expression killed his smile, Hall seeing that the mate didn't know the answer. Confounding his corny tactic further, Hall could hear what sounded like an argument on the stern deck, someone yelling, "It was the Yankees, goddammit!"

"Was it?" asked the mate. "I mean, the Yankees?"

"Yes," said Frank, his cocky assurance of a few minutes ago quickly evaporating. Apart from the improvised LOSHOK packs, the *Petrel* was unarmed. Yes, it was much bigger than the other vessel, but it had no armor whatsoever. Plus, despite his threat to ram them, Frank and everyone else aboard, including the cook's helper, knew an RIB could easily outmaneuver the bigger *Petrel*.

"Dry lab to bridge."

"Come in, Lab," said the mate.

"We're picking up some funny spots on the side-scan since we changed the paper!"

Frank spoke into the intercom, an edge to his voice. "What do you mean, *funny*?"

"Echoes—not many, but some sort of square-ish."

"Aft of that slab we saw?"

"Yes, sir, like I said—after we changed the paper roll."

Frank noticed that the inflatable off the starboard quarter had stopped, for the moment, gyrating slowly in the offshore currents.

"Keep an eye on them!" Frank told the mate as he quickly left the bridge and went through the helo hangar. He slid down the aft ladder to the stern deck without his feet touching a single step, the metal rails giving his hands a friction burn, his senses so alert that in addition to the salty tang of the sea and the peculiarly distinctive smell of fog-saturated air, he could detect the faint odor of the sonar recorder's paper before he stepped over the lab's doorsill.

Frank saw that the spots on the trace, when they were magnified, did look square-ish, but that was all.

It was a fifty-fifty situation. Neither of the technicians had said anything yet, unwilling to commit themselves one way or the other. "Suggestions?" he asked the two men. "Any at all?"

"I—I dunno," said one. The other, teeth clenched, giving his jaw an unappealing, undershot look, shook his head. Frank had left the lab-bridge intercom open for immediate communication.

"What are they doing?" he asked the mate.

"Just circling."

"Circling *us*?" Frank asked in alarm.

"No, I mean just—you know, going around."

"No, I *don't* know—that's why I asked you, you idiot. Be *specific*, dammit!"

There was an awkward silence.

"Bridge?" Frank said.

"Yes, sir?"

"I apologize. I was way out of line."

"That's all right, sir. I've tried to identify any name on the inflatable but can't see anything."

"Good man. Keep looking."

"Yes, sir."

"LOSHOK packs all ready to go," the bosun announced from the lab door.

"Very well." Frank's arms were back in Horatio Nelson mode.

"What'd he say?" Tiny asked the bosun as he returned to the deck.

"He said, 'Very well.'"

"'Very well?'"

"Yeah, like he was Captain Queeg."

"Who's that?" asked the cook's helper.

Tiny, tightening the rope length he'd used to replace his belt, grunted, "Queeg was an old man on a cruiser—"

"Destroyer," the bosun corrected him.

"Whatever," said Tiny.

"So what happened?" pressed the cook's assistant.

"What happened is he went nuts. Under pressure. Caved in. Paranoid. Talked to himself."

The cook's helper looked disquieted. "I do that sometimes."

"Yeah, well, you're nuts too."

"Bosun," called Frank. "Lower our runaround. I'm going out to talk to these jokers. See what the score is."

"I dunno, sir," said the bosun uneasily. "If you don't mind my sayin' so, they're—"

"What would you suggest?" asked Hall. "If they're terrorists, they probably wouldn't try this caper unless they had antitank ordnance. One round of that could easily split us open at the waterline. You know, well as I do, that we haven't an inch of armor on *Petrel*. We'd sink in minutes. I've seen enough dead Americans. More dead bodies than when I was on tour."

The tension increased when the two side-scan technicians reported that the roar of *Petrel*'s engines being brought to full power to bluff the interlopers had scrambled the side-scan's signals to the sea bottom and the return echoes. All they could see now was a massive earthquakelike trace, as if the stylus had lost its head.

"I'll get back to you in ten minutes or so," Hall told them, then ordered the bosun to have the crew lower *Petrel*'s Zodiac inflatable.

Despite Frank's somber mood, a mood that pervaded the entire vessel, Frank, calling the bosun by his first name, tried to inject a little morale-raising humor. "Jesus, Tommy," he said, "I'll be back for dinner!"

There was forced laughter from the crew, the cook's helper the only one to think it was a contender for *Petrel*'s "Best Joke of the Month."

"You take care," the bosun said.

Frank shoved off, the Zodiac's outboard a little rough, spitting now and then as he headed straight for the other, bigger inflatable. Of course they wouldn't be terrorists. Everyone was becoming too paranoid, as if America had been invaded. Looking back, as sailors always do, to the vessel from which he'd just departed, he saw the bosun standing alone on the hangar deck holding up a white rag, pointing downward.

Frank looked down and saw a white rag tucked into the space between the Zodiac's gunwale and floor. It contained a suspiciously generic-looking .38 revolver.

A small, hastily scrawled note said, "Hollow points—remember, hold your breath and squeeze. Don't pull."

Frank didn't know whether to be furious or grateful. He'd told these jokers, now only a hundred yards away, that he'd come unarmed. *Squeeze. Don't pull.* Who the hell did Tommy think he was talking to? Some first-weeker at Coronado? He stuck the gun between his thigh and the Zodiac's floor. The outboard was spitting again. Frank gave it a little more throttle. It choked and stopped, dead in the water. What had he learned at Coronado? "All outboards will fail precisely when they are most needed."

CHAPTER FORTY-ONE

FREEMAN HAD HIS nose in the air like a bloodhound. "Smell 'em?" he asked softly.

Aussie and Sal nodded, Choir's sense of smell sabotaged by the exhaust of the Mercury engine and the bad air mix he'd been inhaling back on the beach. But for his SpecFor comrades, the faint yet distinctive odor of aftershave, cologne, and underarm deodorant told them someone was upwind of them in the fog-shrouded sea, probably no more than two or three hundred yards. The odors were the kind that had betrayed a younger generation of Americans in the jungles of Vietnam, making the same "give-away" mistake as David Brentwood had made by not ordering his team to eat only Arab food. Freeman now went to hand signals, his acute sense of smell indicating there must be at least four of them or maybe half a dozen, up ahead.

Then Choir detected the hushed *slurr* sound of *another* motor. He tapped Sal on the shoulder, Sal doing the same to Freeman, the general hoping that the invisible "perfume boys" somewhere up ahead had not yet detected them. Freeman made a throat-cutting gesture and Choir killed the engine, everyone silent, motionless, listening intently, the current taking them forward. Which way were the bogeys heading?

It was then that *Petrel*'s Tiny saw it happen. The sky opened, the fog riven by sunlight, "Like bloody Moses!" said Tiny. Indeed, the sky suddenly seemed to expand, the common optical illusion at sea when land-generated thermals win the ever-shifting battle with the ocean's air currents. The speed was such that just as during Freeman's battle tour in Iraq, when an artillery round had collapsed a battalion's row of showers to reveal a line of astonished naked bodies, his aluminum boat, Frank Hall's Zodiac, and the sweet-smelling visitors circling near the *Petrel* in their RIB all suddenly saw one another and, a half mile to the east, the Coast Guard's *Skate*.

For a frozen moment no one did anything, not even Freeman, who had experienced a similar unexpected standoff with a Republican Guard platoon when a dust storm had suddenly lifted near Hindiya. Then, he'd fired first; now, he hesitated, the nanosecond lost perhaps because of a fear of committing blue on blue. Friendly fire had caused more than half the coalition's casualties in Iraq.

The 7.62mm burst from one of the six "fake *Skate*" war party unzipped the deadlock, the rounds hitting the sea only three feet in front of Freeman, shocking the general and his team. Choir, making a crucially correct decision, steered at full speed toward the enemy inflatable's bow. Only Freeman was firing, since there wasn't enough room in the boat to permit either Aussie or Sal to shoot.

Choir knew that the slightest variation in the their course would give the enemy RIB a broadside target. His quick action confounded the war-painted crew, now only fifty yards off. Their coxswain, instead of calling Choir's bluff and going full speed at the approaching boat, intuitively but imprudently steered hard astarboard, trying to avoid Freeman's shots. But the general's tracered 9mm hit the front two men, their collapse abruptly shifting the weight in the inflatable so its left gunwale was momentarily submerged, the other four men trying frantically to regain balance. One got off a skyward burst before Freeman's continuing enfilade punched him out of the boat, which heeled farther to port, the remaining three attackers trying to right themselves. It was only two seconds before the three were on their feet, or rather their knees, and stable enough to return Freeman's fire.

But it was too late, for in those two breath-seizing seconds—an eternity in a firefight or car crash—Freeman had ample time to change mags, the steam rising from his HK barrel seen by Frank Hall, who had been banging away with the bosun's gift of the Saturday Night Special. Reopening fire at twenty yards, Freeman pierced the trio's chests with such rapidity it was like a madman frenetically stabbing his victim with an ice pick, the jets of bright arterial blood macabre and, Freeman thought, beautiful against the green of the men's uniforms and beneath the cerulean-blue sky.

Petrel's first mate rang *Petrel*'s telegraph for "Full Ahead" to assist Frank and the men firing from the aluminum boat at the interlopers. Now, as *Petrel*'s bow wave creased the otherwise calm sea, the first mate and his crew braced for what they thought might be a storm of fire from the *Skate*. If, in a terrible blue on blue, *Petrel*'s skipper and the aluminum boat men had mistakenly opened fire on a genuine landing party from the *Skate*, the guns on the Coast Guard vessel would open up.

"Well, shit!" opined Cookie. "What were those guys with the tin boat supposed to do? Those guys in the RIB started shootin' first. It was self-defense, man! If it was me—"

"Shut up!" the bosun said, but Tommy knew the kid had a point.

"Jesus," Jimmy told Malcolm, indicating the floating bodies from the RIB as well as the oncoming Coast Guard vessel. "Maybe they *were* from the Coast Guard patrol boat—I mean, the guys who opened up first. Old man on that Coast Guard probably didn't fire back 'cause it'd be killing Americans for killing Americans, if you know what I mean."

"You mean two wrongs don't make a right?" Malcolm answered.

"Yeah," said Jim, appreciative of the phrase. "That's exactly what I mean. Geez," he added, not wanting to watch the floaters but unable to look away, "*you* think they were from the *Skate*?"

Malcolm shrugged. "We'll soon find out."

Frank wasn't going to second guess his first mate. After all, the officer had good intentions in bringing the *Petrel* forward. But he knew the underwater ruckus made by *Petrel*'s props would destroy any hope of a clear side-scan trace for a while. And so the only comments he made, climbing up to *Petrel*'s deck following the short, fierce firefight on the water, were directed at the bosun.

"Thanks for the weapon, Tom," he said, handing the white bundle up to him.

The bosun gave the bundle to Tiny to hold. A second later a full-bodied oath greeted Frank Hall, Tiny dropping the .38 he'd noisily retrieved from the cloth. "Jesus—it's hotter'n a two-dollar shotgun."

"How'd it go?" the bosun asked solemnly. "The gun?"

"Oh," lied Frank, "went great. Sure as hell glad I had it, I can tell you. One of those bastards holed our Zodiac. Couldn't pick up anyone." Frank was on the deck phone now, the mate telling him he was arranging a deck party to help Freeman's team with the floaters. The *Skate* was back on channel 16, the jamming by the unknown craft having ceased the moment Freeman had finished off the six attacking his tin boat.

The bosun was beaming. Hell, he hadn't been able to do much to help out in the firefight and was glad his .38 had been of some use, confiding proudly to Tiny and Malcolm, "It was probably our skipper who dropped a couple of those bastards."

Tiny watched the bosun walk into the dry lab to join Frank, anxiously standing by the side-scan recorder.

"What's he worried about?" asked Cookie, smoking beneath the A-frame. He sounded nonchalant, but Malcolm noticed that his legs were trembling so much that his stained white apron was shaking as well. Cookie saw that Malcolm had noticed.

"Cold?" Malcolm asked.

"Huh, what? Oh, yeah. Freezing."

"What you expect, Cookie? You haven't got enough on, for chrissake. Put on a windbreaker."

"Cook doesn't like me wearing 'em around the mix."

"Fuck the cook! Put on a windbreaker."

"Yeah . . ." He'd obviously forgotten about what was worrying the captain.

Malcolm put his arm on the young man's shoulder. "We're all cold, Cookie. You'll be all right."

Cookie nodded sharply, tossing the cigarette overboard, which was just as well, Malcolm told Jimmy, who was standing over by portside rail. At the moment, Hall was preoccupied in the dry lab by the fact that the *Petrel* had lost over three hundred yards of trace due to the first mate's "Full Ahead" order. But if he came out on deck and found Cookie smoking anywhere near the LOSHOK, he'd likely shoot him with the bosun's .38.

"Amazing, isn't it?" began Malcolm, he and Jimmy trying to keep out of the way of the guys who were putting over the rope ladder for the approaching SpecFor team, the ropes and wooden steps whacking the side of the ship.

"What's amazing?" asked Jimmy.

"Tommy. First rate bosun. Knew just what to do. He wanted to use the slingshot LOSHOK to try to help the old man, but he knew one slip and he'd kill the old man or these SpecFor guys we're gonna take aboard. But the same guy thinks that dinky .38 he's been haulin' around is accurate."

"It's a piece of crap," agreed Jimmy. "Couldn't hit a barn door at two feet."

"Maybe it saved his life one time," Malcolm mused, out of a sense of fair play.

"Maybe," conceded Jimmy, watching the urgent preparations on the increasingly crowded stern deck while safeguarding the pallet of LOSHOK charges by the A-frame. "Maybe he used it as an oven. Fire three shots out of that thing and you could cook a three-course meal."

Malcolm grinned broadly. It was hardly the time or place for a joke—even a weak one—but sometimes it just happened like that. "I'm gonna tell 'im you said that," he kidded Jimmy. "Put you in the shit!"

"Thanks!" Jimmy kicked the half-dozen small packs of LOSHOK. "Think we'll ever get to—"

"Hey!" said Malcolm, stepping away. "Don't do that!"

"What?" inquired Jimmy, feigning doltlike innocence. "Oh, you mean don't do this?" whereupon he again kicked the seventy-pound mother of all depth charges.

"Jesus, Jimmy, knock it off!"

"Relax, mah boy. Friggin' midget's skedaddled by now under cover of all our prop wash and that Coast Guard tub steaming toward us."

The *Skate* was now only two hundred yards to the east but slowing, its own prop wash slopping forward to overtake and mix with its decelerated bow wave. Along with the *Petrel*, it created a localized chop in which Freeman, Sal, and Aussie found it difficult to haul the dead aboard their commandeered aluminum boat, their outrage at what had happened to Dixon having cooled somewhat by the possibility that they'd perhaps been involved in an unavoidable "friendly fire" incident. It had been unavoidable to them, the men on the spot, but they knew it never appeared as unavoidable to the media or the armchair critics who always knew what you should have done in the millisecond you had to decide.

Freeman was understandably tight-jawed as they hauled in the third of the six bodies. "Look," he said sternly. "No identification!"

Aussie wondered if the general's cryptic comment was a criticism of the dead men for not having identified themselves before opening fire, or whether he was commenting on the fact that none of those hauled in so far had any ID whatsoever. One of them looked Central Asian to him, another Chinese, and the third was racially unidentifiable, having been hit in the upper chest and face.

"Where in hell did they come from?" asked Salvini. "I mean, were they sent from the sub to run interference?"

"Maybe they came out of that cave," said Choir.

"I'll bet—" Aussie began, and paused for breath as he braced his feet against the inside of the tin boat's starboard drop seat and, aided by Freeman, began hauling in the fourth floater. "—I'll bet Choir's right, that these pricks are the same ones who did the sicko job on young Dixon. Probably came down out of the cave then dragged their RIB from a hide on the beach and came out in the fog to do the *Petrel* 'fore she could find their mates in the sub." The fourth floater, another Asian, now tumbled into the boat, which rocked precariously.

"Watch it!" cautioned Choir. "I've had enough dunking for one day." He added, "Why not let *Petrel* haul these shit bags out?"

No one answered his question, but their silence was a reply. Their earlier guesstimates notwithstanding, they were not sure whether these bodies were hostiles or U.S. Special Forces like themselves, caught up in a tragic blue on blue. Aussie's hypothesis that the bodies were those of the hostiles who so savagely murdered and tortured Dixon was no more than that—a hypothesis. Special Forces, like Freeman's, like David Brentwood's failed team in Afghanistan, always went on foreign operations without any identification that might cause political embarrassment should they be captured or killed. And the fact that two different branches of the armed services often sent out their own without telling one another was no help. Plus, as Choir acknowledged, foreign terrorists teams would certainly use someone fluent in English.

"What's this one?" Aussie asked as they hauled in another body. "Chinese?"

"No," said Freeman.

"Japanese?" proffered Choir.

"Vietnamese?" suggested Aussie. "They're heavy as a brick in the water, but you can see they're all in pretty good shape. No extra weight. Damn, look at that! Fog's rolling in again." It came in like a giant billow of smoke, and within a minute the *Petrel* and the *Skate*, each vessel's radar allowing them to maintain station two hundred yards apart, were at times completely hidden from view. With the sixth body nowhere to be seen, Choir sped up the Mercury before they lost sight of *Petrel*.

Unintentionally, just as *Petrel*'s and *Skate*'s engineers had done, he further sabotaged *Petrel*'s side-scan outgoing sonar waves. Not surprisingly, the disturbance angered Hall, who, as tired as everyone else on the oceanographic vessel, now learned from the *Skate*'s captain that the five unidentified dead men killed by Freeman had definitely not been sent from the *Skate*.

This told Frank that the six-man commando unit sent so cunningly to board *Petrel* would not have been dispatched unless the sub was still in the area, lying low. "Mate," he ordered the first officer, "get the GPS coordinates for that slab we had a trace of a while back. GPS, as good as it is, has a possible error margin of a hundred feet. That's not much on land, but out here it can be like looking for your car on the wrong parking level and—"

"Like the *Seinfeld* show," said the mate, "when Kramer—"

"I don't watch TV," Frank cut in abruptly. "Take your steering directions from the dry lab. I'll stay down here."

"Sir?"

"Yes?

"I have to take a dump!"

"Where's the third mate?"

"Feeling sick. She's pretty upset."

"About what?"

"Well, you know," began the mate awkwardly. "She told me she signed on to do, you know, retrieval, oceanographic work, not a war. Guess she wasn't ready for this?" He indicated the bodies being hauled up from the tin boat by the stern's hydraulic arm.

"New York wasn't ready for 9/11," retorted Frank, punching the intercom bar for the third mate's cabin.

A groggy, sickly voice barely managed to say, "Yes?"

"Riley. It's the captain speaking. Get your ass up to the bridge. *Now!*"

The third mate's silence was a tacit recognition of Hall's zero tolerance for malingerers, Frank telling her everyone on the ship was needed. If the fog kept socking them in, it would be an ideal opportunity for an injured sub awaiting its chance to make a run for it come nightfall.

When the third mate dragged herself up to relieve the first mate, she was whey-faced. A tall, lithe young woman who normally looked as if she could handle anything, her male counterparts could see that Sandra Riley looked bedraggled after her ordeal, dazed by the bridge glass's reflection of the bright shaded stern light that formed a sharply defined cone in the swirling fog.

Frank, who had just come up from the dry lab, tapped the GPS coordinates on the chart. "Soon as we get those bodies aboard, Sandra, we'll come about and backtrack to this GPS location. See what we get in the trace. We lost a gob of it during a damn paper change."

Sandra took Hall's use of her first name as a good sign—more often than not he simply called her Riley. "If it's the sub," she mused aloud, "maybe they'll take advantage of all this noise."

Frank's usual equanimity was edgy with fatigue. "You an authority on antisubmarine warfare now?" He knew better, but the perversity that runs with bad temper and the feeling of his own impotence regarding the sub was venting itself.

"I just meant that with all the noise the *Skate*'s engines are making, screwing up our side scan, it would be a good time for a sub in trouble to surface—"

"Yes, I know. Make a run for it in the fog."

"Exactly!" It was said in a gutsy, uncompromising tone.

Frank turned to watch the work crew bringing aboard the general and his three comrades, all of them old friends who'd trained at one time or another in SpecOps at Elgin in Florida as well as at the SEALs' school at Coronado in California. They'd all carried the monstrous logs at Coronado, running along the public beach while young beach beauties Sandra's age, only a few feet away, sunbathed in the scantiest thong bikinis the sweating, grunting SEAL trainees had ever seen. "What beauties?" the SEALs' instructors had barked, their faces masks of incredulity. "Ain't no women here. You're hallucinating. Pick it up, Salvini. Hup, two, three . . ."

Frank made a mental note to apologize to Sandra later. But now, her self-assertiveness, her tone, which some skippers could easily have convinced themselves was bordering on insubordination, was too recent for him to humble himself. It was a trait which he did not admire in himself. "We'll need to be right on the spot," he continued, businesslike. "We spotted a slablike shape against a slope. Unless we're on the southern side of it, our scan'll miss it—the sandy slope'll wall it off from us."

"I understand, sir."

"Very well. I'll be down in the lab. Once we're there, I'll give you helm instructions from the lab."

"Very well."

Very well. Was she sticking it to him?

He saw Freeman, who entered the dry lab, strode over, and shook hands vigorously. "Good to see you, Frank! I need room for my men to rest. That goddamn sub is still here. I know it. Get that Coast Guard ship to do a search grid, but no overlap with yours. Can't afford to waste time."

That's the general, thought Frank. Hasn't seen you in ages, and right off the bat he's telling *you*, the ship's master—no, *ordering* you—what to do.

"You're assuming *Petrel*'s going to do a grid," said Frank.

"Of course. Aren't you?"

"Yes, I agree with you. Those people are still—"

"People?" Freeman cut in crossly, his body odor dominating the dry lab. "They aren't *people*. They're goddamn animals!"

As yet Hall hadn't heard about what had happened to Dixon, who, he remembered, had aged overnight after his swim buddy's death. Frank didn't press the general for any details of what exactly had taken place. It wasn't the time. Freeman left Frank to it and turned his attention back to the five bodies laid out on the stern, pulling back the blanket from each one, squatting down, staring at them.

"I think he's enjoying it," Malcolm commented to the bosun,

who was looking down at *Petrel*'s barely visible wake as it proceeded slowly into the general area of the problematic slab. Sal and Choir, also on the stern deck, were wondering aloud what had happened to the missing floater, still lost in the fog.

"I think that floater was a swimmer," cut in Aussie. "Faked us out. Big bloody drama, clutching his chest and falling from that RIB. Bastard's probably ashore by now, draggin' 'imself up that S trail."

"Possible," said Freeman, but the general, as Sal, Choir, and an equally perplexed Malcolm looked on, was still looking at the five whose floating days were over. Aussie, meanwhile, carefully went through the dead men's sodden camouflage-pattern uniforms for any ID.

"Definitely not all Chinese," said Choir, glancing over at Aussie from the portside rail. "You've lost your bet, boyo."

"The hell I have. They all look Chinese to me."

"Guy looks like he tried to hang himself," said Sal, leaning over and pointing to a dark bruise ringing one of the dead men's throats.

"Should have," said Aussie as Sal let the blood-soaked blanket fall back over the corpse's face. "Would've saved us the trouble."

"Yeah," agreed Sal, standing up, arching and massaging his back, yawning.

Malcolm couldn't tell whether it was the way Salvini arched his back that angered him or the SpecFor warrior's yawn, the soldier's manner appearing to him and Jimmy as inappropriately cavalier, downright disrespectful in the presence of the dead. Freeman was now pulling the fog-shrouded blanket back from the man Sal had referred to.

"I know they're terrorists," Malcolm told Jimmy, "but Jesus—know what I mean?"

"Yeah," Jimmy said, lowering his voice and looking across the deck toward Freeman. "He's supposed to be a legend. Tiny says his troops used to call him 'George C. Scott.'"

Malcolm looked blank.

"You know—General Patton."

"Oh. Yeah?"

"Scuttlebutt is that he's been sidelined ever since Clinton. Apparently criticized Bill in 'ninety-eight. Told him the White House didn't know dick about handling a terrorist situation. Said they were wasting their time, firing a cruise instead of sending in helo snatch-and-grab squads—take some of the towel heads up an' tell 'em, 'Talk or you'll be the first A-rabs to walk in space.'"

"So Clinton canned him?" asked Malcolm.

"No, the Pentagon did. Said Freeman was a loose cannon. Now they're beatin' the crap out of towel heads."

"So how come Freeman's still sidelined?" pressed Malcolm.

Jimmy shrugged. "Pentagon's like anywhere else, I guess. Once you're out, you—" Jimmy stopped as Freeman made his way to the stern's A-frame and, standing by them, stared thoughtfully into the fog, as if willing his tired, deep blue eyes to see farther.

"Where'd you say the *Skate* was?" Malcolm asked Jimmy, in case the general suspected they'd been talking about him.

The general remained staring intently astern. He turned, looked directly at the two men, frowned darkly, then resumed staring out into the fog.

The two men moved away toward the dry lab. "He must have heard us," said Malcolm softly.

Jimmy, turning for a last look at Freeman, almost tripped on the dry lab's doorsill. "No," he told Malcolm, "I don't think he heard us."

"C'mon, Jimmy. Did you see that frown?"

"It wasn't meant for us," replied Jimmy. "Something's bothering him."

Jimmy was right. Something was bothering Freeman, something he'd seen but couldn't identify. Whatever it was, it was like a wasp hovering about, worrying you, when all you wanted to do was rest.

Right now, however, his first priority was to secure sleeping space for Sal, Aussie, and Choir and order them to rest, as if the three veterans of a dozen foreign wars needed a command to sleep after their grueling hours afloat and ashore. And the general's second priority was to get rest himself. Besides, the last thing he wanted was to discuss with Hall or anyone else his failure to stop the sub in the crescent bay.

His team's failure, everyone's failure so far, stalked his sleep as he lay on a mattress brought to the dry lab, his snoring so loud that one of the side-scan technicians put on a pair of cranials.

"Goddamn," the technician muttered, "I can still hear him."

As a sailor, one of whose qualifications is the ability to live 24/7 with constant close-quarter noise, the tech's complaint about Freeman's train-whistle breathing was evidence, Frank thought, of the extraordinary tension aboard the *Petrel*.

In Washington, D.C., public opinion was overwhelmingly in favor of taking out Penghu. Both the Joint Chiefs and the Taiwanese government pointed out the extraordinary danger of allowing China to have a massive air base only fifteen miles from the island nation—two and a half minutes away by fighter-bomber. And, as many other American leaders and newspapers pointed out, most noticeably the *New York Times*, "If Taiwan, the only other democratic bulwark in Asia besides Japan, were to be lost, American power and influence, as well as its strategic and economic interests, would suffer irreparable harm."

And the French were gloating, *Le Monde* commenting in an editorial that "once again Washington has to recognize that in its war against terrorism, in a conflict of such elasticity, its conventional force is passé and its navy has become what the Chinese call a 'paper tiger.' "

The President said he didn't give a damn what the foreign press said, especially France and Germany. The American people, however, did give a damn, and together with the Penghu military danger being pressed home with increasing fervor by the Pentagon, State, and Taipei, the President sought and received Congressional approval to "neutralize" the Penghu threat.

And so as *Petrel* approached the halfway mark of its search grid, the President ordered all battle groups to stand by, "pending imminent action against Penghu—collateral damage notwithstanding." Which meant that whoever was to be tasked with the action would not allow the presence of Taiwanese hostages to impede the mission.

CHAPTER FORTY-TWO

ADMIRAL JENSEN AND Admiral Crowley had something in common. Jensen had been plunged further into depression over the promise of the NR-1B failing to materialize to rescue his all but fatally wounded reputation. Crowley, on the *McCain*, watching CNN's report on the mounting public pressure, dared to hope that he might now have the chance to redeem his reputation as a superior decision maker, following what had already become known among those who'd survived the kamikaze attack on their beloved boat as "Crowley's clanger."

In the *McCain*'s blue-tile inner sanctums, officers and other ranks quietly wondered aloud whether they'd get a chance to avenge their dead with whatever the boat had left in her vault. Situated deep in the boat, these vaults or fortified ammunition magazines held over four million pounds of "payback." There was everything down there from sparkling "virgins"—Standoff Land Attack Missiles—Expanded Response, or SLAMERs—to C-model air-to-ground, joint standoff missiles, each armed with a five-hundred-pound warhead with a mid-course accuracy of plus or minus fifty-two feet.

"That would do it," said an ordnance chief petty officer in the vault. "Got enough here to turn that friggin' Paygoo—"

"Penghu," one of his fellow red jackets corrected him.

"Pay*goo*," continued the CPO, looking about at the bright metal "coffins" that contained the "virgins" and the plethora of other land attack and air-to-air ordnance. As yet none of it was armed, but they were ready to go.

"If we get the call," said the other red jacket.

"We'll get the call," the CPO said confidently. "That CNN skirt—one with the hooters—said there's protest mobs outside the White House demanding we do somethin'."

"Protests *for* war. Man, that's a new one."

The CPO was still thinking about "Paygoo." "Could turn it into a parking lot after we're finished with it."

"After they fill in the craters, Chief," said a green-shirted cargo handler.

"Yeah." The CPO smiled.

"Yeah," joined in the ordnance tracker. "If we get the order."

"We'll get it," the CPO replied, his tone not brooking any dissent. "Who else is there? We're Johnny on the spot. Besides, we're the ones who got whacked."

Admiral Crowley, anticipating, *knowing*, he'd soon be called in to launch America's counterattack against Penghu, retired to what the Navy grandly called his "stateroom" for his daily ten-minute deep-diaphragm breathing, taking advantage of the lull in the normally thunderous roar of the "roof" directly above him. He switched on the TV, pressed "mute," and lay flat on his back, his pillow under his knees. His son had got him doing the "destressor" routine, the admiral rejecting the idea at first, huffing and puffing about New Age cults.

"It's not a cult, Dad," his son had said. "Deep breathing, meditative techniques, are as old as the hills. Will you just try it? You'll feel better when you do it."

So the admiral was trying it, but with the door closed. He didn't want the crew to think he was one of those damn yogis. And it *was* relaxing him—he could feel the tension of this terrible day abate somewhat. Of course, he had yet to write the families of all the men and women who had died, and that wouldn't help his tension level. John Cuso had offered to help, and Crowley had accepted. They both agreed there would be no computer-generated crap, or fake "original" signatures. They'd write every one of the letters. Shipmates of those killed would, as usual, be a big help—providing personal details and, where appropriate, a humorous little anecdote to give the letters a more human touch. The padre would help too, but right now he was giving last rites to the dying and preparing for what would be the massive burial at sea.

CNN was doing its entertainment section. "Hollywood celebs caution a rush to judgment" was about one well-known singer-actor who'd apparently "terrified her fans" by threatening to leave America if Bush invaded Iraq. She was now threatening to do it again, a mob of screaming adolescents jabbing the air with "Peace for Penghu" and burning Old Glory near the perimeter rope in Lafayette Park across from the White House. Another smaller but just as vocal group was holding signs promising to pay the singer's fare to the Penghu. "Neither group," Marte Price reported, "is clear on exactly where Penghu is."

The *McCain* was sailing into night as the show was broadcast, the ship darkened, all lights below rigged for red. Admiral Crowley entered the Combat Information Center and in a voice as calm as ice told John Cuso, "I've been thinking, John. If I were terrorists, I'd attack us at first light."

The incoming secret three-letter-coded message was received by John Rorke's USS *Encino* at four hundred feet below the surface of Bashi Strait via the attack boat's extremely low frequency aerial, which it periodically played out hundreds of yards behind it from a keel-flush integrated spool set on its port side. ELF was secure, being out of view of aerial reconnaissance or other shipping that might be in the area, but it was so slow—its transmission rate this morning one letter every twenty-six seconds—that it was used more often than not to instruct a submarine to come to periscope depth and raise its communications mast in what *Encino*'s crew called "the quick pop-out." At periscope depth, *Encino*'s radio mast quickly pierced the sea/air interface and, hopefully before any hostile got a chance to discover the mast by satellite infrared recon, received a three-second burst message from COMSUBPAC HQ in Hawaii.

"Must be urgent," *Encino*'s executive officer said.

"It had better be," said John Rorke. "I don't like exposing myself for anything less."

"How 'bout your honey, Skipper?" quipped the navigator.

Rorke gave an obligatory grin, but when the navigator had said "your" honey rather than "a" honey, it made him inwardly wince, and he saw that the executive officer sensed it. A certain amount of sexual innuendo was part of a Navy man's life—hell, any man's life, he thought—but cooped-up men sometimes went over the line. It wasn't the words they used—Rorke knew the lexicon from Bangor, Maine, to Bangor, Washington, and he was no prude, but he'd found that whenever he'd started getting serious about a woman, the innuendos and unending sexual "jokes" made him feel defensive—no, protective—about her. Alicia evoked in him a respect for women that usually waned when he was simply chasing "poontang."

The XO had shot the navigator a warning glance, but the latter was busy confirming *Encino*'s position, having taken advantage of the brief "pop-out" of the ultrahigh frequency mast to get a fix before the masts were retracted into the sub's sail. This would allow him to correct for the ship's inertial navigation system, which, despite twenty-first-century computers' linked gyroscopes and movement-sensitive accelerometers, could often drift up to 1,700 yards. It was an important correction, enabling the sub's captain and the handful of officers privy to such information on the boat to know exactly where *Encino* was. This was especially useful, as Rorke's mentor, Admiral Jensen, had once said, "if you actually want to hit something with a torpedo."

Once submerged well below periscope depth, Rorke and the XO watched as two weapons officers from the sub's missile department simultaneously opened two small green combination safes. Both officers extracted one of a half-dozen black plastic capsules from each, with the number on each of the nontransparent capsules received via the UHF burst message being the same. The code phrase within each of the two extracted capsules was also the same, in this case BLAIR KEITH.

The fact that both capsules contained the same name, as duly witnessed by Rorke and his XO, allowed all four officers to concur that the President's order for *Encino* to fire all twelve of its Tomahawk land attack missiles at the target identified only by coordinates was valid. None of the crew would know what the target was, not even the weapons officer, who now, with deliberate yet unhurried pace, punched the given coordinates into his red-eyed firing procedures console. Only the navigator, his computer verifying his manual chart plot, knew the coordinates were for an island off southwestern Taiwan. But he did not know exactly what on that island was being targeted. In this war, as in peacetime patrols, the sub had remained submerged, cut off from the world and news of it for months at a time, night and day distinguished only by whether sections of the sub were rigged for red. Not even the coveted fifty-word familygrams, whose delivery could give the sub's position away, were being received. Only Rorke, who'd been rushed from the plane to the sub's dock to take command of *Encino* after the sub's captain had unexpectedly died at sea from a heart attack, knew about the present situation between the two Chinas.

His mind no longer on Alicia, on women, on anything but the care he must take to arrive secretly at the launch point an hour away, Rorke reviewed all the known idiosyncrasies of the *Encino*. The crew was already in "ultraquiet" mode, signaled by simple voice command from Rorke. No klaxon had sounded his order, and no klaxon would sound "Battle Stations" at launch point. There would be no noise on the sub that might alert hostiles. All mixing machines in the galley, all washer-dryers, and so on, no matter how quiet their rubber mountings, were to be turned off. In the galley the cook's menu changed to ground prime beef hamburgers—better than any in the civilian world—ready to be quickly cooked in a silent microwave, its ear-piercing "done" alarm permanently silenced, replaced by a colored light indicator. Those not on duty had to be in their bunks, and, if using Discmans, Walkmans, and the like, were allowed the use of only one earpiece. The chief of the boat, otherwise known on *Encino* as "Old Testament," ritually informed every newcomer to the boat, "God help the man I find curtained in his bunk who doesn't hear an order because his eardrums are being bombarded by some rap crap!"

A towel hastily pulled around his waist, an auxiliaryman caught in mid-shampoo, all water noise cut off as "ultraquiet" was answered, emerged from the stall, mumbling obscenities, his hair still streaked with suds. A torpedo tech made way for him, flashing him a mocking "Come hither!" look that the suds man returned with a murderous glare. Every one of the fifteen officers and 149 enlisted men now knew this was no drill, and in their bunks men turned to their private comforts: a picture of family, a Bible, girlfriends, and, for some, a passage from the Koran; for others, there were dreams of what they'd do if God, or Fate, spared them from fatality in this strangest of conflicts of constantly shifting "trouble fronts."

Rorke had not told them that America had been attacked in the Northwest. Some were bound to have loved ones there, and why burden men on the boat with the anxiety of not knowing, of being unable to do anything out here deep in the netherworld of ocean? The best they could do, that he could do, Rorke knew, was get on with the job. Though badly shaken by the loss of the *Utah*, he was confident that he could get the 360-foot-long boat to launch point at precisely the right time—providing he could keep *Encino* in perfect trim. *Encino* did not have the bow thrusters some other boats had, which allowed them to hover at launch point, but barring any unforeseen circumstances, he told himself, he should have no trouble.

The more superstitious among the crew, however, who nursed their captain's death and recalled Rorke's clumsy arrival—he'd slipped and fallen while coming aboard on the rain-slicked gangway—took these as two very bad signs, several of the crew believing in the theory that things come in threes.

"Eternal Father Strong to Save" was the hymn played over *Mc-Cain*'s PA to the carrier's five-thousand-plus men and women, the boat's starboard aft elevator space crowded with off-duty personnel for whom the ship's quartermaster had distributed song sheets. The religious and nonreligious who had gathered here were as diverse as American society itself, but all were bound by a patriotism so deeply felt and honored it aroused sniggers and embarrassment among other Western nations, except, ironically, in Russia, once its bitterest foe. But no one could be embarrassed now as the stentorian voice of the padre led the huge ad hoc choir in rough unison with such feeling that no one but the most self-indulgent cynic could fail to be moved by the swell of love for fallen comrades, so intense it could be heard by lookouts aboard the Aegis cruisers guarding the flanks of the huge man-o'-war.

Admiral Crowley had determined that there would be no burial in the light of day for the enemy to take advantage of. When morning broke, he and the entire battle group would be ready to attack Penghu, the President surely giving first licks to *McCain*, whose air wing had been so grievously harmed by the PLA air force and for which everyone on the carrier held Beijing, its protestations notwithstanding, totally responsible.

A complaint was brought to Commander John Cuso that "Eternal Father Strong to Save" was "sexist," said it referred to the creator as being masculine.

"What do we do?" asked the chief petty officer from the section in which the complainant originated.

"I'll file it," promised Cuso. "Consider it later."

"Yes, sir."

When the CPO left, Cuso balled the complaint in his fist and chucked it into his wastebasket. "Filed."

CHAPTER FORTY-THREE

MARTE PRICE DIDN'T like the CNN makeup studio in Port Angeles. She said it reeked of fish. Everything reeked of fish, her producer told her, the smell coming from the thousands of dead fish in the strait.

When Charles Riser arrived in the cab, the odor of Jack Daniel's was still on his breath, though he'd vigorously brushed his teeth. He knew he would have to begin with an apology. It wasn't only good manners, but a tactical necessity, if she was to believe what Wu Ling had told him: that General Chang must have discovered the rumored deal between Beijing and Li Kuan's fanatically American-hating terrorists.

What surprised Charles was Marte Price's immediate and

good-natured acceptance of his contrition. A woman who clearly didn't hold petty grudges, he thought. He told her the story about how Mandy was murdered by Li Kuan's thugs in Suzhou.

"And this General Chang tried to help you find out where Li Kuan was?"

"Yes. Then he disappeared. His girlfriend—"

"Wu Ling, right?"

"Yes." Charles was impressed by her attentiveness and memory.

"You told me you told State," she said, "but that they don't believe you, or rather, they think you're making a mountain out of a molehill—not of Amanda's death, but that your bereavement has made you paranoid."

"Something like that." She was remarkable, insightful and quick. She paused and patted the pockets of her jeans. Her top, "on-camera" half was captive in a no-nonsense, gender-equality black business jacket and a high-collared, almost prudish, white blouse which was mocked by her lower, more casual attire. He liked her—a lot. He could tell she believed him about Chang's discovery of a Beijing-Kazakhstan deal, which, if it could be proved, would result in crippling trade sanctions against China—the removal of its highly coveted U.S. "preferred-nation" status.

"Mr. Riser, I have contacts—good contacts—at State," she said. "They've suspected China of making such a deal with Li Kuan for months and—".

"They have?" cut in Charles. "Then why on earth—"

"Charles—may I call you Charles?"

"Of course."

Charles Riser, she saw, was a decent man, a genuine cultural attaché, not a spy using the "cultural" cover. But he obviously didn't understand the enormous economic war between the U.S. and China that was going to be one of the defining U.S. strategies of the twenty-first century, as the battle between Japan and the U.S. had been in the latter half of the twentieth.

"The problem, Charles, is that State, the administration, needs concrete proof of such a deal before they can act."

Riser fell silent for several moments, and she saw there were tears in his eyes. "They *always* get away with it," he said. "They should have got that bastard Kuan in Afghanistan."

Marte didn't respond at once. There was no need. She knew what he meant. Why *did* the Li Kuans of the world, who murdered, raped, his child, so often evade punishment? Six Americans, the best of the best, led by David Brentwood, had died inside some damn cave in Afghanistan, and still Li Kuan was at large.

Marte touched Riser's hand. "I'm sorry I can't do any more. You understand—rumor, speculation, is one thing. It's *concrete* evidence we need."

He felt selfish, and after a long pause, nodded. He understood. He turned attention away from himself. "How are things up here?"

"Not good. Jensen is dispatching two new state-of-the-art sub-hunter hydrofoils from San Francisco, in a couple of those monster Globemasters. But all our ships that were sunk, including the *Utah*, were *supposed* to have state-of-the-art antisub stuff aboard."

"This Jensen," Charles asked. "He's the sub admiral, right?" He didn't really care; he just wanted to hear her talk. The last woman who'd touched him like that had been his wife, Elizabeth. It seemed a thousand years ago. He felt utterly exhausted, unable even to will himself to move.

"Jensen is—*was*—COMSUBPAC Group 9," replied Marte. "He sent a Coast Guard ship, the *Skate*, in to help. In horrible search conditions. Everything socked in by fog." There was a pause. "Look—" she began.

Her producer was anxious and gestured at her. In three minutes she was to give a report on the sea of refugees still moving south into Oregon and California.

"Have you got a picture of Amanda?" she asked Charles. "Anything we might use if something breaks?" It was a question she'd asked scores of bereaved parents during her reporter's career.

He had a lot of pictures of Mandy, one with Wu Ling.

"'Course," said Charles, "you've got one of this—" He paused. "—animal." It was the same computer-enhanced photo of Li Kuan that the CIA and other agencies had, the terrorist's pockmarked bald scalp and hazel European eyes in stark contrast to his otherwise distinctly Chinese features. The pockmarked scalp gave Kuan what Charles told Marte was a particularly sinister appearance, even for a terrorist.

In her twenty years as a correspondent, Marte had seen terrorists and other cold-blooded killers, such as Ted Bundy, who looked almost angelic, so Li Kuan's appearance did not unduly affect her. "Yes," she said, handing the photo back to Charles, "we already have this on file. Everyone has, Charles. It's the only one, and as you can see, not a particularly useful one."

She was trying to explain to him that you just can't stick someone's photo on TV, even that of a terrorist, and say they're linked to Beijing—that they're in cahoots—without proof. And there had been absolutely no evidence from any of the media feed she was getting that the Muslim terrorists had anything to do with China's push against Taiwan.

"But," Charlie Riser countered, "Muslim terrorists everywhere hate Americans."

"Yes," she conceded, "they do," but she knew it was a non sequitur, Charlie Riser understandably fixated on the terrorists because of his daughter's murder. Marte empathized. She remembered the terrible murder of Daniel Pearl, the *Wall Street Journal* reporter who'd been captured by the Taliban in 2002, horribly tortured and then executed, his grisly death videotaped by the terrorists. Pearl left a grieving wife and an unborn son behind. Even the hard-bitten types amongst the international media had been shocked.

Charlie Riser looked over at her and said, "I have a gut feeling that Li Kuan is behind these sub attacks. You know," he told Marte, "he tells Beijing, 'You help us hit the Great Satan and we'll be no trouble in Kazakhstan.'"

Marte Price's producer gave up on his earlier polite tone. *"Marte! Ten seconds!"* he shouted.

She put her hand on Charles's. "I'll do what I can, talk to Freeman—see what he has." With that, she rose quickly and got back in front of the universal eye.

"Five seconds, Marte."

"Proof," she said to Riser. "Concrete proof. If your friend Chang manages to smuggle out any concrete proof to Wu Ling—call me."

Then she was back on air.

State had been looking for Charles everywhere, and when he got back to Seattle, the tall girl was waiting, trying to be very stern. "Washington expected you in D.C. today."

"Did they?"

"Yes, and I've been told you're to leave on this evening's flight from SeaTac."

"I'm embarrassing the department."

"Well—yes."

"All right," he sighed. What else could he do? He'd been trained in diplomacy. It was all he knew. "I've done my best," he said.

The tall girl from State could have sworn he wasn't talking to either her or himself. It was as if someone else was in the room.

CHAPTER FORTY-FOUR

FREEMAN'S "JIMMY LEG," as his team had always referred to the sudden jerks the general's limbs would make while he was asleep, was getting worse—and alarming to anyone who'd never seen the medical condition.

"Is he okay?" one of the side-scan techs asked Frank Hull.

"He'll be fine," responded Frank, whose eyes were glued to the profile coming up on the new roll of paper.

"Geez, I wouldn't want anyone to see *me* like that."

"He always wants to be near the action," said Frank. "Besides, I don't think anyone's told him. You could, if you want."

"I don't think so."

The other technician, like Hall, was watching the slowly emerging outline of the sea bottom, never tiring of the side-scan sonar's magic. You sent down an invisible sound wave, and back it came, morphed into a visible line that formed a part in the larger jigsaw pattern of echoes whose overall picture should soon tell them if there was a sub down there or not. The tech hoped not—he'd witnessed enough action for a lifetime, the sight of the terrorists that Freeman had killed ironically more troubling to him because, unlike the American dead from the multiple sinkings, rigor mortis had not yet set in. The one Freeman had been staring down at looked as if he was still alive, eyes open. The penny-on-the-eyelids thing one of *Petrel*'s crew had tried failed to keep the eyelids shut, the coins falling off because of residual muscle movement that had sent the pennies running across the deck, which Tiny confessed had "totally freaked" him.

"Those hydrofoil sub chasers Jensen's sending up to Everett," the tech said to Frank, "they should be here soon, right?"

"Half an hour, maybe more," replied Frank, eyes still on the trace. "Everyone goes slow in the fog."

"And," put in the other technician unhelpfully, "it'll soon be dark."

Freeman's leg shot out.

"Jesus Christ—"

"Settle down," Frank told the tech. "If that slab we saw earlier *was* the sub lying low, it might be gone by now, under cover of our prop disturbance during the firefight."

"Looks like we're back at the site, Captain!" one of the techs said excitedly.

Frank nodded.

Freeman's "Jimmy leg" had started up again, which caught young Cookie's attention. Overloaded with a tray bearing thick white mugs of coffee and hot chocolate for dry lab and stern watches, he stepped over the lab's door. "No beer, I'm afraid, gents," he announced cheerfully, resolved to show that corpses on deck didn't scare *him*. He could handle it.

"Thanks," said Frank, without looking up. "Away from the recorder, son."

"Don't have to worry, Cap—"

"Stop engines!" Frank shouted into the intercom. Barely any movement resulted, but in the slight yaw of the ship, Cookie lost his balance, an avalanche of white mugs spilling chocolate and coffee crashing onto the dry lab's floor.

"Wha . . . ?" Freeman was up, one arm around Cookie's neck, the other holding the K-bar's blade an inch from the man's throat.

"Could be the sub!" Hall said loudly, the small, black sound-reflective six-by-six-inch squares on the mud bottom, just a few feet east of the "slab." The squares were not rubberized ane-choic tiles, or they would not have reflected the sonar signals. Like the gaps seen on the space shuttle that had shown where the heat-shield tiles had fallen off, Frank believed he was seeing bare metal squares on the sub, that the tiles had either fallen off through wear and tear or been shot off earlier by Freeman's team during the fight at the falls.

Freeman had sheathed his knife, quickly apologized to Cookie, and stepped to the left of the recorder. The stylus was flashing back and forth now under the lab's night lights. He said nothing, his attention riveted on the profile.

"Bosun!" Frank called. "You have a weight on that LOSHOK pack?"

"Yes, sir. It's ready to go. Same depth, sir?"

"Yes. Thirty-two fathoms. Stern party, stand by to lower. Minimum noise. They can hear us, but I don't want their Passive to pick up the splash when we drop the LOSHOK. I'll start *Petrel* slow ahead—make them think we've found nothing and decided to go on."

"Yes, sir." The bosun strode out onto the stern. "Jimmy, Mal, Tiny—over here."

Frank called Sandra Riley on the bridge. "I think we've found the sub," he said. "Can you see the *Skate*?"

"No, sir. Fog's too thick. But I've got her on radar. She's about a mile to starboard on the north-south leg of her search grid."

"Any sign of those two hydrofoils?" Frank asked, conscious of the fact that while the *Skate* was heavily deck-armed, she had no depth charges of any sort. "I don't want to use the radio to contact *Skate*," he continued. "If it *is* the sub down there, it could be trailing an aerial—to pick up our transmission."

"I assumed that it would have made a run for it under cover of our engine noise during the—"

"Yes," agreed Frank. "I don't know why they haven't."

Freeman cut in, telling Sandra, "I think we winged the son of a bitch, sweetheart. Not on the hull proper, but its ballast tanks. Like having puncture holes in your inflatable. You can still move, but slowly, and you'd have to send a swimmer out through the sub's air lock to repair the holes. You can't do that quietly."

Frank was nodding his agreement.

"Anyway," the general concluded, "this LOSHOK of yours should do it. Rip the damn boat open like a can o' sardines!"

On deck, Tiny was on standby, ready to lower the seventy-pound pack of explosive overboard once Frank gave him the order. He didn't like it. The captain's assumption that it was definitely the sub, and the flamboyant general's talk of what "should" happen, made him nervous. So did the dynamite. "Truth is," he told Jimmy, "you don't know from one minute to the next what's gonna—"

"Hey!" cut in the bosun. "Rain-in-the-Face, knock it off. You have that LOSHOK chain weight taped down? I don't want that friggin' chain to rattle and roll on the way down."

"It won't," Tiny assured him, lifting the combined weight of 130 pounds with one hand as if it was a bunch of grapes.

Jimmy checked the fuse length for the sixth time, the prima-cord calculated to assure detonation of the LOSHOK just above its hull, if in fact it was the sub.

"What'd you call me?" Tiny asked the bosun.

"Rain-in-the-Face."

"Yeah, well, I don't care. I'm tellin' you guys, I don't think that profile *is* the sub. It's a slab of limestone and a few flakes fell off. Slab of limestone's like assholes in these parts—everyone's got one."

"What about those loose tiles they're talking about?" countered Jimmy.

"Tiles, smiles—BS!" said Tiny. "I had a peek at that trace when Cookie lost our drinks. I didn't see anything. Those spots the old man saw could be anything. This strait's full of shit that people're chucked overboard. You know how many Coke cans and crap we pick up on sonar?"

"Ah," said Jimmy dismissively. "You're just scared, Tiny."

"You bet your ass I'm scared. Those hydrofoils hear a bang, what're they gonna do? Everyone's so trigger happy these last few days. Did you see the sonar trace?"

Jimmy shook his head.

"Malcolm?" asked Tiny.

"No."

"Lower and cut," called out Frank. "Carefully."

The bosun lit the fuse and Tiny played out the charge's line, the weight barely causing a ripple as it broke the foggy sea's surface and was released in free fall.

"Full ahead," ordered Frank calmly.

The *Petrel*'s sonar immediately picked up the echoes from the bunched chain weight going down directly below the LOSHOK, and it seemed off course. Had the turbulence of *Petrel*'s engines combined with the deep currents to create a side push? Frank wondered. Would it make any difference? Was it the sub or—

The detonation sent the stylus crazy. A second later the sea's surface exploded in an enormous eruption of green bottom ooze, sand, and pebbles whooshing high into the fog, sending a shock wave against the *Petrel*. The profusion of dead fish and other marine life that rose to the surface added to everyone's surprise as they watched intently for signs of a sub's wreckage. The *Skate*, now notified by radio about what Frank had assumed was the sub, reported she was steaming toward the oceanographic vessel to assist, but at only one-third of full speed, in the event of striking unseen wreckage in the fog. Frank could feel his heart racing in expectation, but the only thing identifiable in the dirty slurry so far was the mass of crustaceans and rock cod.

"There's something!" shouted young Cookie.

"Calm down!" Tiny snarled. "There's nothing but—"

"No, I see it too," said Malcolm. "Starboard aft."

"Me too!" added Jimmy, snatching one of the slingshots and one of the baseball-size lumps of short-fuse LOSHOK packs.

Sandra focused her binoculars in the direction the crew were pointing. An irregular shape with a metallic appearance could be seen, despite the muddied sea that was spreading like a huge blanket in the chop created by the LOSHOK's explosion. Sandra called the dry lab. "It's a ray," she told Frank. "A manta ray. A cephalic fin missing."

Relief and disappointment swept through the crew. Cookie suddenly began throwing up. Frank, hearing him, dispatched one of the techs to help the youth. "But don't let him mope around. Tell Cook I said to go easy on him but to keep him occupied—light duties."

"Yes, sir."

Soon the chaos of sound from the LOSHOK's bang subsided and the *Petrel*, having turned about, headed back a hundred yards or so, Sandra doing an excellent job of using the ship's bow thrusters to relocate the exact GPS position.

The slab was gone.

Then there was another metal-like sheet in the fog. It was vertical, and from mere inches above the sea's surface, it suddenly rose to four feet high, then six.

"Holy—Sub astern!" Tiny shouted so loudly that third mate Sandra on the bridge heard him clearly, as did Frank, in the dry lab. Intuitively, Sandra brought the *Petrel* sharply about in a tight U-turn, the ship heeling hard aport, toppling Aussie, Sal, and Choir against their bunks' side boards and bringing the *Petrel* face-to-face with the ominous-looking and fog-shrouded black sub surfacing a hundred yards off.

Frank quickly organized one of the most primitive and ancient defenses known to man on the stern of his state-of-the-art oceanographic vessel. "Grab the six slingshot packs and run up to the bow!" he hollered to the stern work party.

But there were only four packs left, Freeman having grabbed two of the baseball-size lumps and quickly stuffed them into his battle vest. With a sharp tug on the bow-knotted davit lines holding the Zodiac to *Petrel*'s side, the general rapidly played out the line, lowering the Zodiac.

A sleep-dazed Aussie appeared on deck, holding his MP5. "What's going—"

"Get in the boat!" Freeman said. "We're going fishing!"

"Be careful!" Frank cautioned Freeman. "It might be surrendering."

"It's turning!" *Petrel*'s bow lookout shouted, and everyone, including the approaching *Skate* a mile off, which Sandra had alerted, heard the noise. It was a tortuous creaking sound of metal against metal, the kind Aussie and Freeman had heard when they faced the Russian-made T-72 main battle tanks in the Iraqi desert. It made the four slingshot crewmen even more nervous.

Through his binoculars, the bosun, who'd momentarily given Freeman a hand by passing down the general's gun, could now see the source of the nerve-grating sound: the submarine's prop rubbing against its tapered metallic sheath, which had collapsed under the pressure wave of the seventy-pound LOSHOK depth charge.

"Where the hell's the *Skate*?" someone shouted, another startled by the sputtering then quickly ensuing *purr* of their Zodiac's runabout.

"*Skate*'s coming!" the bosun assured the crew.

She was, but on her radar the two blips were so close together, the captain couldn't tell which was which, and it was too risky to open fire in the fog and noisy confusion. The *Skate*'s heavy machine-gun operators, however, were itching to fire, so much so that the captain repeated his earlier order, "Hold your fire!" Following the sub's carnage in the strait, everyone wanted so badly to get even that blue on blue remained a constant danger.

One of *Petrel*'s side-scan technicians ran to the dry lab's door. No one was there. "Son of—" He realized they must all be up at the bow. Though hanging on to the lab's roll bar at the time, he'd forgotten the violent U-turn, glued as he was to the trace. He snatched the PA mike from the wall. "Captain, dry lab. A bubbling sound from the sub, as well as the prop noise. Could be flooding her tubes."

"Maybe," answered Frank. But what should he do? he wondered. It would be impossible to see a torpedo running at them in the fog. Anyway, the sub was only a hundred yards off, now nose-to-nose with his boat. Even if the *Petrel* moved left or right, the sub could get an angled shot, or if she opened up with small arms fire, the *Petrel* would be virtually defenseless.

"Get the packs ready," he told Jimmy, Malcolm, and Tiny, while taking up one of the slingshots himself. Then he shouted up to the bridge to Sandra, "Go full ahead, close as you can for us—then veer away!"

She signaled with a thumbs-up.

Frank asked, "Where's the Bic?"

Tiny handed him the cigarette lighter. "High tech!"

The small orange light that the *Skate*'s captain, now half a mile away, saw through his binoculars, was not the flicker of Tiny's Bic, however, but the flame from the .50 protruding from the sub's sail like a short, stubby stick in the fog. Its burst ricocheted off *Petrel*'s forward deck bulkhead like supersonic stones thrown against a steel door. One of the .50's rounds struck Malcolm in the back of his neck, felling him in a pool of blood that neither Jimmy, Frank, or Tiny saw, the three busy tossing their LOSHOK packs, the force of their thrusts reduced by the nerve-shattering fire of the heavy machine gun, as the trio hit *Petrel*'s deck. They crawled forward, tight up against the protection of the capstan as several rounds from the sub struck the spool of anchor chain, creating a shower of sparks as *Petrel* heeled hard aport at full speed. The wash of *Petrel*'s prop was now clearly visible to the sub's machine-gun crew, who kept pouring their fire into the big target as it withdrew.

Seeing Malcolm and dragging him into the forward lab, Frank then reached the bridge, where he saw a pale-faced helmsman, the bridge glass a milky spiderweb of bullet holes, the sparkling glass fragments crunching under his boot. Hall was surprised that he hadn't heard the glass being hit. "Where's Sandra?" he asked.

"Chart room!" answered the helmsman, his voice a strangled whisper.

Sandra's face was cut badly and bleeding as the bosun and two other crewmen knelt beside her, doing their best with tweezers to remove the tiny glass slivers. Her white blouse and pants were splattered with oil from the compass mounting, and the chart of Juan de Fuca Strait was smeared with blood.

Aboard the Coast Guard's *Skate*, the sonar operator heard the underwater whoosh of a torpedo launch, the *Skate*'s computer telling him it was running at fifty knots. The *Skate*, two hundred yards off in the fog, was seconds from impact on its present course. The captain reacted swiftly, ordering a 180-degree turn to starboard away from the unseen line of the torpedo.

It took him into the path of the second torpedo fired by the sub during the noise of the *Skate*'s turn. The explosion lit up the night in a bonfire of pyrotechnics that tore the stern quarter off the *Skate*. The ship was going down, its nose sticking up at a forty-five-degree angle. It slipped under in minutes, no time for lifeboats, the cries of its crew, many afire, lost in a cacophony of sounds, a firecracker string of its own ammunition cooking off in its superheated superstructure, its death throes further illuminated by raging fuel oil fires.

Soon all that was left was the burning oil slick silhouetting the frantic two dozen or so survivors trying to extricate themselves from the flaming patches of sea, the fire's updrafts doing nothing to disperse the heavier sullen fog that had now swallowed up the retreating *Petrel*. The crew of the oceanographic ship, unarmed and in shock, were rallying to help their own wounded. An oiler on deck, one of those who'd helped make the slingshots, was suffering from an ugly head wound, hemorrhaging to death.

"We've gotta pick up those *Skate* guys!" someone said.

"We can't," answered the bosun. "*We're* not out of the shit yet. Sub's got—dammit, it's a warship—it's got everything. We slow to pick up survivors, we'll end the same way. 'Sides, those hydrofoils'll soon be here."

"They'll slow right down," said a winch man. "Always do inshore 'cause of all the logs an' crap floating about. Plus there's so much wreckage in the strait they can't risk speeding. Hit something with one of those foils at any speed, you go A over T. Quick smart."

On the *Petrel*'s bridge, blacked out, as was the rest of his ship, Frank Hall knew there was only one decision he could make.

"Where the heck's Freeman?" the first mate asked softly.

"In trouble," replied Frank, "if he doesn't watch that .50."

"They'll hear his outboard if he gets too close."

"I know," said Frank.

Which was why Freeman, at the tiller of the *Petrel*'s Zodiac, had cut the outboard, hauled it in, and joined Aussie, using paddles to move west of the sub which now seemed strangely still, as if, like some giant marine predator, it was undecided what to do immediately following the destruction of its Coast Guard prey. Or was the sub's prop so disabled, Aussie wondered, that in an all-out run on the surface it could reach only a knot or so? The awful noise generated by the prop was so loud that he knew it would serve as a homing beacon for the hydrofoils, which would soon be on the sub's radar.

In the eerie silence of the fogbound sea, the crescent bay's shore, five minutes behind them, might have been a hundred miles away, and the sound of their paddles seemed extraordinarily loud to Freeman and Aussie. Perhaps because their sense of hearing, initially scrambled by the explosions of the torpedoes, was now straining to pick up any sound in the water about them, they both heard the faint rasping sound. It wasn't the same noise as that of the prop, and had it not been for the small but persistent glow from the *Skate*'s dying fires, Aussie wouldn't have seen the bulbous baseball-size head of a snorkel tube rising from the sub. He stopped paddling and, not daring to whisper, tapped Freeman's arm twice, the snorkel rising agonizingly above the sub, the enemy craft about two o'clock to the Zodiac.

Was the sub going to dive, go on batteries for a while despite the grating prop noise, far enough again to lie low and stop all engines? Given the depth reading he recalled on the *Petrel*, Freeman knew that it wouldn't be too deep for a swimmer to exit through an escape air-lock hatch and replace or "putty" in a few replacement anechoic tiles.

Skate was gone, *Petrel* bloodied and unarmed, and, given the fog, the two hydrofoils might not get to the sub before she dived, which it looked like she'd do at any second, because there was no one on deck. Freeman was as vain a man as any other, but he'd never allowed vanity to block efficiency, and he knew that, his A-grade fitness notwithstanding, Aussie Lewis was a younger man with more strength in his arm. So he passed the two balls of LOSHOK to Aussie and quietly tipped the outboard's prop shaft into the water, just in case.

With his mouth against Aussie's ear, he intoned, "Tape one of 'em around the snorkel."

They resumed paddling, Freeman estimating it would take them five to six minutes to reach the sub. The snorkel was still inching up, rasping, the sub's skipper obviously preferring to raise it in air rather than waiting till he was submerged, where the sound would travel four times as fast to the hydrofoils.

The problem, Freeman knew, was that it would be difficult if not impossible to maintain position in the current *and* tape the charge to the rising pipe. The current was getting stronger. They had maybe ten minutes.

CHAPTER FORTY-FIVE

RORKE'S ABILITY TO maneuver the "Big Cigar," as *Encino* called their 360-foot-long sub, had duly impressed the executive officer, especially given the level of instability in the 6881 class, caused by its sail being located farther forward than on the earlier boats of the class. Though launch site was still minutes away, the XO foresaw no problems with the launch. *Encino*'s "load-out" of torpedoes and Tomahawks, following normal procedure, contained a number of variants. Of the dozen cruise missiles in the launch tubes forward of the sail, four had single thousand-pound Bullpup HE warheads, four were armed with 109D runway-cratering submunitions warheads, and the final four were capped with a doomsday "city take-out" 150-kiloton nuclear warhead.

With all presets entered into *Encino*'s fire-control computer console, the attack boat rose to a point sixty feet below the surface, its speed now down from thirty knots to three. Rorke had decided to start with the four 109Ds, the navigator confirming that the intersection of the coordinates was midway down Penghu's runway, now presumably packed with PLA fighters.

The sound of hydraulics and valves opening as the twelve forward vertical tubes were flooded in the sequence Rorke had decided upon were noises that none of the boat's officers and men wanted to hear. They had no qualms about their part in the new post-9/11 American policy of talking softly and carrying the biggest stick you could find. But flooding, then opening, the "caps," or lids, on each of the forward-angled twelve VLTs violated the submariner's counsel of perfection: "Thou shalt stay silent." The gurgling and bubbling sounds were worse than most "sound shorts," or acoustic faults, in a boat, signaling to any hostile within hundreds or even thousands of miles away where you were. And in this case, telling them you were about to launch a weapon—whether it be an antiship harpoon, torpedo, or, as now, the Tomahawk cruise missiles.

"Up attack scope!" said Rorke.

It was unlikely there would be any ships nearby, and *Encino*'s sonar hadn't picked up anything unusual, but a visual sweep was needed just in case. Despite the awesome responsibility he had for launching such tremendous firepower, Johnny Rorke enjoyed the anticipatory moment of looking through the scope. He had not "danced" with either of the boat's "ladies" since the *Utah*. He liked the physical sensation of watching the scope's oil-sheen column rising to his command, the sensation of flipping down the scope's arms, gripping their criss-cross nonslip handles and his eyes marrying themselves to the scope via the sensuously soft rubber cups that shut out all light in the CIC, including the luminescent green of the two target trackers' computers and the bloodred of the weapons officer's screen.

He moved as one with the scope, sweeping smartly through a 360-degree arc and back again, the reverse sweep to assure him he hadn't missed anything during his clockwise rotation because of the different azimuth. All seemed clear.

"Down scope."

With flight instructions for each missile in the computers, Rorke initiated what would be a ripple launch. The first missile fired would be one of the outermost of the six-tube configuration on the starboard side, followed immediately by the corresponding missile of the portside six.

"Commence launch," said Rorke. This was for the crew's benefit, as the countdown the weapons officer had already initiated was an automatic, computer-controlled function.

The crew heard the explosive charge that, along with an enormous whoosh of compressed air, ejected the cruise missile, thrusting it through the thin plastic membrane at the top of its launch tube into the sea, from sixty feet below the surface. The boat lurched slightly as the 2,650-pound Tomahawk exited the boat, seawater immediately rushing into the empty launch tube, the Tomahawk's booster firing underwater, twenty-five feet above the sub. The missile, broaching the sea's surface, shivered with the tremor of the booster's fiery exhaust, the missile's protective wing cover popping off, tailfin shrouds also discarded, four tailfins extending to steady the Tomahawk's angle of flight.

At a thousand feet, only seconds after launch point and as another missile left *Encino*, the first Tomahawk's solid-fuel booster fell away, its job done, the turbofan jet taking over, stubby wings extended. Its terrain control matching system helped to guide it, the missile flattening out at ninety feet above sea level en route to its target, virtually skimming the sea, the radar cross section no more than eleven square feet. Its approach was doubly protected by the *Encino* jamming the PLA radars. Traveling subsonically at plus or minus 500 mph, this small radar signature of the Tomahawk should be lost in the post-typhoon sea clutter, the missile and the eleven other Tomahawks following—a six-million-dollar "train" of explosives that Rorke's crew, many ardent followers of the old *Six Million Dollar Man*, dubbed the "Six Million Dollar Slam"—scheduled to reach Penghu in approximately twenty-four minutes.

Admiral Crowley was bitterly disappointed upon hearing that *Encino* was given the job of "missiling" Penghu. Why hadn't they given it to him? He'd played it smart, very smart, conducting the burial at night in blackout conditions so he'd be ready in the event any Bizarro/terrorist/kamikaze attack was launched at him in the morning when an enemy would assume the ship would slow for such a burial. Or didn't Washington think *McCain*'s battle group was up to it because of the kamikaze hit?

The padre, a good friend of the battle group commander, tried to soften the blow. "God works in mysterious ways, his wonders to perform," he reminded the admiral.

"Is that so?" Crowley retorted churlishly. "Where was he when that kamikaze holed my roof?"

The padre assured the admiral that the Almighty had a plan.

"Well, I'm damned if I can discern it, Padre," Crowley said, his tone softening for the sake of friendship, if not because of religious belief.

The rain of cruise missiles on Penghu brought shock and awesome devastation, the huge billows of copper-red smoke rising, reeking of burning Avgas and atomized fish fertilizer from the once picturesque stony-bordered farms, the clouds of war obscuring the island clearly visible to satellite reconnaissance. The problem was, Typhoon Jane's residual tail winds had "increased the CEP," as the Pentagon put it.

"In English, please," Eleanor Prenty demanded.

"Circular error probable, ma'am. It means the diameter centering on the target within which there is a fifty percent chance of hitting."

"Error probable?" said Eleanor. "My God, you're telling me that they didn't hit Penghu?"

"No, our missiles *did* hit Penghu. No question about—"

"But not the runway and all the radars?"

"No, ma'am. I mean that's right, you're correct. We—"

"Give me a percentage, Commander. What percent did you hit? Eighty? Sixty?"

" 'Bout forty to fifty."

"What's the *Encino*'s load-out?" she asked, knowing that sometimes the subs carried extra cruise missiles, housing them in the torpedo racks.

The Pentagon man didn't know if the twelve Tomahawks were the *Encino*'s full load of cruise missiles or whether there were some in reserve.

"Well, find out," she told him abruptly.

"Yes, ma'am!"

"Use my phone."

It was very highly classified information, and the Pentagon messenger, albeit a commander, had to have written authority from the Chief of Naval Operations to be given one of America's launch platform's precise "load-out."

Eleanor Prenty waited impatiently. If *Encino* didn't have reserve Tomahawks, then someone else would have to be tasked to finish what *Encino* had begun and to pulverize the Penghu runway before the PLA could use it as a base from which clandestine attacks could be launched against Taiwan—even during an official cease-fire that the Secretary of State was hastily trying to broker between Beijing and Taipei, both Chinese capitals sticking firmly to their positions that the other one had reopened hostilities.

The commander from the Pentagon had the answer to Eleanor's question twenty minutes later. SSN *Encino*'s multiple launch, as ordered by the President, had exhausted the submarine's load-out supply of twelve Tomahawks.

The President didn't hesitate. "Draw up orders," he told the Chief of Naval Operations, "for *McCain*'s battle group to take out that runway."

"How about vertical launch from the Aegis cruisers?" asked Eleanor. "*McCain*'s pretty badly—"

"No." The President was adamant. "It's important politically as well as for the Navy's morale—which is the lowest I've ever seen—to have *McCain* do it. Have the carrier's air wing launch the attack. Stand-off weapons. If we can take Makung out as their forward air base, we'll have a lot more leverage to force Beijing to the table."

"Makung?" asked Eleanor.

"Penghu's city. Where the runway is."

"Oh," said Eleanor. "Yes, of course. Mr. President, do you

think Beijing's got anything to do with this sub attacking us in the Northwest?"

The President had obviously thought a lot about it, as he had about the myriad fronts going on in the war, clandestine and overt, all over the world as the U.S. struggled to keep the upper hand. "I don't think so, Eleanor. Nor do the Joint Chiefs. It seems more like a terrorist group to me. Trouble is, we Americans have—let's face it—a lot of difficulty accepting the fact that a bunch of Muslims could develop a weapons platform so quiet, so able to pierce our defenses—like this midget sub the Navy's hydrofoils are now finally closing in on."

"Finally" seemed a bit rich to Eleanor. Admittedly, it had felt like months and months dealing with the Northwest attack, along with everything else, but crises always seemed longer at the time. In fact, it had been much shorter, and the Navy had done darned well to get the hydrofoils on their way, because the new craft had barely finished sea trials.

"Problem is," the President said, "we think of Muslims, we think of Iraq, Iran, Afghanistan. Desert and oil." The Chief Executive paused. "Had you ever imagined Arabs as submariners?"

"No. Well, I knew some Russian submariners who were Muslim, but no, not further than that."

CHAPTER FORTY-SIX

AS FREEMAN AND Aussie neared the bow of the sub, the snorkel pipe stopping then beginning to inch up again—its slow ascent no doubt an attempt to keep its rasping to a minimum— the two wondered if the sub's sonar had picked up the noise of their paddling. The fogbound sea was considerably calmer now than when they had shot at the sub much earlier that day. Or was the sub's scope sliding up for a visual check? But what was there to see in the fog, besides the *Skate*'s dying firelight?

Aussie glimpsed the *Petrel*, her stern's hydraulic arm silhouetted against the oil slick's fire. Having heard the rasping of the sub's snorkel being raised, Frank Hall had no doubt decided to move the oceanographic vessel in quickly to pick up as many *Skate* survivors as possible.

Freeman, meanwhile, reached for the waterproof matches in his vest and flushed. It was his usual physiological reaction upon realizing he'd uncharacteristically forgotten a vital detail. This time it was the short fuse on each of the fist-sized LOSHOK packs he'd given Aussie, which would allow only two seconds. No way you could duct-tape, light the fuse, and get clear. There was no time to convey his concern to Aussie other than by speaking. And they were only ten feet from the sub's starboard fairing, which Aussie would have to board to place the charge. "Cut the second pack's fuse and tape it to the first," the general whispered hoarsely. "That'll give us more time."

Four seconds, Aussie thought, to tape and run.

Their Zodiac bumped gently against the sub's side.

A beam of light struck out from *Petrel*'s foredeck toward the *Skate*'s burning oil spill, looking quickly for survivors. Aussie and Freeman heard a dull thud, then saw a head appear above the sub's stubby conning tower, followed by a quick order in a language neither Aussie nor the general understood. Then they heard another, more excited, voice, and saw a .50 caliber barrel poking up from the interior of the conning tower and sticking straight out in the direction of the *Skate*. The gunner appeared next, and then whoever was giving the orders, either the sub's captain or the officer of the deck.

Good God, Freeman thought. The bastards were going to shoot the Coast Guard survivors as well as the men on the *Petrel* who were trying to rescue them.

A long, ragged flame spat into the fog from Freeman's HK, the 9mm rounds chopping into the sub gunner's head and into the officer's right shoulder. But the officer managed to swing the .50 around and squeeze off a loud burst. A bullet struck Freeman in the chest, knocking him out of the Zodiac as Aussie, already on the sub's fairing below the conning tower, plunged his K-bar into the officer. The officer grabbed at his throat in a vain effort to stop the pulsing jets of blood that showered Aussie's face, then the officer's body crumpled noisily, the wooden stock of the .50 falling back with a whack against the sub's collar.

Aussie heard a commotion below. One more step up the side of the conning tower and he glimpsed the ruby-colored glow of the sub's small control room, the body of the sub's gunner slumped awkwardly, blocking the hatch. Seeing a bald head below the dead gunner, and arms desperately tugging at the gunner's feet, trying to clear the hatch, Aussie fired a burst down the hatch well, the man's head exploding. Then he lit the first fuse and dropped it, the reverberation of the LOSHOK's explosion so severe that it momentarily stunned Aussie, though he was still outside the conning tower and unable to hear anything.

The charge, he realized, must have either bounced off the body-stoppered hatch or the open hatch cover itself. He'd have to heave himself up, drop down into the conning tower, and clear the body. But one glance into the smoke-choked hatch—the LOSHOK fumes rising up, stinging his eyes, throat, and nose, told him another burst was unnecessary. What had been the enemy's decapitated body, or rather, what was now an indistinguishable bloody pile, had fallen down through the hatch onto the control room's floor. He squeezed another burst off anyway, for insurance, dropped the second two-second charge down and slammed the hatch shut. This explosion was a muffled *whoomp,* no smoke emerging from the tightly sealed sub, except for a white puff rising from the snorkel.

"A new Pope!" he shouted, his outburst a mixture of adrenaline and anger, wondering if the general was still alive, and sure that no one in the midget sub had survived. An explosion like that, he knew, would create a dense and toxic mix even in a full-sized attack boat.

The pinhead of light automatically activated by the saltwater showed Aussie where the general, dead or alive, was drifting, about twenty or thirty feet off the sub's starboard bow, not far from the Zodiac. Aussie slung his HK tightly to his back, discarded his boots, and dived in, swimming with all his strength to the Zodiac. He hauled himself aboard, pushed the outboard's starter and, hungry for air, gasped as he steered the Zodiac toward Freeman, cutting the motor almost as soon as he'd started it.

"Fire a goddamn flare!" the general was shouting, his voice imperious. "Don't you know anything?!"

In fact, Freeman's bonhomie in the freezing water helped the general to tolerate the painful bruising that was spreading across his chest, the round from the sub's .50 MG not a dead-on hit, but a powerful angled shot all the same, and one that had shredded all but the last two of the Kevlar's sandwiched layers.

The *Petrel* saw the flare, as did the two closing hydrofoils, one of which approached the Zodiac with a suspicion underscored by an array of weaponry that was as impressive as it was late.

"Well, at least they can help *Petrel* pick up those poor bastards from *Skate*," Aussie told Freeman, who was now hurting badly.

The general was not given to hyperbole regarding his enemies, but what occurred next he would describe as simply "astonishing." From the mini Vesuvius that was the submarine's conning tower, there emerged three ghostly figures in the flare lights, their clothing steaming with white smoke that clung to them like dry ice, their faces hidden by maniacal-looking goggles and the snouts of gas masks.

"Son of a bitch!" shouted Tiny, thunderstruck. "Pricks are still alive!" Two of them were manning the .50.

"Everyone inside," shouted Hall from *Petrel*'s bridge, as Aussie and Freeman were being helped aboard. "Secure all hatches. Lights out!"

"Secure all hatches!!" repeated Frank. *"And stay inside!"* With that, he pushed *Petrel*'s Full Ahead button, shouting into the down pipe to the engine room, "Everything you've got, Chief!"

The crew, bodies involuntarily trembling with the thunderous reverberations, had never felt anything like it.

Frank snatched up the bridge's microphone. "Stand by to ram!"

"Shit!" It was Cookie. In the blacked-out galley, it suddenly dawned on him what Hall intended. "The hydrofoils should—"

The bosun's attempt to explain to young Cookie how hydrofoils were like jet boats on water—very fast in clear weather but too delicate for this—was cut short by a firecracker noise forward, the sound of *Petrel*'s already multipunctured bridge glass collapsing in a resounding crash. Now all firing from the hydrofoils ceased, the *Petrel*, at fifteen knots, having to cross their lines of fire.

The 110-foot-long sub and its conning tower were rendered momentarily visible with each burst of the .50, only one man remaining at the gun.

Frank was steering by the flashes of the .50. He wasn't watching the sub through the fog-inhaling hole that had been *Petrel*'s bridge, but by lying on his back, guided by the image of the .50's spitting flame in the mirror from Sandra's compact. He held it up for several seconds at a time, and could alter his course with a tap on the "sensitouch" joystick.

"Hold on!" he shouted over the PA. But with the PA's wiring, among other things, now severed in the hail of the sub's machine-gun fire, no one heard him beyond the bridge.

The shock of the *Petrel* hitting the sub aft of the conning tower was so severe that it flung several crew members across the mess. The bosun's cheek split against the bulkhead stiffener, and young Cookie literally tore the big electric motor off its mount as a flying avalanche of broken crockery and foodstuffs injured him and five other crewmen amid an outburst of profanities and alarm so loud Hall heard them coming up through the stairwell.

The *Petrel*'s bow was so high now, after smashing into the sub's conning tower, that the broken plates and other debris began sliding back. But just as quickly, everything began to subside, *Petrel*'s forward half coming down as it slid off the sub's deck. As Hall leaped up, running to the bridge's starboard wing, he saw that the sub's aft was severely creased—cracks appearing—heard the machine gunner and dropped to the deck. Aussie, racing along the *Petrel*'s port side, came out firing on its forward deck, not taking his finger off the trigger, killing the be-goggled and black-snouted gunner before the terrorist could swing the .50 from Frank on the upper starboard side to him.

Then, in place of the unrelenting gunfire, there was relative calm. But not silence, as the oceanographic crew, though hesitant at first, now poured out on the stern to watch the death throes of the submarine. In *Petrel*'s deck lights, which were now back on, they could see water cascading into the deep, three-foot-wide gash aft of the sail, the sub's nose rising in a strangely majestic way. The excited voices of the *Petrel* crew and the faint cheers of the hydrofoil crews ceased momentarily, for no matter how evil its man-driven intent, the boat itself now seemed possessed of a dignity in death. Its bow, so high in the air that it momentarily rose above the level of *Petrel*'s foredeck, sent several men racing back toward *Petrel*'s winches, frightened by the awe-filled ascent of the sub's bow. For the first time, a flag was glimpsed on its forward staff, which could only have been placed there by one of the three gas-masked ghosts who'd emerged earlier from the LOSHOK's toxified air.

Once the sub, slipping from view in a hissing steam of burst pipes and shattered machinery, slid out of view, the cheers on hold during her final moments erupted into the dank, dark air, a hydrofoil sapper unit already on their way to destroy the cave and its antechambers.

"We can now report," began one of Marte Price's colleagues in Atlanta, "that this unprecedented assault on America's navy is finally over." The announcer, a Hollywood face in his early thirties but with a marked British accent, turned to his coanchor. "And it's fitting, Joanne, that it was the Navy's hydrofoils that finished the job."

"*Bullshit!*" came a chorus of outraged *Petrel* crewmen. Sandra, in temporary relief from the morphine shot the second mate had given her, shook her head slowly in disgust. It was Freeman's team who'd done it, first slowing and then damaging it further, and finally Aussie Lewis disabling it so it couldn't escape, enabling the *Petrel* to finish it off. The hydrofoils were late to the show.

"It's fitting indeed, Ryan," replied the fair-haired coanchor with the "to die for" looks. "I know all America and our allies in this ongoing war against terrorism will heave a great sigh of relief and extend their gratitude to the U.S. Navy."

"Best in the world," said the anchor, shuffling his papers with an air of efficiency and confidence de rigueur for those who wanted to get ahead—even if, as Freeman sourly observed, "they don't know what the hell they're talking about."

"Sure as hell don't. It was you guys who did it," commented Tiny. "I dunno—first reports are always cocked up."

"Hydrofoil guys are taking the damn credit," voiced Jimmy.

"No," said Freeman. "Not their fault. It's nighttime, no one can see a damn thing. Probably talked to a reporter on the radio phone. Static all over—hydrofoil guy says the sub's sunk, rammed by *Petrel*. Reporter can't hear it probably, thinks what he heard was 'petrol'—probably thinks the sub was afire and rammed. Line cuts out and all he's heard is that the sub's sunk. Every war I've been in—you're right, son—first reports are always 'cocked up.'"

"It'll get straightened out," said the first mate.

Though the rush of relief flooding over them was a well-known experience for the team and the veterans of the Iraqi wars among *Petrel*'s crew, for most, the surge of success, exaggerating their own part in "getting the sub," bordered on hysteria. It was infused in part by the real and present danger they had faced on board what had been an essentially defenseless ship while being machine-gunned. The death of one of their number and the condition of Sandra would dampen their celebratory remarks later on, but right now the sudden turn of fate from being victims to victors was too powerful for them to moderate their behavior. Cookie was all but unmanageable in his adolescent fervor, raining insults down at the fog-shrouded depths where the broken sub now lay.

"General's a bit sullen," the cook told Aussie while lighting up a cigarette.

"Uh-huh," Aussie replied noncommittally. Criticism of Freeman by those in his own team was one thing, but Cook wasn't in the team. How could he be expected to understand the present reserve of a man generally known for his garrulousness and forthrightness, Aussie thought, a man who had become a legend because at crucial times he had neither behaved nor thought like other men.

"He's probably exhausted," added the bosun, sensing Lewis's quiet disapproval.

"Guess we all are," said Aussie, but in truth he had also been struck by Freeman's increasingly down mood. Was it churlishness that he, Douglas Freeman, would not reap the glory that was the fuel of his insatiable ego? Another Patton or MacArthur?

Walking past the general, now a solitary figure in the penumbra of the deck lights, Aussie said lightheartedly, "I lost a good pair of boots back there."

The general, leaning on the gunwale, his focus somewhere in the fog, didn't respond.

"History'll know, General."

"Have you ever seen such fanaticism?" the general asked Aussie. "That machine gunner? Those three coming up out of that hellhole after you'd blasted them silly?"

Aussie thought back, a string of desperate firefights crowding his memory. "Maybe once," he said. "Funny thing is, it was a Republican Guard, during that punch-up we had 'round Hadiya."

Freeman stood up and looked across at Aussie. "To hate America that much. That's what we're up against, Aussie."

Aussie nodded. "Formidable."

"That's the word."

"Well, General, we've won this round."

"Yes," said Freeman, right thumb and forefinger massaging his forehead. "There's something—" He paused. "—something bothering me." He stopped massaging himself and, arms akimbo, took a deep breath. "Know what I mean? A feeling. I've missed something."

"We'll find out more when we bring that sucker up," said Aussie. "Go through it. Might find out who did it—Chinese or towel heads."

Freeman unexpectedly laughed. "You want to win your bet?"

Before Aussie could answer, Freeman added, "A few Asians so far, only a couple of Chinese."

Aussie was glad to see the general loosening up, and promised himself as soon as they got ashore at Port Angeles he'd try to contact Marte Price, set her straight about just what did happen, make sure Freeman got his full measure of recognition—well, the team too. He was encouraged to do it because, after his chat with the general, he realized that what the cook and no doubt others had interpreted as a sullen exhibition of petty ego was in fact a leader's concern. The general, famous for attention to minutiae, was bothered by something like a detail in a persistent dream that takes flight the moment you wake, yet remains in the background of your mind all day.

CHAPTER FORTY-SEVEN

ADMIRAL CROWLEY HAD just had his second and last coffee of the day. Any more and he knew he'd feel on edge. Especially after the kamikaze attack, which, despite the absence of the kind of proof that would stand up in a court of law, everyone on the carrier believed was instigated by the Communist Chinese air force to cow, or at least slow, the carrier from advancing further into the Taiwan Strait and effectively refereeing the two-China "incident," as Beijing was calling the two-China war.

Now, Crowley's voice was at once serious and upbeat as he addressed *McCain*'s air wing.

"Gentlemen, we all know just how badly the Navy's been hit at home. There isn't a man or woman on the boat who hasn't known or lost someone during the rampage of that sub's attacks in the Strait of Juan de Fuca. A lot of folks on the other vessels in our battle group have also lost loved ones. But I'm here to tell you that initial reports of the sub's demise have been confirmed."

There was whooping and clapping throughout the aviators' ready rooms and the other departments in the boat.

"Admiral Jensen, COMSUBPAC Group 9, has verified that two of his hydrofoil fast patrol boats witnessed the kill."

"Who were they?" Chipper Armstrong asked his squadron intel officer. "The terrorists?"

"No verification on that, Commander."

"Now, gentlemen, I have a second announcement." Everyone who'd done at least one tour with Crowley knew that the big news always came last. "As you know, one of our SSNs missiled Penghu. Satellite BDAs confirm wind deflection, courtesy of Typhoon Jane, extended the missiles' CEP. Some PLA planes were destroyed, but not—I repeat, *not*—the runway, 'least not enough to prevent quick repair. The President has therefore asked if we can do the job before the PLA can land aircraft resupply."

There was some braggadocio, but others were silent. There was that big hole in their roof.

"Any flier has the right to pass this one up without prejudice to his service record."

The admiral waited for reports from all the ready rooms listening to him. All pilots and aircrew volunteered to go.

"Very well, gentlemen, it's time. Kick the tires and light the fires!"

Resounding cheers were heard throughout the carrier, and in minutes, unseen even by some high in Primary Flight Control, scores of invisible colored jackets flooded the deck forward of the carrier's island and the kamikaze's bomb crater. The crater, having rendered catapults three and four on the carrier's aft port side inoperable, was now roped off, with a six-man line stationed in front of it to yell at any of the deck personnel who might back up and impede maneuvering aircraft once launch operations got under way. Elevator 1, starboard midships, forward of the island, clunked and emitted its deep hum as it descended yet again to the hangar deck to reload. High up in Vulture's Row, the salty sea wind chilling their faces, two off-duty sailors—a young barber from Ohio and a young woman, Angela, a purple-jacketed refueler from Arkansas—held hands in the darkness, saying nothing. Their rapt attention had been captured by the wondrously unique ballet of soft yellow flashlights far below them, strobing through the sea spray in a strangely hypnotic dance of war.

The scores of deck personnel holding the flashlights were all but invisible. The only thing that approached it in Angela's memory was a performance by the Black Theater of Prague that she had seen as a schoolgirl, the players invisible, only *things* moving on the pitch-black stage, as if by magic. The soft yellow bulbs of the flashlights were conveying the same eerie yet comforting display of connectedness and separation, as if countless glowworms were "coming together, coming apart," as the song goes, joining, separating, and rejoining as the "foreign object debris walkdown" continued, only personnel on the starboard end of the inspection line coming into full view as they passed through the apron of subdued orange light at the base of the island.

"Isn't it beautiful?" Angela asked her beau.

Despite the cranials they were wearing to protect them from the brain-dulling crescendo that would soon break loose below, the young barber heard her. He'd heard every word she'd said from the moment they'd first met on the boat. "Yes," he replied. "It is. Like you."

She elbowed him playfully, their hands still locked together, her grip tightening as the foreign object walkdown ended and the colored shirts went to work, kicking the tires and lighting the fires. Then fierce purple-white jet exhausts pierced the night, the engines' feral screams shattering any remaining world of glowworms, the afterburners momentarily illuminating the colored jackets whose earlier, gentler ballet was now a rougher thing altogether. Yet within what at first seemed a chaos of disorganized crew running, kneeling, and signaling pilots with lighted wands, there was an organization so intricate and fast that it would make the busiest civil airport appear indolent, the carrier's night launch all the more impressive given that only catapults one and two were operational.

Angela glimpsed a plane handler wanding the first striker, Chipper Armstrong's Super Hornet, into position. For an instant the ambient light silhouetted Eagle Evans in the Hornet's backseat as the catapult's tow bar was lowered into the shuttle, in position to pull the fighter along the deck. With the nose wheel housing's holdback rod acting like the reins on a caged stallion, the turbofans could now reach full power before release. The shuttle's pull, in concert with the plane's own thrust, would catapult the plane off the deck, providing all went well, the night launch and recovery the ultimate test of an aviator's skill.

Hunkered down in the CAT control pod set almost flush into the deck, the yellow-shirted "shooter," or catapult officer, initiated the flow of superwet nonradioactive steam, provided by a secondary loop off the carrier's reactor plant. The shooter double- and then triple-checked the combined deck-and-ship speed in regulating the steam pressure flow. Too little pressure and the fighter-bomber, unable to attain takeoff, would be pushed into the sea. Too much, and the aircraft's nose wheel would be torn asunder.

Chipper Armstrong, all preflight checks completed, red-ribbon-tagged ordnance pins out, raised his arms high, as if surrendering, but in fact showing the shooter that his hands were nowhere near the controls.

The shooter, seeing that the green shirts had completed the final checks, gave the okay to Armstrong, who selected "Afterburner" for the Hornet's twin turbofans and snapped off a salute. The shooter pushed the button and the Hornet rushed forward, Armstrong's and Evans's bodies slammed back under the G force, the plane hurtling down the deck, speeding from zero to 150 miles per hour in two seconds. Evans experienced an involuntary erection, his eyes rammed back hard into their sockets, and then the plane was aloft, Chipper taking over the controls.

As they banked, RIO Evans glanced back at the rapidly shrinking deck, seeing an F-14 Tomcat, one of the four fighters assigned to ride shotgun for the Hawkeye, moving into position, its toy-sized launch crew swarming around their charge. If all went well, the F-14 would be off the deck in under three minutes, longer than usual because of the extra maneuvering required forward of the crater. Despite one sailor in the crater's warning line being knocked down by the combination of crosswind and jet blast freakishly angling off the catapult's blast shield, all went well. *McCain*'s squadrons assembled "upstairs" for a standoff attack on Penghu to finish what Johnny Rorke and *Encino*'s crew had begun.

On *Encino*, neither the officers nor men knew anything about the instructions given to Crowley and his crew. Now they received orders to turn about and head for home, the submersed "blue"-crewed six-month patrol ending. Upon return to Bangor, through the Juan de Fuca choke point, the sub's "gold" crew would take over after food, lockers, and vertical launch tubes were restocked.

McCain's sixteen planes—eight Super Hornets, four A-6E Intruders, and four Tomcats—selected for the mission against the "high-value fixed land target" of Penghu were about to attack. Each surface-to-land missile contained a GPS receiver/processor able to pinpoint the big 1,366-pound missile's position to within fifty-two feet. And each missile's erasable programmable read-only memory had received four missions from the pre-launch loader: three possible missions for Penghu, a fourth or alternative target being the PLA-occupied Kinmen Island, a hundred miles west of Penghu.

In Chipper Armstrong's Super Hornet, Evans had already selected the first of the three Penghu programs—1.35 minutes before impact the imaging infrared seeker would be activated, each missile's infrared seeker head "fan-scanning" through 180 degrees and back again in ninety-one seconds. Should anything happen to Chipper's plane or any other of *McCain*'s birds, "Mother," the E-2C Hawkeye, could take over control of the missiles via Hawkeye's "pancake," or rotodome. And via *McCain*'s Super Hornet and Intruder pilot and bombardier/navigator crews, the "standoff" missile's five-hundred-pound blast fragment warhead had been programmed for "instantaneous" rather than "delayed" fuse.

McCain's "Hit Parade," as the crew of just over five thousand called the strike force of Hornets, Intruders, and Tomcats, were under strict instructions—namely for the benefit of the "nuggets," the rookie aviators—that the SLAMs must be careful of "fratricide," by which they meant the destruction of a SLAM by either the explosion or debris of the missile fired just ahead of it impacting. The rippled fire of Tomahawks from Johnny Rorke's *Encino* had prevented "too fast a rain," as missile instructors often stressed, because of the time between each launch.

Chipper was scheduled to be first to push the button, the other SLAMs to be fired at fifteen-second intervals, the Hit Parade's launch points well beyond the range of anything PLA's air-to-air missile batteries might have hurriedly put into place on Penghu.

It would be hit and run, *McCain*'s planes returning to the safety of the carrier battle group's protective screen, for whom there would never again be a "Bizarro" incident. Any bogeys or friendly marked plane approaching the CVBG would be assumed hostiles. And unless proved otherwise by radio-recognized "friend or foe" code, they would be shot down.

"Weapons free" authority was confirmed by Chipper Armstrong's six "range known" homing antiradar missiles, fired by Tomcats getting close in at ten miles. Low in the protective sea clutter at ten miles, the missiles homed in on either side-lobe or more direct "back" radiation, to take out whatever early warning radars the PLA might have managed to erect on the island. Although these half-dozen eight-hundred-pound missiles, streaking through the now typhoon-swept sky at Mach 2, were burning low-smoke solid propellant, their vapor trails—two of them crisscrossing—were plainly visible to the crews of *McCain*, the two Aegis cruisers, and the battle group's destroyers and frigates. Only the CVBG's forward and rear subs were unable to witness the HARM attack, the kind of antiradar onslaught that destroyed Saddam Hussein's early warning network in April 2003.

Any concern Mother's electronics crew might have had about an unintended crisscross of two HARMs quickly evaporated as all six antiradar missiles struck their respective targets, the thousands of tiny steel cubes in their warheads swarming the radars' sensitive antennae.

Penghu, now "electronically blind," had no effective defense against the ensuing onslaught of sixteen SLAMs, Penghu's runway so badly pitted by the SLAMs' cratering sub munitions that on SATPIX it looked like a moonscape.

There was collateral damage, but as with the CIA's post-9/11 attitude, aboard *McCain* there was "Before Iraq" and "After Iraq." After the civilian shields Saddam had used to smother targets, which had cost so many American men and women their lives, the phrase "collateral damage" no longer evoked undue alarm in the administration. Similarly, there had been a hardening of hearts among the Australian, British, American, and Polish soldiers of the 2003 coalition, and deep suspicions of white flags.

CHAPTER FORTY-EIGHT

RESTING IN *PETREL*'S dry lab, lazily watching the fog clear as the ship slowly limped back toward Port Angeles, her bow and bow thrusters in critical shape, Aussie, Sal, and Choir were struck by the general's refusal to feel relieved. Even though Marte Price, following up on the initial and incorrect CNN report, had made it abundantly clear that it was *not* the hydrofoils who were instrumental in the terrorist sub's destruction but Freeman's "brave, heroic team," and *Petrel*'s gutsy captain and crew, Freeman was still frowning as he walked about the ship, unable to relax.

"So what if some folks still believe the first news reports and haven't heard Marte's follow-up?" mused Sal. "The general knows what went down."

"Yeah," joined in Choir. "There'll be a White House reception, medals galore, that's what it'll be, lads, 'cept for Aussie here and his BIGS."

"BIGS?" said Aussie, who was as familiar as his comrades with most military acronyms. "What in hell is BIGS?"

"Aussie's big grenade screw-up!"

"You little Welsh squirt," Aussie said. "I ought to bash your head in."

Sal chortled.

"You too, you Brooklyn bastard!" said Aussie. "I incapacitated the damn thing. It couldn't move." Aussie saw Freeman passing by the lab doorway as he headed along the passageway out to the deck. Hoping to bring him out of his mood, Aussie called out, "Isn't that right, General?"

Freeman paused, the frown creasing his forehead so severely that Aussie felt like saying, as his mother used to when he grimaced sourly over homework assignments, "If you don't get rid of that scowl, you'll stay that way." Young Aussie used to frequently check himself in the mirror.

"What's that?" asked the general, stopping, but so preoccupied that he hadn't heard.

"I was just telling these two no-hopers here that it was me who stopped the sub long enough to—"

"Yes, yes," Freeman said, disappearing from the doorway as he strode away.

Aussie waited several seconds, then looked at Sal and Choir. "What a friggin' rain face! Never seen 'im so down."

Sal put his finger to his lips and jerked his thumb toward the stern deck where, having turned sharply on reaching the deck, Freeman had bent down, pulling back the blanket from the terrorist with the badly bruised neck. Once again he irritably threw the blanket back over the man's face, stood up and walked slowly away.

"What's with him?" said Sal.

Aussie shrugged. "Don't think *he* knows."

"Maybe," said Choir, laughing and quoting an old detergent jingle, "he doesn't like 'ring around the collar'?"

"There's definitely a bee in his bonnet," began Choir, then stopped. Freeman was standing at the corridor doorway again, having reentered the ship's passageway directly from the A-frame, out of view of those in the dry lab.

"It's not a bee," said the general. "It's a goddamn wasp, and I don't know where the hell it's coming from." With that, he moved off.

"So?" asked Choir. "Where's his wasp coming from, my hearties?"

Neither Sal nor Aussie knew.

The question was finally answered at precisely 3:00 P.M. a mile west of Port Angeles, when the *Petrel*, in thinning but still persistent fog, received the news—as did the rest of the world—that the USS *Harold Ward*, a fiberglass-keeled minesweeper of 895 tons, had just sunk between Cape Flattery and Vancouver Island. "A Coast Guard patrol boat was sighted in the area, but it's doubtful if it was able to rescue any of the survivors, as the minesweeper sank so quickly that—"

"Suffering Jesus!" exclaimed Freeman.

In that serendipitous confluence of forces where unconnected links are finally connected, the general had it: Choir's offhand joke about "ring around the collar" and the general's obsession about the bruise ring about the collar, or neck, of the terrorist on deck came together in the shock of yet another ship going down.

Frank Hall told Freeman it would take another hour at least, at *Petrel*'s present crawl of one of two knots, until they reached Port Angeles.

"Frank," said the general, his eyes alive with urgency. "For God's sake, let me have the Zodiac!"

"General, I had no intention of refusing it. You and the boys take it, but the news guy said that that minesweeper had *sunk*— nothing about an explosion. Media's so hot to trot these days they're automatically assuming it's been torpedoed or something. Ships do sink for a host of other—"

"It's been torpedoed, Frank," said the general. "There's *another* goddamn sub! Don't you see? That's why there were so many goddamn sinkings in a few days. It was a goddamn duo at work!"

"Then where the hell's it come from?" asked Frank. "I mean you—Darkstar's gone over the whole coast."

"I don't know, Frank. That's why I need the Zodiac."

Frank let Freeman have the Zodiac, Aussie meanwhile cursing the fact that there were no boots on the *Petrel* to replace the pair he'd lost on the sub after diving off to help the general. He ended up borrowing a pair of young Cookie's runners.

"Move it, Aussie!" shouted Freeman, already in the Zodiac as Jimmy and the bosun lowered it from the davit.

One of the side-scan technicians gave Freeman a sonar tracking beeper he'd requested. It was used on occasion by the technicians to test their hydrophones in the lab.

"Bring combat packs!" Freeman called out.

"He's keen," said Jimmy, watching the general using the Zodiac's pike to keep the inflatable from crashing into the side as the *Petrel* engaged a strong offshore current.

"He lives on adrenaline," replied the bosun, his muscles stiffened from the *Petrel*'s last tension-filled twenty-four hours. "I want a massage."

"So do I," said Aussie, lacing up the runners and pulling on his gloves. He threw over a line down then, so he, Sal and Choir could rappel into the Zodiac, its outboard already spitting, coughing, then roaring to life, the general checking the gas level. "Full?" inquired Aussie.

"We're only going into Port Angeles," said the general.

"Well hell—couldn't we have waited till *Petrel*—"

"*No*! Now listen to me, Aussie. Go get the first mate, tell him I want him to get some syringes from the ship's first aid kit and take a blood sample from each of those damn terrorists."

"DNA samples?" said Aussie.

"Right," replied the general. "We'll take them with us. We might be able to ID them through Interpol."

"You think so?" said Aussie dubiously.

"Well, it's worth a try," said the general, adding, tongue-in-cheek, "Might help you win your bet."

Aussie grinned. "They're not all Chinese. I'm not that stupid."

"Go on," said the general. "Hurry up. Tell him to get those samples fast and put 'em in a cooler. I want to be off this tub in ten minutes."

While the Zodiac, bow up, skimmed the gray water through varying densities of fog, Freeman's brain was racing, his chain of connected memories now complete, his penchant for detail at the fore, his mental files rapidly flipping back to the café, the waiter's dirty fingernails and the angry ring of irritated flesh around the throat and wrists taking him back to remembrances of his long days and nights in Vietnam, especially in the South, where, as he was now reminding Aussie, the Viet Cong, having gotten dangerously close to Saigon right under the noses of the Americans and their own fellow South Vietnamese, had executed one of the greatest military maneuvers of all time.

"Cu—" he began, then stopped, swerving the boat, heeding Sal's shouted warning that there was a deadhead in front of them, one of the many floating logs that were always breaking loose from the huge timber rafts hauled across the strait, or the fallout from storm-uprooted trees along the coast.

"Cu Chi," the general told Aussie as the Zodiac straightened out on its fast run into the harbor.

"Gotcha!" Aussie shouted above the outboard, the engine markedly noisier than when he and the general had used it to approach the sub. "This Merc needs a tune-up," he told the general.

Freeman took no notice, telling Aussie instead that it would be his job to drive the Humvee that he'd told Hall to book ahead by radio.

"Hope it's there!" shouted Aussie. "Everyone's probably left town by now."

"It'll be there," the general assured him, though Aussie was certain Freeman had no way of being that sure.

"Sal," the general called out. "I've been thinking. Soon as we hit the beach, you call Fort Lewis. Tell Brentwood to grab a Huey and get his ass up here. Tell him we'll meet him at Laurel and Railroad."

"You want him to bring that Bullpup?"

"Hell, no. Better his sidearm."

"Roger."

"There's the Humvee," said Freeman, slowing the Zodiac to twenty knots, well in excess of harbor approach regulations. A purse seiner loomed ahead in the fog, one of its crew giving them a frantic "slow down" signal.

"Sea rage," quipped Aussie, waving at the purse seiner, the man's shouting eliciting a full stiff-arm Italian response from Salvini.

The Humvee driver was waiting for them. "General Freeman?" he asked, unsure of just who was whom, since none of the four Special Forces team wore any insignia or rank. But it was Freeman who had the leader look.

"That's me," he told the driver.

"Sir, a Captain Brentwood is waiting at—"

"Guess he got your message," cut in Aussie.

"Good," answered Freeman, without breaking his stride, turning to Sal. "Don't worry about making that call. Brentwood's here."

Sal looked about the fog-wreathed beach. "Where?"

"In town, you dork," said Aussie.

"Well, least he could do was bring us an ale," put in Choir.

"Son," Freeman told the Humvee driver, "you can wait here—take a little unofficial furlough, or head back to Fort Lewis."

The driver was nonplused, not knowing whether to be grateful or insulted at not being needed.

"Ah, yes, sir. Fine."

Freeman sensed his disappointment. "I'd love to have you along. Fort Lewis tells me you're a real Andretti." The general smacked him affectionately on the shoulder. "Maybe next time."

"Ah, yes, General."

As the four SpecFor warriors piled into the Humvee, the egalitarian Aussie commented pompously, "He didn't know who Andretti was."

"Who is he?" asked Sal.

Aussie pushed the starter button. "You're jerkin' me off."

"No," said Sal. "Who was Andretti?"

"Race driver," said Aussie.

"Yeah," said Sal. "Mario. I know."

"You're gonna get it, Brooklyn. Right up the ass!"

"Promises!" responded Sal.

"Go to the hospital after we pick up Brentwood," Freeman cut in abruptly, his tone signaling an end to Sal and Aussie's banter. "I want you people on your toes. If I'm right about the minesweeper, this is going to be dicey."

In the back, Sal glanced at Choir. Whenever the general said "you people," it was a warning that the mission could be extraordinarily tough. The problem for Choir was that he thought the general was getting ahead of himself, so he made a side wager with Sal that the minesweeper hadn't been sunk by a hostile.

The onetime Medal of Honor recipient looked even thinner than when Aussie and Freeman had last seen him on the firing range. He was standing at the deserted junction of Laurel and Railroad in full combat gear, and, even with its bulk, looked as if he'd lost weight. The sidearm on his right hip, Aussie noticed, was holstered back to front so that his still-functioning left hand could cross-draw it if necessary. Why on earth had the general asked him to come along? he wondered.

Brentwood had to use his left hand to get aboard the Humvee, his right arm still a stiff L-shape, its hand a perennially bunched fist.

Choir asked him anxiously, "What happened to that minesweeper, David? You hear anything?"

"It sank."

"He knows *that*, you dodo," Aussie told Brentwood. "But *how'd* it sink?"

"Don't know," said David, who then asked Freeman, "Where we going, General?"

"Hospital first."

When they got there, Freeman asked Aussie to grab the five terrorist samples. Obviously in a hurry, he strode ahead to the front desk to arrange for immediate testing of the samples. Aussie came in a minute later, looking concerned.

"It's all arranged," Freeman told him. "Dr. Ramon here will do it for us soon as he can."

The doctor nodded to Aussie, who exchanged greetings.

Returning to the Humvee, Aussie, in trepidation, told the general, "*Petrel*'s mate has screwed up. He only took four samples."

The general frowned. "Didn't you *check* 'em?"

"I thought there were—but you know, sir, we were in such a damn hurry."

"Not good enough, Aussie!"

Back at the Humvee, the general was all business. "Listen up. We're going to the East-West Café. We'll be there in five minutes. There'll be no time for dessert, so here's the drill. . . ."

Freeman was wrong—it took them eleven minutes to reach the café because of the traffic lights in the town. Not that many people were out and about; most of the refugees hadn't returned yet. As Aussie waited on the second-to-last red, fingers tapping impatiently on the Humvee's wheel, David Brentwood asked him, "Do you mind not doing that?"

"Doing what?"

"Drumming your fingers," he said, causing Sal and Choir to look straight ahead and not risk a "What's eating him?" glance.

Then the general said, "Don't censure me, boys. I wouldn't do this if I didn't think it was necessary."

Their silence told Freeman that he was the only one in the team convinced there was a second sub in the choke point.

The light turned green.

CHAPTER FORTY-NINE

"SHOCK AND AWE, gentlemen," Freeman told them as the Humvee dropped Choir off in the alley behind the East-West Café. Aussie then made a sharp turn to bring the wide, stocky, no-nonsense vehicle to a pronounced stop in front of the café. Freeman, armed only with his HK 9mm sidearm, strode in, Aussie immediately behind him, HK at the ready. He was followed by Brentwood, then Sal, who, with his shotgun turned about, stood guard at the door.

About a dozen diners, including some with young children—one in a high chair—looked up, startled. Everyone had stopped eating. They were obviously refugees returning to the town, hungry and exhausted. At first they had been reassured by the sight of the Special Forces team, but then were suddenly terrified by Freeman's thunderous order: "Everyone out! Now! Leave your cell phones on the table. Write down the number. If you lie, we'll backtrack through the phone company and you'll be in violation of the Emergency War Powers Act. Move!"

Only one elderly man, with stubby beard and no teeth, refused to leave his steaming wonton soup. "I'm too old to be frightened of guys who—"

He had to finish his sentence outside, Sal having taken a firm grip of the man's worn lumberjack collar and literally dragging him out, the old man's hands flailing, spittle-sprayed obscenities filling the air. "Be safer out here, buddy," Sal told him, and Sal was telling the truth, for when Salvini reentered the restaurant, he heard a high-pitched Oriental voice in the kitchen beyond the string bead curtain screaming to someone back of the kitchen, "Cor 911! Cor 911!"

"Good idea!" said Aussie evenly.

"She the same waitress as before?" Freeman asked Brentwood.

"Yes," confirmed Brentwood.

Aussie checked two side rooms without taking his eyes off the Vietnamese woman who was yelling beyond the curtain. He was struck by the fact that though she was clearly frightened, she wasn't cowed. There was fight in her eyes.

"What are you afraid of, ma'am?" asked the general. "We're Americans, not terrorists."

"Soldiers!" she said contemptuously.

The restaurant's back door, about six feet beyond the kitchen at the end of a passageway cluttered with piled boxes of noodles, burst open. It was Choir pushing one of the waiters ahead of him, Aussie immediately relieving the waiter of the cell phone he was in the process of using.

"Over here!" ordered Freeman, standing in the kitchen, the young woman glaring at him from the kitchen's chopping block. The man looked more frightened than the woman, who had obviously been the object of dispute between the two waiters Freeman had seen when he and Brentwood had been in the café. Among all the other SpecFor training courses, one had been about quickly ascertaining who the alpha male was in any hostage-taking situation. Freeman, though a stickler for multilayered training, had always been skeptical of the course. "A ten-year-old kid can tell you in two seconds who's the boss in a room," he used to say. Here, the woman was clearly the alpha. Aussie heard a noise directly above, looked up and saw a trapdoor opening.

"No, please!" shouted the man. "My mother!"

"Jesus Christ!" said Aussie, a nanosecond away from wasting her. The old woman said something in Vietnamese and withdrew.

"No pickup till after six, I think," joked Aussie. No one laughed, but his attempt clearly infused the man with more terror of the unpredictable.

The young woman was retreating farther back, almost touching the wall-suspended array of ladles, noodle strainers, and other utensils. No knives, Freeman noticed—they were to her left in a wooden rack near a kitchen stool and corner chopping block. The SpecFor team had been in the restaurant for less than two minutes—a fast entrance, a quick push to see who was whom, and to clear out those Freeman had decided were innocent bystanders. Now he strode up to the waiter and told him to show his wrists. The irritated skin rash had almost vanished. Freeman reached up to the man's collar. "Stay still!" The bruised ring, or more accurately, half ring, around the waiter's throat was not nearly as dark as when the general had seen it when he and Brentwood had eaten in the café.

Freeman turned from the waiter and in a move whose speed and violence surprised even Aussie, advanced on the woman, who seemed to shrink in size beneath him. He grabbed her by her left ear and wrenched her toward him. She gasped in pain, but nothing more, her eyes glinting with hatred and determination. He pulled her out from the wall of appliances.

"Don—Don't hurt her please, sir!" implored the waiter.

Brentwood's eyes avoided the scene, focusing on the bubbling vat of fat by the chopping block.

"I won't *hurt* her!" bellowed the general, his eyes maniacal. "I'll *kill* the bitch if you don't take me to the tunnels!"

The waiter's pale face turned gray and he tried to speak but couldn't.

"Then I'll kill Granny upstairs!" shouted Freeman. His voice had taken over the café like a storm. "You bastards think I don't know what's going on? Eh? Eh? Those collar marks, the ones on your wrists. Your filthy damn fingernails. Your ring around the collar, buddy, comes from hauling your buddies out of cave-ins in the tunnels. Only way you could get in and out in Cu Chi—only way you *can* get a tunneler out in a cave-in—two ropes from your wrists to his feet—gotta get 'im out before he suffocates. Then you put the pull collar 'round your neck, lie down, roll over and haul him out. Or maybe it wasn't your buddies, eh? Maybe a torpedo warhead you were hauling down to the cave, with all your other supplies, eh? That's why we didn't get any infrared spots on the ground. You terrorist bastards were all underground like goddamn rats!"

The man had said nothing, but the rest of the team, except for Sal at the front door, looked at one another with something akin to awe. They realized they were witnessing the stuff of the Freeman legend. Aussie alone, however, knew that the general's shock was not over with.

"Well?" Freeman thundered. "You going to tell me?"

The waiter caught the woman's eye, as did Aussie. Her message was clear: "Stand your ground! Don't tell them!" The waiter, however, probably habituated by a lifetime of running slavishly from the exhausting kitchen through the beaded curtain to serve the class to which he aspired, and despised, was torn between reality and hope, his mind obviously a tumult of indecision.

"All right!" bellowed Freeman, drawing his sidearm. "Tell me!" He was holding her at point-blank range.

The waiter was trembling but shook his head.

The shot threw the woman back with such violence that her head slammed into hanging utensils, her shout of pain startling Sal, who quickly looked around from the front door, the crash of utensils like cymbals. He could smell the acrid cordite wafting through the beaded curtain.

Brentwood and Choir, their previous awe now overcome by shock, stood literally open-mouthed at what the general had done. Aussie was for once speechless, seeing the woman writhing on the floor as Freeman grabbed her by her bullet-torn blouse, now covered in blood, and hauled her roughly into a sitting position against the wall.

"All right!" Freeman yelled at Aussie. "Bring down that old bitch. I'll shoot her too!"

Aussie gave the waiter an "I don't like it but what can I do, mate?" glance, footing the chopping block stool across the floor below the trapdoor.

"Hurry up!" ordered Freeman. "Bring her down."

"No, no," the waiter said, his voice cracking. "I show you."

"Right!" said Freeman, turning to Choir. "Choir! Over here!"

Choir didn't move. "But—" he began.

"Goddammit!" Freeman roared. "Don't *but* me. We're a team. Work as a team. Get that bitch's body out of here, give her to the cops. Then grab the old lady and stay in touch with me." The general looked across at Aussie, who'd been about to assist the woman with his first aid kit. "Leave her alone," barked the general. "She dies, she dies. Give Choir this joker's cell phone."

Aussie wordlessly passed the phone he'd taken from the waiter to the silent Welshman, who was obviously upset.

"Tell him your number!" the general ordered the waiter, who, dry-mouthed and trembling, was barely able to speak. "Try calling the number from the other phones," Freeman ordered, indicating the half-dozen or so cell phones that had been left, as per his orders, on the café's hastily vacated tables.

Within a minute the team all had working phones.

"Give me the one with the best battery," Freeman told the others, his schoolyard bully's tone not going over well with David Brentwood. It wasn't an aspect of Freeman he'd seen before.

While Choir carried the bloodied, pain-wracked woman outside, the others began to climb aboard the Humvee. Then they heard a police cruiser's siren and saw its flashers approaching, a group of the previously ejected diners huddled across the street like homeless waifs, waiting anxiously to see what the police did about what one man in the group angrily and correctly described as the "grossest violation of civil liberties" he'd ever seen in America.

Freeman holstered his sidearm as the other four helped Choir to carry the wounded woman toward the police cruiser.

"Spray and Wash's not gonna get *that* out!" said a callow adolescent who, with some other teenagers, had been drawn by the gunshot and was now pointing at the blood on her blouse.

"Hey," a portly sheriff called out as he lumbered out of the cruiser, his partner grabbing the first aid box. "You kids move along."

"What happened, Wally?" asked the teenaged boy in an overly familiar tone.

The sheriff's eyes narrowed. "Don't you sass me, George Daley. You get on home. From what I hear, your grades need all the help they can get."

There was a burst of laughter from the gaggle of young girls in the group. "You tell 'im, Sheriff," someone shouted, and George Daley sullenly moved off.

The general and sheriff conferred hastily by the cruiser, the sheriff hitching his belt several times and nodding, Sal hearing him say, "You betcha," and "Wish we had more time to get enough guys up here to . . ."

"I figure," the general told him, "that those bastards'll be reloading with torpedoes and restocking after sinking that mine-sweeper."

The sheriff knew the general was right, and agreed that the first thing the SpecFor team had to do was get to the tunnel that the waiter and others had been using to service the second sub. Second, they were to find the tunnel used to service the sub that had already sunk, to make sure both tunnels could never be used again.

Freeman called out to Salvini, "You go get Grandma. Frisk her. Put her in a cab and catch up with us. The cab driver can wait here. And Sal, cuff her."

Sal merely nodded.

Seeing Sal's resentment—a resentment apparently shared by

the rest of the team—Freeman pushed the waiter roughly aside. "Salvini, you hear me? You have a problem with my orders?"

"No—sir," said Sal, helping the waiter up, the prisoner looking up pleadingly at Sal, his eyes betraying some sympathy for these four American soldiers who he saw had to serve under such a brutal commander—one as tough as Li Kuan, even though the smaller Kuan bore no physical resemblance to the big American. But Li Kuan had the same hard eyes as this man whom the sheriff had called "General Free-man."

The waiter understood English well enough to realize the full intent of the ruthless general's orders: that his aged mother, contemptuously referred to by the American as "the old bitch," would be forced to follow the general's Humvee in the cab so that if her son balked at revealing the tunnel's entrance, they would kill her. No, no, he wouldn't kill her. If she were dead, then what would he bargain with?

No, the waiter concluded, this crazed general would do what Li Kuan would do in such a situation, what he'd done to the American girl in Suzhou who'd overheard the plans between Beijing and Kazakhstan—that Beijing would supply the experienced Vietnamese and Chinese tunnelers for the Muslim terrorists' continuing Holy War against America, and Li Kuan would arrange the logistical support via "sleepers" in and around the Olympic peninsula. This supply tunnel complex, not nearly as elaborate as the giant two-hundred-mile underground complex at Cu Chi in the sixties, would be ingenious nevertheless. No, the waiter told himself, one had to face reality. This American general who'd shown not the slightest hesitation in shooting his beloved My-Duyen, whom the whites called "Sally," would not kill his mother outright, he would torture her, as Li Kuan had tortured the young American girl in Suzhou to find out what she knew before he'd killed her. The waiter, now in the passenger seat of the Humvee, wanted to bury his head in his hands, but the tight nylon strip binding his hands behind his back prevented him from doing so.

Freeman was driving—Choir, Aussie, and Brentwood in the back.

"Once the fog lifts we'll call in cavalry troops, soon as we locate the position," Freeman told them.

No one responded. Aussie wanted to, but held his tongue. Knowing their silence denoted disapproval, Freeman elbowed the waiter in the side. "How many people you reckon you and your sub buddies have killed, Mao?"

The waiter stared sullenly through the fog that was rushing toward them in huge gray billows.

"How many so far?" Freeman asked his prisoner. "Would you say around ten thousand? In an undeclared war?"

"World is at war," said the waiter. "You Americans invaded Iraqis."

"Oh," said Freeman, swinging the Humvee around a pothole, but not fast enough, jolting Choir out of his nap. "You think we didn't give those towel heads enough warning? Six months not long enough? Who's in charge of this operation, Mao?"

"I don't know."

"Who gave you orders in Port Angeles?"

"E-mail."

"Li Kuan's e-mail or from bin Laden's leftovers—who?"

"I don't know."

"You serve on the sub, Mao? Or you strictly a tunneler?"

"Tunnel."

"Same tunnel for both subs? Or did they have to take their turn, Mao? Or did each sub have its own garage?"

"I don't know this."

"Aha," said Freeman accelerating. "You just know about the tunnel you're taking us to, right? You bring the supplies—what, in a van?—and just drop them off."

"Yes."

"You lying bastard," said Freeman, braking hard as he swerved to miss a fallen branch, barely visible in the fog. "You're a hauler! Look at your throat, Mao. You're a goddamn hauler of everything from rice to outboards to ammunition to kill Americans!"

Now Aussie, Choir, and Brentwood were more attentive. What they'd seen as the general's "over-the-line" behavior in the East-West Café was now temporarily mitigated by their outrage at the horrendous loss of life, to say nothing of the loss in ships, caused by the midget submarine. Still the four SpecFor warriors, unlike Freeman, were not convinced there was a second sub, believing that the minesweeper, if it hadn't gone down from natural causes, had most probably been destroyed by a mine.

The general's questioning of "Mao" was reminding them, however, just how horrific the terrorist submarine attacks had been. And if the general was right about a second sub, there would be more to come.

The fog lifted with the rapidity of a stage curtain. What had been a gray, damp world along eerily deserted Highway 112 as the Humvee sped west toward the inland point five miles south of the Strait of Juan de Fuca that marked the big bend between Pillar and Slip Points—the latter seven miles farther west—was now a world so bereft of fog that every tree and bush was clearly visible. The longitudinal reading Aussie had taken earlier on the winding cliff-face path as he'd climbed high enough to see over the fog had given them the exact position of the cave behind the falls, the cave in which Peter Dixon had been so gruesomely tortured and murdered.

"Tunnel entrance near here," Mao told Freeman, who slowed the vehicle to sixty, waist-high brush, sandy, loamy soil, and burned-out forest racing by. To their left, looking south, they could see the grandeur of Mount Olympus and the sun-drenched snowcaps of its surrounding peaks. The general fixed his eyes on the waiter, who, despite the general calling him "Mao," looked only partly Chinese to Aussie.

"Further," said Mao sourly.

"How much further?" snapped Choir, his finger jabbing the man's neck. Choir still didn't approve of the old man crossing the line, shooting the woman like that, but if he was right and there was a second sub, time would be running out before it either struck again or decided to flee.

"Aussie?"

"General?"

"Call Sal. Tell him we're—"

A loud pop from the right rear wheel was followed by the roar of the Humvee taking rounds, Aussie realizing that Freeman and his team would have been dead or badly shot up if the general had not immediately sped up.

"Five o'clock!" yelled Aussie. "Hundred yards. Light PK. Three men." He grabbed the handhold, Freeman swinging the Humvee off the road and into the loamy ground, mowing bushes down before the vehicle that was back up to sixty miles an hour. Aussie and Choir were returning fire as Freeman swung hard left, enabling his men to get off a quick broadside before he just as violently swung the Humvee back hard right, driving, accelerating, straight for the light machine-gun post that Freeman barely saw through the narrow slit between the rim of his Fritz and the Humvee's bulletproof glass. The machine-gun post was now only twenty yards in front, seconds away, rising and falling with the Humvee's passage over the rough ground.

"L'audace!" Freeman shouted. *"Toujours l'audace!"*

Aussie's next burst hit one of them in the shoulder. The trio broke and ran, the gunner, frantically hauling the PLA light machine gun, jumping over a log.

"Hold!" yelled Freeman, the Humvee hitting the log. The vehicle's high clearance easily, if shudderingly, passed over it, momentarily throwing Freeman's steering off, the Humvee clipping the fleeing gunman with the right fender. He was down, the gun thrown four feet away. Freeman braked, shoved the stick into reverse and backed up. They heard a sound like a branch cracking. Then he was off after the other two. Fog was moving in again.

"IR!" Freeman shouted.

Aussie reached over and, given the bumpy ride, deftly managed to "crown" the general with the infrared goggles.

"Ah—there they are, the bastards! Three o'clock, hundred yards!" With that, Freeman again abruptly changed course, the vehicle fishtailing then suddenly straightening, Mao's head smacking the right door's glass, the windshield not as peppered as Aussie expected. The general had no doubt put the fear of Allah into the machine-gun trio by unhesitatingly attacking without pause.

"Damn! They're gone!"

"The tunnel," said Choir.

"Where's the entrance?" Freeman asked Mao.

Mao was silent.

"You think your buddies are trying to save you?" asked Freeman. "They're trying to kill you, Mao. So tell me, where's the entrance?"

Mao remained silent.

Freeman looked into the rearview mirror. "Aussie, tell Sal to bring Granny here." The general glanced across at Mao, the waiter badly shaken by the attack. "See how much your buddies care, Mao. They wanted to kill *you* as much as they did us. Either way—" Freeman tapped his watch. "—you've got thirty seconds to show us *exactly*, I mean *exactly*, where the hidden entrance is. Otherwise I'll shoot Granny."

Mao was stroking his face, beaded with perspiration. He shouted, "She not my granny. She my mother." He began to sob.

"Then," said Freeman, eyes afire and drawing his 9mm, his face so close to Mao that their noses were all but touching, "I'll shoot your goddamn *mother*!"

Brentwood had a flashback to the portrayal of Patton drawing his ivory-handled pistol, about to shoot one of his soldiers who, trembling, said he couldn't take it anymore. Brentwood felt revulsion. First the young woman, now the older—

Mao was nodding so vigorously he looked as if he was suffering from an acute neurotic disorder. "I—I show you."

"Get 'im out!" said Freeman.

Aussie, his adrenaline still up from the speeding firefight, hopped out the passenger door and hauled Mao after him. The fog was clearing as Mao, stumbling, barely able to walk, began dry retching.

"No, no!" said Aussie. "You throw up on your own time. Show us the friggin' entrance." Aussie saw Brentwood's jaw clench tightly. What the hell had happened to David anyway? he wondered. Did he hunker down in the Humvee just because he couldn't fire from mid-seat, or was he scared, so scared that he wouldn't have fired if he'd had the chance? And now David was giving everyone a censorious look. Well, the trouble with Davy, Aussie concluded, was that he hadn't seen the sea literally red with American blood, pieces of goddamn meat, heads floating about, thousands more than were killed on 9/11. So he had a big trauma in 'Ghanistan. All soldiers in combat have traumas; warriors live with it—night sweats, the screaming, recurring nightmares. But Aussie knew that he himself had no compunction about pushing Mao to his limits. The bastards had killed the young Coast Guardsman Jorges Alvaro near the falls, his body still not found, and the SEAL diver Albinski, and poor, bloody Dixon. This lot was as cold-blooded as—

"Jesus!" said the general, his blasphemy now a measure of his immediate if begrudging soldier's admiration for the ingenuity of the tunnel's camouflaged entrance.

"Best *I've* ever seen," concurred Aussie.

Freeman ordered everyone back ten yards. "All right, Mao," he said. "Go open it."

Mao looked blankly at him.

"Work the combination safe," added Aussie. "You know, the old booby trap."

"C'mon," said Freeman impatiently, all of them startled by the ringing of Choir's phone.

"Son of a bitch!" said Aussie. "Put that friggin' thing on vibration!"

It was Sal informing them that he should be there in "about five."

Mao approached the camouflaged tunnel entrance, its trapdoor not horizontal, as one would expect, but vertical, a soil-impacted root end of a fallen, charred spruce. The roots' four-by-four trapdoor had been exquisitely carpentered so that any saw marks were invisible to the naked eye.

Mao swung open the door and pointed inside the hollow tree trunk, the actual entrance to the tunnel being a second four-by-four trapdoor flush with the earth.

"You all set, David?" Freeman asked Brentwood.

As it dawned on Brentwood that the general expected him to go down into the tunnel, the cold-clammy feeling of incipient panic closed in and his head and neck felt feverishly hot.

"Didn't think I told you to bring your sidearm for nothing, did you?" said Freeman. "Fort Lewis CO says you can take out a dime at thirty feet. And you're lean as a stick—like these guys." He pointed at Mao. "You know what it was like in 'Nam. Most of us'd get stuck halfway down the damn shaft, never mind the damn tunnels, which are even narrower." Freeman turned around, asking for a 7-flashlight. Aussie took out his from his combat pack.

CHAPTER FIFTY

DAVID BRENTWOOD FELT all eyes on him, even Mao's.

"In 'Nam," Freeman told David quickly, "guys tried to take regular weapons down tunnels. Couldn't move. Only thing that'd work was this." He tossed Brentwood the 7-shaped flashlight. "Best shape for tunnel rats. That and a sidearm. It's the only way." Brentwood still hadn't moved. Freeman walked closer to him. It was as if they were in a confessional. "There's another goddamned sub on the coast, David. We could use a whole division like we did in 'Nam to search and destroy and we still wouldn't find the damn hiding place. Only way to find it there—in 'Nam—and now here is to go down the tunnel. See where it leads. I'll call in airborne cav once we find the hideaway."

But it was Mao, not the general, who would change Brentwood's mind. The waiter, no longer shaking now that he'd given in, sneered at Brentwood, possibly in an effort to regain some dignity from his own capitulation to the general. The sneer was an unmistakable accusation of cowardice.

Brentwood slid the flashlight switch on and looked at the bulb, its light difficult to see in the flood of sunlight that, after the dreary world of fog, had revealed the Northwest wilderness in all its glory. He glanced up at the mountaintops, the sun so bright it hurt his eyes, the enormous rain-washed green apron that swept down to the coast one of such striking primeval beauty that he knew—if he survived—he would never forget it. And the smell rising from the moss—no longer that of bone-cold damp, but of reinvigorated life. He hated to leave it.

Aussie crawled into the darkness within the partially hollowed tree and, edging his way past the trapdoor that was flush with the earth—no booby trap—waited till David had descended into the shoulder-high shaft. Then he handed him the sonar location beeper, the flashlight, infrared goggles, canteen, knife, and David's short-barreled Heckler & Koch 9mm self-loading Compact, its control lever easily switchable from left to right for left-handed shooters. "Good luck, mate!" Aussie said softly.

As David moved farther into the tunnel, not even the IR goggles helped. The only things he could see were the tiny wriggles of mice chewing at the base of what appeared to be a crude candle holder set into the tunnel wall, the walls and ceiling in the rain-soaked terrain supported by five-foot-high, four-by-four wooden joists, the rodents and residual warmth from the extinguished candle in the holder emitting just enough heat to be detected by the IR goggles. But beyond this, the tunnel was a black, disorientating unknown.

The air was foul and damp, his back only inches from the N-shaped tunnel. He could hear his heart banging against his chest, as he had in the Afghan cave, so loud that his fear, locked in battle with reason, was convincing him that anyone else in the Stygian darkness ahead must have heard him move in and was lying in wait. And to his train of fear, other terrors quickly attached themselves: the veterans' stories of how the Viet Cong had booby-trapped the tunnels with pits of razor-sharp punji sticks hidden by thin, dirt-covered membranes of stretched cloth, and how captured U.S. claymore mines had been rigged in the tunnels' side walls with invisible fish-line trip wires only a few centimeters above the floor. He was struggling to find a hope that he might get out alive.

Trying to make himself concentrate on how to get through, he recalled that a GI had gone down a tunnel, smelled another man coming toward him in the dark, and, rather than fire, had lain flat, "damn near melting into the earth," his buddies had said. The VC had fired first, emptying an AK-47's full thirty-round mag, its rounds whipping over the GI, no more than twenty feet away. The GI survived without a scratch, firing just once at the Kalashnikov's flash, killing the VC. And he remembered how the tunnel rats who had survived said it had taken hours of painstaking work, probing gently every inch ahead with your knife for the little Russian-made "butterfly" mines that would blow your hand or foot off. And the kind of unbelievable pain in neck and elbows as you crawled ahead, the pain David Brentwood was starting to feel now. To reach the coast, where Freeman said the cave was, would take hours, and if the tunnel snaked, had security "double back" loops and sucker dead-end tributaries, it would take an eternity.

But then in the pitch-blackness of the stinking tunnel, David accepted the possibility that if Freeman was right that there was another sub, this tunnel might not be part of an underground complex like Cu Chi, which had held hundreds of fighters, living and working underground, with medical and kitchen antechambers, as well as weapons and ammunition storage. The man they called Mao didn't live in the tunnel, after all. He lived in Port Angeles and used the tunnel solely as an underground supply road to the cave, an underground throughway to prevent their sub resupply line from being spotted by the infrared-equipped American satellites and UAVs such as Darkstar. The munitions, torpedoes, and mines could be stored deep in the cave, but food—even the American and Russian nuclear subs needed food supply—had been routinely transported in by Mao and his friends. And what better cover than a restaurant?

Had Freeman thought of this? he wondered. That if this was a supply tunnel, wouldn't it be as straight as possible to the coast? And why bother booby-trapping it? The terrorists had dug the tunnel not as they had in Vietnam, as a conduit from which to attack American ground troops, but merely as a supply line. And why impede an escape route from the cave with dangerous booby traps?

The rushing of blood in David's ears didn't go away, but it subsided. He switched on the flashlight, and in that instant knew he was right.

Ahead, instead of narrowing, the tunnel widened to twice its width for about thirty feet, then dipped down and broadened into what seemed a holding area, about as big and high as a good-size delivery van. The dimensions of the excavation at once impressed and told him that in order to get rid of the dirt—always the tunneler's big problem—the terrorists must have started digging from the sea cave, so they could pass the massive amounts of soil back and dump it into the ocean. That way, if seen from the air, it would have been attributable to the runoff of the 112-inches-a-year rainfall.

By the time David reached the "holding area," his confidence was growing, and he sped up his pursuit of the escaping terrorists who Freeman hoped would lead them—via David's sonar beeper—to a second lair.

Beyond the holding area, using his flashlight in quick on/off snatches, he saw flattened cardboard. The labeling in Japanese and Chinese told him nothing, but the manufacturers' stamps, with their illustrated pictures of contents, indicated that the boxes had contained dried noodles, rice, and other such foodstuffs. He sat down, getting his breathing under control. He was so dehydrated from the strain, his initial freeze-up at the entrance to the tunnel, and the constant bent-over position required to negotiate the five-foot-high tunnel, that he wanted to gulp down all the water in his canteen. But warning himself not to drink too much, he rescrewed the cap and slid the canteen around his belt behind his back. Then he resumed his trek, walking slowly, moving his flashlight from side to side in rapid sweeps.

In fifteen minutes he had passed through what he estimated must have been a quarter mile of tunnel. This wasn't a tunnel rat's crawl, he thought, this was Nascar. He checked his beeper. It was working fine. He couldn't stand up and his back was aching, but, his "dead" right hand notwithstanding, he was in reasonably good physical condition and anticipated that he would soon reach the cave or the branch-off that had to exist if Freeman's theory of a second sub lair had any substance.

He heard a sound like a spit and the flashlight flew from his hand, flung somewhere behind him. He dropped to the floor and, through the IR glasses, saw a smudge of white—heat—in the tunnel, probably twenty feet away, and double tapped his compact's trigger, the two rounds striking a human form that collapsed into an indistinguishable shape. He could hear someone moving, running, away. And then he was running too, the hunchbacked position slowing him more than he would have believed, the human diaphragm not built to sustain a sprinter long in such an unnatural position, the man fleeing from him obviously much shorter. Passing the stilled body, he saw it was a woman, her face no longer there. Two hundred feet farther he had to stop.

Sweat pouring off him, Choir Williams prodded Mao with the barrel of his HK, he, Freeman, and Aussie wearing full battle packs, not knowing what they might need if there was another sub lair, or what Freeman had begun calling a "branch plant" of the terrorists. They were close to the coast.

Aussie Lewis could hear the surf ahead. "We must be damn near the cave!" he said, looking over at Freeman.

The general heard him but refused to comment. Instead, he beckoned Mao with a gesture. "You led me on a wild goose chase, comrade," he said. "This tunnel's leading to the cave we already found. I told you what I'd do to Mommy, eh? Didn't I?"

"I only know the cave tunnel," said Mao. "We bring—we brought food to the cave. That is all. I swear. You kill my mother—you kill me—I can tell you no more. I only know this tunnel."

Freeman believed him, and saw that Choir, red-faced with exertion, also believed him. He thrust his gloved finger hard in the direction of a thick treeline that Aussie felt certain marked the high cliff's edge. "There's a—" he began, and had to stop for breath, which made him more irritated. "—a goddamn sub nearby. I know it."

"Permission, sir?" said Choir, a rarely used formality in the team.

"Go on," the general said.

"There *is* a sub nearby, sir," said Choir. "It's at the bottom of the bay. We sank it."

Below them, the damp of the tunnel was penetrating David Brentwood's uniform, his perspiration chilled now that he'd stopped. Ahead in the quick sweep of his flashlight he saw a wall of rubble blocking the tunnel, no doubt the effects of the hydrofoil sapper unit's demolition of the cave. Suddenly, David was revisited by the ghosts of panic, of losing his squad in Afghanistan, in another cave. And now he'd just shot a woman to death. And where had the other two terrorists gone? A side chamber? Behind him? He started back then stopped, heart thumping again. How many had died in the tunnels? Sealed off. The air was fetid in the darkness, and he could smell the disgusting odor of decomposing bodies, probably buried in the demolition of the cave.

Then, through his infrared goggles, David saw a smudge of heat leaking from the rubble. A moment later he saw a sudden white blossom, then a *thwack!* punched him off his feet. He was being fired at—two of them. The first bullet struck his vest low left, the second cracking above him as he lay flat on his back, IR goggles knocked askew, as he returned fire in the direction of the flash. There were no ricochets, which confirmed his marksmanship, his double-tap rounds obviously having passed through what he now realized must be a narrow cleft between the demolition rubble and the left side wall of the tunnel, his initial panic evicted by the sheer concentration required if he had any hope of getting out alive.

Above him the SpecFor team and Mao had heard the faint, muffled shots. Choir noticed that Mao was smiling, and jabbed him with his HK. "Better not let the general see that, laddie."

But Mao, the tunnel "mule," as the load bearers were called in Vietnam, was grinning because he'd detected movement high in a tall cedar atop the cliff's edge. The Americans were in for a surprise, and this time, unlike in the Humvee, Mao knew he could keep himself out of the line of fire.

In response to Choir's warning, Mao nodded as if apologizing for a lapse in judgment, and waited anxiously for the party to move on. He selected a solid-looking log ten feet off to his right, a fir that would protect him from the Americans' return fire if any of the three infidels were lucky enough to survive the sniper's fire. The waiter resented the name "Mao"—he was no Communist, but a true believer, and now he prayed to Allah, blessed be His name, that the marksman's aim would be sure.

"There must be at least two of them down there," said Freeman. "That's the way I read it. Dammit, I sent David down there thinking there was another—" He paused, then said, "I guess you guys were right. No second sub. We're almost at the cliff's edge above the cave." He shoved the silent receiver into his vest pocket and moved forward.

The sniper's first shot rang out, Freeman's Fritz helmet literally spinning about his head as he fell. The second shot penetrated Aussie's vest and left rib cage. The third shot never came, Choir's 9mm parabellum cutting into the tall cedar, a clump of its branches breaking, plummeting down from what had been the sniper's position. The figure fell, then abruptly jerked to a stop, the sniper's safety line coming to its end, the body, arms out, dangling like an inverted cross. Choir then walked angrily over to the big fir log behind which Mao was cowering, his mud-caked face twitching, and clipped a full magazine into his HK. "You saw him up there, didn't you, laddie?" he said. "You didn't warn us."

"No, no!" Mao pleaded, rolling over onto his back like a beaten dog, his hands still cuffed beneath him, pushing him closer into the protection of the log. "No, please—"

"We'll make sure," said Choir. Seeing Freeman with his bullet-scarred Fritz back on, the general stripping Aussie of his Kevlar vest and administering first aid, Choir raised his HK to his shoulder.

"No!" Mao screamed. "No, please, sir! I tell you about other cave! Okay? Other cave right nearby, around headland behind cliff vines. Yes, yes. I swear!"

Choir called out, "General, there's another cave on this cliff face." The Welsh American looked down at Mao. "How far around from the falls?" he asked sharply.

"Two, three hundred yards maybe from other cave. West— yes, west of other cave. Tunnel here going to chicken bone."

"Chicken bone?"

"Finish him off!" yelled Aussie, more to mask his pain than to offer advice. "Give him a full fucking—oh, shit!"

"Don't be a baby," Freeman admonished, plunging in a vial of morphine. "This isn't an inoculation." It was an open team secret that the tough Australian had fainted when he'd gotten his two-in-one smallpox and cholera shot before Iraq.

"Finish him off, Choir!" repeated Aussie.

"I'll finish him," said Choir.

"Chicken bone—" Mao was frantic, licking his lips, rushing to explain. "Tunnel here!" He was pointing down. "Tunnel goes into—" He rolled over onto his stomach and made a Y shape with his arms and hands. "Chicken—"

"You mean the tunnel divides into two?" said Choir. "Two tunnels?"

"Yes, yes!" said Mao, his voice muffled by the mud and grass growing by the log.

With that, Choir raised his 9mm submachine gun and fired a long burst into the cedar tree, the hanging body jerking violently, emitting a scream. It sounded like a woman.

"Told you the whore was faking it," said Aussie. "Would've dropped a grenade on us if we'd—Jesus, General! That hurt!"

Eyes closed, Mao awoke from his nightmare, first in utter surprise, then in delirious relief. "Thank you, thank you, sir. Thank you. I take you to cliff ledge near cave."

"There a sub in the cave?" asked Choir.

"I never been in cave. Only know about ledge. I take you—"

"Shut your mouth!" It was Freeman, his baritone sounding extraordinarily stentorian. "And listen to me, you slimeball. You're going to put on Aussie's Fritz—his helmet—and his uniform and you're going to lead us *quietly* through this grass and timber up to the cliff's edge. And very quietly you're going to be the first one down. As well as wearing Aussie's helmet, you're going to have duct tape around your mouth, and so god-damned tight, *laddie*, that if you try to take it off, you'll fall from the rope right down to the fucking cliff."

The general, though his line of sight was obscured by the wind-bent treeline along the cliff's edge fifty yards away, was recalling the view of the falls and cliffs from the sea farther down the coast. "I'd say it's about a hundred and fifty, two hundred feet down to the rocks," he continued. "You take us right to this friggin' ledge you're talking about, and you make any noise—*any* fucking noise—and I'll push you off myself! Then we'll have Grandma join you, you traitorous son of a bitch. Go on, get up!" Freeman grabbed him by his collar. "We let you people come into this country and this is the way you repay us. Attacking America. By God, I ought to—" Freeman shoved him back, Mao falling and bashing his head against the fallen log, only the moss saving him from cracking his skull.

Choir helped him to his feet, color now flooding back into the man's face.

"We forced to do this," said Mao with unexpected passion. "Otherwise Li Kuan kill all our families in China, in Kaza-khstan. Kill everyone."

Freeman jabbed his finger hard into Mao's chest. "You're a terrorist. I'll give you three minutes to get that gear on." Free-man turned to Choir. "Cut him loose. I'll rappel down the west side, you and Mao go down over there by that big arbutus."

"Which one's that?" asked Choir.

"Jesus Christ, man! The red bark—twenty paces."

Freeman had a parting comment for Mao. "If my boy down there is dead—which I think he is—I'll cut your fucking throat!"

It had been only seven minutes since the sniper's fire, and about ten since the beeper had died, but to Choir it seemed no more than two or three seconds, everything having happened so fast. He was about to ask the general whether it wouldn't be bet-ter to call Fort Lewis in now when Freeman turned to Aussie.

"You up to calling Fort Lewis? Get their airborne cav over here."

"No sweat," answered Aussie, dragging himself over to a small copse of cypress for good cover, now having only his Kevlar vest to keep him warm, his load vest as well as his helmet having been given to Mao.

"Maybe we should wait for them, General?" said Choir.

"Hell, no! By that time these bastards'll have burned all their codes and vanished. Then," he indicated Mao, "all we'll have is this bag of shit. The cav can mop up."

Choir was tugged by conflicting emotions. Freeman, whatever else you might think of him, was "guts personified," and in SpecOps command that was the ultimate accolade. But the point-blank shooting of the young woman in the café, who might have already succumbed to her massive chest wound, was clear evidence that Freeman would have no hesitation killing Mao's aged mother as well. There was a line, even for Special Forces, that Choir knew you didn't cross. He recalled the SAS Brit who gave up his and his team's position rather than shoot a little Iraqi shepherd boy who'd wandered into their hide. Freeman had surely crossed the line with his behavior in the restaurant, and, as Choir readied the nylon line for his and Mao's rappel from the cliff's top to the ledge that led across the face of the vine-curtained cave, the Welsh American found himself adopting a fatherly, almost friendly, tone with the terrorist as he gagged him with the duct tape.

"Now just calm down," he said. "Breathe through your nose. Don't panic. But I'm telling you, laddie, you make any noise, you do *anything* wrong, and he'll . . ." Choir couldn't bring himself to say it, so alien was it to all his experience fighting by the general's side.

Mao understood and nodded, his labored breathing producing a faint nasal whistle that didn't worry Choir because of the over-riding noise of the crashing sea below and the wind through the thickly vined vegetation of the cliff that Mao had assured them screened another cave. The same Mao, Choir reminded himself, who had sworn he was telling the truth earlier.

Freeman signaled to Choir to synchronize watches, then both

of them began feeding the rope through their gloves over the cliff's edge. Mao began his rappel.

In the tunnel below them and back from the cliff, David was still hunched, his neck and leg muscles taut with the pain that radiated up and down his back. He was trying to regain his hearing, his ears still ringing from the three shots he'd fired from his Compact. He felt a warm wash of air from the radiant heat of its barrel. It felt good in the dripping wet cold of the left-hand tunnel he'd entered through the narrow gap in the rubble of the tunnel that led to the waterfall cave. He wondered if the two terrorists were still in the tunnel or if they'd reached what he guessed must be a second lair in the cliff face. If they were still around, he hoped they didn't have IR goggles that would pick up the Compact's residual heat. *Stupid*, he told himself. If the terrorists had IRs, they would see his body heat anyway if he advanced down the tunnel. He could only hope they'd be more interested in escaping than trapping him, because they must have heard the shooting above them. It had sounded as if a sniper had gotten two shots off before the replying stutter of an HK.

David placed his Compact into the wooden, lifeless grip of his injured hand, and felt for his 7-flashlight. He pulled its head hard against him, slid the on switch forward, saw a pinpoint of light and switched it off, returning the Compact to his good left hand. The danger, he thought, was that if the two terrorists he was following had reached the second lair, at least one of them might be waiting at the tunnel's exit, under the lair, to finish him off, while the other busied himself with the means of escape. They could have a Zodiac, possibly one of the "big jobs," as Aussie referred to the thirty-foot RIBs, that in a pinch could quickly ferry away twenty or more sardine-packed personnel. That would rapidly take them eastwards, back into the protective shroud of fog where they could then land, melting back into the perennially green canopy of the peninsula, to later reassemble and launch yet another attack.

David stopped, noticing that one of the five-foot-high joists lining the tunnel had come loose from the wall, bringing down what appeared to be a candlestick holder with it. A butterfly mine underneath? The fallen joist seemed to have been pushed out over time by an inch-thick root growing horizontally along the tunnel, the root itself about three or four feet in length.

He slid his Compact into his waistband and quickly made two cuts with his K-bar, resheathing it and extracting the root, rubbing the root hard back and forth against his trousers to remove the slippery mud coating. Then he made several small nicks on one end of the root so he would have a better grip. With the Compact, which had eight shots left, and the thick three-foot-long root in the wooden grasp of his injured hand like an officer's swagger stick, he started moving cautiously again down the tunnel. It took a slight curving turn to the left, the wide angle of the turn obviously designed to accommodate much longer containers than the cardboard boxes of food; perhaps crated segments of torpedoes, he thought.

He paused again, the persistent ringing in his ears now joined by a sound like wind in trees. The falls? They were possibly only two hundred yards or so to the east, and if he was that close to the coastal cliffs, he knew the tunnel would soon end. Infrared spots of residual heat, like those captured by IR cameras showing the images of parked cars that in fact were no longer there, speckled his IR glasses. *Slowly*, he counseled himself. Above him, outside somewhere, Freeman, Aussie, and Choir, and maybe Sal too, would be moving fast, coming down a trail on the cliff face, or some such thing. Exactly how, he couldn't be sure, because unlike them, he'd never seen the cliffs in the area. He'd only heard about them secondhand from news reports of the sinking of the sub.

David Brentwood, who was determined to redeem himself for what had happened in Afghanistan, his bootlaces tied so tightly his feet were throbbing, knew that any temptation to rush, to get it over with, had to be restrained by common sense. The terrorists, if they hadn't already fled, would be waiting for him. In that case, perhaps he should wait in turn, until Freeman and company made their move and he heard them. He could smell paper smoke, which, together with the fetid air of the tunnel, was partially depriving his brain of oxygen. But should he make a dash for the exit, which couldn't be far away? The terrorists would be watching the seaward side of the lair as well, not just the tunnel exit. He had assumed that the roar he was now hearing was that of the falls the team had spoken of where they had attacked the sub, but, disorientated in the tunnel as to precisely what direction he was heading, he couldn't be sure. And everything was becoming fuzzy with the lack of oxygen. He thought he heard movement ahead, or was it behind him? He stopped again and knelt down, almost tipping off balance because of the oxygen depletion and the lack of sensation in his right arm. He reached out with his left hand and duct-taped the 7-flashlight to the end of the thick, three-foot-long root.

CHAPTER FIFTY-ONE

WHERE IN HELL was Douglas Freeman? More to the point, Marte wondered, what was he looking for? She'd heard by now of his mythical second sub, but it might be simply rumor. "There's a thousand bucks in it, Sheriff," she told the well-fed lawman.

Wally got up from his desk and hitched his pants. Lord, she was a looker. No spring chicken, but experienced, like you could get right to it. "CNN tryin' to bribe me, Ms. Price? That's serious."

"Oh heavens, no," said Marte, smiling, touching his arm, tossing her head back, the sheen of her hair caught in the sheriff's green desk lamp. "It's Walter, isn't it?"

"Most folks call me Wally."

"Wally?" she said, as if right there and then nothing else was important to her. "Wally—yes, I like that. Most nicknames— well, to be frank, I don't like them. But *Wally*. It's friendly sounding, isn't it?"

He knew what she was doing. Did she think that coming from New York, she could pull a fast one? Think he was some kind of rain-forest hillbilly?

"I just think," continued Marte, "that you folks in law enforcement have done a marvelous job up here—the rescue work, people leaving in droves, and all that. I'd simply like to make a contribution to your benevolent fund. As one grateful American to another. I'm sure there are police officers' families in need?"

Wally nodded. "I knew some of those deputies on duty at Birch Bay."

She remembered the attack against the oil refinery. "General Freeman knows me," she said suddenly.

"They've headed out on 112—road to Callam Bay." He showed her where it was on the station's wall map of the Olympic Peninsula. "Cameraman going with you?"

"You rather he wouldn't?"

"No, no, I mean I think you need a man along."

"Really?" A feminist edge there, he saw.

"I mean—ah, you know—one of you drive, the other one navigate sort of thing. Very deserted out there. I'd lend you a deputy, but with all the townsfolk returning—"

"Look, Wally, there might be other media people arriving here, now the *Petrel*'s in port."

"Uh-huh," said Wally, rubbing his chin thoughtfully. "I'm not sure *where* General Freeman is. Could've gone east back to the 104, down to Hood Canal. Bangor Base. Imagine Admiral Jensen'll have a few questions to answer. Bit late with those hydrofoils. 'Sides, I think most reporters'll want to get first dibs at interviewing the *Petrel*'s crew. Helluva thing they did."

Marte was careful not to crack a smile as she began writing her check, her pen slowing, however, when she realized the sheriff might be right. The *Petrel*'s crew *would* be a huge story. And if all Freeman wound up with was simply a bunch of leftover terrorists in the bush? Still, she'd learned that Freeman had a kind of sixth sense about things military.

"Whoa!" said the sheriff. "I can't take a check, ma'am." He was astounded by her naiveté. "I mean, ah, cash'd probably be better."

"Oh, yes, of course. I'm sorry. I wasn't thinking. Where's the nearest ATM?"

"Man, there's been a run on them. I don't think—"

"I've only got four hundred in cash. I'll need that for a cab. Can you trust me?"

"Hell, sure I can trust you."

"Soon as I get back." She gave him a smile.

Lordy, he could have sworn she licked her lips. Walter gave her a wave.

"We on?" asked the cameraman, his tone utterly devoid of enthusiasm.

"There's no second sub," he added wearily. "I'll *bet* you there's no second sub."

Marte Price told the cab driver to go faster, worried that the car a half mile in front was Fox or possibly England's Independent Television Network. "Those Brits have been all over us like measles since Iraq," she told her cameraman. "I swear they got the nod into our market because they went in after Saddam Insane with us and the Aussies."

The cameraman shrugged disinterestedly.

Marte wanted the cabbie to catch up and overtake the vehicle ahead, her fold-up binoculars out of her bag. "It's another *cab*!" she blurted, a realization that convinced the CNN veteran that it was media up ahead. Rental cars were seldom used by the media because the paperwork and Homeland Defense "Purpose of Rental" security form took too much time to fill out.

Salvini had spotted the car way back, and saw it closing fast now. Terrorists? he wondered. He called Aussie Lewis.

Aussie wasn't surprised to feel the sudden vibration in his tunic pocket, the morphine Freeman had administered having temporarily banished the pain, putting his brain in reverie. "Where the fuck are you, Brooklyn?"

"In this cab with Grandma," Sal replied. "Listen, I've got a bogey up my ass. Looks like another cab. No one else is supposed to be out here. The boss told Sheriff—"

"Yeah, well," cut in Aussie lethargically, his laid-back tone annoying Sal.

"Could be a hostile," said Sal urgently.

"Okay," Aussie answered pleasantly. "Pull a left—block the road. Show 'em your weapon."

There was a pause.

"Well, that's what I was gonna do. You okay, Aussie? You sound weird."

"Took one in the rib cage. Not deep, though. Other guys takin' care o' business."

Aussie definitely sounded high. "Got a GPS loc for me?" asked Salvini. "I must have gone past the mile post you gave me."

"Oh, yeah," said Aussie accommodatingly. "Sure. Hang on, mate."

"You on morph?"

"Oh, yeah," Aussie's voice said lazily. "On the morph."

"Jesus! Call me back with your GPS." Sal dropped the phone onto the cab's passenger seat and braked hard, Mao's mother yelling something at him in Vietnamese as he blocked the road and stepped out with the shotgun.

Marte's cab slowed. "Keep going," she told the driver. "There's another hundred in it."

"Lady, I don't care if there's another million in it, I'm stopping right now. That guy's holdin' a shotgun—all I got is my dick, an' I plan on keepin' it."

"Stan," Marte told her cameraman. "You drive." She turned back to the cabbie. "You stay here." She handed him two hundred, adding, "We shouldn't be long. I'll pay for any damages."

The cabbie counted the money. It was more than he'd expected.

"Go, Stan!" Marte instructed her cameraman.

"Slowly," he said.

"Fine, but go."

"Take off your panties," the cameraman told her.

"What?"

"You're wearing white panties. I think we'd better start waving them."

"Pervert. Don't turn around."

He didn't, but did look into the rearview mirror.

When the cab pulled up to him, Sal told Marte she'd have to turn back. No media. Too dangerous. As they spoke, he could hear firing, which he was sure must be echoing up from the sides of the cliffs. In fact, he was hearing the distant linoleum-ripping sound of Aussie's HK.

With the morphine now wearing off, his pain returning, Lewis had been in no mood for the four terrorists he saw popping up out of the ground a hundred yards away from what was supposed to be a patch of skunk cabbage. All four were armed and in a clump, running for their lives through the brush toward him, heading for the road. Aussie flicked off the safety.

"Aw shit!" he murmured after his first burst, seeing that the four, though having been in a bunch, now had the sense to disperse.

Like every SpecFor warrior, Aussie Lewis knew "Stop!" in at least eight languages. *"Zhàn zhù,"* he called out now. "Claymore!" Every enemy of the United States knew what "claymore" meant. Aussie thought of it as the terror that had pulverized so many of Uncle Ho's Viet Minh into "ground Minh."

Three of the four were suddenly standing dead still. The fourth, in what Aussie called "obvious Freeman shock"—maybe he'd heard what had happened in the Port Angeles café—was walking around in circles, calling for someone.

Aussie cut them down without the slightest compunction. They had attacked his adopted country, his home, and besides, they were in civilian garb, and thus, he told himself, armed spies under the Geneva Convention.

"You should go back to Port Angeles," Sal told Marte and her cameraman. "Put your panties back on and interview those people."

"Don't be a smartass!" Marte snapped. "What people?"

"People who got kicked out of the restaurant. They can give you a story." He'd taken care not to mention the woman being shot, and he felt badly about having to steer the reporter in that direction. The shooting story was sure to come out, but it was the only way he could send her and the cameraman away from the firing. Anyway, seeing that some media type was going to get the story, it might as well be Price, whom he'd heard had once been buddy-buddy with the general.

"Who's the old lady?" asked Marte, looking into Sal's cab.

"Informant," Sal said, before he had time to think. His job was fighting, not arguing.

The old lady was shaking her finger at the three of them.

"What's she saying?" Marte asked. "Do you know?"

"Says you should go away. Big trouble up ahead."

Marte looked disgusted. "Do one thing for me—what's your name?"

"Mickey."

"All right, Mickey. Will you at least tell the general—if he's still alive—that I was here first and I'd appreciate it if he gave me first crack at his story."

"I'll do that."

As their cab headed back, the cameraman told Marte, "His name's not Mickey."

"Gee," said Marte, her voice cold with sarcasm. "I thought it *was*." She asked him to toss back her panties. "And I'd appreciate it, *Stan*, if you didn't perve at me in the rearview."

"There might be a good story in town," he said in a conciliatory tone.

She didn't answer.

"You know," Stan continued, "up at the hospital? That sub commander's crush—what was her name, *Elisha*?"

"Alicia," said a somewhat mollified Marte. "Alicia Mayne."

"Yeah, the one with the burns. You know, I heard that deeper burns aren't as painful as first degree burns because third degree burns destroy all the nerve endings—you don't feel the pain."

"Still needs skin grafts by the dozen, that one."

"Yeah, but they can work wonders now. Friend of mine told me they have this kind of synthetic skin that's revolutionized burn recovery."

"Well, she couldn't look worse than some of those Hollywood bimbos," said Marte. "Pay ten grand for a facelift and they look like they're from a waxworks."

"Boobs look real."

"Just drive, Stan."

CHAPTER FIFTY-TWO

IF MURPHY'S LAW had run amok through the Strait of Juan de Fuca during this disastrous week for America, Freeman thought, Murphy now seemed absent as he, Choir, and Mao, having successfully rappeled down the cliff face without incident, now reached the footpath-width ledge that ran across the base of the cliff. High tide was in, waves broaching the ledge here and there, disappearing behind the ragged bottom of the thick tangled-vine curtain.

Freeman was about fifty feet across from Choir and Mao, and both could see the entrance. There was a smaller curtain about fifteen feet wide and thirty feet high within the much larger curtain of vegetation, like a smaller door set within a hangar door.

Another outfit might have used Mao at barrel point to go ahead, to be first man inside, to take the first fire if surprise wasn't achieved, but Freeman didn't want to do it that way. Surprise was not gained by creeping approaches in his school, which taught that slow approaches bred defensive attitudes in what was supposed to be an offensive force. Freeman signaled to Choir to make a walk speed approach along the slippery ledge, then a fast entry. It suited his preference for audacity: *L'audace, l'audace, toujours l'audace!*

Choir gently pulled Mao back, cuffed him with a nylon strip, and turned his face into the cliff. Mao's breathing was still labored but, Choir could tell, easing now. "Wait here," Choir whispered.

He glanced down, checking his grenade array, Freeman already having done so. Then both of them began making their way along the ledge, Choir from the east side of the heavy vine door, Freeman from the west.

Freeman's biggest worry, given the bright sunlight, was whether any part of their shadows would pierce the screen of vegetation, like that of someone passing by an ivy-covered trellis. Momentarily, he glanced up at the rim of the cliff, its overhang of fresh-smelling vegetation a vivid green fringe against the blue sky, and he saw why he and Choir hadn't spotted any sentries, other than the tree-hidden sniper. A human form against such a wild, natural setting would at once arouse curiosity in anyone at sea. Anyway, he hoped he and the rest of the team had decimated the core of the supply unit in the firefight at the falls cave and against the six-man Zodiac near *Petrel*, along with everyone on the submarine they'd sunk.

He saw a cloud about to swallow the sun. Choir, seeing the general looking up, got the same message. They'd pause a second or two longer, the door still ten feet away, and then make their move in the shadow of the passing cloud.

They heard pulley chains then, and the two halves of the vegetation-screened door began opening like a stage curtain. No voices. The sun, hidden in cloud now, had not cast shadows, but neither did it illuminate anything more than a few yards of a semidark cave whose back wall neither Choir nor Freeman could distinguish. Some kind of gantry was faintly visible, and the first thing coming to Freeman's mind as he and Choir dropped down on damp, ice-cold rock, was stage scaffolding. He couldn't see anyone, but if the terrorists had escaped, then who was running the chain and pulley? Admittedly, it would require only one man, but where was he? Or she? Terrorists these days were equal opportunity employers.

Then Choir glimpsed a faint wink of light.

It was David's 7-flashlight sweeping from about twenty feet inside the tunnel as he approached the tunnel's exit that led directly into the cave. And it immediately drew fire, the last twenty feet of the tunnel suddenly exploding with tracer pouring from the back wall of the cave into the tunnel at the flashlight.

The shooters had assumed the enemy tunnel rat was right behind it, holding it, but David was now at least five feet away, left of the flashlight. The long root handle, to which he'd taped it for just such an eventuality, was in the wooden grasp of his "useless" right hand. David's left arm came up from his prone position, Compact in hand. His first shot imploded one of the two terrorists' heads, and the second was just as accurate, born of constant practice on the Fort Lewis range, also killing its victim instantly. Choir and Freeman held their fire at the remaining terrorist, lest an errant round strike David, the bang of his Compact's 9mm as distinct to Freeman as the sound of his own weapon.

"David?" Freeman shouted.

"General!" The exultation David felt, combined with the smell of the sea air that was now flushing out the stink of gunpowder, sent his adrenaline racing.

The cave lit up then, and Freeman swung his HK up, its burst taking out the light, a hot glass rain showering down on him and Choir. But in that instant of light turned on by the terrorists, Freeman had glimpsed enough to know now that what he'd assumed was scaffolding was in fact a dry dock, and in it was a long, black-tented vessel, only its prop and prop guard visible.

Choir had time only to glimpse it too, but he'd noticed something Freeman hadn't—the prop had exactly the same number of blades and prop guard as the sub they'd sunk. For an instant Choir felt as if someone had walked over his grave, that the sub had been resurrected, but he told himself that was not possible. No way.

Choir and Freeman, at the front of the cave, crawled quickly to the bottom beam of the dry dock. The two were about fifteen feet apart, with David just inside the tunnel exit at the cave's rear forming the third point in an ad hoc triangle of fire. But to stay there, to wait, was to die. They had to get up.

A shaft of light pierced the cave on Freeman's right, and three men came out, firing wildly, their intent obviously to flush out the Americans. But having already glimpsed the layout, Freeman,

Choir, and David, because of their training for instant memorization of hostile layouts, had no fear of blue on blue, and cut the terrorists down within seconds. What they weren't prepared for was the utter surprise of seeing the black tent moving toward the front of the cave, two hydraulic launch rails sliding out ahead of the dry dock through the now open, vine-covered door into the high tide's water, which was almost flush with the cave's lip that was the ledge.

The black tent moved slowly at first, its conical top plucked up by an overhead "fingers" claw that had been screwed into the cave roof. Freeman saw that on his right side of the cave there was a thick side spar, a short, canvas-covered walkway projecting out from the cave's westerly wall, presumably coming out from either a natural or manmade antechamber in the rock wall adjacent to the black tent. Several terrorists—probably four, certainly no more than six, by the sound of their footfalls—had just entered the conical tent via this covered walkway as the tent was being raised higher and the vessel started to move. Freeman could see that once the as yet unrevealed bow hit the water and the camouflage tent was completely drawn off, the vessel would be into the water and away, like rescue boats that could be launched in seconds from rocky shorelines, sliding straight from dry dock to sea. Choir and David paired to maintain suppressing fire, but David's ammunition was getting low.

"Cover!" Freeman shouted, and dashed toward the rising tent that now, above the vessel's waterline, revealed the shape not of a sub, but of a fast patrol boat with U.S. Coast Guard colors. Freeman pulled the pins of his grenades and lobbed one, two, three, forward and midships, the last one onto the stern deck. Three of them went off in quick succession, the craft aflame. The fourth HE grenade exploded as the vessel was only halfway out of the cave, its stern still inside and on fire.

David, having located the pulley/chain button, pushed it, thus shutting the door, jamming the patrol boat half in and half out, because of the resistance of its high superstructure, aerials, and radar antennae.

The vine curtain was now on fire, and fuel tanks began exploding, spewing out sheets of flame over the starboard deck's canvas-shrouded torpedo tube, the concussion lifting Freeman off his feet, covering him in flame and throwing him back toward the center of the cave, where Choir quickly extinguished his burning clothes with a throw of "fire sand" from one of several contingency buckets lined up by the wall.

Spitting and cursing, eyebrows singed, Freeman was up on his feet, facing seaward, when he saw a door burst open on the deck of the burning boat. Three terrorists emerged, firing furiously at David, who coolly returned fire, "heading" one of them, who fell back into the burning shroud of the tent. Choir felled the second. And then there was the general—not in uniform, of course, but General Chang nevertheless. As Freeman squeezed off another burst before Chang could hit him, he realized, with the force of a physical blow, seeing the Chinese general's wig fly off like a blood-sodden pelt, revealing a pockmarked scalp, that he was looking at Li Kuan.

The cave was an inferno, Freeman telling David and Choir to disengage, an unnecessary order, given that there was no more resistance, the downed terrorists scattered about the cave floor. Freeman knew the fight was over, but feared that the torpedo tubes—the warheads doubtless having been loaded to sink more minesweepers or anything else in the choke point—would explode, the cave instantly becoming an oven, consuming all the oxygen and everything within.

"Move out!" he shouted. He couldn't see David.

Then Freeman heard a loud *crack*, saw Choir fall, and the drydock frame behind him engulfed in flames, knots in the wood exploding like more gunshots.

Choir was all right, but had twisted his ankle. As he fell, he could have sworn that the body of the pockmarked terrorist leader on the fiery stern deck had twitched. Muscles contracting probably.

Freeman, his right hand holding his HK, his finger on the trigger, thrust his left hand under Choir's right shoulder to serve as a crutch, and the two made their way through black, toxic smoke that was now pouring out from the interior of the burning boat. They heard a tremendous crash behind them, the drydock's front section having collapsed, the boat's stern higher because of it. Choir saw a figure clinging to its rail. It was the pockmarked terrorist issuing forth such a feral scream of rage and pain that Choir knew he would never forget it.

"Mother of God!" he blurted, the hot smoke scorching his throat. "He's still alive. We should finish the poor devil off."

"Don't bother," said Freeman, glancing back at Li Kuan, a.k.a. General Chang.

"Jesus!" said Choir. There was another ungodly scream. "He's melting, General! His body's—" Choir was coughing violently. "His body's actually melting!"

"Let the bastard melt!" said Freeman, who was thinking about a young American woman called Amanda, so full of promise and hope, brutally tortured, then murdered and dumped in a stinking canal by Chang/Li Kuan's thugs because she'd overheard what had now been revealed in the cave—the Communist Chinese government's plan to quell rebel Muslim nationalist movements on its Xinjiang border by offering to oversee a Muslim attack on America. Chang, or Li Kuan, as young Mao knew him, had clearly blackmailed immigrants, just as Mao had told Freeman, to cooperate in providing the sub and torpedo boat with supplies, the Asiatic Muslims providing crews and gunmen.

By the time the *wokka wokka* of the airborne cavalry units from Fort Lewis could be heard in the skies over the U.S. side of the Juan de Fuca Strait, the threat was over.

For now.

It would be the FBI's and Homeland Defense's joint responsibility to backtrack, to go through Seattle and Vancouver importers' invoices and find out which importers bought which supplies and, just as important, who transported them to Port Angeles on the lonely Washington coast.

Outside the smoke-filled cave, Mao, who'd had ample time to turn around carefully on the ledge and cut through the nylon cord cuffs by rubbing them against the barnacle-encrusted rocks, moved across the ledge, helping Freeman and a cordite-reeking David Brentwood assist Choir along the narrow ledge and then, in a painfully slow descent for Choir, down to the rocky foreshore.

EPILOGUE

"IT'S NAIVE," FREEMAN told Marte Price Port Angeles during her "exclusive" hospital emergency room interview, "to believe that there aren't more sleepers all over the country."

"You really believe that, General?" Marte pressed.

"Marte—" he began, drawing back as the nurse applied a malodorous salve to his burns. "Smells like damn fish!"

"Do you really believe that?" Marte asked again. "That there are sleepers all over the United States?"

Freeman was sure she believed it too, her repetition of the question merely an attempt to have him answer in a form best suited for TV. This was *Larry King* grist. "I do," said Freeman, asserting, "Most Americans—the experience of 9/11 and this last week notwithstanding—are far too sanguine about the extent of the sleeper danger." There, she had her quote, and it was the truth. "And the Canadian border's a walkthrough," he added, almost as an afterthought.

This last comment was the one that grabbed headlines and caused a diplomatic fracas between Ottawa and Washington, D.C. It drove the "modern miracle" stories of what was occurring daily in America's hospitals off the front pages. The space age technology of these miracles, wherein radical DNA-based techniques had greatly reduced burn healing and recovery times to months rather than years, barely got a mention amid all the war news.

Sal, as he put it, was "highly pissed off," missing the action in the second cave, his day ending by having to return Mao's mother to the restaurant, where she berated him again, in rapid-fire Vietnamese.

Mao was turned over to the FBI for further questioning with an "In consideration—leniency" note from Freeman stating how helpful the blackmailed terrorist had been.

Sal had joined Choir and David at the hospital to visit the general and Aussie. While David was waylaid by Marte Price, who wanted a follow-up interview with the Medal of Honor winner, Choir and Sal went to the second floor to see Aussie. They had to wait, the patient's curtains closed as a harried nurse checked his wound and recorded his vital signs. Despite their relief that the military operation was over, Sal and Choir, now they had a chance to talk about it, were still troubled by Freeman's behavior in the restaurant with the young woman and his actions en route to the second cave with Mao.

"Maybe," said Sal, checking to see that no one was within earshot, "he should give it up."

"Yes," concurred Choir. "You fight these fanatics too much, you become like them. End justifies the means, right?"

"Right."

And so one can only imagine the two men's astonishment, indeed their shock, when they saw a gum-chewing sheriff's deputy walking by with a young female patient, the woman in a washed-thin V-necked nightie. Sally—Mao's would-be love— glared hatefully at them, a dark, saucer-sized bruise visible even through her nightie. She quickly drew the V of the nightie closed, as if rebuking two leering adolescents.

Sal and Choir stared at each other. "Point-blank!" said Choir. "He fired point-blank!"

"Shit!" said Sal. "He must have used a nonlethal round! A rubber bullet."

"But wait a minute—what about the blood?"

"Fake, mate!" came an Aussie drawl from behind the curtains. "Those blood samples taken on *Petrel* from the terrorists we whacked. I told the general one of 'em was missing when I went to get 'em from the Humvee, that we only had four instead of five. Cheeky bastard bawled me out for it, and—"

"He'd taken it," put in Sal.

"And after he'd fired the rubber round into Mao's woman, *who* dragged her up, her blouse covered with blood?"

"Cunning old prick," said Sal.

"Silly bitch thought she'd been hit," continued Aussie. "Well, she had been. Those nonlethals hit hard, mate."

"You shit," said Sal. "You—"

"Ah, don't get your balls in a knot," continued Aussie. "I found the vial on the floor—guess he couldn't do everything at once. If he tried to put it back into his pocket, we would have seen that. Anyway, once I confronted him, he *ordered* me to keep it quiet. If young Mao even suspected it'd been a put-up job to scare him witless, there's no way he'd've told us about the tunnel. Everything was riding on that. Fuck, if we'd—"

"Excuse me!" It was a burly head nurse, and even with the starched white uniform, she looked as if she'd stepped right out of the World Wrestling Federation's ring after crushing Jesse Ventura. "We'll not have any of that foul language here, thank you very much. There are children here, you know."

The SpecFor trio were utterly cowed. Terrorists, they could do. This, they couldn't handle. "Sorry, ma'am," they said contritely.

As she left, there was a moment of silence, Sal and Choir feeling guilty for ever doubting the general.

Down on the first floor, Freeman stood impatiently in the phone cubicle outside Emergency, the stiffness in his chest from the impact of the sub's .50 round against his Kevlar spreading up to his neck and shoulders. He could tell that if he didn't get something to relieve the discomfort, as the hospital staff referred to pain, he would be in for a Motrin-sized headache. Trouble was, to get a pill in Emergency required a consultation with an M.D. So instead he took a combat vial of morphine from his jacket and jabbed it into his upper arm.

"Junkie!" exclaimed a disgusted young woman hurrying by with an open-mouthed teen. "In the hospital yet. I dunno."

Freeman felt badly—stupid thing to do—and was about to hang up the phone so he could go and explain, but then he heard Charles Riser's voice on the other end.

"Mr. Riser?"

"Yes?"

"General Freeman here. You've probably seen the news, Mr. Riser, about what's been happening up here in the—"

"The sub and that other boat, yes. Thank God."

"Mr. Riser, I hate to fall back on a cliché, but I can't think of anything better than to say I've got some good news and bad news. Well, I guess it's all bad for you. Li Kuan and General Chang are—*were*—the same person. Chang being in prison was a lie—just a smoke screen."

Freeman waited, giving Charles Riser a chance to absorb the shock. It was only seconds, but seemed infinitely longer, before Riser, whom Freeman imagined must have had to sit down, get his thoughts together, replied, "Is—Are they . . . ?" his voice taut with tension.

"He's dead," said Freeman. "Shot the son of a bitch myself."

There was another long pause before Riser inquired, "You're sure he's dead?"

"Deader'n a fucking doornail—excuse my Latin."

"You actually saw him die?"

"Mr. Riser, I saw the scumbag *melt*. I can go into details if you like, but I'm sure—"

"Please do," said Riser.

Charles Riser's next door neighbors were concerned for him. It was late, 1:00 P.M. on the East Coast, and they could still see him, in his tartan robe, roaming around his house, from kitchen to dining room to front hall and back to the kitchen, clutching a large, gilded portrait of his daughter to his chest.

"He's talking to her," said the neighbor's wife. "I think he's crying."

"Don't think so," her husband said, peering over her shoulder at Riser. "Looks to me like he's celebrating. Maybe both."

Marte Price, the embodiment of unflustered professionalism, was becoming flustered. She had just clipped on the Medal of Honor winner's throat mike—the emergency room a terrific backdrop, as Stan told her—everything set to go, and what did she see? The elevator opening and John Rorke, the captain of the USS *Encino*, who the White House confirmed had launched the first blow against the PLA's Penghu garrison. Together with the *McCain*'s air arm strike, it had forced Beijing to the cease-fire table with Taipei.

As Freeman reentered the room, he heard Marte ask her cameraman, "Who's the woman with him?"

Stan was busy adjusting the tripod and the focus. "What?" he said.

"The woman with Commander Rorke," said Marte.

Stan glanced over. "In the wheelchair?"

"Yes, Stan. In the *wheelchair*. It's the only one I can see."

The couple were now over at the admissions desk, obviously ready to check out, he in the stunning white dress uniform of a United States naval officer, she in a flattering, loose-fitting blue silk dress.

"She's the one who was in the hospital room when we barged in for that interview."

Marte remembered the occasion. "But that's not her," she said emphatically. "That woman was badly burned."

"She *was*," said Stan, adjusting the down angle of the video. "She still is on most of her upper body, but haven't you been reading the papers? They've had photos of her and some of the other burn victims. Pretty impressive, I can tell you—some sort of miracle skin wrap that's revolutionized—"

"Damn!" said Marte. She had the legendary Freeman on tape, the Medal of Honor winner all miked up and ready to go. And now a naval hero and a medical miracle were about to get away.

"Excuse me," she told David Brentwood, unclipping his mike and dropping her clipboard.

She scuttled over to the admissions desk. "Commander!" she called out, but she was positively beaming at the woman in the wheelchair. Quick pleasantries were exchanged between Rorke and Marte.

"This is my wife, Alicia," he said, his pride evident. "And Alicia, this is Marte—"

"Oh, I recognize you," said Alicia, her smile pleasant but not obsequious—and extraordinarily painful to her, though she didn't give any indication of it.

Would they be so good as to let CNN do a "quick" interview?

Marte asked. "Just a few minutes?" she lied. "I know it would mean so much to the people who—" She stopped as she saw John Rorke looking down with concern at Alicia.

Alicia knew it was her call. Talking tired her—there was so much subcutaneous healing yet to occur, and her face was still so sore that the slightest breeze at times became unbearable. "Fine," she said. "Where would you like us to go?"

"Over here," said Marte, and, returning with them to the camera, ever so politely edged Freeman and Brentwood out of camera range. "David, would you be willing to wait a few minutes?" Marte asked.

"Sure," he said. He felt relaxed for the first time in over six months. He'd called Melissa, and knew he'd be home by tomorrow evening. "I don't mind. Take your time."

"Thank you," said Marte, turning triumphantly to her cameraman. "You see, Stan, things happen in threes."

Freeman watched her do the interviews, realizing again how people who don't actually do a job, any job, from gofer to legend, ever understand how much goes into making things happen. He rose to leave, feeling exhausted and slightly woozy from the morphine, but he managed to interject a brief invitation between camera takes. "Dinner tomorrow night?" he asked Marte.

She smiled knowingly. "Last time you invited me out, General, you thought I was too hyper—needed to relax. How did you put it? Rest and recreation. Calming down. Will eight o'clock be all right?"

"Done," the general replied, and left.

"You see," Stan told Marte. "Things happen in fours."

"You ready to roll?"

"Yes, *ma'am*."

On the second floor, as the nurse, taking Aussie's vital signs, finished up and closed the bed curtains, Choir and Sal sat down, and soon the three warriors were busy talking over the mission.

"Then I guess the boss would never have harmed the old lady," said Choir.

"Guess not, eh, Aussie?" added Sal.

The usually voluble Aussie didn't answer. He didn't know. It was an old world but a new war, this battle with terror. Nothing quite like it. In many ways this world war was like all wars, but still it was different. But for now, the hemorrhaging in the Northwest, at least, had been stanched.

The big news of the day, however, which dominated all the networks, was that the elderly blind woman and her black lab guide dog who had been missing following the sinking of the ferry *Georgia Queen* had been found by a U.S. Coast Guard cutter. Though both cold, voraciously hungry and thirsty, they were together and otherwise all right, having huddled together on an ad hoc raft of Styrofoam packing that had been rapidly drifting out to sea through the choke point.

GLOSSARY

AAM—Air-to-Air Missile
AAR—After Action Report
CAP—Combat Air Patrol
CEP—Circular Error Probable
ChiCom—Chinese Communist
CIC—Combat Information Center
CIWS—Close-In Weapons System
COMSUBPAC—Commander Submarine Force, U.S. Pacific Fleet
COMSUBPAC-GRU 9—Commander Submarine Force, U.S. Pacific Fleet, Group 9
CVBG—Carrier Battle Group
CVN—Carrier Aviation Nuclear
DA—Direct Action
DEFCON—Defense Condition (There are five levels.)
DIREC—Digital Recon Camera
ELF—Extremely Low Frequency
EPROM—Erasable Programmable Read-Only Memory
EWO—Electronics Warfare Officer
FITCOMPRON—Fighter Composite Squadron
FLIR—Forward Looking Infrared
HARM—Homing Anti-Radar Missile
HK—Heckler & Koch
HUD—Heads Up Display
LOSFABS—Low Silhouette Fast Boats
LSO—Landing Signals Officer

OOD—Officer of the Deck
PRC—People's Republic of China
RIB—Rigid Inflatable Boat
RIO—Radar Intercept Officer
ROC—Republic of China (Taiwan)
SALERT—Sea, Air, Land Emergency Response Team
SEAL—Sea, Air, Land Warrior
SITREP—Situation Report
SLAM—Standoff Land Attack Missile
SLAMER—Standoff Land Attack Missile—Expanded
    Response
SOC—Special Operations Command
SOSUS—Sound Surveillance System
TLAMS—Tomahawk Land Attack Missiles
UAV—Unmanned Aerial Vehicle